3.25

❤ P9-DEA-958

*He came out of the darkness.
She could see his face,
so beloved . . . so dear.*

His touch burned across her, his lips forging a trail of tension that began at her chin and hurdled downward. Her hands caught and held in the dark thatch of hair on his head as she hung on for dear life. He was taking her with him . . . to places she'd never been . . . and if she didn't hold on, she would never find her way back. She gasped and lost her hold on Chance. She reached behind her to hold onto the bed. It wasn't there! She fell backward and down . . . down . . . down. And heard him calling her name.

"Damn you, Chance McCall!"

Her cry broke the silence of the dream. Jenny bolted up in bed, gasping for breath, aching in places she'd never known she could ache for a man who was gone.

For a man who came only in her dreams and was driving her mad . . .

Other Books by
Sharon Sala

DEEP IN THE HEART
DIAMOND
FINDERS KEEPERS
LUCKY
QUEEN
SECOND CHANCES

SHARON SALA

Chance McCall

HarperTorch
An Imprint of HarperCollinsPublishers

This is a work of fiction. Names, characters, places, and incidents are products of the author's imagination or are used fictitiously and are not to be construed as real. Any resemblance to actual events, locales, organizations, or persons, living or dead, is entirely coincidental.

HARPERTORCH
An Imprint of HarperCollins*Publishers*
10 East 53rd Street
New York, New York 10022-5299

Copyright © 1993 by Sharon Sala
ISBN: 0-06-108155-8

First HarperTorch paperback printing: August 2003
First HarperCollins paperback printing: August 1993

HarperCollins®, HarperTorch™, and ♦™ are trademarks of HarperCollins Publishers Inc.

Printed in the United States of America

Visit HarperTorch on the World Wide Web at www.harpercollins.com

10 9 8 7 6 5 4 3

Once in a lifetime, if we are fortunate enough, we love that someone special. When it happens twice, we are blessed.

This book is dedicated to the people who find that love is better, the second time around.

ACKNOWLEDGMENTS

Special thanks to the wonderful people of Odessa, Texas, who opened their hearts to a stranger asking questons.

And to the Odessa Chamber of Commerce who treated me like a member of their family: to Linda Sweatt, Stacey Burkhart, Chrissy Roehrman, Pat Owlfley, Molly Reid, and Frances Durham.

To Glen Atkins, Lynn Riggs, Joe Johnson, and John Middleton, of The Chuck Wagon Gang for sharing the organization's fascinating history. Keep up the great work!

To Pearl Collins of Henderson's Drug.

To Bonnie Ruth Brannigan at The White-Pool House for helping me remember my own roots . . . and for laughing with me.

To the people at the Barn Door for their hospitality.

To the waitress at The New Brewery, thanks for sharing the hospitality of your city.

And a special thanks to my aunt, Grace Ryan, a long-time resident of Odessa, who shared her home with me while I searched her city for its flavor.

Prologue

A strange anxiety seized him. It was time! Suddenly he couldn't get away fast enough. He grabbed the can he'd brought from the station and began walking through the house, methodically pouring a thin, steady stream of gasoline on and over everything. Walls and floors, furniture and clothing; nothing escaped his treatment.

He walked out of the house, tossed the empty can into the back of his truck, and stood for a moment in the shadows of the yard, watching the house take its last breaths. He shuddered, dug into his pocket, and pulled out a book of matches. They were from Charlie's Gas and Guzzle. He stepped up onto the porch, kicked the door open, and yanked the safety match across the pad. It flared instantly. Chance gave it a toss and ran.

The air inside the house ignited before the match ever hit the floor. Chance reached the pickup just as the first window blew, shattering glass and wood across the front yard. He started the truck, put it in gear, and accelerated. The glow of the flames was bright in the rearview mirror over the dashboard. The hair on the back of his arms smelled singed where he'd come too close to the flames. Chance McCall had just burned every bridge connecting him to Odessa. He headed out of town with the sound of sirens fading away behind him. It was time to leave. He never looked back.

1

Jenny stood in the shadows of the hallway adjoining her father's office and watched the sunlight behind the desk shine directly into the stranger's eyes. He didn't blink.

Jenny thought maybe he was blind and then quickly discarded the notion. Blind men couldn't be cowboys, and Marcus was hiring extra help for roundup.

Jennifer Ann Tyler was small and delicate, an unlikely heir to Marcus Tyler's vast ranching operation. Thick dark curls and wide, china blue eyes enhanced her doll-like appearance. That deception was her greatest asset. Although she was only eleven years old, she was as tough as the leather on her scuffed cowboy boots.

She was such a fixture on the Triple T Ranch that her father, Marcus Tyler, didn't even acknowledge her presence as she sidled quietly into the office and listened to him hiring the temporary ranch hand.

"That's the way we'll leave it for now, McCall; part-time until roundup is over. After that, we'll see. Understood?"

The young man nodded silently as he continued to stare into the light.

Jenny wondered if he was "touched" in the head. Everyone knew you weren't supposed to look directly into sunlight. When you turned away, it made you see fairies that weren't really there. She continued to stare at the man's profile and waited, watching with interest as her father moved around his desk.

Marcus Tyler was a self-centered, domineering man. Years ago, he'd become a father and buried his wife within the same month. The thing uppermost on his mind at the time had been making the next payment on his bank loan.

With the passing of each year, he'd packed an extra pound onto his once wiry frame. And each year that passed, he'd become more and more of a stranger to his only child. Close-cropped, graying hair and cold, blue eyes only added to his commanding demeanor. Jenny was a feminine reflection of her father's stubbornness and bore the same mutinous expression when crossed.

On the Triple T, Marcus's word was rarely questioned and, when it was, Jenny was the only one who ever got away with it. She was also the only one who saw the young man who was applying for the job silently nod his acceptance to the terms of his employment.

"I can't find the payroll sheet you need to sign," Marcus muttered. "Wait here. I'll be right back." He marched out of the room, absently noting Jenny's presence but choosing to ignore it. Unfortunately for Jenny, he did a lot of that.

Jenny took this as her opportunity to check out the new employee. She shoved her hands into the hip pockets of her faded blue jeans and approached the silent young man seated in front of her father's desk, still staring into the light.

"Hi!" she said, as she walked up behind him.

The sound of the child's voice was so close and unexpected, it startled him. He turned, blinking rapidly as he tried to clear his vision.

She chewed the inside of her lip and rocked back and forth on the heels of her boots as she stared at the cuts, discoloration, and subsiding swelling on his face. Her eyes widened perceptibly. It was the only reaction she allowed herself at the sight of him.

"What's your name?" she asked.

"What's yours?" he countered.

"Jennifer Ann Tyler."

"Hello, Jennifer Ann," he said softly, letting his gaze sweep across the doll-like face of the little tomboy. He noted the grass stains on the knees of her jeans, the three-corned tear in the sleeve of her plaid shirt, the wind-blown curls and scuffed boots, and wondered if her mother would have a fit. It would be much later before he discovered she'd never known a mother's love.

Jenny permitted herself a deceptively sweet smile. She raised an eyebrow and rocked a bit more on already rounded boot heels. Finally the young man allowed himself a smile that didn't get past his eyes.

"My name is Chance . . . Chance McCall. Am I to assume you rule the roost around here, Jennifer Ann?"

Satisfied with his capitulation, she ignored the last part of his remark and concentrated on the next point in question. Fixing a hard stare on the left side of his face, where fading bruises and healing cuts drew her attention, she asked, "Does it hurt?"

Chance knew what she meant, but his answer was deceptive. The injuries to his face were healing fine. It was what was inside of him that was still sore and festering.

"Yes, it hurts," he said, his voice quiet and low.

"I'll fix it," she announced, and charged from the room. Before he could think, Jenny was back clutching something tightly in a grubby fist.

Chance watched, mesmerized by the lightning quick movements of her tiny fingers as she peeled the sterile coverings from two adhesive bandages decorated with stars and stripes. She stuffed the wrappers in her pocket and carefully peeled back the covering from the first bandaid. Satisfied that she was now ready to proceed, Jenny stepped close to Chance and peered at the cuts and bruises, squinting one eye just a bit to judge the best place to administer her first aid.

Chance sat spellbound, touched beyond words as the little girl gently placed the strips of sticky bandage across his cuts and bruises. The tip of her tongue worked out of the corner of her mouth as she pulled the last bit of cover from the sticky plastic.

"There!" she said, patting her work with a butterfly-light touch, "that will help."

"It already has, Jennifer Ann," Chance said, as he swallowed a huge lump in his throat.

Footsteps announced Marcus's return and sent the

child scurrying out of the room. Chance blinked and she was gone. He ran a tentative finger across his cheek, just to assure himself that he hadn't imagined her. But the bandages were there. He allowed himself a smile. It was the first in so long, it felt strange. The adhesive pulled across the flesh of his face as he regained his composure. He ignored Marcus Tyler's look of surprise and then dawning comprehension as he stared at the strips of red, white, and blue. Chance picked up a pen from the desk.

"Where do I sign?" he asked, and sealed his future on the dotted line.

It had been raining since midnight last night and hadn't let up once all day. The water ran in torrents off the roof of the bunkhouse and onto the already over-soaked Texas earth.

Chance paced in the empty bunkhouse, from an easy chair, past the row of beds, and back to the window. He never thought he'd be sorry that he didn't have to be out working in this miserable weather, but in his present frame of mind, boredom overrode good sense.

His shoulder muscles bunched, straining against his soft denim shirt. The shirt was old, chosen especially for his current problem. His long, blue jean clad legs traveled the distance between the spare furnishings in the bunkhouse with stifling repetition. He stopped at the window, squinting against the dismal sight through the muddy panes of glass. He stared blankly at his reflection. *I wonder if they would recognize me now.*

The old scars across his face were barely visible. The thin young man who'd driven onto the Triple T over two years ago with nothing on his mind but crawling into the nearest hole was gone. He'd grown four more inches and, at twenty years old, stood three inches over six feet without his boots. His dark brown hair was streaked with gold, bleached from the hot, endless days working in the sun. His features had changed from the softer gentleness of youth to those of a man, with hard, sharply defined cheekbones, a square jaw, and a mouth that rarely smiled. But his dark eyes were still the same . . . and still hiding a world of hurt.

"Dammit!" he muttered. He flexed his arm again and looked down in disgust at the reason for his confinement. His left hand was in a cast halfway up his arm, thanks to a cranky horse and a mutinous steer. Only his fingers had escaped the doctor's plaster. He wiggled them in frustrated boredom.

If it weren't for the weather and his injury, he'd have been riding fence or working on the constantly faltering innards of some truck or tractor. But the persistent rain had ended that escape. The doctor had been adamant about keeping the cast dry and Chance damn sure didn't intend to go through having his wrist set again.

Juana Suarez walked through the open door of the library. Marcus looked up, frowning at the interruption.

"What?" he asked sharply.

"I'm sorry to disturb you, Marcus," she said, "but it's raining very hard . . . and Jenny will be getting off the bus anytime now. Don't you think you should go pick her up?"

Marcus sighed at the intense worry evident in the

housekeeper's soft brown eyes. She was right, but he was waiting for an important phone call. If he left, sure as the world he'd miss it.

"Can't you go?" he asked. "I'm waiting for a call."

"No, it is not possible," she said. "The ranch wagon *esta' mal . . . muy mal.* It does not work at all. And with Chance's injury . . . . it will be a while before he can fix it."

Marcus grinned at his housekeeper's lapse into Spanish. It always happened when she was upset or nervous. When he glanced out the window he saw the wisdom of her concern. The rain continued to pour.

"I'll take care of it," he said. She started to leave when he called out, "Juana?"

"Yes?" she answered.

"Thanks for reminding me," he said.

She smiled and walked away.

Juana had come to work for Marcus Tyler when Jenny was six months old. She'd been widowed fairly young and had no children of her own. Juana had been the fourth in a long line of nannies that Marcus had hired, but she'd been the keeper. She'd taken one look at the tiny, dark-haired baby and fallen in love. She moved in that same day and never regretted it.

Marcus glanced at the clock, trying to figure a way out of his dilemma when something Juana had said registered. Chance! Because of his recent injury, he was probably still in the bunkhouse. He grabbed the intercom phone that connected all of the ranch outbuildings to the main house.

◦　◦　◦

Chance jumped and turned away from the window as the phone rang loudly into the silence, startling him into hurrying to answer its summons.

"Hello," he answered.

"Good," Marcus said, "you're still there. I need a favor."

"Sure." Anything would beat this enforced inactivity.

"I'm waiting for a phone call. Go pick Jenny up at the school bus stop. I don't want her to walk home in this rain. Okay?"

"Okay boss, my pleasure."

He liked the feisty little girl and it was fortunate that he did, because whenever he was around the ranch house, Jenny Tyler walked in his shadow from dawn to dusk. She always had more questions than he could answer, and offered more advice than he needed, but he dealt with her patiently. He sensed her need for companionship as much as he craved her company.

He stepped onto the porch and then shivered. It was chilly, a result of the early spring rains. He ducked back inside, grabbed his heavy sheepskin coat and shrugged into it. He lifted a sweat-stained Stetson from a hook by the door, and jammed it on his head as he hurried outside into the downpour.

The rain showed no sign of abating as Chance pulled out of the driveway and onto the blacktop road that was a quarter of a mile from the bus stop. He shivered and turned on the heater, warming the pickup truck's interior against the chill Jenny would be feeling.

The worn windshield wipers scraped frantically at the downpour, staying about two swipes slow of a clear view of the road, but Chance was so glad to be out of the bunkhouse he didn't much care that they needed replacing.

His relief at being released from the bunkhouse quickly turned to concern as he neared his destination. What he saw made him brake to a sliding halt in the water running across the roadway.

"What in hell . . . ?"

Two figures were barely visible through the sheet of water pouring off the truck roof and across his windshield. They were rolling around in the ditch, kicking up mud and sending grass and water flying about in wild abandon.

Chance hit the ground at a run and jumped into the ditch. Ignoring his cast and the loss of his hat, he grabbed at a flying arm then cursed as it slipped out of his grasp. Dodging a kicking boot, he braced himself astride the muddy pair and tried to pull them apart with his uninjured hand.

"Dammit to hell, Jenny. Stop it!" he yelled. It was futile. The little tornado on top was bent on destruction.

"Make her quit, mister. Make her quit," a boy begged from the bottom of the ditch.

Jenny's fury was obvious as she pummeled the face and body of her victim.

"Jenny! I said, stop it," he repeated loudly, and grabbed at her coat sleeve. His hand came away with nothing but mud and grass for his effort.

Jenny was too lost in anger to listen to Chance's demands. She swung her fist and landed another blow. This time it connected with the already bloody nose of the boy beneath her.

"Yeowch!" he yelled, and covered his face with his

arms. "Jenny, I'm sorry. I already said so. Please! Don't hit me no more."

She ignored his plea.

Chance braced himself in the mud, swiped his coat sleeve across his face to clear his vision and reached for a firmer grip on Jenny's flailing arms. He connected and pulled. She flew backward, landed on her rear end in the water running down the ditch, and then gasped in angry shock at the interruption.

The sorry-looking trio silently faced each other, oblivious to the thundershower that continued to pour down upon them. Chance's chest was heaving, his mouth firm with concern and determination as he looked at Jenny's face. She was furious.

The boy was another matter. He looked like a whipped pup. Rain diluted the blood that was seeping from his cut lip and bloody nose. It ran in pink rivulets down the front of his coat and shirt.

"Get in the truck, both of you!" Chance ordered, as he began dragging them from the ditch. He met with mutiny.

"I'm not riding beside him," Jenny spat as she climbed into the back of the pickup truck. Ignoring Chance's outstretched hand, she sat mutely in the continuing downpour.

Chance swiped at his face in frustration. He'd lost his hat, his cast was getting wetter by the minute, and the little beggar wouldn't get out of the rain.

"I'll walk, mister," the boy mumbled, and started across the road toward a house that was barely visible through the downpour.

Chance grabbed at the collar of his coat. "You're not

going anywhere until I find out what's going on." He flinched as thunder rolled above them, and knew that they were all in danger from the intermittent lightning that flashed sharply across the sky. "What in hell was going on here, boy? And what's your name?"

He glanced back at Jenny who quickly looked away. Embarrassed by his concern, she hunched her shoulders against the rain pelting her head and back and sniffled loudly. Chance swallowed a curse.

"Melvin Howard," the boy mumbled, in answer to Chance's question. He pointed. "I live just over there a piece."

"Well now, Melvin," Chance drawled, pulling the boy closer, unwilling to relinquish his hold on the only voluble witness, "we're all gonna be a hell of a lot wetter unless one of you starts talking. I know Jenny. And she doesn't start a fight for no reason." He fixed Melvin's drooping figure with a hard stare that demanded an answer.

"I didn't hurt her none," Melvin said defiantly, now that he was safely out of Jenny's reach. He leaned forward and whispered in Chance's face, trying to manage a man-to-man demeanor. When he tried to grin the cut on his lip pulled. He settled for a shrug. "I just made a little ole pass at her. You know . . ."

"You did what?" Chance asked. But before the boy could answer, Chance had him pinned between the bed of the pickup truck and his hard, unyielding chest. "How old are you anyway?"

"Nearly fifteen," he said, hitching his soggy jeans before they slipped down around his ankles.

"Listen, you little worm, if you ever so much as lay

another finger on Jenny, I'll put both of your arms and legs in one of these," he threatened, shoving his cast roughly under Melvin's nose. "Do you understand?"

"Yes . . . yes sir!"

"Now, Melvin," Chance said softly, "you apologize to Jenny. And when you get home you'd better tell your parents what you did, because I can promise you that Jenny's father will be calling."

Melvin gulped. "I'm sorry, Jenny," he mumbled. He snuck a quick look at her defiant face, saw no mercy for him this day, and dashed across the road toward home as if the devil . . . and Jenny . . . were still after him.

Chance turned to Jenny. The expression on her face twisted a tiny pain in his chest. She looked as if the world had just caved in around her. He held out his hand, trying to coax her from her seat in the rain.

"Come here, Jennifer Ann," he said softly.

She ignored his outstretched hand, climbed out of the back of the truck and crawled into the cab, sitting as far away from Chance as she could.

He bit his lip, rescued his soggy Stetson from beneath the wheels of the pickup, trudged around to the driver's side, and got in.

"Jenny, look at me."

She stared out of the window, her head turned away from Chance as she ignored his request.

"You're pretty mad, aren't you?" he asked quietly.

She nodded.

"Did he scare you, Jenny?"

Her blue eyes pierced him with a look that caused another pang of sympathy to shoot through him.

"Are you mad at me?" Chance asked.

"No," she finally mumbled, and swiped at a lump of mud and grass that was caught in the button of her dripping coat.

"Do I scare you, honey?" he asked.

She shook her head.

Chance was almost afraid to ask the next question. "What did he do to you, Jenny?"

The look she gave him broke his heart. He suspected that Jenny's last hold on childhood had all but vanished today. She had faced a very grown-up problem.

"What was it, honey? You can tell me."

Jenny took a deep, shuddering breath as the tears began to roll down her face, making little clean tracks in the streaks of mud. She moaned and flung herself into Chance's outstretched arms as she began to sob.

"He touched me here," she said, brushing her hands against her chest, "and he tried to kiss me." She shuddered with revulsion as she remembered the uninvited indignity.

"Jenny . . . honey . . . it's going to be okay," Chance said, patting her awkwardly with his soggy cast. "Shoot, after what you did to Melvin, he'll have nightmares for weeks about making passes at girls."

Jenny giggled between sobs. "I did nail him good, didn't I, Chance?" She pulled away from his arms and sniffed loudly as she looked to him for approval.

He smiled. "Here," he said, digging a damp handkerchief from his coat pocket. "Blow!"

Jenny grinned, accepting the handkerchief as well as the command.

Chance started the truck, made a U-turn in the road,

then headed back toward the Triple T. They were nearly home before either of them spoke again.

"You want me to talk to your daddy, Jenny?"

She thought for a moment. "Maybe you can come help me tell him?" she said.

He nodded.

They were about to turn into the driveway when Jenny slipped her hand on Chance's wet jeans and patted his knee. "Chance?"

"What, honey?" he asked, as he maneuvered around a big pot hole in the washed-out road and pulled up in front of the main house.

"Thanks," she said softly.

"You're welcome," he answered. "Now come on inside. Let's go find Marcus."

They made a dash for the house, laughing at the splash Chance made when his boot went into the deepest part of a puddle, soaking his jeans to the knees.

"Madre de Dios!" Juana cried, as she opened the door to meet them. "Get inside, both of you. I have some hot chocolate waiting. And Jenny! You go change your clothes. What in the world happened to you? Did you fall down?"

Jenny's laughter suddenly disappeared. A wave of scarlet swept across her cheekbones. Chance knew she was probably embarrassed at having to admit what Melvin had tried to do. He slipped his arm around her shoulders and hugged her gently. A silent look passed between him and Juana warning her not to press for answers. Her eyebrows arched, but wisely, she refrained.

Jenny sighed, leaned against the solid comfort of

Chance, using him, as always, as a buffer between herself and the world.

Juana saw the girl slide her arm around the young man. Something was going on. What had Jenny done now? She'd find out sooner or later, she always did.

"Is Marcus in his office?" Chance asked.

"Yes," Juana answered, "but don't you think you should change before . . ."

"We need to talk to him . . . now," Chance said.

Jenny slipped her hand in his and led the way. Suddenly she didn't want to face Marcus. Somehow this had become her fault, and he didn't suffer fools gladly. She knew that from experience.

"Marcus, got a minute?"

Marcus Tyler looked up in surprise, momentarily at a loss as to why Chance was standing in his office with Jenny, and then remembered that he'd sent the young man to the bus stop.

"Oh . . . sure," he said, shoving aside a stack of papers and standing to wave them toward the fire burning in the fireplace. "What's up?" He eyed Jenny, wondering, not for the first time, why God had given him a girl baby, and at the same time taken away his wife. He had never known what to do with her.

Jenny almost stepped on Chance as she shuffled in behind him, willing him to start the conversation. Talking to Marcus had always been difficult for her. Admitting that she needed him from time to time was impossible. If she did that, then she would also have to face the fact that he didn't need her . . . at least, not enough.

"It seems Jenny had a little problem at the bus stop today," Chance said.

Marcus glared. He didn't like problems.

A knot began forming in the pit of Jenny's stomach. Just the look on his face told her this was going to make him angry.

"So?" Marcus asked. "She seems okay now. What happened? Jenny, what did you do?"

Chance bit his lip. Damn this man! Why did he always assume that the problem originated with Jenny? Why couldn't he see that she was upset?

"She didn't do anything but defend her honor," Chance answered, and then sucked in a sharp breath, willing himself not to jeopardize his job. He needed this security. It was all that kept him going. But he also knew that Jenny had even less security than he. Money or not, Jenny was on her own, too.

"What do you mean?" Marcus asked.

"I mean that a boy made a pass at her. It upset her . . . it scared . . ."

The phone rang. Marcus grabbed it as if it were a lifeline.

"Hello?" he said, and motioned for Chance and Jenny to wait.

Jenny sighed and leaned her forehead against the wet, steamy back of Chance's coat. This was not going well. It was to be expected.

Marcus nodded to himself, shuffled through a stack of papers, and then began making notes.

Chance stared, dumbfounded by the lack of interest Jenny's father had shown in what had happened to her. He felt her fingers sliding beneath his coat sleeve, searching for his hand. He cupped the small hand in the warming strength of his own and squeezed gently.

Marcus looked up, remembered that Chance and Jenny were still waiting, and sharply ordered the caller to hold. He covered the mouthpiece and said, "Jenny, go change your clothes. You're dripping. Chance, thanks for picking her up for me." He waved them away and went back to his conversation.

Chance cursed softly beneath his breath and let Jenny lead him from the office.

"It's all right," she said. "He's busy. And I'm fine."

"Well, I'm not. Come on, honey. Let's go get you some dry clothes and then find that hot chocolate. We've got a phone call to make to Melvin Howard's folks. And when I'm through talking to his father, Melvin will probably have to eat his supper standing up."

Jenny smiled. The pain that was coiling inside her heart began to unwind. Chance would take care of it. She should have known not to worry. And the thought of Melvin, pimples and all, getting a whipping for what he'd done made her giggle.

"Yeah, and I bet he has to eat soup. His mouth will be too swollen to chew. I really got him good, didn't I?"

Chance fought the urge to push his way back into Marcus's office and shake him. "Yeah, honey. You sure did. You got him good. Now come on, let's go find Juana."

They went down the hallway toward the kitchen, hand in hand, dripping mud and water with every step.

A string of firecrackers exploded, dancing its way across the dusty driveway with a string of little boys following along behind. Shrieks of excited laughter erupted from them.

It was the Fourth of July, and the Triple T Ranch was holding its annual barbecue. Half the populace of Tyler was present along with all of Marcus Tyler's employees and their families.

It was a triple celebration, because it also marked the founding of the Tyler Ranch in Tyler, Texas, and the birthday of Jennifer Tyler, Marcus's only heir.

Sixteen years earlier, Marcus Tyler had purchased a section of Texas land with the help of the Federal Land Bank. He'd installed his pregnant wife, Lillian, in the run-down ranch house and headed back to town for some groceries and supplies. He'd returned to find Lillian in the last throes of labor. Marcus delivered his daughter, Jennifer, as capably as he'd done everything else in his life, and less than three weeks later his wife had died of complications resulting from childbirth.

"Ooowee, Marcus," Conrad Hancock said, "that little girl of yours sure has grown up. It won't be long before you'll be beating the boys off the front porch with a stick. Just look at her. She'll have the young bucks in a fight for sure before the day's over."

The group of men standing beneath a shade tree, visiting with Marcus, laughed. Each of them began offering words of advice and warnings.

Marcus turned and stared at his daughter, seeing her for the first time through the eyes of his friends. He was suddenly uncertain as to how he would deal with a budding woman. Leaving her to her own devices didn't seem as wise as it once had. All sorts of implications presented themselves as thoughts of boys and teenage problems took root in his mind.

He frowned. The iced tea warmed in his hand as he stared at his daughter, who was perched on the top rail of the fence. She wasn't paying any attention to the young men who'd begun a game of horseshoes on the other side of the yard fence, trying to impress her with their prowess. She was watching Chance, but her father thought nothing of it. She always seemed to be within shouting distance of his foreman.

Marcus smiled at a carload of late arrivals and waved at the tall man who was busily directing traffic to the designated parking areas. Since he'd made Chance foreman he'd had all kinds of time to devote to his chief goal, thinking up new schemes to make more money.

"Say, Marcus," Hancock added, "that boy of yours, that foreman there." He pointed with his cigar. "Old Thurman here wants to know who his people are."

Marcus shrugged. It was not something he'd ever wondered about, and it suddenly struck him as strange that he had not. In all the years that Chance had worked for him, not once had he asked for time off, or to go home for a visit. Surely he had family somewhere?

"I don't know," Marcus answered. "But I can find out. Chance, come here a minute," he yelled.

Chance turned toward the sound of his boss's voice and waved an acknowledgment as he directed another carload of latecomers toward the proper parking area.

The group of well-to-do ranchers and oil men standing with Marcus beneath a large shade tree watched Chance's arrival into their midst with varying degrees of calculation.

His long legs moved with unconscious grace as he dodged the laughing kids and crowded buffet table. He carried his strength and power well. More than one of the men recognized the hard, hungry look in his eyes and the grim line around his mouth. In earlier days they'd looked the same, unyielding and unforgiving.

"Boys," Marcus said, as Chance came to a halt beneath the tree's welcome shade, "I'd like for you to meet Chance McCall, my right-hand man and, as of last month, my new foreman."

"Gentlemen," Chance said, touching his forefinger to the wide brim of his gray Stetson. He knew these men represented power in oil, horses, cattle, even the stock market. His keen gaze missed none of the looks he was receiving. *What in hell is this all about?* he wondered. "Is there something you need, Marcus?"

"Now that you mention it . . ."

Chance stared at the stranger. The man was hefty, and he shoved the cigar he was chewing to the other side of his mouth before he spoke.

"We been watchin' you standin' by that gate directin' traffic and ol' Thurman here"—he gestured with his cigar toward another man in the group—"remarked that you look mighty like a man he used to know."

There was no outward sign of the panic Chance felt. Instead, a sardonic expression spread across his face. His eyebrow cocked, and a cold smile slipped into place. They were going to have to ask. He wasn't volunteering a damn thing. Besides, he assured himself, there was no way they could know.

The big man laughed heartily as he continued. "I like this boy. He don't give nothin' away. I could use him in my company. Bet you're a hell of a poker player, McCall."

"No way, Hancock," Marcus said. "I didn't invite you out here to steal my best man."

"Will that be all?" Chance asked, as he started to walk away.

"Say, boy," Hancock persisted, "you never did say if you was kin."

"Well," Chance drawled, "could be because you didn't mention who it was I looked like."

"Hell, if you ain't right," Hancock laughed. "Say Thurman, what did you say that man's name was?"

"Logan Henry . . . an oil man from down around Odessa way. Met him at the Permian Basin Oil Show a few years back. Now there was a party. The Chuck Wagon Gang out of Odessa had the best barbecue I ever did eat. No offense to you, Marcus, but them good old boys are professionals at puttin' on a feed."

Jenny was sitting on the fence, out of reach of the exploding firecrackers and frenzied guests, yet within earshot of the conversation going on between Chance and her father's friends. She saw the shock in Chance's eyes as the man's name was mentioned. It startled her and then made her nervous. That he could have secrets had never occurred to her. But it did now, and Jenny being Jenny, would not be the one to let it die.

Chance belonged to her. It was understood. He had from the first day he'd hired on. It didn't matter to Jenny if she was the only one aware of this arrangement. If he had problems, she had problems.

Chance didn't waver. "Never heard of him." He turned to Marcus. "You need anything else, boss?"

Marcus knew Chance was angry. It was the only time he'd ever called him boss. The anger surprised Marcus and made him curious, but he decided to let it go.

"No. Go on and enjoy yourself. Have a good time. Get some barbecue and cold beer. Let these jokers park their own cars. If they get stuck, they can get themselves unstuck later."

Chance touched the brim of his hat in a brief, almost rude good-bye to the staring men, spun on his boot heel, and disappeared into the noisy crowd.

"I think you touched raw flesh, Hancock," Marcus muttered as he watched Chance walk away. "Real raw." It surprised him and then made him wonder. In all the years he'd known this man, it was the first time he'd ever seen him lose any control over his emotions.

Jenny jumped down from the fence and followed Chance's retreat. Twice she lost him in the crowd before spotting the wide-brimmed gray hat he was wearing. Although he was nearly a head above most of the crowd, Jenny wasn't more than four inches past five feet. At the age of sixteen, it didn't look as if she would exceed that height.

"Chance!" She focused on the Stetson. "Chance!" she called again, only louder. "Wait for me." She knew he heard her. She saw hesitation in the movement of the hat bobbing above the crowd.

Chance heard her call, but continued to move through the crowd, desperate to get away from the memories that had been so rudely and unexpectedly resurrected. Then he sighed at the persistent tone in her voice. He knew Jenny. He might as well give up because she wouldn't. He turned around and tried to pinpoint her location.

Jenny saw his face. She stopped short and bit her lip, shocked by the pain and anger evident in his expression as their eyes met across the crowd.

Damn. How long had she been standing there? He felt naked. She'd seen too much of him . . . of things that were better left buried. He took a deep breath, suppressing all of the old fears that had crawled out of the hole in his mind.

"Jenny! Here I am!" he called. He pushed his way back toward her. "Happy birthday, girl." He smiled gently at the way she almost preened. Then he grabbed her hand. "Hang on. I'll get you out of this mess."

Jenny clasped his hand, relishing the feel of hard calluses and gentle strength. She let him lead her through the crowd. She didn't care where he was going, it didn't matter. All she'd wanted for the last few years was to follow Chance McCall into eternity. Then curiosity got the best of her.

"Where are we going?" she asked, as they left the merry-makers and headed toward the stables.

"Do you want your birthday present or not?" Chance asked, grinning at the expression on her face. This small bundle of nervous energy never bored him. In fact, she'd been the single reason he'd stayed as long on the Triple T as he had. If he'd moved on years ago, who would have taken care of Jenny? It damn sure wouldn't have been her father. He was always too busy being boss. Chance knew what it felt like to have no one. Being Jenny's "someone" had given him as much pleasure as it had her.

"Wait here," he ordered, then returned before Jenny had time to fully appreciate the sight of his backside in those form-fitting jeans.

"Here." He handed her a long, nearly flat box wrapped in bright red paper. "Happy birthday, Jennifer Ann," he said gently, smiling at her eagerness as she tore the decorative wrappings.

He'd spent most of one afternoon choosing this gift. It had been all he could do to keep it hidden from her as long as he had. He had no secrets from Jenny, at least not many. There *were* the women he sometimes took out, but they were just that. Just women for expediency's sake, never for love.

"Oh!" The sunlight caught the beaten silver rosettes that decorated the hand-tooled leather of the new bridle. "Chance! It's beautiful!" She threw her arms around his neck, hugged him tightly, then swept a quick kiss across his cheek just before he pulled out of her arms.

"Sweet sixteen," he teased.

Jenny wiped the smile from his face when she leaned forward and softly finished the rhyme, "And never been kissed."

Suddenly all the noise and excitement of the day faded. Chance was shocked by the thoughts that flooded his mind. His body pulsed. For a moment his breathing stopped. Her face imprinted into his memory as if he were seeing her for the first time—pouting, slightly parted lips, with her dark, shoulder-length hair blowing gently in the wind. He was shaken by the need to lay her down in the dust and . . .

Startled by his desires, he stepped back, needing to put distance between them. She was just a kid, too young . . . and so damned beautiful it made him ache. He had to stop his thoughts and the look growing in her

eyes before things got out of hand. He suspected Jenny
was just trying out her new-found womanhood on the
first available man. Little did he know how she longed
only for him.

"Now, that's not so, Jenny," he chided, trying to lighten
the tension of the moment. "You have been kissed. I
seem to remember a certain young man named Melvin
some years back. Of course, he got a bloody nose for his
troubles. Could be word got around." He laughed and
started to pull her hair, when Jenny caught his hand and
cupped it to her face, pulling him close again.

Chance's heart skipped one beat, and then another,
as Jenny closed her eyes and rubbed her cheek against
the palm of his hand. He couldn't move. Every body
part that could, stiffened, including some that had no
business doing so. *God in heaven, make this stop or
never let it end!* He wanted to touch her but didn't dare
move.

When had she blossomed into this woman-child?
Where was the laughing urchin who'd dogged his steps
for the last five years?

A stray gust of wind blew a lock of her black, silky
hair across his face. His mouth opened to object and
instead tasted the errant strand as it slid across his lips.
He shuddered and gripped her arms, uncertain whether
to push her away or pull her beneath him.

Her breasts taunted him, pushing firmly against his
shirt. The tank top and coordinating shorts she was
wearing accentuated her slender, sun-tanned legs.
Chance closed his eyes and swallowed a groan as he
imagined those legs wrapped around him. The image
was too much for him to bear, and he cursed and jerked

away as if he'd just been slapped. This feeling was simply a reminder of what he'd been running from when he'd stumbled into the Triple T. Jenny was still a child. He had no business thinking about her . . . not like this.

Jenny opened her eyes and smiled at the expression of pure shock and lust on Chance's face. *Thank God!* she thought. *Now to give him something else to think about.* She leaned forward, slid her arms around his neck before he could move away, and planted a lingering kiss at the corner of his mouth.

Chance inhaled. The world stopped. Jenny was kissing him. She'd kissed him plenty of times before. But never like this. She'd never moved her lips across his mouth in this yearning, searching motion. She'd never made that soft, almost kittenlike sound of satisfaction as the tip of her tongue traced that old scar at the edge of his lower lip. He was just thinking of turning enough to cover her lips with his own when she withdrew and sighed.

"Thanks for the birthday present, Chance."

She dusted the seat of her shorts and waved good-bye as she walked away, clutching her birthday bridle tightly. She willed herself not to giggle, or run, but the urge to do both was strong, as was her awareness of the fact that she still didn't have an answer as to why Chance had bolted from the visit with Marcus and his friends.

Chance valiantly fought the need to help her with her dusting as he watched her hands brushing against her backside. He took a deep breath and swallowed curses.

Jenny stopped and turned, her curiosity and determination getting the better of her.

"Chance?"

"What?" he mumbled, still in shock from the kiss and his x-rated thoughts.

"Who's Logan Henry?"

The look of lust he'd been wearing was replaced by something that Jenny had never seen before. It grew and grew on his face until she became afraid. What had she done? What had she said? Long seconds went by and still she waited for her answer. Finally he spoke.

"Just a ghost," he said. His words were harsh and angry.

"Well," she announced, "I don't believe in ghosts."

Chance stood silently, stunned as her words sank in. When he finally answered, there was no one left to hear. "I wish to hell I didn't."

2

He moved with grace and power. Bare to the waist in the noonday heat, his jeans loose and beltless so that a scant inch of white from his briefs showed, reminding Jenny that there was more to him than the eye could see. His hat hung on the corner post of the corral, his denim shirt draped between the rails.

His dark hair curled slightly at the neck, a reminder that he'd missed his last two dates to get a haircut. Sun blistered down upon his bare back, turning his skin to an even deeper shade of brown. Sweat poured down from his hairline, over his sharp, chiseled jaw and down the tight band of muscles across his belly. A powerful man, thirty years old, and in his prime.

Hidden by the shrubbery that bordered the yard, Jenny watched him move, mesmerized by the sensual pull that existed between them . . . always. She licked her lips; an unconscious movement that mimicked Chance when he tried to catch a drop of sweat that hung at the corner of his mouth. He missed, and Jenny swore softly to herself as she watched the errant perspiration hit his chest and flow down into the waistband of his jeans.

In the old days, she would have been right beside him, laughing, talking, offering suggestions that he would gently ignore. Jenny blinked back tears. She missed the old days. And she missed Chance.

She'd learned over the last few years that whenever she appeared, Chance disappeared. At first she'd been dumbfounded. While she'd been growing up, he'd been her rock, her dependable companion. Hurt and anger had followed on the heels of being ignored. Confrontation between them seemed inevitable until Henry, an aging wrangler who'd been more father figure than her father's employee, had delicately pointed out in his sparse vernacular that Chance didn't hate the sight of her. She just reminded him of things he couldn't have.

"What can't he have?" Jenny remembered asking.

"You," Henry had answered.

Suddenly everything had fallen into place. Jenny had lived with the love of Chance McCall for so long, it had become familiar property in her heart. She'd taken it for granted that when he finally realized she'd grown up, his reciprocation would be automatic. The idea that Chance saw boundaries between them was appalling to her. She lost sleep at night trying to figure out ways to get past his overdeveloped sense of propriety but it was useless. The more she tried to get past his walls, the higher they became.

Finally, in despair and disgust she had begun to ignore him. It had been the single most difficult thing she'd ever done in her life, and it accomplished nothing. She had circles under her eyes and had begun to lose weight she couldn't spare. Juana had noticed Jenny's pallor and had sent her outside into the sunshine to soak up some of the Texas summer. All that did was put her right back in the vicinity of the man who had stolen her heart. And so she watched him, mesmerized.

Chance held the long length of water hose in one hand and a soft, soapy sponge in the other as he moved back and forth along the length of his pickup truck, methodically washing away the week's worth of dust and grime from the exterior. It was Saturday, the fourth Saturday of the month. Tonight he would go to town and lose himself in the wild atmosphere of a local bar. He had no preferences. One time it would be one club, the next month another. Sometimes he'd meet a woman, sometimes not. They weren't important, but at times, necessary. He'd spent the better part of the last seven years trying to forget that he'd fallen in love with the boss's daughter on her sixteenth birthday. And he'd lost sleep at night wishing that it was Jenny beneath his hot, aching body and not a damned, lumpy mattress.

Memories of his past and the secrets that lay between them always kept him at a distance. Yet nowhere on the Triple T could he work and not come face to face with reminders of her presence. She was an integral part of his life. Telling her how much he loved her would be impossible, though. Just as impossible as facing how much she loved him.

Her life with her father had not changed. Marcus seemed to care for Jenny, but he was never around when she needed him.

When she'd graduated from high school, it had been Chance who'd stood at the foot of the stage with camera in hand, mingling with parents of the other graduating seniors. Jenny had accepted her diploma. He'd snapped the picture. And the smile on her face as she'd walked toward him had nearly stopped his heart.

Marcus had missed her graduation, as he'd been away on one of his constant trips. He'd refused to cancel, though he'd offered to hire a professional photographer to commemorate the occasion and then presented her with a new car as a graduation present. Jenny had refused the offer of a photographer but calmly accepted the car and his off-hand apology. She didn't need her father. She had Chance.

College had loomed on the horizon, an ominous reminder that Jenny would leave the Triple T . . . maybe for good.

Chance had alternated between dismay that she would be out of his sight and relief that it was what he needed to put their relationship back into perspective. Only that hadn't worked. After one semester, she'd transferred to a school closer to home and commuted.

He hadn't realized until after she'd come home that Christmas, how she'd suffered from the distance between them, and how much he'd missed her company.

❖   ❖   ❖

"Somethin' smells good," Henry said, shutting the kitchen door with a slam. He raced Chance for a place by Juana's fireside.

"Jenny's coming home today," she said, as if that explained everything.

Chance's stomach knotted, reminding him of something he'd spent a sleepless night trying to forget. Jenny!

Her first semester at college was finally behind her. Houston seemed a lifetime away. The lines around his mouth tightened as he stepped closer to the warmth of the free-standing fireplace in the corner of the room. How was he going to get through the next three and a half years without seeing her? And then a worse thought arose: What if she fell in love with some college boy and never came back at all?

"Where's Marcus?" Henry asked. "Chance saw a pack of coyotes yesterday when he was out checking on that new crop of calves. Reckon we should hire that hunter and his dogs like we did last year and get rid of them varmints before they get rid of them new calves?"

Juana shrugged. "He called about an hour ago. He's going to stay over in Dallas again tonight."

Chance frowned. Dammit! He was doing it to her again! Jenny would come home . . . and no one would be there for her. The selfish son-of-a-bitch! It was Christmas, for God's sake!

Henry sidled over to the cabinet and snuck a couple of Juana's freshly baked oatmeal cookies, stuffing one quickly into his mouth before she could catch him.

"Figgers he wouldn't be here," Henry muttered, bent on talking and swallowing at the same time. "Shuda' took care of it on our own anyway."

Juana glared. "You've had enough cookies."

Henry grinned.

"I'll call the coyote hunter myself," Chance said. "Mind if I use the phone in Marcus's office? I think the man's number is in his Rolodex."

Juana nodded and handed Chance a cookie as he walked past her.

Henry frowned. "How come you told me not to eat no more and then gave him a cookie?"

Juana's eyebrows rose. "Because you're already three ahead of him. That's why! I saw you sneaking cookies earlier. I'm no fool, Henry Thomas. You go on with Chance and get out of my kitchen. I want things special for Jenny."

Henry grinned and then the smile faded. "Don't know how special it'll be when she comes home to a damned empty house again. I know you'll be here, but you know what I mean."

Juana nodded. "*Es verdad,*" she said softly, and then looked in the direction that Chance had gone. "But Jenny won't mind . . . not as long as that one is here."

She and Henry stared at each other, absorbing the truth of her words. They'd long been aware of the affection Jenny had for Chance. And they'd watched it grow from a child's dependence to a woman's love. Henry, more than anyone else, knew how much Jenny meant to Chance. But he didn't understand the man. There was a line in the big man's mind that he couldn't seem to cross.

Only Chance knew what made him keep Jenny at arm's length.

"The man's on his way," Chance said, as he walked

back into the kitchen. "Come on, Henry. I told him we'd meet him at the west pasture."

Henry nodded and grabbed one last cookie on his way out the door.

Juana frowned as she watched them leave. But she wasn't frowning at the fact that the old cowboy had sneaked another cookie. She was worried about the silence that had enveloped Chance when Jenny's name had been mentioned.

It was spitting snow. Tiny flakes mixed with minute pellets of ice that bit into Chance's already frozen cheeks as he parked the ranch's four-by-four truck and made a run for his quarters. Having a house to himself, however small, was going to be a welcome respite tonight. It had been rough spending holidays alone in the bed-lined bunkhouse when he'd first signed on at the Triple T. Then he'd had to face the fact that everyone on the ranch had someone . . . somewhere . . . except him. Now, because he was always alone, tonight would be like any other.

He pushed the door open, and it slammed itself shut as he made a beeline for the fire burning in his stove.

"Merry Christmas," Jenny said softly, letting her eyes feast on the tall cowboy who'd just come in from the cold.

He spun around in surprise. She stepped out of the shadows and walked toward him. He forgot to speak. My God, how she'd changed! Too much! He didn't know what to say to this Jenny. The girl who'd gone away to college had come back a woman.

"Here, let me help you out of that coat," she said, and began unfastening the heavy sheepskin jacket, brushing away ice and snow as her fingers journeyed from button to button.

Her blue eyes burned as clear and hot as a summer day. His hands caught her fingers as the last button came open just below his belt buckle.

She looked up, trying to get her gaze past his mouth but failing. Those lips, usually so hard and unyielding, had softened and curved into a smile of welcome.

"Merry Christmas, yourself, Jennifer Ann," Chance whispered as he slid her arms around his waist and wrapped her inside his coat. Her cheek lay against the steady rhythm of his heart as his arms enfolded her. She inhaled sharply and blinked back tears. She was home!

"I missed you," he said softly.

Jenny swallowed hard, twice, before she trusted herself to speak. "Don't tell me that," she teased, her eyes flashing a warning he didn't want to interpret. She leaned back, bracing herself against his arms. "I know all about those women in town, mister. You don't have time to miss anyone."

His heartbeat doubled as the blood hammered against his chest. "You're too well informed for my peace of mind," Chance muttered, and tightened his hold on her waist. It felt wonderful to be holding her, touching her.

"You have no secrets from me," she teased.

Oh, but I do, Chance thought.

Chance knew he shouldn't. He knew it would be a mistake. But he couldn't help himself, or stop Jenny. He stared at her face, inhaled sharply, and lowered his head.

His mouth was cold on her lips, moving gently, tentatively and, for Jenny, too achingly slow. She sighed, shifted in his arms, and stepped forward, aligning herself completely against his body, relishing in the muscles that tightened beneath her, the feel of desperation with which he held her.

Chance shuddered. He yanked his head up like a drowning man desperate for air. He started to step back . . . away from her arms, but Jenny wouldn't let him go. Instead she slipped her fingers inside the edges of his front pockets and gave his jeans a gentle tug.

"Don't do this," she begged. "Don't turn away from what's between us. What's always been between us."

He shook his head. "You don't know . . ."

"No," Jenny said. "*You* don't know. You don't know that I almost didn't survive this semester. You don't know that I was so homesick I almost quit twice."

Chance cupped her cheek. "I knew leaving home would be rough for you, honey. And I'm sorry Marcus wasn't here when you arrived. But I'm sure it was unavoidable. He'll be here tomorrow."

"Don't kid yourself . . . or me. Marcus will come home when he's ready and not one second sooner. To hell with whoever comes or goes around here. Besides, I wasn't homesick for him. It was you that nearly had me running home. It was you I dreamed of, and you I missed."

His eyes burned with unshed tears. His mouth worked, but no words would come. The need to tell her what was in his heart was almost overwhelming. And then she spoke, her words sending him reeling.

"I love you, Chance."

It was this declaration that had broadened the gap between them. And it was what stood between them . . . always.

He continued to move along the truck's red exterior with his water hose and sponge. It was a damn shame that he couldn't wash away the ghosts in his life as easily as the dirt came away from his truck. Jenny's persistence during the past three years had nearly sent him over the edge. He needed to claim his woman, and he needed to get the hell out of Texas. Both were necessary, but neither seemed possible.

He jerked the hose sharply and began to rinse the soap off the grill. The water trickled to a slow stream and then came to a complete stop. He cursed beneath his breath as he dropped it to the ground and started back around the truck, thinking it had become caught and trapped the flow of water. He couldn't have been more wrong.

Jenny stood at the tailgate of his truck, wearing a green bikini and a taunting grin as she held up the hose, indicating impishly that she'd just twisted it into a knot.

"Dammit, Jennifer," he said, "turn it loose. I've got places to go tonight. I can't be messing around like this."

The "places to go" was what did it. Jenny knew good and well that he "visited women" when he disappeared once a month. She wasn't a fool. But the fury that grew with each impending fourth Saturday was getting the best of her. If he wasn't such a pig-headed idiot, he could be "visiting" her instead of strangers. She reacted without thought, intent only on delaying his trip.

"Fine," she drawled. "You want water . . ." She released the kink, knowing full well that the water was going to come gushing through the limp hose and cause the end that he'd just dropped to do a dance on the muddy ground beneath him.

The look on Chance's face when the hose came to life between his legs was priceless. One minute he was straddling limp, gray rubber, the next he was trying to dodge the wild, snakelike slither of the nozzle as it spewed mud and water alike over him and his freshly washed truck.

Jenny doubled over with laughter. By the time he'd caught the hose and halted its wild behavior, he looked as if he'd just pissed his pants in a hog wallow.

Chance stared, aimed the gushing hose away from his soaked jeans, and inhaled the sight before him. He knew damn good and well that Jenny's outfit was intentionally seductive.

Her breasts were covered just to the point of indecency with small triangles of green, drawing the eye straight toward her long brown arms and legs, her flat stomach, and her curves that taunted and teased. He'd just straddled a cold shower that had had no effect on the instant heat that rushed through his body at the thought of making love to Jenny in the cool mud—peeling that little green bit of nothing off of her one inch at a time and burying his hot, aching body in her softness until neither of them knew the way home.

"Think that was funny, do you?" he asked. The glint in his eye should have warned her, but she saw it too late to run.

The spray hit her square in the chest and knocked

her back against the truck. She gasped, trying to catch her breath as the water pummeled her breasts. And then it seemed to take on a life of its own as it awakened her body with powerful and continuous strokes.

Chance jerked in reflex. His eyes narrowed and his lips thinned as he watched her nipples taunt him through the thin, wet fabric. He stood transfixed while the water touched her in a way he dared not.

"Holy hell," Chance muttered. Jenny's face was alive with passion. It was move or die. He moved. The hose fell to the ground, writhing wildly as it spewed water onto the already muddy earth. Chance backed blindly, knowing that he had to put as much distance between them as possible before he burst.

Jenny was just as shocked as Chance. This wasn't supposed to happen.

A long silence hung between them. It took all Chance's willpower not to gather her in his arms and carry her off to his bed. Jenny's face was a mixture of torment and confusion, but it was nothing next to the knot she'd pulled in his gut. She looked up in time to see him stagger over to the faucet and turn off the water.

"Chance . . ." she began, when his curt order halted her.

"Get the hell out of here, Jennifer Ann. You had no business pulling a stunt like that. Stay away from me, dammit. Just stay away!"

Shocked tears flooded her eyes, but she'd be fried in hell before she cried in front of him.

"I live here, mister," she yelled back in his face. "But if that's the way you want it, it won't be for long. Marcus wants to marry me off like a damned brood mare. He has never even acknowledged my existence, and now, all of a sudden, he sees me as a marketable asset. You don't want me around. Why the hell should I not comply? Why the hell not? I've yet to meet a man who ever wanted me anyway."

Chance couldn't move. Marcus wanted her to marry? He'd heard nothing about it! The thought made him sick. He couldn't imagine another man with his hands on Jenny. In his heart, she belonged to him. But, in the real world, she never would.

She watched the shock appear on his face. *Good!* she thought as she struggled to her feet and started back toward the house, gaining momentum with each yard that separated them.

"Jenny, wait," Chance called, but it was too late.

She was too hurt and mad and blinded by tears to stop. Her ears roared and the world turned dark as she staggered into the backyard and collapsed onto a lounge chair. She *was* hurt, and God knew she was mad. But words weren't necessary. An inspiration had occurred to her. If Chance thought he didn't want her . . . then she'd see how he liked it if someone else did.

But that Saturday night, for the first time since he'd arrived on the Triple T, Chance McCall didn't come home at all.

The men were laughing about the boss's wild weekend when Jenny came through the door of the stable area in search of a horse for her daily ride. The sudden silence was not soon enough to quiet the pain that shot through her when Chance's name was mentioned.

She didn't have to hear it from them. She'd been the first to know that he hadn't come back from his Saturday night fling.

She'd sat dry-eyed, numb and sleepless, as she watched the driveway for a pair of headlights that never appeared.

The next morning she and Marcus shared something rare . . . breakfast.

"Jenny, it's great to be having a meal with you," he said, letting his eyes wander across the face of the daughter who'd suddenly become a woman without his noticing.

She was so precious to him, yet such an unknown. He could make a deal with the best businessmen, pick out a stud horse that would make him millions, yet he knew nothing about what made his daughter tick. And he knew it was his own fault. Every chance he'd had to act as father to his girl, he'd delegated to someone else. He sighed. Hindsight was always clearer that foresight. But looking back was not Marcus Tyler's way. He was forever and always looking toward the future. And the future for him seemed to warrant delivering his daughter safely into the hands of another man . . . namely a husband.

She smiled and nodded, lost in the overwhelming memory of Chance's refusal to admit he loved her. And she didn't think she was mistaken. She could actually feel the intensity of emotion whenever they were together.

Marcus knew something was wrong. It was unusual

for Jenny to be so silent. He said the first thing that popped into his mind. "How would you feel about Jordan Whitelaw and his son Darrin coming to dinner tonight?" He'd barely started to whitewash the question with reasons when she agreed.

"That would be fine with me," she said. "I have a new red dress that I've been wanting to wear. It's the perfect opportunity. I think I'll call my hairdresser and see if she can't work me into her schedule this afternoon. I need a trim."

Marcus nearly dropped his fork at her response, but he wasn't going to question his good fortune. "That's great, honey," he said. "Whatever you need, just go ahead and get it. Buy yourself some new dresses— Buy a whole rack. We should do this more often."

His eyes lit up as he envisioned a table full of family, with him at the head. A son-in-law . . . grandchildren . . . he could hardly wait, unaware of the undercurrent of reasons boiling inside his daughter.

Jenny nodded and smiled again. She felt a little guilty at letting Marcus assume she was interested in meeting eligible men. But if this served its purpose, it would be worth it. As far as she was concerned, she'd already met the only man she'd ever want. She just had to find a way to make him admit he wanted her too.

Thinking about the dinner tonight almost made her shudder. She knew what it would be like, being put on display for the studs that he intended to parade before her. That was how Jenny categorized the so-called eligible men into whose company she would be tossed. She wondered grimly if she was going to have any choice, or if she should even care. If their presence brought Chance around, it would be worth it.

∘   ∘   ∘

Jenny grabbed her leather gloves from the hall table, shook the leg of her blue jeans down over the top of her boot, and tucked her brown plaid shirt inside her belt. She picked up her hat, shoved it on top of her head, and headed out the door. She needed some air. Last night's dinner had been a disaster. Darrin Whitelaw was nice, but he wasn't Chance. She'd gone to bed sick to her stomach with guilt and frustration.

Her daily rides had become the only thing she could look forward to, and today she needed a challenge. The stud horse she had in mind was a good choice. It would take all her skill and strength to keep him in line.

"Henry, is Cheyenne available to ride today?"

The look on his face told her volumes. He was fully aware of the fact that Jenny and the foreman were in love. And he also knew why she wanted to ride that unruly stallion. He suspected that it matched the turmoil in her heart.

"He's here," Henry drawled, "but he ain't bein' friendly."

Jenny knew what he meant. She bit her lip and kicked a divot out of the dirt floor of the stables.

"Well, I'm not feeling any too friendly myself at the moment," she answered sharply. "Maybe we'll suit each other just fine."

Henry shrugged and walked off to saddle the horse. He knew better than to argue. Jenny was capable of handling the animal. He just didn't like the idea of her taking any chances.

Chance walked past the barns, leading two young

horses toward their stalls, satisfied with the daily training session that they'd been through. The breeding program they'd initiated was working out very well, and he saw a lot of potential ahead for the Triple T line. Crossing Cheyenne's fiery endurance and clean lines with the dependability and faithfulness of their better mares was resulting in some fine colts.

He heard Jenny's voice before he saw her, and then when he watched Henry walk away with a look of resignation on his face, knew that he'd better investigate. He handed over the two horses he'd been leading to one of the ranch hands and started toward the stalls where the riding horses were stabled.

"What the hell are you doing?" he asked when he saw Henry leading Cheyenne out of his stall.

Henry shrugged and pointed over his shoulder with his thumb as he pulled a saddle blanket down and slapped it across the powerful stallion's back.

"Jenny's goin' ridin'."

"Not on that she isn't." Chance took the reins out of Henry's hands, yanked the blanket off the horse's back, and tossed it to one side as he returned the horse to its stall.

Cheyenne yanked back on the reins and danced sideways, rebelling at the premature return to the small, confined area of his stall. He was antsy enough knowing that mares were close by and ready to breed. It was what he was born to do, dominate and lead. Being confined within the space of a stall when his instincts told him to be gathering a herd was making him too randy to ride.

"Well, I ain't gonna be the one to tell her," Henry drawled, and disappeared down the shadowy hallway.

Chance grimaced as he slipped the bridle off of the stallion. He moved him to one side, stepped out of the stall, and fastened the door. Ignoring the horse's neigh of discontent, he walked to the other side of the stables, saddled and bridled one of the riding horses, and led him to where Jenny was waiting.

Jenny turned around at the sound of the approaching horse and then frowned.

"That's not Cheyenne," she said.

"No, ma'am, it's not."

They stared, man to woman, appraising the other's determination in this issue.

Jenny shrugged. She hated to admit it, but she'd been apprehensive about riding the stallion anyway. She'd seen the look on Henry's face. She'd just been too stubborn to admit she was wrong. Chance had called her bluff.

"Doesn't much matter," she mumbled, and reached for the reins.

"Come here," he said, and cupped his hands to give her a leg up on the horse. She vaulted into the saddle.

She stared down into his eyes. The sounds around them muted and faded until Jenny forgot everything and everyone but the man who was gazing up at her. He was so familiar, and yet such a stranger.

Who was this man, Chance McCall? Why did he shun her when every other man in the area would give his eyeteeth to bed her? Her silent questions went unanswered as Chance handed her the reins. Their hands touched, inadvertently, and then with purpose. His thumb rubbed across her knuckles as he pulled absently at the stirrup.

"Are you okay?" he asked.

Jenny felt like crying. She knew he was trying to get past the truck washing incident and reestablish a line of communication. It was obvious to her that Chance was as miserable as she.

She nodded. "I'm fine."

"Riding anywhere special?" he asked softly.

"Just riding," she answered, willing silently—almost begging—that he would accompany her.

But he shrugged and then stepped away. "Be careful."

His eyes devoured as his voice seduced. Jenny shivered.

"As always," she answered, and watched him walk away.

3

Chance stared down at the dust on the floor of the corral and tried to ignore the circle of people outside the arena. He'd been given orders to parade Marcus's latest acquisitions before the crowd, and that's just what he intended to do. But from the way some of the younger men were ogling Jenny, he felt like he should rope and halter her and lead her around with the horses. She was the one Marcus had put on show. It made him mad as hell.

She perched on the top rail, ignoring most of their catcalls and jests, giving them only the attention that manners demanded. Her cool, touch-me-not demeanor only intensified their behavior.

Jenny heard the young men's teasing invitations, but she wasn't interested in them. Her sole interest in the proceedings lay in Chance's reactions.

Her father's announcement had been cool. Inviting

some horse buyers out for an afternoon showing of some of his newest purchases and then following that up with some of the stock he had for sale was not out of the ordinary. But Jenny saw through his plan. It was solely for the purpose of assembling as many eligible men as possible at one time, and she knew it. What other explanation could there possibly be for the fact that most of the prospective buyers were under the age of thirty?

"Chance!" Marcus called. "Bring that mare that just foaled. Run her and the baby out here and let these men have a look-see at the latest results of our breeding plan."

He nodded. Henry led away the horses that had been on display as Chance went to get the mare.

She whickered a hello as Chance entered her stall. "Come on, momma," he said softly. "Some VIPs want to look at you and your baby, here. If you play your cards right, you might wind up eating your oats off of china instead of out of a feed bag."

His sarcasm was lost on the horse. She led easily, a gentle, docile horse with clean lines and a strong build. The foal stole the show as it nickered and kicked, its stubby tail flying high behind long, delicate legs as it ran short, nervous circles around Chance and its mother.

Jenny laughed. She clapped her hands at the foal's spirit and quickly forgot the reason why she'd intended to remain aloof. The baby was too dear to resist.

She vaulted down from the fence and walked into the arena. Her hand slipped into her pocket and then she was holding it out in front of her, calling softly in a quiet, crooning tone.

The foal stopped short, its tiny ears upright and dark eyes watching nervously as the stranger came close. The mare whinnied softly as Jenny's familiar scent reached her nostrils. Her muzzle extended as she reached hungrily for the treat she knew was waiting.

Jenny smiled, one eye on the baby, the other on the mother, whose soft nostrils stroked her palm as the mare delicately nibbled the sugar cube out of her hand.

The foal was curious. Jenny could see its interest from the corner of her eye. Slowly she slid a second cube out of her pocket and extended her palm. The foal sniffed the air, and then made one quick sidestep, just to remind Jenny who was in charge. But the smell was enticing and curiosity won out. Jenny's heart thumped as the foal walked toward her on those matchstick legs. She held her breath, and as the crowd watched, her patience overcame the foal's fears. The sugar cube disappeared into the tiny mouth.

Fascinated in spite of himself at the way she'd coaxed the mare and foal to her will, Chance couldn't resist the dig.

"You have them all eating out of the palm of your hand, don't you, girl?"

Jenny looked up. He said one thing, but she knew he meant another. His remark referred to the men outside the corral, not the horses.

"Not all," she answered. "Not yet. But I'm not about to quit trying. Sometimes . . . the ones hardest to get are the best. And if I can't have the best"—her stare made him forget what he'd been about to say—"then I don't want anything at all."

He was speechless. He watched her walk away and

resume her seat on the fence as the crowd clapped and cheered in appreciation of the impromptu show. The noise sent the foal running to the opposite end of the corral. The mare nickered nervously and Chance quickly led them both away.

"Well, hell," he muttered, as he fastened the mare and her foal back into their stall. "That was futile for the both of us, lady. Your baby showed off . . . and I got put in my place . . . as usual."

The only problem is, I don't know where my place is. I know what I want, and I know what I can't have. And I'm expected to exist somewhere in between. That's not existing, that's hell!

He slammed the latch shut and pushed his Stetson down tight on his head. Dust billowed beneath his boot heels as he stomped back out into the arena to see what his boss wanted of him now. But he knew it didn't much matter. As long as that line of men was waiting to get their hands on Jenny, his life wasn't worth a damn.

The men were given free rein to wander the horse barns. It was Marcus's way of letting them talk among themselves and come to a decision about whether or not to purchase some of his stock. He didn't much care. He wasn't particularly wanting to sell. He'd staged the entire event for Jenny's sake.

After she'd finally agreed to meet *one* young man, he'd been inspired to try bigger and better things. This horse showing was simply a means to an end. One never knew what would strike sparks between a young man and woman.

A few months ago it had dawned on him that she had little to no social life. He'd been dumbstruck. The only explanation he could come up with was that she had to be lacking in opportunity. Therefore, he'd decided he had to provide.

In the past, he hadn't given Jenny's welfare much notice. But when it had finally occurred to him that Jenny should be thinking about settling down and raising a family, he'd clung to the idea with bulldog tenacity. He had no idea that his daughter was using his lineup of possible suitors as a means of making his foreman jealous.

"Look, son," Devlin Walters said. "It can't hurt to be nice to her. Hell, it shouldn't hurt at all. I'd be proud to call her daughter." And then he grinned and nudged his son as they pretended to look over a herd of geldings in a side corral. "I'd be even prouder to get her daddy's money in my pocket. She's pretty as they come and built like a brick . . ."

"That's entirely beside the point," Jason Walters said.

His father was like a broken record. He'd been pushing him to marry for a year. And when they'd gotten the invitation to come out to the Triple T, his father had lost all reason. It wasn't that Jason didn't like Jennifer Tyler. Any man who deserved to call himself a man would like to take that female to bed. She was pretty and rich—a deadly combination.

The problem was, she wouldn't have any of it. He'd spent the entire day giving her the best of his male repertoire and all he'd gotten for his troubles was a sorry-ass smile. Half the men here had at least gotten her to speak. If she wouldn't even talk to him, how the hell did his father expect him to get to first base . . . let alone farther?

"Look, Jason," Devlin said, "you're a good-looking boy. You take after your mother's side of the family . . . and God knows they've got more looks than brains." He blushed as he realized what he'd just implied, but continued as if it didn't matter. "What woman could resist you if you gave it your all?" He lowered his voice. "Get her interested . . . and then get her pregnant. It's the surest way I know to snag a reluctant woman, and that's a fact. Give it a try. It can't hurt."

Chance couldn't believe what he'd just heard. Fury boiled in him as he dropped the saddle he'd been carrying and walked around the corner of the corral. The two men jumped as if they'd been shot, and looked at each other in guilty silence.

"That's where you're wrong, Mr. Walters." Chance's drawl was deceptively soft.

The younger man shivered. He saw pure, unadulterated anger boiling behind those dark eyes and wished he'd stayed at home.

"It'll hurt a hell of a lot," Chance continued. "If your son goes anywhere near Jenny Tyler, I'll tell her what you said. And if by some wild, off-chance, you decide to try me and take her out anyway . . . you'd better pray to God that she comes back in the same condition in which she left." He stared pointedly at the younger Walters and whispered, "You touch her . . . I'll break your neck."

Devlin Walters blustered. He was furious they'd been caught out, and furious that a mere hired hand was reading him the riot act. If it had come from Marcus himself, that would have been another matter altogether.

"Look here," he said. "You have no right talking to us like that. What we said . . . why . . . it was just in jest, you understand. But that's beside the point. Miss Tyler's welfare is none of your business."

"That's where you're wrong," Chance said softly. Jenny *is* my business. Has been since she was eleven years old. And don't you forget it."

Jason Walters decided that if he made it home in one piece today, he didn't give a tinker's damn what his father wanted, he was going back to college. Another degree never hurt anyone . . . and it was a lot less painful than what this implied.

Devlin Walters might have tried to push the boundaries of good conscience and continue the argument, but Marcus and Jenny were coming toward them.

For one long moment, the three men stared at one another, each waiting to see if another was willing to stir up trouble.

"So, Dev," Marcus said, as he slapped the elder Walters jovially, "I see you've met Chance. I was going to introduce you, but I see you've beat me to it." He smiled at Chance as he continued, unaware of the undercurrents seething between the men. "He's my other right hand," Marcus said. "The Triple T wouldn't be half the place it is without him. And don't get Jenny started on his accomplishments . . . she'll never shut up. She thinks he can do no wrong."

Jenny saw the looks the men were exchanging. Something had happened, of that she was certain. But what remained a mystery.

"We introduced ourselves," Chance said, then gave Jenny a long, telling look and walked away without looking back.

Jason Walters breathed a sigh of relief. "It's been really nice meeting you, Jenny," he said. "But my dad and I were just saying that Mom is expecting us. In fact, she expected us home over an hour ago. We've got to be going, right, Dad?"

Devlin shook hands with his host, winked at Jenny just to prove to himself that that damned foreman didn't own all the rights, and let his son lead him away.

"I'll be right back," Marcus said. "I'll just walk them to their car."

Jenny nodded. She had no intention of following him. Her sights were set on locating Chance and finding out what had been going on. It didn't take her long. He was slamming saddles and bridles around the tack room as if he'd just lost his mind.

"What's wrong with you?" Jenny asked, as she grabbed a bridle out of his hand before he flung it across the room.

His hungry gaze swept over her like wildfire. Her slim waist and flared hips were nothing but a reminder of what he'd overheard. It made him crazy to think about any man putting his hands . . . or anything else . . . on her.

"Nothing," he said, turning away.

She shoved a fist against his chest and stopped his retreat. "Bull! Don't give me that," she said. "I saw the looks . . . I heard what you *weren't* saying. I want to know, and I want to know now."

"Well, sometimes you don't always get what you want, Miss Tyler." Chance's drawl was slow and cruel.

Jenny gasped. It was the first time in their entire relationship that Chance had ever . . . knowingly . . . insulted her. Tears sprang to her eyes. She blinked furiously, angry with herself for giving in to the feeling and angry with him for causing it.

Chance groaned. He'd seen the tears, and he knew she didn't deserve pain.

"You don't have to remind me," Jenny said, and spun around, intent on putting as much space between them as possible before the tears began to run.

"Wait!"

She stopped but refused to turn around.

"What?" Anger kept her back straight and defiant.

"I'm sorry," he said quietly. "But there are things in my life that you don't understand. There are things I can't change." The pain was thick in his voice as he finished. "I wish to hell I could . . . but I can't. And as for Walters and his son . . . don't mess with them. . . . Okay?"

Her pause showed him that she'd gotten the message.

"Okay," she said. When she turned around, he was gone.

Jenny stuffed her hands into her jacket pocket, stepped off the porch, and wandered down toward the barns. She'd been aware of the activity in the main corrals all afternoon but had been stuck inside the house entertaining the latest of Marcus's friends who'd come calling. The horse show had come and gone, but Marcus had obviously not given up. Neither had Jenny. She was back to her old plan of trying to make Chance jealous.

Today, it seemed hopeless. He kept ignoring her and the silent treatment she was receiving was breaking her heart. After the incident at the horse show, he'd dodged her with precision and determination.

"How's it going?" she asked, smiling at Henry.

She rested her chin on her forearms and leaned against the top rail, watching the last of the mares being led out to the corral where Cheyenne was standing at stud.

"'Bout the same as usual," Henry drawled. It didn't take a mind reader to figure out what had been going on up at the house. And it was obvious from the look on his Jenny's face that she was less than excited about the prospective son-in-laws her father had paraded through the Triple T. "How 'bout you?"

Jenny snorted. It was enough said.

Chance came around the corner of the barns. The surge of excitement at seeing her dimmed as he realized what she'd been enduring. She hadn't been lying to him. After the array of men Marcus had paraded before her the other day, Chance had no doubts that he was serious. Marcus Tyler really was searching for a husband for his daughter. What hurt Chance most was the fact that Jenny didn't seem to give a damn who won the prize, the prize being her. This passive Jenny was not the woman he knew.

"Is this the last one?" Henry asked, as Chance walked up beside them.

Chance nodded. The trio stood in silence as the mare was led to the impatiently waiting stallion, then whinnied apprehensively even though she was ready to be bred. Her shrill scream sounded of panic, and Jenny blinked back tears as she watched the powerful stallion dancing and circling the mare, finally cornering her as he mounted, biting sharply at the back of her neck as the mating began.

"What's wrong, Jenny?" Henry asked. He'd seen the sudden spurt of tears and been shocked by the fact that she had then buried her head in her arms, refusing to watch what had always been commonplace for her.

"It doesn't matter to Marcus whether or not I love the man I marry. It only matters that I live with him, sleep with him, and produce offspring . . . hopefully a boy. He's never asked me if I liked any of these men, or even loved one. As far as Marcus is concerned, I'm just a damned brood mare for the Triple T. That's what's the matter. Dammit, Henry. He doesn't even know me!"

Henry's mouth twisted with concern as he turned to stare at Chance.

Chance returned the stare, unblinking, giving away nothing of the pain shooting through him.

Henry shrugged, patted Jenny awkwardly on the shoulder and walked away, unable to alleviate any of her fears. He'd like to punch Marcus Tyler in the nose. The man couldn't see what was right in front of him. It was all up to Jenny. She was the only one who could stop Marcus, but she didn't seem to give a good damn what happened to her. Henry sighed. He knew the reason why.

Chance's heart swelled in his chest, making it harder to speak, to bring each breath painfully past the constriction in his throat. He saw the defeat on her face and knew it was because of him. She didn't care about herself because she thought he didn't care about her.

"Jenny . . ." His voice was low, the pain of her words sharper than a knife in his belly. There had to be a way to take away the horrible distance between them.

She stared up at him through a veil of unshed tears, for once allowing her vulnerability to show. "Unless you can say it, Chance McCall, don't even talk to me."

He knew instantly to what she was referring. And there was no way he was ever going to say the words aloud. If he did, there'd be no turning back. How could he tell her he loved her? What would he have to offer but a past full of ugliness and shame. And love? It was too small a word for the feeling he had for her.

She watched the pain and indecision sweeping over his face. Then he recoiled as if remembering himself . . . and his place. His mouth tightened and his fingers knotted into fists as he turned and walked away.

"Oh, Chance," she whispered. "You're going to be the death of us both. Why? God in heaven, why?"

"Jenny, I'd like you to meet Nelson Turnbull," Marcus said. "His father and I grew up together back in Missouri. Imagine my surprise when Nelson showed up at the cattlemen's dinner today as one of the speakers."

"Imagine," Jenny drawled, and limply shook the hand of the tall, sandy-haired man who was eyeing her breasts with more than normal interest. "So," she said, willing to play their game, "exactly what do you do, Mr. Turnbull?"

"Nelson, please. And I'm a stockbroker from New York."

Jenny recoiled inwardly. "How interesting," she murmured. She walked over to the bar and got herself a glass of cola. "Anyone?" she asked, as she tipped her glass to her lips.

"I'd love a whiskey, neat," Nelson said as he slid onto the cushioned seat opposite the bar.

"Nothing for me, thanks," Marcus said. "I've got a few phone calls to make. I'll leave you two kids to get acquainted and then maybe we could go out to dinner?"

"That would be great!" Nelson said. "My treat of course."

"Of course," Jenny muttered to herself, and let the sharp tang of the cola slide down her throat too fast. She coughed and gasped as quick tears stung her eyes. It was just as well. It was a good cover for the real tears that brimmed as she watched her father's exit.

"We've just been set up," Nelson said. It was the wisest thing he could have done. It took the edge off of Jenny's resentment.

"It's not the first time," Jenny said, sliding the requested whiskey toward him with a skilled move.

"But I'd like it to be the last," Nelson said quietly.

He stared at her, his pale green eyes mentally undressing the small but shapely heir to the Triple T.

He'd heard through the Dallas grapevine that Marcus Tyler was parading eligible bachelors through the Triple T. Gossip claimed the daughter was a looker, but gossip didn't even do this woman justice.

Jenny had long ago left the scruffy urchin of her childhood in the Texas dust. She was a well-groomed, fashionable female with more than ample curves. Her shoulder-length black hair was perfectly cut and styled. Her face was china-doll perfect in features and proportion. But there was one aspect of Jenny that had remained the same over the years. Her wide, clear blue eyes missed nothing and, at the moment, were as cold as ice. She might look feminine, but she was still as tough as they came.

"So," she asked, "where are you taking us for dinner? I'm not going to pretend you haven't already made reservations. I need to know how to dress."

Nelson tipped his glass in recognition of her astuteness and smiled.

"Dress up, pretty lady. We're flying to Dallas. I've got the company jet. I'll show you a night on the town you won't soon forget."

It was quite a distance from Tyler to Dallas by car but, by air, less than thirty minutes. This one was out to impress. It was no surprise to Jenny when Marcus came through the door moments later wearing a practiced look of regret.

"I'm going to have to beg off dinner. It seems a problem has come up that I can't ignore. Have fun without me, okay?"

Jenny shrugged. It was to be expected. She'd go along for now. Maybe this one would be the trigger to ending Chance's patience. She couldn't believe he would let her marry someone else. Although she had no intention of letting it come to that, he didn't know that. And she knew of no other way to break down his defenses.

Nelson didn't even try to hide his elation.

Less than an hour later, Chance watched the couple leave. He stood on the front porch of the bunkhouse and watched the sequins sparkle on her dress. He heard the laughter in the man's voice as he called back to Marcus, who was waving good-bye.

The pain that swept over him was almost more than he could bear. He staggered backward until his boot heels hit the side of the bunkhouse and stopped his momentum.

"Damn your sorry soul to hell, Logan Henry. If you'd only stayed on your side of the tracks . . ." The bitter regret echoed in his soft whisper, resurrecting a ghost who should have stayed buried.

Just for an instant, Chance felt the pain, and the shame. He closed his eyes and, once again, saw the blood, the fresh earth covering the grave . . . and felt the fire.

He leaned his head against the wall, balled his fingers into fists and, as he turned to go inside, swung viciously toward a face that hovered in his mind. Knuckles rasped angrily against the rough wood of the house as flesh instantly gave way to blood that flowed. But he didn't care. The pain in his heart was far worse.

Jenny returned with daybreak. By afternoon, at Nelson's persistent insistence, they'd gone riding. She was showing him her world and exactly what was expected from the future heir to this dusty empire.

Her heart was heavy, her smile a pasted affair that grew stiffer and less frequent as the day progressed. But she stood her ground.

She knew Chance saw everything they did and that kept her going. If he would just get jealous enough to make a move . . .

She caught herself daydreaming just in time to dodge a low-hanging tree branch. But her sharp warning was not enough to save Nelson from a bump on the head. His near-hysterical reaction made the horse bolt and it was only through skilled riding that Jenny saved him from a hard tumble into a ditch. His unreasonable anger and acute discomfort mirrored obvious incompetence. It only reminded her how out of place this man was on a ranch.

They rode into the stable area. Jenny was leading Nelson's horse as he held a handkerchief to his head to stem the flow of blood. She stared pointedly at Henry who sauntered out to take their horses, and breathed a sigh of relief as the older man wisely made no mention of the wound. She looked around, hoping for a glimpse of Chance. He was nowhere in sight.

She sighed, swung her leg over the saddle horn and slid to the ground, then helped Nelson down from his mount.

"Have a good ride, Jenny?" Henry asked.

She sent Henry a frown he promptly ignored. "It was fine." She grabbed Nelson by the elbow, herding him toward the house before any more remarks could be made. She wasn't quite fast enough.

"A good shot of whiskey'll take the edge off of that," Henry called, and pointed toward Nelson's makeshift bandage.

Jenny spun around and motioned wildly behind Nelson's back as she pushed him toward the house. It was slightly humiliating to have gone riding with such a greenhorn, and she knew that Henry was chiding her for her choice of partner.

"Shut up!" she mouthed silently to Henry, and accentuated her warning with a sharp glare.

He grinned, tilted his hat, and led the two horses off to be brushed down, and then watered and fed.

"Oooh," Nelson moaned, as he stumbled on the uneven ground.

He was humiliated and angry with himself. He wished he'd never set foot on Texas soil. The only thing that kept him going was the thought of bedding and wedding Jenny Tyler and investing all that money.

"You'll be okay," Jenny said. "I'll get Juana to put an ice pack on it for you and then one of the men can drive you back to your motel in Tyler."

"I don't think I'm up to that," Nelson mumbled, seeing an opportunity arising from the incident. "I'm going to have to impose on your hospitality. I'll ask Marcus if I can spend the night. My head hurts too much to consider the drive."

Jenny wished she'd never seen Nelson Turnbull, but it was too late for that. She'd already encouraged him more than she should have, simply by going out to dinner last night in such a flamboyant manner. Offering him a bed was the least she could do after almost leaving his head on that limb back in the pasture.

"Certainly," she said. "There's an empty bedroom next to Marcus. You two can talk business to your heart's content."

Upon entering the house, Marcus began an instant commiseration at the sight of blood.

Jenny stomped off to her room, stripped herself of her clothes, and spent the next twenty minutes standing beneath the shower crying mad. She wasn't really crying, she told herself as she blew her nose with the washcloth.

It didn't count if she cried in the shower. The tears just washed down the drain.

She turned off the water and stepped out of the shower, blew her nose once more for good measure, and began to dry herself. *If Nelson Turnbull isn't gone when I wake up tomorrow, I'll send him down the damned drain, too!*

4

"*Jenny Tyler, where* are you going? Your daddy's still got company at the table."

Jenny jumped, startled and guilty at being caught slipping out of the kitchen door.

"You scared me," she accused, glaring at the housekeeper who was standing in the doorway.

Juana glared back. "I'm waiting for my answer."

Jenny sighed and slumped against the kitchen door. She eyed the stubborn expression on Juana's face. She'd seen it before.

"I'm going for a walk," she muttered. "He doesn't need me," she said, tossing her head toward the dining room.

"Marcus may not agree with you, young lady," Juana argued. "You and I both know a certain young man at that table was invited especially for your benefit."

Jenny bristled. "I'm well aware of Marcus's invitations.

They've been frequent and none too subtle. Nelson Turnbull wasn't gone two days when this man was shoved in his place. Why does he do things like this? Doesn't he think I'm capable of finding someone on my own? I don't want to sit across the table from any more men who spend half their time flirting, and the other half wondering how much Marcus is worth."

"Whatever he's doing, you're letting it happen," Juana said.

Jenny blanched at the truth of Juana's accusation. Still she argued. "I'm right and you know it. But he's crazy if he thinks he can treat me like his damned breeding stock. I am no longer on the market. And, I'll pick my own man." With that, Jenny pushed her way out the kitchen door, letting it slam sharply behind her.

Juana sighed as she watched Jenny stomp toward the barns. She knew the true cause of Jenny's anger had little to do with Marcus's manipulations. Jenny had already picked out her man. He just wasn't cooperating.

Chance stalked through the horse barn, angrily pushing a bucket back into place against the wall, muttering under his breath about the carelessness of the horse trainer who'd been hired less than a week ago. But he knew that the empty bucket wasn't the cause of his discontent. He'd seen the arrival of fancy cars and well-dressed men over three hours ago. The knowledge that Marcus had just dangled another prospective son-in-law before Jenny's eyes tore into his gut. The thought of another man with similar plans to those of the Walters men made him sick with fury. Why was she letting her father do this? The Jenny Tyler he knew would never stand for it.

He'd been at the Triple T for almost half his life, and for the first time since his arrival he was giving serious thought to leaving. He'd stood just about all of the torment he was capable of absorbing. He was thirty years old and the foreman of the Triple T. But, in *his* eyes, he was nothing more than a glorified hired hand with secrets that were eating him alive.

He tripped over a loose length of lariat and then turned and kicked it, sending a cloud of dust flying as his curses echoed. A flock of roosting pigeons took to the air with a flutter of wings and feathers.

Jenny was speechless as she watched him lose his temper. For the past week, he'd been trouble waiting to happen. The first time she'd seen him really mad had been years ago when Melvin Howard had made a pass at her. She remembered he'd threatened to break Melvin's arms and legs.

That was just about the same time Jenny had admitted to herself that she was in love with Chance McCall. No one else had ever measured up to the man who'd become her friend and champion.

"Son-of-a-bitch," Chance muttered, leaning his forehead against the rough wall of the stable hallway. He had to get a grip on himself.

"Chance! What's wrong?" Jenny asked softly.

"What are you doing out here?" he snapped at the unexpected sound of her voice. "Surely your . . . guests . . . haven't already left?"

"What do you care? You've made your decision

regarding us . . . or lack thereof," she said. "Whatever happens to me now is my business."

That wasn't exactly what he needed to hear. He knew he'd more or less given her free rein. But it wasn't what he wanted. . . . It was just what had to be.

Jenny sauntered around in front of him until she was less than inches away from his face, pinned between him and the stable wall with a look on her face that would melt angel wings. She was daring him. He could feel it. Something stirred inside him. Something wild . . . and demanding. She refused to move . . . and then it was too late to ignore.

"You shouldn't have come out here, Jennifer Ann," he growled, just before he swooped down on her.

Jenny's mouth opened to respond to his warning. But his lips demanded more from her than words. His groan of defeat was nothing compared to the swell of elation that swept through her as Chance lifted her off her feet and into his arms.

Nothing in her life had prepared her for the demand of his mouth as it swept across her face and neck. She sighed in supplication and wrapped her arms around his neck. Chance's body shuddered beneath the touch of her hands and the feel of her belly brushing against the ache behind his zipper.

He turned and caught the tip of her finger between his teeth. Eyes locked, breathing slowed and then quickened as he sucked the tip of her forefinger into his mouth and rolled his tongue around it.

Jenny moaned softly and leaned against him as she lost control of her body.

"Hell," he said softly. He started to pull away, dimly

realizing that he'd just stepped over a boundary he shouldn't have, when her whispered plea sent his sanity flying with the rope he'd just kicked.

"No, Chance," she said. Her lips burned across his mouth and neck. "Don't you dare stop now. Not now! Please make love to me."

It was a plea he could not resist. His arms tightened around her. He stared at the passion on her face. Her body was soft and pliant, curving against him. Pain shot through him, marked by the swell of his anatomy demanding relief. Chance responded to her mouth with his as he turned, taking them both into the shadows of the empty stall behind them.

"This is wrong," he muttered, as he gently pushed Jenny onto the sweet-smelling hay and tested the fabric of the dress she was wearing. It was delicate and pink, and it made him ache. "You weren't made for cowboys and haystacks, Jenny. You were meant for furs and diamonds and more money than I'll ever see."

"No, Chance. You're wrong. I was meant for you. From the first day when I put bandaids on your face, to the day you saved me from Melvin, I've known. It's just taken you longer to find out."

Her voice curled around his heart and stopped his breathing. He couldn't think past the clear blue gaze and the open trust on her face. She didn't know what the hell she was talking about. She couldn't have loved him that long ago, she'd only been a kid. And then she moved, fitting herself against the swell behind his zipper, and sighed.

He rocked against her, unable to resist what she offered. She moved with the thrust of his body and moaned. Chance shuddered. His movement was exciting her. Her mouth fell open slightly as her neck arched, spilling a dark curtain of hair across his arms and onto the hay. It was more than he could take.

"This is wrong, Jennifer Ann. But, God help me, I can't stop."

Her sleepy smile gave him permission as his hands slipped beneath the neckline of her dress. They brushed across the crests of her breasts and then she kissed him, capturing the sigh that slipped out of his lips.

He was lost. His fingers slid across her shoulders, moving the dress straps down and off. His hands shook as his palms cupped and caressed her bare skin. Nubs hardened and peaked beneath his touch, taunting him by their presence until he could no longer resist a taste. They were sweet and soft, then at once achingly hard beneath his tongue. He shuddered and moved above her, lost in the feel of so much woman beneath him.

Jenny's fingers tore at his shirt, needing the feel of his skin against her body, the heat growing between them. The snaps of his shirt popped apart. She sighed as her hands came in contact with flesh and blood . . . and the man himself. The muscles she discovered came to life beneath her caresses as she moved across his back in a foray of discovery. She was at once elated, and then fearful of the unknown awaiting her.

"Jenny, slow down!"

His command was lost as passion fed the mounting ache between her legs. She moaned, whispering his name quietly into the silence, needing more than he was giving, unwilling to give up what had begun.

Her lower body shifted and he fell into the valley

she'd dug into the hay, allowing him access to a part of her that had previously existed only in his dreams.

"Sweet Jesus!" His voice rasped as an ache swelled into a pounding fury. The need to bury himself in her was fast becoming a reality. His hands slid up the bare skin of her legs, moving of their own accord as they swept across her belly, fingering the lacy wisp bordering the nylon barrier that lay between him and heaven.

She shuddered as his fingers slid lower. And then the gasp and moan that slipped past his ear told him more than words could ever have revealed. He was in virgin territory in more ways than one. He'd bet his little finger that Jennifer Ann had never made love to a man. The thought was sublime torture. It was a justification of every dream he'd ever had that she'd know only him, and a fear that he couldn't be the one to take her when he knew he'd never be the one to keep her.

His head dipped as he rested against her breasts. It was torture to breathe and not move. But finally . . . slowly and surely . . . he regained control of his passion. He couldn't have Jenny in the way that he wanted, but he'd damn sure make certain that he'd be the first to show her what passion meant.

"What are you . . . ?" Jenny's question was lost in the gasp that followed as Chance's hands slid beneath the nylon barrier. Her eyes widened as she stared up into the face of love. "No . . ." she began. Then he sent her sanity spinning out of control.

His fingers stroked and pulled, rubbing slowly at first, back and forth against her hot, swollen flesh until Jenny thought she was going to die. Her hands dug into his shoulders as he gave her love in a way she'd never imagined, and would never forget. Her bones melted beneath his touch as his lips swooped, coaxing away, with soft words and sweet touches, the last of her inhibitions.

Tears blinded Jenny's view of his face as a fever swept through her body. Everything within her seemed to swell and pulse toward the point in her body that Chance had possessed. Suddenly she lost control and cried aloud, frightened by the overwhelming need to be carried away by the touch of the big man above her.

"Let it go, Jenny," he pleaded, "ride with the feeling, baby. I can't go with you, but let me take you away."

His name was a chant as she arched beneath his fingers. Light burst behind her eyelids in an explosion of colors as heat spilled in her body. She moaned as Chance wrapped her in his arms and buried his face against her neck. She felt his tears, and even in her innocence, knew the strength of mind and character that it had taken for him to give her joy and deny himself fulfillment.

"I'll never forgive you for not being inside me when this happened," Jenny whispered, blinking back tears from the overwhelming passion she'd just endured.

"And I'd never have forgiven myself if I had," he said. "This shouldn't have happened, and I can tell you it won't happen again."

He crawled to his feet and then stopped short, unable to walk for the pain. He leaned over and grabbed his knees, taking deep, harsh gulps of air as he tried to regain control of his rebellious body.

Jenny shakily pulled herself up. Tears streaked silently down her face as she methodically picked hay from her hair and clothing.

Chance took a deep breath and straightened just in time to see her shutter her expression. He'd hurt her, but the pain inside him was infinitely worse. She didn't know that he wanted to go out and shoot the next man who even looked at her twice. In Chance's eyes, she'd become his woman. But he couldn't have her. All he had were ghosts and a monthly paycheck. Not enough to take and keep the heir to the Triple T.

"Go back to the house, Jennifer Ann. And don't ever come out here alone again." The harshness in his voice was all she heard. She was too blinded by the pain to see the shattered expression in his eyes.

"Go to hell," she said softly, as she walked past him.

"I already have, Jenny. I already have," he whispered, as he watched her walking away.

She walked into the sunlight and out of his life.

The next two months *were* hell. Jenny darted from one beau to the next with butterflylike persistence. Frenzy seemed the norm.

But Juana knew differently. She'd seen Jenny's face the day she'd come back from the barns. She'd picked the last bit of straw off her back as she'd passed through the kitchen. The bitter, sardonic smile that had been on Jenny's lips had shocked her. Whatever had happened between her girl and the foreman was obviously over.

Juana also heard complaints from the men about the quiet anger that Chance was letting fester. He was at once swiftly critical of everything and everyone, and then instantly furious with himself for losing control.

Everyone was walking on eggshells and Marcus Tyler seemed to be the only one oblivious to the reason.

It was Marcus's weekly meeting with Chance that stopped their cycle of self-destruction and nearly erupted in chaos. It took every ounce of dignity and self-control Chance had left, not to kill the man Jenny walked in with just as the meeting was coming to an end.

"Marcus," Jenny said, "Nelson and I are going riding and we thought you might . . ." She stopped short.

The look of total devastation came and went so quickly that only Chance saw her pain. It was inevitable that this meeting would happen, but it was more than bad luck that she was with this man when it did. He was the only one who'd managed a return engagement in the constant string of men who'd been paraded through the Triple T. His mere presence was a threat to Chance's sanity.

"Sorry," she said as her world shattered quietly into tiny pieces, "I didn't know you were busy."

"It's okay, Jenny," Marcus said, unaware of the tension. "We were just finishing our weekly update. And as for the riding invitation, I'll have to pass. As soon as Chance and I are through, I've got to fly into Dallas for a meeting. I won't be back until tomorrow."

Chance saw the look of expectation that swept through Nelson's eyes when he realized that Jenny would be alone. His fingers curled into fists and he actually took a step forward before the silent plea on Jenny's face stopped him short.

"Oh hell," he said softly, not caring who heard him or what interpretation they made of the remark. "I'll be outside if you have anything else to say to me, boss. I need some air."

Chance walked past Jenny without saying a word, and left the men staring at each other in stunned surprise.

Pain twisted and coiled around Jenny's heart. *I can't take much more of this,* she thought, sinking limply into the chair beside the doorway.

"I wonder what's wrong with him?" Marcus mumbled, and then shrugged. His foreman was an enigma he'd long since given up trying to understand. What he cared about was performance, and Chance McCall was one of the best. The Triple T had never run so smoothly.

"You two run along and have your ride. I'll see you tomorrow, Jenny," Marcus said, as he began shuffling papers on his desk. "Nelson, you come back soon, you hear? It's real nice having a young man like you around the place to help out."

Jenny couldn't believe it. Nelson Turnbull didn't know steers from heifers, and barely knew the ass end of a horse. Why couldn't her father see what was staring him in the face? She had been coming apart for months, and he thought she was having the time of her life.

But Jenny knew it was partially her own fault. She hid her feelings very well. Suddenly her frenetic rebellion of the past few months caught up with her. She sighed, looking up with barely disguised distaste at the man who'd been sniffing at her heels as if she were a bitch in heat. She buried her face in her hands, ashamed of her behavior, and knew that Nelson Turnbull's time was fast running out. After today, she'd tolerate no more unexpected visits from Marcus's "friends."

If he wanted to expand his properties, he could buy

more land. Chance didn't want her and Marcus didn't know what to do with her. For two cents, she'd move out, take her marketing degree, and put it to use.

"Come on darling," Nelson urged, "let's go get our horses. We've got several hours of good daylight left before I need to leave."

Jenny sighed. There was no way to get out of this ride. It had been her idea. "Okay," she said, "but you have to let me choose your horse this time. Last time you nearly took a header. Cheyenne is too much horse for you."

"Nonsense," he argued, getting a look on his face she'd come to recognize as mutiny, "I can handle anything you've got."

Jenny kept her mouth shut. It was one of the few times that she didn't feel the need to argue with total idiocy. It was probably because she could not have cared less.

"Henry! Saddle Cheyenne," Nelson ordered, as they entered the stable area.

The wizened cowboy squinted his eyes even tighter than usual and spat. Tobacco juice sliced through the air, landing within inches of the highly polished, obviously new boots that Jenny's latest dandy had seen fit to wear.

"Sorry. Didn't see you comin'," he muttered, watching with satisfaction at the shock and disgust spreading across Nelson Turnbull's face. He ignored Jenny's frown. She saw through his opinion of Turnbull, but he didn't care.

"Indeed!" Nelson said.

"Don't think you oughta try that horse today, Mr.

Turnbull," Henry said. "He's been actin' up some. A couple of the mares are in and he's more ready to ride them than for you to ride him."

"My God!" Nelson gasped, and cast a glance toward Jenny who was leaning against the wall trying to pick something off of her pant leg. "You shouldn't talk of such things in front of the lady."

"Oh shoot," Henry said, "Jenny has seen it all, ain't you darlin'? It's just part of life on a ranch. She's gonna inherit all this one day. She has to know how it works."

"Never mind," Nelson said. "I'll saddle him myself." He pushed past Henry, ignoring his calls of concern, and stomped toward the stall where the stallion was stabled.

The horse tossed his head at the sight of the stranger. Nelson gritted his teeth, yanked a bridle off a peg on the wall, and pulled the door wide.

"Come here, you son-of-a-bitch," he muttered. "I'll teach you who's boss."

It took Jenny a moment to realize what was happening. She'd only caught the last of Henry's explanation. But the look of pure panic on the old cowboy's face was enough to send her running toward Nelson with arms outstretched, yelling frantically for him to stop. It was too late.

Nelson had the stall open and had taken a step inside when the stallion screamed a warning. Nelson jumped back in shock, unaware of the intensity within such an animal when the need to mate was upon it. In reflex and fear, Nelson swung the bridle, catching the horse across the forehead and the tenderest part of its muzzle.

The stallion reared in defense, using the only

weapons it had, and pawed the air with iron-shod hooves. Nelson staggered backward in stunned surprise. He felt the wall at his back, saw the horse in his face, and knew his life was in danger.

Jenny ran. She saw Cheyenne roll his eyes in pain and fury and knew what was about to happen. It did.

The stallion was unfamiliar with intentionally inflicted pain. He'd never been struck or beaten in his life. That, and the scent of a stranger, sent him out of control.

"For God's sake, run," she screamed, yanking Nelson outside the stall as he stood frozen to the spot, unaware of the deadly hazard he'd unleashed.

Nelson fell to one side, for the moment safely out of the path of the sharp hooves slicing the air. The massive stallion saw daylight through the open door and headed for it with nostrils flaring and teeth bared to anyone who stood in his path. A mare whinnied frantically in the corral outside, sensing the turmoil and smelling the stallion's presence. Her call only incensed the stallion more.

Henry could see that Jenny was in trouble. The stallion wanted out and Jenny Tyler was in the way. If the horse would just keep going, Jenny would be safe. All they had to do was let the horse have his head. They'd catch him later. The only thing that mattered was getting everyone out of the way unharmed.

Unaware of the unfolding incident, a ranch hand was just about to unload the feed he'd hauled from town. He pulled up to the barn, backed into the open breezeway, and blocked the stallion's only avenue of escape.

Unfortunately, the horse saw the feed truck about the same time that Henry did. Cheyenne reared, pan-icked by the shouts and Nelson Turnbull's erratic actions as he crawled on hands and knees along the wall, trying to get out of the way. Fear shortened Henry's life span. The horse was penned in . . . and it knew it.

"Hellfire," Henry muttered. "He'll stomp her for sure."

He shouted loudly and threw a bucket toward the stallion, hoping to divert its attention from the woman in its path. It was useless. The stallion was upon her, and then there was nothing but dust and screams and the sound of running feet.

Jenny curled tightly into a ball, making herself as small and inconspicuous as possible as she tried unsuccessfully to roll out from under the thrashing hooves of the frantic animal.

Chance came out of nowhere.

Henry didn't know where he'd been, but he saw where he was going and knew it was suicide.

Henry's shouts and Jenny's single scream had sent him running. The sight of Jenny underneath that horse had been terrifying. He knew he wouldn't be able to move the stallion in time to save her from injury. But he could put himself between her and the hooves. He dived to cover Jenny's body with his own.

With luck they would survive. Without doubt they still faced serious injury, even death. Yet there was no hesitation in his actions. If she died, he was going with her.

"Don't fight me!" he yelled, and shuddered with relief as he felt her go limp. His arms tightened around her and they rolled, constantly trying to outguess the direction of the stallion's hooves. It was useless.

"Jesus bloody Christ," Henry yelled, and waved at several of the ranch hands who'd come running at the sound of the melee. "Get that damned truck out of the door, and get some rope. That horse is gonna kill them both."

In a panic, the ranch hand trying to move the truck flooded the motor instead. It remained in position, a metal boundary through which the horse could not run.

The men finally snared the horse, but could not pull him away from the couple on the floor. By now, Cheyenne was crazy with fear. He pawed and bucked, angry at the confining ropes around his neck, intent on nothing but escape and the mares in the corrals nearby.

Chance couldn't see, but he sensed what was happening. He could think of nothing but protecting Jenny from harm. He kicked and rolled, more than once feeling the slicing blows of the horse's hooves bouncing off his body. Each time he imagined them to be free from danger, the horse moved and the death dance continued. And then one of the ropes around Cheyenne's neck slipped. It gave the horse just enough leeway to jump one last time. And when he did, his hooves came down on Chance.

The first blow caught him in the middle of the back. He felt the pain clear down to his toes and groaned as he pulled Jenny even tighter against him. And then lightning flashed behind his eyelids and blackness sent him into hell. He fell limply onto Jenny, his last conscious movement covering her body.

Jenny screamed once. The horse danced above her with thunderous rhythm and then long arms and a strong body pulled her into a haven of safety. Sight was not necessary. She'd know his touch through her whole life. Fear such as she'd never known kept her motionless, allowing Chance the freedom he needed to move them around while dodging the deadly hooves above their heads. And then his groan of pain sent shockwaves of fear rocketing through her body. He went limp and her world came to an end.

Rough hands yanked Jenny out from under his dead weight and pulled her to her feet. She struggled, trying desperately to get away from Nelson Turnbull's grasp.

"My God, Jenny," he cried, "be still. Are you hurt? The damned horse is gone now. It's all over."

"Chance!" She shoved herself free and started toward him. "Let me see him."

Nelson tried to turn her away. "It's not pretty. Let the men take care of him. They've called your father. He'll be here soon and tend to the situation. Let me take you to the house. You must be devastated."

Jenny went cold. The stupid bastard had caused the entire situation and now he wanted her to just walk away from the man who'd saved her life at his own expense. Her hand flew back and the slap that connected with the side of Nelson's face resounded in the shocked silence of the men assembled.

"Get out of my sight!" she screamed. "If you're real smart, you won't ever show your stupid face in my vicinity again. It's your fault that this happened, and if Chance dies I'll kill you, myself. Do you understand?"

Her expression scared Nelson as much as her threat. He sputtered once and then turned and stomped out of the stables, ignoring the ranch hands' disgusted looks. This wild west atmosphere was not where he belonged. And this wild woman was not his kind, either.

Jenny bit her lip, and dropped to her knees as she ran shaky fingers across Chance's body, feeling for the injuries she knew were there. Blood came away on her hands and she moaned. A thin, thready pulse signaled the life that hung on with stubborn persistence.

"Thank God," she muttered, and then yelled, "Henry, get a mattress from the bunkhouse and bring the van!" Her chin quivered as she looked down at the blood on her hands. She wiped them on her jeans. There was no time to cry.

"I'm already there," he answered, hurrying to do her bidding. Jenny might be a girl, but on the Triple T, she had long ago earned every man's respect.

"What in hell is going on here?"

Marcus entered the stables. He'd seen Nelson running for his car. When he saw the condition of Jenny's clothes and the big man lying on the ground, he began to shout. "What happened to Chance? Why is Nelson leaving like that? He wouldn't talk to me."

And then he saw the bridle in the dust and a saddle blanket beneath their feet. "Did something happen to Cheyenne?"

"At least you asked about Chance first," Jenny spat.

Marcus paled. It had been unintentional, but he knew instantly how it had sounded.

"I didn't mean . . ."

"Never mind," Jenny muttered. "Just shut up and help us get him in the van."

"Let me call an ambulance," Marcus said, but the look on his daughter's face stopped him cold.

"No time. Do what I say."

Marcus stared, dumbfounded by the authority in her voice.

Jenny pivoted wildly, searching for a safe means to

move Chance. He had to be immobilized. There was no way of knowing how badly he was injured. She needed something hard and flat and long enough to lay a big man on. The grainery door!

"You men!" She pointed. "Take that door off its hinges . . . now!"

Marcus stepped forward and was pushed aside by the cowboys hastening to comply with Jenny's orders. He stared. This Jenny was a stranger. His conscience tugged. She'd always been a stranger.

The men didn't question her orders, instantly understanding the makeshift spine board that Jenny was going to use. The door came off just as Henry pulled the van up to the stables and backed inside.

"Help me," Jenny ordered, refusing to relinquish her right to this man who lay too still and pale.

The men carefully moved Chance onto the door, carried him to the van and, at Jenny's direction, pushed their makeshift gurney onto the mattress.

"Call the hospital!" Jenny ordered. Her fierce stare burned into Marcus's memory. "Tell them we're coming! Tell them to be ready!"

His quiet acceptance of her orders was uncommon, but so was Jenny's protectiveness of the man he'd known only as his foreman.

"Marcus," she said, just before the van door swung shut on them both, "if Chance dies, I'm going to shoot that horse. Do you understand?"

Marcus nodded. He understood much more than he had moments before. Many things were becoming clear, including the fact that his daughter was in love, past hope, with a dying man.

The van began to move, slowly at first, and then rapidly as Jenny and two of the men who'd come along helped hold Chance safely in place.

"Henry . . ." Fear was beginning to soak in. Jenny sat on the van floor with Chance's head held firmly between her hands, her legs locked on either side of his body to keep it from rolling.

"I know, girl. We'll get him there. Trust me!" He pressed down on the gas.

5

It was midnight. The hour of uncertainty when life hangs suspended between yesterday and tomorrow, waiting, like Jenny, to see what the new day will bring. For her, time had ceased at the hour Chance went into surgery. All of her energy was focused on the double doors at the end of the long white corridor of Tyler Municipal Hospital.

She sat perched on the edge of the chair, relishing the sharp pinch of the stiff seat on the back of her legs. It reminded her that she was still alive. Jenny was praying . . . frantically . . . repeatedly. She'd made so many promises to God that she knew she would never be able to keep them. They conflicted with one another in such a ridiculous fashion, yet she was certain that He understood. After all, He was the only one who knew how desperately she loved Chance McCall.

Jenny sighed as she leaned her head against the cold,

hard surface of the wall behind her chair. *Please God, just give him back to me.*

Her silent prayer stopped along with her breath and heartbeat as the doors swung outward. A man in sweat-stained greens started up the long hallway toward the waiting area. Jenny's lungs expanded, her legs trembled. She couldn't have taken a step to save her life.

Dr. Jonah Walker wiped a weary hand across his face as he tried to ignore an overwhelming fatigue. It had been touch and go one too many times tonight for his peace of mind. Then he saw the young woman at the end of the hall. The strain on her face was obvious. He hadn't been the only one who'd suffered through this long night. Marcus Tyler's daughter looked haunted.

He'd known Marcus for years. More than once he'd hunted quail on the Triple T. But it was the first time he'd been this close to the daughter. Her beauty startled him. For just a heartbeat he wished . . . *If she was just a bit older or I was a bit younger* . . . Good sense and compassion for the waiting woman shamed him. He quickened his step.

"Well?" Jenny asked. Her voice shook. She was blinking back tears and swallowing the denial that kept trying to slip past the lump in her throat.

"I'll tell you this much little lady," Dr. Walker said as he guided Jenny toward the empty lounge and a sagging fake leather couch. "As my grandfather used to say, that's one tough hombre."

"You mean he's going to be okay?"

"I don't know yet just how 'okay' he's going to be, or how long it'll take to get him there, but he's alive, Jenny, and that's a lot more than I'd hoped for when we started."

"Thank you, God!" she whispered, then she buried her face in her hands and wept. It was the first time she'd allowed herself the luxury.

The doctor patted her gently on the shoulder and began relating the injuries Chance McCall had suffered and what had been done to correct them. Jenny listened, her eyes fixed on each movement of the doctor's lips, but little registered except the fact that Chance was alive. Then the room began to spin.

Jonah took one look at the color receding from her face and shoved her head between her knees.

"Can't have you fainting on me, girl," he said. "I'm too tired to treat another patient tonight. You go on home and get some rest. Your friend is going to be with us for quite a while. I've put him in a drug-induced coma to allow brain swelling to subside. Plenty of time for a visit later."

Jenny stared at the patterned tile between her feet as she felt the blood rushing back into her foggy brain. She felt like a fool. "I've never fainted in my life," she mumbled, and pushed herself upright. Her entire body felt like her mouth did after a trip to the dentist. "And I'm not going anywhere. I want to see him. Please, Dr. Walker . . . I have to."

Jonah Walker took one look at the determination and desperation on Jenny's face.

"Well, come on," he said, heading back down the hall with Jenny at his heels. "You can look, but don't touch, okay? And just for a minute. Can't let word get around that I'm easy. Damn nurses give me fits as it is." He paused outside a door marked ICU.

Jenny stepped around the doctor and stood for a

moment, absorbing the whispered voices, the antiseptic and medicine smell of the area, and the gold lettering on the see-through door. *Intensive Care Unit.* Oxygen flowed throughout her system as she took a deep breath and wiped sweaty palms on the seat of her jeans. She put a shaky hand on the glass door and pushed.

"He's going to look rough," Dr. Walker cautioned, and then caught his breath at the expression on Jenny's face.

"I don't care," she said fiercely and slipped inside.

"Damn!" he said, and headed for the shower. "I hope to hell that poor bastard lives to appreciate a woman like that."

Jenny saw him instantly, but it wasn't *her* Chance. He was lost somewhere in the network of tubes and needles that were pumping life-giving fluids and medicines into his badly injured body, trapped in the world of drug-induced sleep because, according to the doctor, consciousness would have been unbearable.

A single sheet covered only what modesty demanded, leaving his long-limbed, well-muscled body, and his injuries, in plain view. Jenny clutched her hands against her belly, fighting the panic that threatened to overwhelm her. This was her fault!

Dear Lord! Jenny pressed trembling fingers tightly against her lips and forced back a scream. She wouldn't . . . couldn't panic, and had no intention of humiliating herself again by nearly fainting.

The need to touch him was overwhelming, to assure herself that life still coursed through him. He was so still. But a promise was a promise, so Jenny settled for a seat near his bed instead. Her eyes focused on the steady rise and fall of his chest as life-giving oxygen was fed into his body.

"Are you his wife?"

The nurse's voice startled her. Jenny shook her head, and tried not to weep.

"Then I'm sorry, miss. In this ward, only family is allowed and then not for long. You shouldn't be here."

Jenny stared blankly into the sympathetic face of the nurse, oblivious to the tears falling freely down her face.

The nurse sighed, pulled a tissue from her pocket, and handed it to her with a warning. "You can't stay long." She walked away, leaving Jenny to her silent vigil.

"Jenny! Wake up!"

Marcus's voice unwound Jenny from her makeshift bed in the lounge. "What?" she mumbled, disoriented by the unfamiliar surroundings. She came instantly awake as she remembered. "Chance! Oh God! Daddy . . . is he . . . ?"

She called me Daddy! How good it sounded! In all of her twenty-three plus years he'd never once corrected her for calling him Marcus. Where Jenny was concerned, he had a lot to regret. Her fingernails dug into his wrist and pulled him from his musings. The question demanded an answer.

"I don't know anything about Chance's condition. Henry and I just arrived. Here, drink this, and don't burn yourself," he said, as he thrust a cup of hot, steaming coffee into her hands. "I'm going to find a nurse. We'll know soon enough how he spent the night."

Jenny tried to blink the sleep and confusion from her

eyes as she watched him stalk down the corridor. If she hadn't been so distraught, she would have wondered about his presence. He'd never been around much when she'd needed him before.

Henry took the cup of hot coffee out of her hands, set it down on the table, pulled her into his arms, and patted her awkwardly. The hug was clumsy but warm, and for just a moment, Jenny felt safe.

He smelled of Lava soap and Old Spice cologne, a deadly combination on anyone else, but on Henry, better than the usual dust, hay, and manure.

"It looked like you needed a hug," he mumbled self-consciously. She was as near to a daughter as he would ever have. It was his right.

Jenny sighed and settled into his arms.

Henry Thomas had worked for the Triple T for almost twenty years. His small, wiry body had not weathered the years as well as it might have. He walked with a limp, an autograph from a horse that no longer existed. His face had more wrinkles than an unmade bed. But he was all heart, and loyal. In Jenny's world, that was all that mattered.

"All the boys send their best," Henry said.

Jenny nodded and dropped onto the lumpy chair that had served as her bed. She leaned back and took a long swallow of her coffee, ignoring the heat as she drained the cup.

"They feel real bad about Chance gettin' hurt," Henry continued. "Kinda guilty-like. But I told 'em it wasn't no one's fault, 'cept maybe that damned green-horn. It just happened."

It was quite a speech for the normally taciturn man.

Jenny stared up at the concern on his face. She squeezed the empty white foam cup and swallowed a lump in her throat.

"It wouldn't have happened if I hadn't let Marcus parade those fools through the house. I only did it because I thought Chance . . ." Her voice shook. "If it's anyone's fault, it's mine." Her mouth quivered and she bit the inside of her cheek to keep from crying.

"That ain't so, honey," Henry said. He patted her knee and slipped into the seat beside her. "Besides, Chance never gave it a thought. He just reacted. You know how he feels about you. He couldn't have no more stood and watched that horse trample you than he could'a stopped breathin'."

Jenny's voice was low and quiet. "But that's just it. I don't know how he feels about me. He's kept me at arm's length since my sixteenth birthday. He's treated me as if I had the plague. But I know how I feel about him," Jenny whispered. "I just hope and pray I get a chance to prove it. If I don't . . ."

The Styrofoam cup she'd been gripping popped, showering itself into bits. She stared down at the mess and sighed. She'd just started to pick up the pieces when she saw Marcus coming down the hall. She leaped up and ran to meet him.

Marcus abruptly blurted out his news. "He's better. Stronger vital signs, they call it."

As Jenny started down the hall to see for herself, he grabbed her roughly by her arm and then let go, regretting the motion, as she blinked back tears.

"You can't see him yet. Besides, you look like hell, girl. You need to . . ."

"I'm not going home. I won't leave him." Her last words were nothing more than a whisper as she buried her face in her hands. "I can't."

"Well now, I don't remember asking you to," Marcus said. "Here!" He shoved two sets of keys into her hands. "You have a room across the street at the motel, a suit-case full of clean clothes on the bed, and your car."

Marcus took a deep breath, suddenly shy in front of his daughter as she flung her arms around his neck.

"Thank you, Marcus," she whispered, then withdrew, every bit as embarrassed as her father. Affection was not something they had learned to share with each other, but definitely something they needed to explore.

Jenny turned the plastic motel key over in her hand, checked the room number, and started toward the exit sign down the hall.

Marcus and Henry watched her leave, each with a different ache in his heart. Henry Thomas loved her like a daughter, but to Marcus Tyler . . . she was a daughter he didn't know how to love.

Jenny's had become a familiar face in Tyler Municipal.

"How's he doing today?" she asked, as she leaned over the desk inside ICU.

"The same," the nurse answered. "Every day he seems to get a little stronger. He's breathing on his own. The incision from surgery is healing well. There are no fluids in his lungs. And you know what a problem that can be when broken ribs are involved and the patient is immobile."

Jenny nodded. She'd heard it all before. "Nothing else?" she asked softly.

"No . . . he still hasn't awakened," the nurse replied, and then felt obligated to continue in an encouraging tone. "But with a head injury such as his, sometimes this happens. Any day now I expect him to open his eyes and glare at us for all the times we've poked him with needles."

"I hope so," Jenny answered, and then hurried to Chance's bed, unwilling to waste a moment of her allotted visiting time. "Hi, mister," she whispered, and feathered a kiss on his stubbly cheek. "Have mercy! You need a shave!"

She spoke in normal, conversational tones, just as she had every day since his accident. Jenny was convinced that Chance could hear her and would wake up when he was ready to deal with the pain on his own. And, just as she had on every visit, she clasped one of his lifeless hands between her own warm ones and rubbed gently, massaging his fingers and the palm of his hands, careful not to disturb the intravenous needles fastened on both arms. She talked about Henry and the ranch . . . clumsy blunders that the new colt had made trying to chase a wily old barn cat. Anything that came to mind. And as she talked, she touched, patted, massaged and caressed, willing him, if only on a subconscious level, to know that she was here.

Up to this point, everything in her life had revolved around this man. She couldn't imagine life without him. He had to get better! He was her whole world and they'd never even made love. He'd hadn't given her the opportunity to share the part of her that belonged only to him.

Why, Chance? Jenny wondered. *Why did you keep me at arm's length? All I ever wanted was to be in your arms. What are you hiding from me . . . and from yourself? Why won't you let me in?*

Where once only darkness and silence had existed, now there was sound. And with sound . . . pain! Gut-wrenching, clear-to-the-bone, pain. When it became more than he could bear, he would concentrate on the gentle touch, and the familiar voice that hovered just beyond consciousness. If he focused hard enough, the pain would be replaced by a nameless something . . . an emotion too far away to identify. He tried. But just when it was within grasp, the blessed darkness would come back to claim him.

"Nurse! Nurse!"

Jenny stepped back from Chance's bed as the ICU team answered her call for help. She'd been sitting by his bed, talking and touching, just as she had for the past week, when she'd seen him move. Not an involuntary muscle spasm, but a specific motion toward his midriff where tight bandages bound healing ribs.

Oh God! Jenny thought. *Chance!*

It was the first conscious thing he'd done since diving beneath the horse's hooves to protect her.

His mouth stretched into a grimace and opened just enough to let a tiny moan escape. It was just as well it was gone. It had been hanging around inside his head for days, teasing and taunting, threatening to become a full-fledged scream, but hadn't quite managed to make the transition.

"Don't move, please," the nurse cautioned, as he began to pick at the needles and tubes tying him to the bed.

"What?" he mumbled, as he tried to form the word around a tongue too thick and swollen to articulate clearly.

"You've been injured," she answered. "Doctor will be here shortly. You're in a hospital. Please don't." She grasped his hand. "You'll dislodge the needles." The nurse's firm voice stilled his movement as he digested her words.

Hospital? Hurt? How? Unfortunately the deep breath he took before speaking got him pain instead of answers. His lungs expanded against his bruised and broken rib cage and sent oxygen spiraling into an already aching head.

The pain forced him back into darkness. His body relaxed, regaining the inert status it had maintained for days.

Jenny groaned softly, her joy at his first signs of recovery erased as he sank back into his personal twilight zone.

Dr. Walker came into the ward just as the nurses completed their check on Chance's intravenous hookups.

"Coming around, is he?" he asked, as he made a thorough sweep of the big man on the bed before grabbing the chart one of the nurses thrust in his hands. "Jenny! Out!" he ordered, and then cushioned his words with a cockeyed grin. "Wait for me in the lounge."

Jenny nodded and willed herself to walk away from Chance's bed without disgracing herself. She didn't know whether to laugh or cry. *Surely this is a good sign.* The door shut behind her.

It was late that night before she made it across the street to the motel. The sight that greeted her as she turned the key and opened the door never failed to make her groan. She didn't know which was worse, the shag rug in three shades of burnt orange with contrasting green floral curtains and bedspread, or the red and black velvet painting of a matador and bull hanging in glaring prominence over the head of the bed.

However, this time the room decor took a back seat to her jubilation. Chance was getting better. She thought she would just rest a minute before calling home to let Henry and the boys know.

The next conscious thought she had was realizing it was morning. She jerked awake, heart pounding wildly, as she grabbed the telephone that was ringing.

"Hello?" she croaked, and then cleared her voice, trying to sound alert. She hadn't fooled her caller.

"Sorry I woke you, Jenny," Dr. Walker said. "Thought you might like to know he's waking up again. If you hurry, you may be able to talk a bit. Don't think he'll go back out as fast again. He's probably learned that less movement is better at this point in his life." He chuckled at his own wit before disconnecting.

She's here again! Chance thought, and shifted slightly, careful not to disturb anything still tying him to the bed. Through all the time lost and the few times he had any conscious memory, he'd known she was by his side. Some inner peace always came over him knowing she was there. Then he would relax and the panic he felt at not being able to communicate would ebb away to a far corner of his mind.

The sound of her voice, soft and low as she talked to someone nearby, drew him closer and closer to waking. He fought back the comforting darkness as his mind reached toward the sounds. A touch on his forehead, a petal soft caress against his cheek, made consciousness necessary. Now her voice was low and close to his ear. He focused on the sounds, struggling to string them together into coherency.

Jenny suppressed her exhilaration. His eyelids fluttered. He knew she was here!

"Hey you," she said quietly, "I'll bet you're getting tired of hearing me talk all the time, aren't you? Why don't you tell me to shut up and go home?"

It was nonsense, but it was something . . . anything . . . to say. She had no intention of leaving. But the big man on the bed had no way of knowing that.

His hand moved. It startled them both when he grasped her hand and then clutched, using the flesh and blood lifeline to pull himself from the pit of darkness.

"Don't go," he begged, his voice dry and raspy from disuse. Slowly, slowly, the light of day came back into his world.

"Dear God, thank you!" Jenny whispered. His fingers gripped her wrist with surprising strength. She let out a long, slow sigh of relief. "You came back to me!"

He started to nod and then winced, blinking painfully as he realized it hurt less to speak than to move. He licked his lips, suddenly aware of the mundane nuisance of a dry throat and cracked lips.

"Here," Jenny urged, and pressed a cool, damp cloth to his mouth. She'd been doing so for days, but this was the first time he'd responded by sucking the moisture from the fabric. Jenny wanted to laugh. She wanted to cry. Never in her life had so much gratitude and joy overwhelmed her at such a small, insignificant gesture.

"Are you in pain? I can get a nurse . . ." Her voice trailed off as his grip tightened.

"Not much . . . now," he whispered. "Don't go."

He stared, transfixed by the dark fall of hair, the intense blue eyes, and the generous curve of her lower lip. A heart-shaped face of rare beauty, a womanly body. Each feature was so familiar, yet for the life of him he couldn't remember her name.

Awareness began pooling in the pit of his stomach, and crawled ominously toward a heart thumping with panicked irregularity. His breathing quickened. A film of moisture beaded across his forehead and upper lip. He stared down at their locked fingers and dropped her hand as if he'd just been burned. The panic inside him threatened to overflow.

Jenny sensed his increased agitation. She stepped back in shock. What was the fear she was seeing on his face? He turned his head away from her and closed his eyes. Her heart sank.

She forgot to be calm. She forgot to be quiet. "What? What is it?" He was blaming her for the accident! He was going to hate her forever!

He turned and stared. Blankly . . . horrified.

And then nurses were at the bedside. "What's

happened? What did you say? What have you done?"
Their accusing stares weakened her knees.

"I don't know," she whispered, and wrapped her
arms around herself in panic. "All of a sudden he just
withdrew . . . like he'd never seen me before. I don't
know why . . ." Her heart stopped. She looked into the
face of his fear. And then she knew. His thoughts came
through as clearly as if he'd just spoken aloud.

Jenny took a deep breath, reached down and took his
hand. He flinched but allowed the touch.

"Do you know where you are?" she asked.

He hesitated. Admitting his fears aloud was as frightening as knowing that they were there. He finally answered.

"No."

"Do you know who I am?" Jenny asked. That he hesitated sent her hopes plummeting.

"No," he muttered, and slipped his fingers out of her
hand.

"Dear God," she said, and sank down onto the chair
by his bed. She shuddered, trying desperately to hide
her fear and dismay from him, aware that even in his
confusion he was looking to her for strength. Unaware
of the doctor's arrival behind her, she continued, taking
a deep breath as blue eyes locked with brown, each
reading the panic on the other's face.

"Do you know who you are?" Jenny whispered. Her
heart broke as he shuddered, letting out one long sigh as
he answered.

"No."

"It's okay," she said, and wiped the beads of sweaty
panic away from his forehead. "I do."

He closed his eyes, briefly relishing her cool, familiar

touch on his forehead in a world where there were suddenly no constants.

"My name is Jenny Tyler. And you, Chance McCall, are the man who saved my life."

Jenny watched in despair as a single tear slipped from the corner of his eye and ran beside a new bruise and an old scar. *I'm afraid it's going to take a lot more than bandaids to fix this hurt, my love,* she thought.

Dr. Walker slipped his hand on her shoulder and patted her as he spoke. "This is not uncommon you know. Now Jenny, once again, I'd like for you to wait outside while I examine this fellow."

She nodded, resisted the urge to lean down and press a kiss against the bitter twist at the corner of Chance's mouth, and walked away.

The glass door of the ICU closed behind her. She staggered down the hallway, leaning weakly against the wall as she fought back rage at the unjustness of this new development. But, just as suddenly as she felt despair, she found relief.

"Well! I just wasn't as specific as I should have been with my prayers," she muttered to herself as she dug around in her purse for change. "I asked God to let him live. And he did." She headed down the hall toward a pay phone.

He heard her footsteps as she came out of the elevator and began the long walk down the tiled hallway toward his room. Over the past few weeks, her walk had become as distinctive to him as her voice, her scent, and her touch. His heart skipped a beat and a familiar panic welled before he turned to face the mirror over the sink. He leaned forward and braced himself as he stared at the reflection of a stranger's face. The muscles in his arms corded and flexed as his fingers gripped the cold porcelain. The door opened behind him. He shuddered and sighed, then pivoted.

"Are you ready?" Jenny asked. She didn't know who was more nervous. His nostrils flared at her question but his stare never wavered.

Chance was coming home today. But Jenny knew that he was not happy about the news. The hospital was the only familiar thing in his world and she was taking him away from it.

Dr. Walker came into the room and saw the look of distrust on his patient's face. His heart went out to the big man. It would be hard to go on pure faith that everything one had been told in the past few weeks was the truth. It was a lot to ask when a man didn't even recognize himself in the mirror. But it was time for the next step and that meant getting back into the real world.

"Well, son," he said, "I can't say I'm sorry to see you go. After all, when I send one out of here walking, I've done my job." Jonah Walker chuckled at his own wit and combed his fingers through his hair. "You've got a big job ahead of you, boy. You don't need to worry about anything except a slow recuperation at your boss's expense. Everything else will come back to you when it's time. Memories are funny things. Sometimes they have their own reasons for hiding. It's all up to you . . . and this little lady here." He gestured toward Jenny. "Whether you know it or not, she's a big part of the reason you came back to us."

Chance nodded slowly and let his gaze rake over the

woman who stood silently beside the doctor. Finally he held out his hand.

"Thanks, Doc."

"Don't mention it," Jonah said. "You all right?" He sensed the nervousness in Chance's handshake.

Chance took a deep breath. He glanced around the small room, relishing the comfortable familiarity. His gaze collided with blue fire staring at him, willing him to answer. He knew that no matter what he discovered when he left, it would be all right as long as she was there.

"Yes," he answered quietly. "I'm just fine, Doc." His gut pulled sharply as he caught the woman's smile of relief. He wasn't sure what she'd meant to him in the past, but he damn sure knew what she meant to him now. She was his lifeline. And he wasn't about to let go.

6

"*Welcome home,*" Jenny said. She parked the car in front of the main house. The confusion on Chance's face was obvious. "Don't worry about it," she said. "I know nothing looks familiar, but give yourself time. It will come, I know it."

"I lived here?"

Chance stared. The Spanish-style rounded archways and red tiled roof sprawled out in all directions. The house spelled money. He didn't have to remember his name to see that.

Jenny looked away. She hadn't expected him to question her plans to install him in a guest room in their house.

"Not exactly," she began, "but I thought that it would be better if . . ."

"Take me where I belong."

The tone of his voice could not be denied. She bit

her lip to keep from arguing and started the car, backed away from the driveway, and drove toward the bunkhouse.

Chance relaxed. They'd already explained his status on the ranch as that of foreman. He had no intention of jeopardizing it by being housed where he didn't belong. He watched as they approached a small, frame building that looked as if, once upon a time, it'd had a single coat of whitewash. Now it was as colorless as the Texas dirt upon which it stood. A group of men were waiting on the porch. From the expressions on their faces, they were waiting for him.

"Man, we're sure glad to see you back, boss."

He stepped out of the car, took a deep breath, and smiled awkwardly. Boss! The word sounded strange. And there was no use putting off the fact that he didn't remember a damn one of their names.

"As you've probably already been told," Chance said, "what sense I ever had has been kicked out of me. You'll have to give me some time until I can learn your names all over again."

One small moment of silence met his announcement and then one of the men answered and had them all laughing with relief.

"Hell, boss. It don't matter what you call us. We've all been damned idiots so long, we'll answer to that."

"Welcome home, boy," Henry said. "Come on inside. I'll show you where you bunk." He waved to disperse the crowd of ranch hands. "Marcus ain't payin' you to flap your jaws, boys. Go find somethin' to do."

At Henry's orders, they disappeared, relieved that the initial meeting between them and Chance was over.

Jenny saw instant rapport flash between the two men. It hurt. Chance didn't remember Henry, but it was obvious that the trust was instantly there. It made his distance from her all the more painful.

"I'm going back to the house," she said. "When you've had a chance to settle, you're both to come to dinner tonight. And don't argue. You'll have to answer to Juana, not me, so wipe that look off your faces right now."

She pivoted, grabbed his bags from the car, all but threw them on the porch, and drove away in a cloud of dust.

Chance stared. What had set her off like that?

Henry sighed. He could see Jenny's suffering. And he knew what it had taken for her to give Chance some space.

"Come on, boy. Let's take a tour of the residence. It won't take long. There's only a couple of rooms to gawk at. Get yourself some rest and then be ready at seven. I'll walk you up to the house. It don't pay to argue with the lady. I learned that the hard way years ago."

"Did I learn that, too?" Chance asked, grinning slightly at the resigned expression on the old man's face.

"Oh, you learned a hell of a lot more than that, boy. I just ain't gonna spill the beans on what. You're gonna have to remember them lessons all on your own."

Something about the way Henry smiled as he spoke told Chance much more than words could ever have done. He had a feeling that there was a long history between him and the boss's daughter. He just hoped it was one he could learn to live with.

"Chance! It's great to have you home," Marcus said, as he opened the door.

Home! The word sounded strange. Nothing felt familiar or even remotely comfortable. He'd spent the entire afternoon going through everything in his quarters, and learned absolutely nothing more than what he'd been told about himself. It was strange that he didn't have a single, solitary personal memento. No pictures, no letters, no nothing.

"Thank you, sir," Chance said, uncomfortable as to how he should address the man he knew was his boss. Marcus Tyler had visited him twice in the hospital. That was all he knew of him.

"Just call me Marcus. You always have," he said quietly.

Chance nodded. Henry pushed past them and scooted into the house.

"I smell food," he said. "If my nose don't deceive me, Juana's outdone herself in your honor, boy."

The two men grinned at each other as Henry hobbled down the hallway toward the dining room, and then Chance swallowed his smile as Jenny appeared.

She was wearing a soft, white, Spanish-style dress that floated around her body, only hinting at the shapely form beneath. The low-necked yoke was colorfully embroidered with brilliant pink and cool teal. The hem brushed the top of her knees as she walked toward them, drawing the eye instantly to her long, tanned legs.

Twice Chance started to speak, but each time the words never got past the lump in his throat. *My God, but she's beautiful!*

"Did you bring it?" Jenny asked.

"What?" Chance asked.

"Your appetite." She smiled. "Juana's been cooking

for two days. If you don't like Mexican food, you better not say so. Just push it around on your plate and fake it."

"I don't know what the hell I like," he said. "But I'm willing to try just about anything."

The words came out meaning one thing, but the look on his face told Jenny he was thinking about an entirely different subject. He hadn't taken his eyes off of her since she'd walked down the hall. If looks fed hunger, he'd already have eaten his fill . . . of her.

Marcus watched them—his daughter and the man who'd stolen her heart—and wondered how this mess would ever end. Even before the accident, Chance had made no overtures toward Jenny, at least none of which he'd been aware. Now, with his lack of memory standing between them, how could Jenny ever hope to conquer the extra odds?

Marcus kept his worries and his thoughts to himself. It was time to play host.

"Okay," he said. "I don't know about you two, but I'm heading for the dining room. Henry's already got at least a five minute head start and that could mean trouble."

They laughed, the tenseness of the moment broken by Marcus's words.

"He's right, you know," Jenny said, as she slipped her hand in the crook of Chance's arm. "Come with me. I know where Juana keeps extras just in case."

Her hand felt small and trusting . . . and right. And somehow, Chance made it down the hall, and through the meal without making a fool of himself. It was difficult, because he didn't want the food that was placed before him. He'd suddenly realized that he wanted something entirely different. He wanted Jenny Tyler.

* * *

It was strange the things that came instinctively. Chance had no problem knowing what needed to be done around the ranch. He would find himself nearly through with a task that he had no recollection of starting, although the first few days he'd done little more than observe. At times he would get light-headed and have to rest. He was constantly frustrated by his lack of endurance, but his physical strength was gradually returning. It was his lack of mental capacity that kept him on edge. He didn't remember a damn thing before waking up in the hospital and staring into wide blue eyes and the face of an angel.

The angel might have a sweet face, however it did not match her disposition. She hovered and cajoled, scolded and protected, until he was afraid to zip up his pants without asking permission. Regardless of his annoyance, he still sensed her presence, or heard her coming, long before she would make herself known. For some reason, he'd tuned in to Jenny Tyler and try as he might, could not tune her out. He wasn't even sure that he wanted to. Even if she did ride him for doing too much too soon, there was always that small lilt of anticipation that kicked him in his gut when he heard her voice or saw her smile.

"Chance! That's too heavy for you! Let one of the other men finish loading the fencing material."

He turned with a frown and dropped the fence posts he'd been carrying back into the bed of the pickup truck.

"Jennifer Ann, why don't you find something to do

besides wet nurse me? I've got enough sense to know if I've started something I can't finish."

Jenny's mouth dropped. He'd called her Jennifer Ann! Even if it was instinctive, it had come from a part of him that she thought she'd lost. Her eyes watered and her chin wobbled as she tried to speak. It was no use. Words wouldn't come. It didn't matter. Words were not what she needed as she flew into his arms.

Chance caught her, but he wasn't certain why she'd just thrown herself into his arms. All he knew was that it felt right holding her, and that it wasn't enough.

"Hell, girl," he growled. "I'm sorry I was so cranky. But dammit, Jenny . . . you hover. You're going to have to let up or I'll never get anything done." His voice softened as he felt her arms sliding around his waist. "And, I'm sorry I yelled."

"It's not what you told me. It's what you called me." Her voice was muffled against the front of his shirt.

"Called you? What are you talking—"

"Jennifer Ann. You called me Jennifer Ann."

Adrenaline spiked through him. His arms tightened around her shoulders as he nuzzled the top of her head. Something vague, yet familiar, hung just out of reach of his memory. It was the first hint they'd had that recovery was possible, maybe even imminent.

"That's good, isn't it?" His plea for assurance was as strong as his arms around her shoulders.

"Yes, Chance, that's good." Jenny leaned back and stared into his face. "Life is good."

She slid her hands up the front of his shirt and relished the life beating beneath her fingertips. A smear of dust on the corner of his chin caught her eye. She started to wipe it away and then stopped. It was time to let go. He could function with a smear of dirt on his chin. He had before. He would now.

"So!" she said. "Go back to whatever you were doing. I'm going shopping."

He grinned. She'd not only loosened her apron strings, she'd just cut him free. "Thank you, Jenny."

She knew what he meant. "You're welcome, mister. But don't think that you're completely off the hook. You're still going to catch hell if I see you doing something to endanger your health. And, just for the record, that happened before the accident too. Don't think just because you saved my life that you're going to get preferential treatment forever."

"No, ma'am." Chance's smile was broader. She started to walk away. "Hey, Jenny!"

She turned.

"When you go shopping . . . you gonna bring me a surprise?"

"Why should I? You're already full of surprises."

His laughter followed her all the way to the house.

"How's he doing?" Marcus asked, as Jenny came in the door.

She smiled and shrugged. "His memory's still shot, but his attitude is normal. He wants me to mind my own business and bring him a present from town."

Marcus watched the look of love on his daughter's face and knew a small moment of jealousy that it was for another man. The emotion was just as strange to Marcus as the thought. His daughter loved him . . . didn't she? He shouldn't worry if she also loved someone else . . . should he?

Jenny walked out of the room. He started to call her back, but then stopped. *What the hell could he say? Oh Jenny, by the way, do you happen to love me? Or have I wasted my opportunities once too often?*

It was a sobering thought, and one that Marcus had no intention of letting slide. Not this time. Not ever again.

"Now just because Dr. Walker has pronounced you more or less recovered, doesn't mean you can fall back into your normal routine," Jenny said, as she turned into the driveway and headed toward the bunkhouse. Chance glared.

She had just driven Chance to his last doctor's appointment and the checkup had been good. Unless he had new or recurring complications, he was released.

"Well, bossy, since I don't remember what the hell my old routine was, I don't suppose I'll be resuming it, will I?"

Chance's sarcastic drawl was not lost on Jenny. She'd almost overstepped her bounds again. And she knew that he was becoming frustrated by the fact that he'd had no other signs that would indicate his memory was returning since the time he'd inadvertently called her Jennifer Ann.

"Good!" she said sharply. "Those Saturday night women can go find someone else."

A dark, red flush crept up his neck and face. "For God's sake, Jennifer! Did I have any secrets from you?"

She grinned. "Not enough to brag about."

Chance bolted. Jenny watched him stomp into the

bunkhouse and slam the door shut behind him. *Good!* she thought. She wanted him to wonder about their relationship. She wanted him nervous about what she knew and what he couldn't remember. It could be the only chance she'd have to get under his skin and find out why he wouldn't have committed to her.

Jenny drove back to the house and parked. She bumped into her father as he came out of the den.

"Where are you going?" she asked, watching him shift a garment bag and an overnight carryall to a more comfortable position. "Another trip, I suppose."

Marcus frowned. The tone of her voice pricked his conscience. He'd never wondered or worried before about what Jenny did when he was gone. This awareness of his daughter was bringing new concerns into his life.

"I've got to fly to Houston, honey," he said. "Want to come? All you need to do is grab a couple of changes of clothes. If you forget anything, you can always go shopping."

Jenny gaped. She was nearly twenty-four years old and never . . . absolutely never before . . . had Marcus ever invited her to go with him. "With you?"

He smiled. The sarcastic tone in his voice was not lost on Jenny. "Hell yes, girl. With me. Do you want to go?"

She sighed. He'd just asked her something that once she'd have given a year of her life to hear. Now was a different story.

"I don't want to be away from Chance."

Marcus frowned. "He wouldn't let you near him when he was well. Don't take advantage of the fact that he doesn't remember that, missy," he said.

A deep, abiding pain began to curl in the pit of her

stomach. "You didn't have to remind me, Marcus," she said sharply. "I don't forget anything. I'm not allowed to."

"I didn't mean it the way . . ."

"Drop it," Jenny said. "Have a safe trip."

He knew he'd hurt her. He could see her blinking back tears. But it had been years since he'd seen his daughter cry. He suspected it would be a lot longer before she allowed him that familiarity. A parent had to earn the right to love. Of all the things he'd earned and accumulated in his lifetime, the right to love his only child was not one of them.

He frowned and then sighed. Apologies were not in his vocabulary. "I'll be back late tomorrow," he said. "If you need me for anything, check the papers on my desk. There's a phone number and the name of my hotel where I can be reached in emergency."

Jenny nodded.

"Jenny—"

"Have a safe trip, Marcus," she said. She wasn't in the mood for any more of his advice.

And then he was gone.

Less than fifteen minutes later, Juana came into Jenny's room with a piece of paper in her hand.

"Jenny! Where's Marcus?" she asked.

"He's gone, but not forgotten," Jenny said, ignoring the look of rebuke she knew Juana would be wearing. "Does he have a message?"

Juana nodded. "I think it will be important to him," she answered.

"Give it to me," she said. "I'll phone his hotel. When he arrives, the message will be waiting."

Juana nodded and handed Jenny the message. "Are you going to eat dinner here tonight?"

Jenny shrugged. The thought of a long, lonesome evening loomed. And then an idea surfaced. "Yes! In fact, we're all going to eat here. Let's have a cookout on the patio. Thaw some steaks. I'll tell Henry and the boys."

Juana teased her. "Don't forget to tell Chance. It would be a shame if he—"

"Shut up, smarty," Jenny said, softening her words with a smile. "You know entirely too much about me for my own peace of mind."

"I know I love you, *niña*," Juana said. "And I don't want to see you hurt."

"I'm not going to be hurt. Chance wouldn't hurt me."

"This Chance is not our old Chance, and you know it," Juana reminded her, and silenced Jenny with a look.

Jenny headed for her father's study. She shuffled through the papers on his desk and finally located the brochure with the hotel address and number that he'd circled. She dialed the number, read the message twice to the desk clerk, and then hung up with a feeling of accomplishment. Marcus's plans would not go awry and neither would hers. She had a special plan for tonight after the meal. She was going to resurrect some old home movies. The men always loved to see themselves in action, and she knew that Chance was in many of the shots. Maybe this would help jog his memory. It couldn't hurt.

Chance watched Jenny flit from one group of men to the other, playing hostess one minute, and reverting to "one of the boys" the next. She kept slipping glances in his direction when she thought he wasn't looking, but, true to her claim, she'd more or less left him alone. He didn't know whether he was relieved or disappointed. His fingers curled around the cold bottle of beer in his hand and knew that holding that beer was not what he wanted to do. Holding Jenny seemed much more necessary . . . and important.

"What's for dessert?" Henry asked, as Jenny scraped the last of the potato salad onto his plate.

"Movies," she answered, and grinned at the men's cheers of delight.

"Show last year's roundup," one called.

"No, show the Labor Day barbecue where Shorty and Pete got into a fight over Hettie Williams," another one said.

"How about the time . . ."

The catcalls and rude jokes flew around the yard as the men hurried to move their chairs onto the flagstone patio where Juana had erected a portable screen. Henry quickly took over the duty of projectionist, thereby assuring himself that he could run whatever film he chose, and took bets on whether Shorty or Pete would be the first to lose their temper when the movie was shown. It was still a source of contention with them that Hettie Williams had ignored them both and gone home with a cowboy from a neighboring ranch. They blamed each other for her abandonment.

Chance turned away and walked into the shadows. It was almost dark, a perfect time for outdoor viewing of the promised movies, and a perfect time to slip away. The need to run was strong, as was the need to remember. The moment he'd heard her announcement, he'd known what had prompted her decision to show the movies.

A feeling of dismay mingled with one of excitement. If he watched, maybe something would trigger a memory that would bring him back to normal. And, if he did watch and nothing happened, it only made his condition more hopeless . . . more final.

"Are you mad at me?" Jenny asked.

He turned at the sound of her voice.

Her hand slid tentatively up his shoulder.

"No, Jenny. Why would I be mad? It's obvious the men are looking forward to the treat."

"Because I think you know why I did it," she said. "And I swear, if this feels like pressure, you have every right to tell me so."

Chance was quiet. Jenny held her breath.

"I want to see," he finally answered. "But I have a favor to ask."

"Anything," Jenny said.

"I think I want to see these without being a part of the crowd. Let me watch from back here, in the shadows. I don't want to run interference between what I'm seeing, and what you might feel obligated to remind me of. Can you do that much for me, Jenny?"

"I'll do anything for you. You've always known that."

She hid her disappointment. She'd envisioned sitting beside him while his past came to life before his eyes, dreamed of seeing remembrance come flooding back. Obviously, he didn't expect that to happen, and thought it was naive of her that she had.

"Roll 'em, Henry," she called as she walked away

from Chance. "And the first one to start a fight has to clean up the party mess."

Chance grinned as the men muttered under their breaths. Jenny knew them well. They'd rather feed pigs than do "woman's work." And a cowboy does not willingly set foot around a pig.

Images danced through the night on the beam of light from the projector and jumped onto the screen, bringing a portion of the past to life. It didn't take long for the laughter to follow, as Henry's weathered face and hitched gait filled the screen.

He was leading a horse toward Jenny, who sat perched on the top rail of the corral. The smile on her face kicked Chance in the gut. And when she vaulted off the fence and threw her arms first around Henry, and then around the horse's neck, he swallowed harshly. It was a Jenny he'd never seen. This one wasn't scolding, or wearing a continual frown of worry. She was unconscious of her beauty, unconcerned with her clothing, and looked to be in her teens.

Firecrackers went off beneath a bystander's feet, telling Chance that it must have been a Fourth of July celebration that was being filmed. A man walked into the picture, and Jenny's face lit up like a roman candle. Absolute and total devotion was obvious. When the man turned around and made a face at the camera, Chance caught his breath. *It's me!* He had no memory at all of the occasion. Jenny was handing him a bridle that he slipped over the horse's head. She was smiling and laughing and clapping her hands as the crowd around her began singing.

It took Chance a minute to decipher the song,

since this movie had no sound. Happy Birthday! They were singing Happy Birthday to Jenny! His breathing quickened and he stiffened as he watched Jenny throw her arms around his neck and plant a swift kiss on his cheek before allowing him to help her mount the horse. Because he was looking for it . . . because subconsciously he'd always known it was there . . . he didn't miss the intense look of love that Jenny gave him before she turned the horse's head and rode off amid cheers and birthday greetings from the crowd.

It was too much! Chance knew that the rest of the night would simply be a rerun of similar scenes and similar people. He didn't have to remember it to know that Jenny Tyler loved him. He'd felt it through the darkness in the hospital, when he had no memory at all . . . when there was nothing in his life but misery and pain.

What he didn't know, and what he couldn't face, was the depth of his own feelings for the boss's daughter, and memory of what, if anything, had ever happened between them. He turned and walked away, hidden by night shadows.

Jenny saw him go and resisted an urge to cry. It would do no good. And it would be too obvious if she bolted after him. *Damn this all to hell*, she thought. *Why can't you remember me, Chance McCall? Injury or not, I'd have to be dead not to remember you.*

It seemed like a lifetime, but it was less than an hour later before Jenny could find an excuse to slip away from the party and leave the men to their enjoyment of the old films.

She didn't need a flashlight to find her way to the foreman's bunkhouse. The moon was three-quarters full, but she could have found her way there in her sleep. Her step echoed loudly as she walked across the planked porch. She bit her lip and cursed under her breath, wishing that she'd had the foresight to be more quiet.

It wouldn't have mattered. Chance had been watching the moonlight and shadows on the drive for nearly an hour. He'd known that she would come. He opened the door before she could knock. They stared, each holding their breath, waiting for the other to make the first move. And when it happened, neither knew or cared. She was in his arms.

"I knew you'd come," he whispered, as he wrapped his arms around her. He trailed kisses against her face and down the side of her neck. "I always seem to know when you're around. I don't know my own goddamn name, but I can always feel your presence."

"Chance!" It was all she could say. His words broke her heart and at the same time gave her hope. Maybe it didn't matter that he couldn't remember the past. It was obvious that he cared for her now.

He pulled her into the bunkhouse and kicked the door shut with his boot heel as he walked them both to his bed. The springs creaked quietly, once, as they stretched out on the old, blue patchwork quilt. Then all was silent. The only sounds in the darkness were of breaths caught and stopped, only to be released as swiftly in passion.

Jenny's world was tilting. There was nothing left but

this big man's body and the touch of his mouth. The whispers in her ear and the feel of him growing beneath her hands as she pulled him closer. The heat of flesh upon flesh as clothing disappeared and the knowledge that something she'd prayed for was about to happen.

Chance moved his mouth across her face, taking and marking with his lips the virgin territory of Jenny Tyler. She melted beneath him, pliant and willing as he unbuttoned, unsnapped, and tasted her, this wild, wonderful woman who'd pulled him from hell. Lush curves spilled from the wisp of bra he unsnapped, filling his hands. He caressed and revered the woman beneath him. Memory had no place in the feelings she evoked. Passion was everything, here and now.

He felt himself swelling against his zipper until he thought he would burst if she moved another inch beneath him, and still he could not bring himself to make the final journey. Something kept holding him back from taking what she was obviously willing to give.

Her lips opened beneath his mouth, and the moan that slipped down his throat sent shudders all the way to his soul. It was at the same time a moan of need, and a moan of submission. He knew that she would not stop him. And it was that knowledge that gave him the impetus to stop himself. That, and the memory of how long this had been between them. She remembered. He did not. It wasn't right.

Jenny felt his withdrawal. The heat on her bare body cooled almost instantly as he lifted himself up and rolled away. Bitter tears sprang into her eyes as she caught her breath, swallowing harsh accusations as he once again pulled away from making love to her. Only she would remember that this wasn't the first time it had happened. Her heart felt about to break into tiny pieces. *He may not remember that he wouldn't make love to me before, but obviously his heart does.*

"Jenny . . . I'm sorry," he whispered. "It would be cheating you if . . ."

"Oh hell, honey," she said sharply, "don't let it bother you." She started to roll away.

"No," he muttered. He slid his arm beneath her bare shoulders and yanked her against his chest. He heard her pain. It intensified his own regret.

"It'll bother me a hell of a lot longer than it will you," he answered. "And I didn't stop for my health, that's for damn sure."

Jenny sighed. Fighting would get them nowhere. She shouldn't have come, and she knew it. Even her own father had warned her about trading on his memory loss for her own gain. It had backfired, just as he'd warned. She had only herself to blame.

"I don't know why you stopped," she said, the weariness in her voice dragging out her words, "but I shouldn't have come. It's my fault, too."

Chance sighed and pulled her against him, pillowing her head against his chest.

"Lie with me, Jennifer Ann. I have this overwhelming urge to sleep, and I don't want to do it alone."

Tears slipped quietly down her face as she rolled over and wrapped her arms around his chest. Everything about her ached, from her head to her heart. But leaving Chance at this moment would have been suicide.

Nearly an hour passed, and Jenny thought he was

asleep. The steady beat of his heart beneath her ear, and
the even rise and fall of his chest, made her almost posi-
tive. But then the sound of his voice, and the content of
his question scared her to death.

"Were we lovers, Jenny?" His voice was a caress
against her skin, his hand moving gently but possessively
up and down her spine as he settled her more securely
in place.

For long moments, she was silent. Finally, she could
answer. And when she did, it was as near to the truth
as she could come and not lose the man in her arms
forever.

"You're the only man who's ever made love to me.
You're the first and only man who taught me what passion
felt like."

Her words were quiet, but the depth of emotion was
there. He heard it. He could feel it humming beneath
her skin. The knowledge gave him roots. If they'd been
there once, when he got well, they'd be there again.

"Good. Just remember that for future reference."

Oh, Chance, Jenny thought. *Without you, I have no
future.*

"I think I'd better go," she said. "You should rest, and
I better check and see if Marcus got the message I left
for him at the hotel."

The mention of her father changed his mood drasti-
cally. Instant guilt swept over him at the knowledge that
he'd just nearly made love to his boss's daughter. He
had no idea what that would mean to the man. *My God!
What I wouldn't do for a memory!*

Jenny knew the moment she'd mentioned her
father's name that Chance would withdraw. It didn't

take a genius to figure out why. Even if he was brain dead, Chance McCall wouldn't step over the boundaries of his character and conscience. She'd give a lot to know what had marked this man.

"Chance?"

"What?" he asked, as she started out the door.

"If you let what happened tonight change what's between us tomorrow, I'll never forgive you."

"It won't, girl. I'll mark it up as a weak moment. But I need to say this . . . and don't misunderstand me. I don't think it should happen again. Not now."

"Why doesn't that surprise me?"

Her laugh caught on a quiet sob as she disappeared into the night. Chance rubbed his hand across his face and sank back down onto the bed. *And what in the hell did she mean by that?*

7

"*Marcus, have* you got a minute?"

Marcus looked up from his desk. Chance was standing in the doorway.

"Come in, come in," he called, waving him inside. "It's so good to see you back to normal." The moment he said that he regretted it. Chance wasn't normal . . . not yet. "Is there a problem you needed to see me about, or is this just social?"

"Actually, neither," Chance said, and closed the door behind him, thankful that he'd made it all the way to Marcus's office without attracting Jenny's attention. What he had to ask would be difficult enough without an audience.

The action surprised Marcus. His eyes narrowed as he took a long look at the man who'd been his right arm for the better part of the last twelve years.

"So, what can I do for you? You know you only have to ask. Sit down, why don't you?"

"I'd rather stand." His answer was abrupt, as was his manner. He began to pace.

Marcus leaned back in his chair and watched Chance walk the room like a caged tiger.

"What was my relationship with this family?" Chance asked.

Marcus answered instantly. "For starters, long-standing trust."

Chance frowned.

"That's obviously not what you wanted to hear," Marcus said. "If you're wanting to know did you have a personal relationship with Jenny, I honestly don't know. We aren't exactly close." He sighed and shrugged. "And I have only myself to blame for that."

"What if I had?" Chance persisted. "How would you have felt about that? To the best of my knowledge, I don't own anything but that pickup truck and a few personal belongings. I found a bank book in my desk. It seems I'm not exactly a spendthrift, but I'm also way out of your league."

"When I started, boy, I didn't own that much and had a pregnant wife to boot. Soon after Jenny was born, I was several hundred thousand dollars in debt and burying my wife. I wasn't exactly strolling down easy street myself."

Chance stared. This was not what he'd expected to hear. "How long have you owned this place, Marcus?"

"To the day? I bought it a week before Jenny was born. We moved in the day she arrived. This Fourth of July, twenty-four years." He frowned. "And I don't remember two damn days of Jenny's childhood that I could string together. I wasted it all building this."

Chance listened intently. There was so much riding on what he learned today.

"And you know what the sad thing is, boy? I'd trade it all for a closer relationship with Jenny. She has little to no regard for me, and I can't blame her."

"That's not true, Marcus," Chance argued. "I don't remember much. But I know what I see now. She may not hang on your every word, but she loves you. She's just independent as hell. That's not a failure." He stuffed his hands in his pockets and paced some more. "But that's not really why I was asking."

"Then, shoot," Marcus urged. "I'm listening."

"Would you resent me being more than a foreman to the Triple T?"

"A few months ago, this question would have come as a complete shock. I can't lie to you about that. But you knowingly dived beneath that stallion to protect my daughter. And she nearly went crazy when you were hurt."

"So what are you telling me?"

"I'm saying that whatever you two decide will be fine with me."

A weight lifted! For the first time in days Chance felt good inside. Even if he didn't remember it himself, he was obviously held in high regard. He didn't think Marcus Tyler would gladly suffer a fool.

"Okay," Chance said, trying unsuccessfully to mask a grin, "then I have another question. And this one may be a little harder for you to answer."

Marcus would have bet money on what was coming next, and he would have won.

"What do you know about my past? Did I have

references when I hired on? Who did I list as next of kin? Have I ever received any outside visitors or mail? Did I—"

"Whoa, boy. I can save you a whole lot of breath," Marcus said. "I don't know a damn thing about your past."

Chance wilted. He'd been afraid that was what he would hear. He just hadn't wanted to face it. Henry had already said as much when he'd questioned him.

"But I do know that you're the best and longest temporary help I ever hired." He punctuated his answer with a grin. "You were eighteen years old. You told me that you could fix just about anything with an engine. From the looks of the old truck you drove up in, I believed you. How you came as far as you did in that thing was a source of amazement to me. You told me that you'd work for board and keep, and you sounded desperate. That was the reason I hired you. I followed a hunch. From your appearance, it would have seemed likely that I'd hired a troublemaker. I couldn't have been more wrong."

Chance stared. "What do you mean, my appearance?"

Marcus sat upright in his chair. "That's right! You wouldn't have remembered. Hell, boy! You walked in my office favoring your right shoulder. Your face looked like you'd gone ten rounds with a bulldozer and come out the loser. You'd been beat to holy hell and back, that's what!"

"Well, I asked, didn't I?" The sarcasm was not lost on Marcus.

"Yes, but don't let any of that worry you, Chance. I have faith in the fact that one day everything will come back to you full force. You've just got to be patient."

Chance shook his head and headed for the door. "I'm real long on time, Marcus, but a whole lot short on patience. I don't want to wait too long to remember what I may not want to hear."

He left Marcus to mull over their discussion.

Marcus didn't like what he was thinking. The idea of Chance and Jenny wasn't as strange as it might once have been. But Jenny wasn't Chance's problem. His past and his memory were holding him back from commitment. And if he knew Jenny, she wouldn't buy either of the reasons on a bet.

"Did you see the boss?" Henry asked, as Chance came through the stables.

"I saw him," he said shortly.

Henry nodded. He didn't have to ask to see that Chance hadn't gotten the answers he'd wanted.

"Henry, what did I bring when I first came to work here? Did you ever see—"

"Say," Henry nearly yelled, "now that you mention it, you did have a suitcase. In fact, when I was helpin' you move to the foreman's quarters a few years back, you tossed it into the storage room off the bunkhouse. Said something about not needin' to move ghosts."

"Ghosts?"

Henry shrugged. "That's what you said."

Tension pulled across Chance's gut. "Where did you say that suitcase was?"

"I'll get it myself and bring it to your room," Henry said.

Chance stared at the aging cowboy's retreat and felt a

strange desire to tell him never mind. Something . . .
some instinct . . . was obviously telling him he was about
to open a big can of worms. He headed toward his quarters instead.

"Here it is! Just like I claimed," Henry said as he
burst through the door and dropped it down on the bed.
"It was a bit dusty. I wiped it off before I brung it over."

"Thanks, Henry," Chance said, staring at the small
brown bag as if someone had just thrown snakes on his
bed.

"Don't mention it, boy," Henry said. "You know, it's
nearly suppertime. I'm gonna head on over to the
bunkhouse and wash up. Juana is fixin' enchiladas
tonight and they're my favorite. You take your time. If
you don't make it up for supper, I'll bring you back a
plate."

"Don't bother," Chance said. "I don't think I'm going
to be hungry."

Henry shrugged. His heart went out to the young
man, but there wasn't a thing he could do or say to help
him. Chance McCall was lost inside himself, and only
Chance could find his way back.

"See you tomorrow, then," Henry called, and shut
the door on his way out.

Chance took a deep breath and then went into the
small kitchen area of the two room house. He opened
the refrigerator, took out a cold brown bottle of beer,
and popped the cap. It went spinning out across the
hardwood floor, metal against wood, and clattered to a
stop beside the wall. He left it there as he drank the

sharp brew, letting it run cold and slow down his throat until his eyes watered. He emptied the bottle, tossed it into a wastebasket, and stared at the suitcase on his bed. He hadn't really needed the beer for fortification. He'd simply been postponing the time that was now at hand.

His fingers curved around the old rusty locks and pressed. One snapped open loudly, startling him with a clear, sharp click. The other resisted. Chance picked at it with his pocketknife and, finally, it too came open with a resounding noise. He tossed the knife onto the bed and opened the bag.

He didn't know what he was expecting, but it was definitely more than this. His hopes plummeted.

It was almost empty. A few old matchbooks lay scattered across the faded cloth lining. An old bolo tie with a longhorn steer head pull was coiled in a corner. He fingered it, hoping to stir something familiar. The matchbooks were an advertisement for a gas station in Odessa, Texas, that probably didn't even exist anymore. The name meant nothing to him, but he stuffed them back into the suitcase for reference. It was a place to start, and Chance had already made his decision.

He ran his fingers along the gathered pockets on either side of the suitcase. One was empty save for a straight pin that caught the tip of his little finger. He cursed and yanked it back, and then searched the other side of the pocket more carefully. An old wallet fell into his hands.

At first glance, it was as empty as the suitcase shedding dust on his bed. He poked and pulled, searching through every pocket, and almost missed the concealed flap. Even before he lifted it, he knew something was there. He could feel the difference in bulk through the dry, brittle leather. As he lifted the flap, the contents fell out onto the bed.

It was a picture of a girl, and it wasn't Jenny. Images swirled around in his head and, for a moment, he thought he heard laughter. Long blond hair, wide-set eyes, and a slender figure were caught in time. It was signed, *Love, Victoria.*

Victoria! The name meant nothing. Neither did her face. He turned the picture over and read the penciled note he recognized as his own handwriting. *V. Henry. Picnic. 1980.*

1980! That was just before he'd come to the Triple T. Depending on the month of the year, he couldn't have been more than seventeen or eighteen. He dropped the picture into the bottom of the suitcase and continued his search. Maybe there was something else . . .

And there was. In the wide stretchy pocket of the lid, he found an old high school yearbook, also from Odessa. *Odessa High School . . . Broncos.* His frustration grew. It took some time to find a picture of a fresh-faced boy with hair too long who bore the name, Chance McCall, class of 1980.

"Well, boy," Chance said softly, as he traced his finger across the page. "You're coming with me. I've got to see a man about a life I've lost, and maybe . . . just maybe . . . you can help."

He tossed the yearbook back into the bag along with the matchbooks. He stuck the picture into his own wallet and headed for the closet. It didn't take long to pack what he needed.

"I'll need cash," he muttered to himself. "I can get

that at an ATM." Then he grinned wryly. "I can't remember a goddamned thing that matters, but I can remember how to get money out of a stupid machine."

He shrugged and continued tossing things into the nearly full bag. It didn't matter. Nothing was important but finding his past, and his memory, and then getting back to Jenny. Something inside him kept telling him that if he'd just remember, then everything would be all right.

The next and last thing he had to do was also the most difficult. There were letters to write. And he didn't know what to say that was going to make this easier. He sat down at the table and wrote the first one to Henry. It didn't take long. There wasn't much to say. He'd simply ask him to tell Marcus that he'd gone looking for his past, hoping that it would help him remember the present. He wrote that if it meant his job, then so be it. He couldn't live in this vacuum any longer and not do something.

The next was to Jenny. This was not difficult, it was downright impossible. Finally, all he could say was that if she was willing to wait, he'd be back.

He folded the two separately, left them laying on the table, and closed the rusty locks on the bag. There was little left to do except wait until later, when everyone would be asleep. He didn't want any scenes. Leaving when no one was around to say goodby seemed the easiest way out.

"Oh holy hell," Henry said to himself, as he unfolded his note and began to read. There was another addressed to Jenny. He didn't need to look to know that it was more of the same. Chance was gone! And, from the sound of the note, he wouldn't be back until he had some answers. The only thing that worried Henry was, if Chance didn't find answers, would he ever come back?

Jenny walked up onto the porch and started to knock when she saw Henry through the screen door.

"Hi!" she called. "Tell Chance that mare is about ready to foal. He'll want to be there. You know how he is about . . ."

Something about the way Henry was standing told her to hush. She started to shake. It was instinctive. And then when he picked up a piece of folded paper, came outside onto the porch and handed it to her, she began to cry.

> Dear Jenny, I need to find some answers from my past before a future is even possible. Please try to understand. If you'll wait . . . I'll be back.
>
> Chance

"He didn't even say he loved me."

Henry heard the pain in her voice. She was bent almost double, as if the simple reading of Chance's message was more than she could bear. He didn't know what to say.

Ever since Chance had awakened in the hospital, with that lost look on his face, Jenny had known that this could happen. It was what she'd feared most in the world. Chance was gone, and she was sure he hadn't told Henry where he was going either.

"Now, honey," Henry said, patting her awkwardly on the shoulder, "he's coming back. He said so."

"When?" she asked. She wanted to scream, but it would have done no good.

This was the part she wasn't going to buy. "Just as soon as he finds out what he needs to know."

"Oh, great," she shouted, wadding up her note and throwing it against the wall. "And what happens if he doesn't find the answers to his questions, Henry? Does that mean he'll come home a wiser man . . . or does that mean he won't come home at all?"

There was nothing he could say. He'd asked himself the same things less than five minutes earlier. He tried to comfort her, but there was no comfort to be had for Jenny.

"Where you goin', girl?" he called, as she ran from the bunkhouse.

"To hell, Henry," she screamed back at him. "To hell. It's the only place I haven't been."

His heart broke for her, and there was a look on her face that scared him. He turned around and headed for the phone in the bunkhouse. He had to call Marcus. He'd better know now, and he'd better know fast. Someone had to be there for Jenny. And, for once in his life, Marcus was going to have to behave like the father he'd never been.

Henry's news pumped adrenaline into his system. Marcus hung up the phone and made a dash for the kitchen just as Jenny burst through the back door. The panic in Henry's voice had told him this was serious. From the look on Jenny's face, Henry had been right.

"Jenny!" She pushed past him and staggered blindly toward her room. "Wait. You need to talk about—"

She turned, lashing out in pain. "With you? You want

to *be there* for me, Marcus? Are you having a father attack again? Well don't bother. I don't need you. I don't need Chance. I don't need anyone, especially a man. All they do is lie and then do exactly what they promised they wouldn't. Did you know that? Is it inbred, or is it a learned thing? Do men practice cutting out a heart by degrees, or is it the preferred method to just give it a yank and to hell with tact?"

"Jenny! Don't talk to your father like that," Juana cried, as she stepped between the pair in the hallway. "You have no—"

"I have no father, you meant to say, didn't you, Juana? Before, it never mattered. There was always you. And then there was Chance."

Her voice was shaking. Her whole body was shaking. And for a moment, Marcus feared she would faint. Her face paled as she leaned against the wall and closed her eyes.

"Honey . . ." he began.

"Now he's gone, too. And God help him if he doesn't come back for me. I'll haunt him in hell," Jenny whispered.

Tears poured down Juana's face as she gathered Jenny in her arms and rocked her against her ample bosom. "*Madre de Dios,*" she muttered. "It's going to be all right. It's going to be all right." She shook her head at Marcus and mouthed, *not now.*

Marcus watched the woman he paid money to clean and cook for him lead his daughter away. He hadn't paid her to mother Jenny. She had done that out of instinct and love.

Juana stripped off Jenny's clothes and urged her into

bed. She tucked a lightweight cover over her and tried to ignore the violent quaking of the girl's slender shoulders. She knew it was shock and that it would pass. But she feared the dull, lifeless look in Jenny's eyes would not. Jenny's world had just been cut out from under her. And, God help them all, there was no one but a lost man who could put it back together again.

"Sleep, baby," she crooned, as she brushed Jenny's hair away from her face. "Just sleep. It will be all better when you wake, and then we'll talk. It's never as bad as it seems after you rest."

Jenny turned her face away and willed herself not to die, at least not yet. If Chance couldn't find himself, she just might have to go help him search. And if that was impossible, then they'd just have to be lost in hell together. She shuddered and swallowed a sob. There were no more tears left. Only a dull, aching pain that kept growing and growing and growing. She closed her eyes and slept.

West Texas was flat as hell and nearly as hot. Chance rolled the windows down to let in air, but the heat only circulated. His air conditioner in the pickup needed coolant, or something else. He'd stopped earlier and lost precious hours trying to fix it. He didn't want to stop and check it again so he just turned it off. He'd have to tough it out until he reached Odessa. And from looking at the map, there was only an inch left to go. Unfortunately that inch would translate into at least fifty more hot-as-hell miles.

It was late afternoon. He'd driven like a madman

when he'd first left the ranch. Putting distance between himself and Jenny had been the only assurance he had that when night came, he wouldn't turn around and go back. He hadn't been gone a day and he already missed her.

"Stop it, fool," he told himself. "Concentrate on Odessa, that gas station, and the yearbook. On the facts!"

He increased his speed and stared down the long, flat road stretching out before him. But there were no answers waiting in the dancing waves of heat that shimmered across the blacktop. Only tumbleweeds and mesquite and, occasionally, a lone herd of cattle, grazing on the sparse forage of the dry, brown land. It made him homesick for the Triple T and the greener, rolling hills and scattered clumps of trees, the creeks that ran into rivers, and the herds of horses running across the pastures.

A lone truck came barreling down the straight highway toward him and honked loudly as it passed, as if the driver was assuring himself that he wasn't the only man left on earth. Chance looked down at the gas gauge. "With a little luck, I should just about make it."

He drove on into the setting sun.

"You want a room for the hour, the night, or the week?" the woman asked, as she stuffed a used-up cigarette into an overflowing ashtray and blew the last remnant of her smoke into Chance's face.

It was dark. The broken neon lettering outside reflected off the lenses of the woman's horn-rimmed

glasses. Chance tried not to stare. His eyes burned, his
nose twitched, but he kept his mouth shut. He pulled
out a credit card and handed it to her.

"I'll be here a while," he said. "I didn't think reservations would be necessary here, or I wouldn't have
stopped."

She had the grace to blush. She fluffed her peroxide
blond hair and pursed her lips. "I don't think there'll be
a problem, sweetie," she said. Her eyes swept over him.
Chance felt like he'd just been bar coded, scanned, and
had a price shining on his butt.

"Let's hope not," he drawled as he took back his
credit card and grabbed the key she slid toward him.

"First room at the far end," she called. "Thought you
might want some privacy."

He nodded as he walked away.

"Oh," she yelled as the door started to swing shut,
"the pool is temporarily out of order."

Chance smirked as he got in his truck and drove
down the length of building until he reached twelve B.
How in hell did a pool get "temporarily" out of order?

*You've picked a winner this time, Chance. Let's hope
this place looks better in the light of day.*

8

It didn't. Chance stepped out of the motel room and stared up at the cloudless sky and the already hot sun drifting toward zenith. He'd overslept. He'd been so damned tired last night, and then hadn't been able to sleep. The intermittent guests in the room next to him had banged themselves and the bedstead against the wall until he'd been ready to kill. The sighs and moans sounded way too pat to be real. He suspected he'd just taken a room in a twenty-dollar a shot, come and go, motel. He wondered if the peroxide blond clerk with the horn-rimmed glasses was the one doing the honors and then doubted it. A man would have to be past desperate to consider that.

His stomach grumbled, reminding him that food had been the last of his worries yesterday. A small diner across the street from the motel beckoned. Judging from the assortment of cars and pickup trucks parked in front of it, the food had to be good. Business was brisk on Second Street.

A stiff wind pulled at the brim of his hat as he started across the street. He jammed it a little tighter and lengthened his stride. As he pushed open the door of the diner a cowbell hanging over it jangled, but the noise was lost in the din of busy waitresses and hungry customers calling for service or just another cup of coffee.

"Sit anywhere you want, honey," a woman said as she sailed past with a coffee pot in her hand. "I'll be with you in a minute."

Chance took her advice. There wasn't much choice in seating. It was either share a table with two elderly men, or take a stool at the counter. He chose the stool. A coffee cup appeared in front of him, full of hot, steamy brew. He drank, thankful for the kick of caffeine and the heat that slid down his throat and nestled in his stomach.

It might be close to ninety degrees outside, but Chance felt cold as ice. Breath constricted, his eyes narrowed, his belly churned behind his belt buckle. He cupped his hands around the thick crockery cup just to have a place to put them. He'd never had such an urge to bolt and run in his life.

"Okay, good lookin', what'll it be?"

The voice startled him as well as the question. His eyes darkened as he looked up at the waitress who was waiting with pencil poised.

"Eggs, over easy, bacon and biscuits," he answered, almost expecting her to point her finger at him and scream in recognition. This wasn't going to be easy. He took another long swallow of coffee and shoved away the fear. *Dammit to hell. This was my idea. Nobody made me come. Now get your butt in gear, McCall, and quit acting like a fool.*

The silent pep talk did wonders for his nerves. That and the second cup of coffee the waitress poured before turning in his order. Chance dug in his shirt pocket, pulled out the old blue matchbook he'd found in his suitcase, and fiddled with it absently, turning it back and forth between his thumb and forefinger as he watched the mirror over the counter, staring at every customer who came and went, hoping that someone would look familiar to him. They didn't.

"My God!" the waitress cried loudly, as she slammed a plate of bacon and eggs in front of him. "Where did you get that old thing? I haven't seen one in years."

She snatched the matchbook out of his fingers and turned it over.

"Yeah! I was right! It's from Charlie's Gas and Guzzle. Hell, honey, where did you come from . . . the Twilight Zone?" Her laugh was shrill. So was her voice. Several people at the counter turned to stare.

Chance didn't know whether to answer, or let her answer for him. She was so bent on talking, he opted for the latter.

"Look here, Marsh. How many years has it been since you seen one a these?" She didn't wait for this Marsh fellow to answer. "Where did you get this, honey?" She shoved it back in Chance's face. "From a flyin' saucer?"

She must have fancied herself quite a comedienne because she repeated her question to this Marsh fellow just to get another reaction.

Chance took the matchbook back from her and smiled before he picked up his fork and began to eat.

She evidently decided that he was one of the strong, silent types, because she tried another approach. "You vistin' or just passin' through?"

Chance chewed and swallowed. "A little of both," he said quietly. He flipped the matchbook over and stared at the logo. "Is this station still here?"

"Shoot no, honey. And for all intents and purposes, neither is Charlie Rollins."

Chance frowned. Who was . . . ? He didn't have to ask. The girl was full of information.

"Charlie Rollins was the owner of this station. The station is gone and, for the most part, so is Charlie. He's got that forgettin' disease. Whadaya call it? You know the one I mean . . . Owlzeyemer's, or somethin' like that."

"Alzheimer's?"

"Yeah! That's it. He don't remember nothin'. His wife died. His daughter come back long enough to put him in one of them homes for old people, and then she left. I heard she don't even visit. I guess it don't much matter. If he don't know her, what good would it do to come."

"Where is the home?" Chance asked, shoving his empty cup toward her. He watched, fascinated as she talked, poured, and waved at a customer who was leaving, all at the same time, and still didn't spill a drop.

"Why? You gonna go see him? It won't do no good. He won't know you."

But she shrugged and gave him directions, and watched thoughtfully as the tall stranger dropped a generous tip by his plate and sauntered outside as if he had all the time in the world.

"Ten years ago, I'd already have had your phone number and you'd have had the hots for me, sweetie," she murmured to herself.

"Hey," Marsh called, tapping his empty coffee cup on the counter as a reminder.

"Comin' right up," she said, watching as Chance walked across the street to his red pickup truck. Something about that man was *very* familiar. She shrugged, stuffed the tip in her pocket, and headed for Marsh.

The Golden Years retirement home was easy to find and the parking lot was nearly empty. Chance grimaced as he parked and headed for the front door. This was going to be one for the books. He couldn't remember a damn thing, and he was searching for answers from a man with Alzheimers. He walked in the door and then caught his breath at the sight. The parking lot might be nearly empty, but the lobby was nearly full . . . of wheelchairs and their aging occupants.

"Can I help you?"

The twangy, nasal question from the young woman behind the desk got his attention. So did the scent of the building. It was overpowering: a combination of antiseptic, cleaning solutions, liniment, and aging bodies.

He shuddered. If he had a choice, he'd just as soon go fast, not linger in a place like this. His depression deepened. Looking for answers here was futile. If it weren't for Jenny, he would have already turned around and headed back to Tyler. But he owed it to her. He couldn't make a commitment to her without being certain that his past was clean.

"I'm looking for Charlie Rollins."

Her eyebrows rose perceptibly. "Are you family?"

Chance frowned. "No. Do I have to be?"

"No," she answered, "but he's never had any visitors."

"Then it's time he did," Chance said, and waited for her to direct him. She pointed down the hall.

"First door on your left past the bathrooms. Don't expect much," she cautioned. "He has good days and bad days."

"What's today like?" Chance asked.

She shrugged.

Every light in the room was on, the window shades pulled up, the curtains tied back. The bed was neatly made, the room immaculate, although sparsely furnished and, at first glance, empty. Chance started to walk back to the desk to ask if there was another place Charlie Rollins might be, when he happened to look down. A pair of legs protruded from under the bed. Chance's heart thumped. *What in hell?*

And then a pair of hands cupped the bedframe and pulled sharply. The strength in the gnarled and knotted fingers was evident as an old man shot out from under the bed. Chance stared. Charlie Rollins was on a creeper. The kind mechanics lie on when working underneath vehicles.

"Didn't hear you drive up," Charlie said, as he got to his feet with surprising agility. "What'll it be? Gas or directions?"

God in Heaven! Charlie Rollins was operating his gas station from his room. At least Charlie *thought* he was operating his station. And if Chance wasn't mistaken, Charlie had just pulled out from under his bed as if it were a car. Chance wondered what he'd been doing under there and hoped that whatever Charlie removed during the day, he put back before night. If not, his mattress was likely to go through the frame and onto the floor.

"Well, boy?" Charlie prompted. "I ain't got all day. I got to get this car fixed before Mabel Geraldine comes askin' or there'll be hell to pay. She ain't got no patience at all."

"Sorry." Chance grinned. "I just need a little information. Maybe you can help?"

Charlie scratched his head. A foggy look began to pass through his eyes. "If I can. Seems like it gets harder and harder to remember things anymore. Guess I'm gettin' old."

Chance nodded. "I'm trying to locate some people I used to know. I heard that they lived around here some time back. The family name was McCall. Did you happen to know anyone by that name? There was a boy named Chance. Maybe he worked for you . . . or lived close?"

Charlie picked at a week's growth of scraggly gray whiskers and began to fidget. "I don't think I know no McCalls," he mumbled. "I know Mabel Geraldine. She wants her car fixed. I can fix cars real good. Do you need yours fixed, boy?"

Chance sighed. This had been a long shot, and obviously a wild one. "No, Charlie." He patted him on the shoulder and then flinched as he felt the sharpness of the old man's bones through the thin shirt. "Is there anything I can do for you? Anything you need?"

Charlie grinned. He couldn't remember when someone had last offered him something. But trying to think of what he could ask for sent him back into a fog. He walked around in a nervous circle and patted his pockets, muttering to himself about losing his wrenches.

Chance tried not to stare. Sadness overwhelmed him. Poor Charlie Rollins. He'd lost his wrenches . . . and his mind. At least the doctors thought Chance's memory loss was temporary.

"I'll be going now," Chance said softly. The look of relief was instantaneous on Charlie's face. "Thanks for the information, Charlie."

"Anytime, boy, anytime." He laid back down on the creeper and positioned himself, watching the tall man's legs from floor level as he walked through the door and out of the room. "You come back, Chance, boy. You come back soon. I'll need you to close for me tonight," he said.

And then he pulled himself back beneath the bed and began to hum "The Yellow Rose of Texas" as he worked.

Chance didn't hear Charlie's last words. It wouldn't have mattered anyway. By the time Chance reached the desk, Charlie Rollins had forgotten that he'd ever said them.

Chance drove up one street and down another, his eyes searching constantly for something familiar. The acres and acres of pump jacks at the edges of the city were mind boggling. He knew from the signs on the highways, that the Permian Basin, on which Odessa rested, was one of the richest oil fields in the United States, maybe the world.

He took careful note of the business he passed. Especially the older ones. But nothing rang true. He watched the faces of the people on the street, hoping that someone would look familiar . . . or that he'd look familiar to one of them. He was desperate for anything that would tell him that he'd once been a resident of Odessa.

Yet the oddest thing kept happening. No matter which side street he took, or how far off the main highway he drove, he invariably came back to Grandfield. The street kept taking him places and then pulling him back. Chance didn't know how. It had to be instinct. It damn sure wasn't something conscious. As far as he could tell, he'd never been here before in his life.

"Did you see that?"

"What?" Bettye Collins asked, as she swiveled the chair back to face the mirror, combed and parted another section of hair on Dotty Parson's head, then snipped.

She had to finish this cut and style. She had a perm due in forty-five minutes and it would take hours to finish. She'd be lucky if the perm lady's hair didn't fall out on the rollers. She'd had one too many home-bleach jobs. Bettye had talked for over an hour on the phone, trying to persuade the woman to wait until her scalp healed and her hair was in better shape, but the woman was adamant. She had a class reunion to attend and wanted to look like a million bucks. It was Bettye's opinion that she'd never look like that, even if she had the money to prove it.

"Did I see what?" Bettye prompted, as she snipped a good inch of split ends off of Dotty's hair.

Dotty Parson's mouth was hanging open like a land-locked fish on the banks of a pond. "That old red pickup truck. The one that just turned the corner and headed east. I swear on my mamma's grave, that was Logan Henry." And then she frowned. "At least it looked like he used to look. You know, before he got all gray and gained that twenty pounds."

"You're seeing things," Bettye said. "Logan Henry wouldn't be caught dead driving an old dirty pickup truck."

"I guess," Dotty said, and frowned at herself in the mirror. "Do you think I'd look good as a redhead?"

"Only if you never set foot outdoors again," Bettye answered. "That complexion of yours would be redder than your hair, and you know it. If you want to change the color, you oughta let me try . . ."

Their conversation turned to more important matters and, for the moment, the red pickup was forgotten. But, later that night, when Dotty went home, she asked her husband if he'd seen a stranger in town that day driving a red pickup truck up and down the streets. He stared at her fancy coiffure in dismay. That and the fact that she'd even noticed another man caused a fight to erupt that totally drove Logan Henry and his existence permanently from Dotty's mind. It was just as well.

Chance was tired to the bone. Tired and disappointed. His visit to Charlie Rollins had been a lost cause, at least as far as Chance was concerned.

He turned into the motel parking lot. The only thing he'd accomplished today was fix his air conditioner. Buying the part for it had prompted him to make an additional purchase. The set of wrenches he'd bought, and had wrapped and delivered to Charlie Rollins, had probably caused all kinds of commotion at the Golden Years retirement home. The way Charlie operated, he'd probably screwed and unscrewed every nut and bolt on his bed so many times, he'd stripped them out. There'd be hell to pay when bedtime came tonight, but a man had to have wrenches if he was going to work on cars . . . and beds.

Chance parked his truck, locked the doors, and pocketed the keys. The motel key slid across his fingers as he pulled his hand away. It reminded him. He headed for the office.

"Well, now," the desk clerk drawled, "if it ain't Mister twelve B. How ya'll been doin' anyway? If I've seen your truck cruise Second Street once, I've seen it cruise by a hundred times today. Whatcha' tryin' to prove? Or better yet, who you lookin' for? I don't want no trouble here. If you find who you're lookin' for, don't cause no trouble."

Chance took a deep breath. He bit back the words that wanted out and smiled. Then he leaned over the counter, stared point-blank at the enlarged pupils behind the thick lenses, and drawled, "The only trouble that's likely to happen around here is if that room next to mine starts jumping again like it did last night. I don't give a tinker's damn who bangs who around this town. But if it takes place on the other side of my wall again, I won't be responsible for what happens. Do I make myself clear?"

The desk clerk blinked twice rapidly in succession. "Well, now." The timbre of her voice had just gone up two octaves. "I had no idea that you were so . . . disturbed . . . last night. Maybe you need a little . . . relief of your own. If you want I can call—"

His hand slapped down on top of the counter, sending dust and papers flying. "Don't even think it, lady. Just remember what I said. Peace and quiet. It's not too much to ask, is it?"

"Fine," she said. "I was only tryin' to—"

Chance slammed the door behind him. "It's what I get for staying in this godforsaken place," he muttered. But it served his purpose. He wanted low-key, and this was just about as low as it got.

He entered his room, slipped the dead-bolt, and dropped facedown onto the bed. Every muscle in his body ached. He'd walked streets and dodged curious questions from locals all day. He'd even eaten his evening meal at a different location just so he wouldn't have to face that waitress twice in one day. He felt like a rabbit hiding from a fox. The only problem was, he didn't know who the fox was. And he damn sure didn't appreciate feeling like the rabbit. Tomorrow was going to be different. He might not like the answers he would get, but he sure as hell wasn't going to hide from the truth.

When sleep finally came, Chance dreamed. Of a small girl with dark curls and eyes so blue it made his heart hurt. Of gentle hands and a laughing face. Then suddenly she changed. She was no longer a girl, she was a woman, lying beneath him, crying for something he couldn't give. Every time he leaned forward to taste her lips, something . . . or someone . . . kept pulling him back. She reached for him and his body ached, swelling at the thought of her soft, womanly curves. She pleaded, silently, tearfully. Hands pulled him away, yanking and tearing. He turned angrily and stared into the face of—

He woke! Instantly, achingly. Cursing softly into the darkness, he rolled from the bed and tore off his clothes in short, angry motions. He staggered into the bathroom, ducked under the shower head, and turned on the cold water full force.

What the hell kind of a dream tore out a man's insides and left them hanging on the bedpost as a reminder? What the hell kind of world had he come from that had twisted him so much inside that he couldn't give himself to a woman like Jenny Tyler? From the things he'd heard said, and the remarks Jenny had made, he'd damn sure given himself to other women. Why not her?

Water ran over his hot, throbbing body in weak rivulets. He pounded the shower stall with the flat of his hands, futilely urging the pressure to intensify. It didn't happen. The only thing that intensified was his need for Jenny, and she was hundreds of miles away.

Chance watched the sunrise from the tailgate of his pickup truck. The room had been stifling, the memories of his dream too fresh. He'd found an all-night quick stop around daybreak and purchased gas, a Snickers candy bar, and a bottle of pop. Hell of a breakfast, but it would have to do. After last night, he wasn't in the mood to meet the day with that nosy waitress in his face.

His long legs dangled as he rested the old high school yearbook in his lap, searching each page diligently for the girl in the photograph. She wasn't there. That had to mean she wasn't a local. There were pages full of loyal athletic fans watching on the sidelines as school heroes ran for touchdowns. Pages with tiny blond girls, practicing for the day when they'd be cheerleaders, but for now, satisfied to be their mascots. Homecoming queens, FFA sweethearts, band princesses, every kind of royalty that public school could produce graced those pages. But no Victoria Henry.

Who was she? The question was driving Chance mad. Had she been a girlfriend? A neighbor? The school yearbook had no answers about her, but maybe someone there could give him some answers about himself.

He'd seen another high school on the far side of town: Permian High School. The big MOJO logo on the building had made him smile. Schools all across the nation had their own claim to fame for their spirit . . . or magic . . . or whatever it was called that made competition, both scholastic and athletic, important.

Chance frowned. He needed some MOJO of his own. God knew he could use all the help he could get to find answers. If it took magic, he was all for it. Maybe Victoria Henry had been a student at Permian High, but how could he check without calling attention to himself?

Chance was still worried that he had something to hide. If that something was so awful that he'd hidden it for the last twelve years, from people he obviously loved . . . He couldn't finish the thought.

He watched the desk clerk inside the office switch off

the neon MOTEL sign and turn on the radio. The day had begun.

Chance was ready, too. He slid off the tailgate, slammed it shut, and tossed the yearbook inside the cab. Then he locked his room and headed for the truck. He had to see a man about a school.

School was out for the summer. Yesterday's investigations had revealed empty classrooms and parking lots. But there was a man trimming shrubbery near the main entrance of Odessa High School.

"School's closed," the man said as Chance walked up to him.

"Yes, sir."

The man never missed a snip as his clippers trimmed the small bush. "No job openings," he said.

"Not looking," Chance said.

The man paused, but he didn't look up. "Then state your business. I haven't got all day."

Chance grinned. The women in this town were full of talk, and the few men he'd run across seemed friendly, but were as tight-lipped as persimmon pucker.

"You worked here long?" Chance asked. The man looked up. *That got his attention.*

"Retiring next year."

Chance nodded. "So I guess you've seen a lot of kids come and go around here."

"Too damn many," he said as he snipped at a stray leaf.

"I'm looking for . . . some of my relatives. They may have lived in this area . . . say twelve or fifteen years ago.

The name was McCall. Does it ring a bell? I've got a picture of the boy, maybe he looks familiar to you."

The yearbook fell open to the page with Chance's picture. The old man stared, and then shook his head. "They all look alike to me," he said. "Damned hoodlums. Always tearing something up that I have to fix."

Chance's hope dropped. This day wasn't starting out any better than yesterday had.

"You sure the name doesn't ring a bell? You never knew anyone by the name of McCall?"

"I told you I can't tell one kid from another. Don't even try," he muttered. He punctuated the end of the conversation by turning his backside toward Chance and resuming his duties.

Chance let the yearbook fall shut with a slap. "Well, thanks anyway," he said. "If you oil that rivet, you won't get a blister," he added, pointing to the clipping shears dangling from the old man's hands.

The man turned and stared, and then nodded his thanks. Chance started to walk away.

"Say!" the old man called. Chance turned. "I don't remember no kid. But I remember a woman by the name of McCall. She used to waitress down at a bar toward the end of town. It went bust when the oil business fell. Whole damn country's going bust if you ask me."

Chance's heart skipped a beat. A woman? "What did you say her name was?"

"I think her name was Lily, or Lucy . . . something . . . Letty! That was it! Letty McCall."

"Is she still here . . . in Odessa?"

The old man laughed. "She's here, and ain't goin'

nowhere," he said. "She's buried beneath six feet of Texas dirt, boy."

Hell! She was dead! Chance's stomach turned. Something dark pulled at him, swirling his thoughts around until he had to concentrate to ask his next question.

"Do you remember when she was buried? What year? If she has any kin living here?" The words came out in a torrent.

"I don't remember the year. But I remember it was suicide. Ain't real common around here."

Chance turned cold all over, all at once. The old man was still talking when he turned and walked away. He didn't need to hear any more to know that somehow, in some way, it had affected him and his life. There was no other explanation for his reaction. Every bone in his body felt like it was crumbling to dust.

He staggered to his truck, crawled inside, grabbed hold of the steering wheel and closed his eyes, willing himself not to black out. The pain inside his head was increasing in thundering increments. If he could have found his way to a doctor, he'd have gone, but by the time the pain subsided enough for him to see, all he could do was head for the motel. The need to crawl inside that pit was overwhelming, just as overwhelming as the need to see Jenny. To hear her voice, feel those blue eyes burn into his soul and cauterize this festering hell. He'd known this wasn't going to be easy, but he hadn't known that it might kill him.

When night came and darkness slipped into every corner of his room, dreams followed, turning into nightmares that pulled and clawed their way out of his soul and left him wide awake in a pool of his own sweat. He stared blindly at the ceiling above his bed, trying not to think about the word. *Suicide*.

The room next door was silent, just as quiet and empty as his heart. He almost wished the busy tart and her constant string of twenty-buck losers was nearby. Then at least he'd have something to think about besides the hell that kept growing in his mind.

A phone rang, persistently. Probably in the office. It rang . . . and rang . . . and rang. Chance blinked, trying to focus on the sound. And while he was concentrating, his eyes closed.

And, thankfully, blessed peace came.

9

Thanks to the school caretaker, Chance had a name. It was a place to start. Letty McCall must have left tracks somewhere in this town, and a suicide would not easily be forgotten. Twelve years ago it would have to have made the papers. Newspaper people were notorious for being curious, though he couldn't forget that he might wind up on the wrong side of the law if he asked the wrong questions. He decided on another route.

Maybe the courthouse would have some answers. If Letty McCall had once owned property, there would be records. Finding that property would be a beginning. That was more than he'd had yesterday. Chance resolutely put the word *suicide* out of his thoughts and headed for the diner. Food first, answers later.

He escaped most of the nosy waitress's questions by asking a lot of his own. It was interesting just what a man could learn by watching people's expressions when certain names were mentioned. Admitting that he'd visited Charlie Rollins yesterday was easy, and it killed nearly fifteen minutes of his meal time. Dodging the issue of his own name was a different story. It took all of his tact not to tell her to mind her own damn business. It was when he mentioned the name, Letty McCall, that he knew he'd hit pay dirt.

The waitress got a look on her face that could only be described as guilty shock.

"Did you know her?" Chance asked, though he knew what her answer would be.

"Yeah," she drawled, and tucked a stray lock of hair back underneath a barrette. "I knew her. I worked at the same bar she did a few years back. Sometimes we had the same shift." She refused to meet Chance's gaze. "It was a real shock when we heard what she'd gone and done. Killed herself and all. I couldn't make it to the funeral. I had to work."

"I suppose her family understood," Chance said, hoping for a reaction. He got it.

The woman's face twisted. "She didn't have no family that I know of 'cept a kid. He run off after the funeral. Never did know what happened to him. If he was anything like her, he's probably dead or in jail by now."

Chance's gut twisted. Some epitaph! And a funeral! This was something he hadn't even considered. The cemetery was a place to look next if he didn't get any answers at the courthouse.

"Look," the waitress said, "I've got to get back to work. The boss don't like it if we socialize too much with the customers."

Chance looked around the almost empty diner. "Yeah, right. You'd better get back to work."

She ducked her head and hurried away.

The more he discovered, the less he liked it. And from the little bit he'd learned so far, he didn't think his family name would be on the social register. In fact, he'd be damned lucky if it wasn't on a police record somewhere. It was time to go.

It didn't occur to him that the waitress would mention his interest to her boss, or that he in turn would make a phone call, passing along a message that a stranger was in town asking questions about a woman who'd long since turned to dust. But if it had, it wouldn't have changed a thing. Chance was on a mission.

"Oooh Della, would you look at that long-legged hunk coming in the door. What I wouldn't give to get him in the back seat of a car."

"For Pete's sake, Tamma. If I didn't know you better, I'd think you were a tramp. What makes you talk like that? Your husband Jimmy Lee would kill you if he knew you even had thoughts about other men, and you know it."

Tamma grinned and shuffled papers on her desk. "Want me to wait on him?"

"I'll do it," Della said. "Just keep your silly self in that chair and your mouth shut. You hear me?"

Tamma grinned and waggled a finger at the older woman as Chance walked up to the counter.

"What can I do for you?" Della asked. She agreed with Tamma's opinion of the man on the opposite side of the desk. Only, in her day, they'd called them "real dolls." And the longer she looked, the more certain she became that she knew this one . . . from somewhere.

"I need to verify ownership of some property," he said. "A woman lived here back in the late seventies, early eighties. If she owned property, would you have a record of it, and if so, could you help me find it?"

"If you have a name, I'll have a record. If she owned property, that is."

Chance nodded. "I have a name. I just need some help locating the records. That is, if you're not too busy."

"I'm not too busy," Tamma offered. Della turned around and glared at her.

"What's the name, please?" Della asked. Her pencil was poised above a sheet of notepaper on the counter.

"Letty McCall."

Her pencil point dug one small hole in the paper and then snapped off at the wood. It was an indication that Chance had, once again, struck nerves. That, plus the fact that her mouth dropped several inches toward her gizzard.

Della looked up, gave Chance a hard, fixed stare, and clamped her mouth shut. She picked up another pencil, wrote the name down, opened a small, swinging gate, and indicated that Chance should follow.

He complied, grinning at the saucy expression on the younger woman's face as they passed her desk. Chance didn't have to look back to know that she was ogling him.

"In here," Della said. "And I need to know exactly

what interest you might have in the McCall property?"
As if I don't already know, she thought.

"Does that mean there is some?"

"Was she a relative?" Della persisted.

"Does she have to be? Isn't the information public knowledge?"

Della bit the inside of her lip and fumed. He hadn't answered one single question she'd asked. In fact, he'd thrown them back at her with some of his own.

She didn't like being bested. She also never forgot a face, and this man's face would have been hard to forget. She walked down a long corridor of books, deftly lifted one from the stacks, and dropped it onto a table in front of Chance.

"Should be in here," she said shortly. "If you have any problems, just yell. We'll be happy to help you out." She stomped away.

"Yes, ma'am," Chance answered, glad to see the last of her. She was too persistent, and she'd given him one of those funny looks. He was beginning to recognize a pattern.

It didn't take long to find the name, but it only gave the date on which the property had been purchased. He noted that it was around the same time that he'd been born. He jotted it down. He would need a city map. He headed back to Della.

"Excuse me," he said. Both women looked up. "But how do I find the address? This only gives a date."

"You'll need to go to the Administration Building . . . to the office where taxes are paid. They'll have an address there."

Chance nodded. "Well then," he said, trying to get

past her belligerence with a smile, "if you could just furnish me with a map of the city, so that I can locate the Administration Building, I'll be on my way."

Tamma jumped to her feet and pushed past Della.

She reached beneath the counter. "Here you go, mister," she said sweetly. "I have a copy of the city map you can have free of charge. Let me just jot down my . . . I mean our phone number here in the office . . . just in case you get lost . . . or something." Her eyes danced.

Chance resisted the urge to laugh as she shoved the map across the counter. The phone number glowed in red ink. She wasn't just obvious, she was blatant. And she didn't care who knew it. Those kind were trouble with a capital T and exactly what he didn't need.

"Thanks, ladies," Chance said. He tipped his hat, and made a dash for the door. He didn't know which was the more dangerous, the woman with a grudge or the one wearing hot pants.

Della watched him leave. Even his smile was the same. She glared at Tamma, who'd already retreated to her desk. Then she made a run for her own. The pages of the phone book fanned her face as she searched for the name. There! She didn't hesitate. It had been years since she'd done more than pass the time of day with people like this, but she deserved to know. Della considered it her duty.

The numbers beeped in her ear as she punched them in. The phone rang, three, four, five times, and then was answered.

The voice was the same, and Della guessed that the face hadn't changed that much either. People like her had money. They didn't have to age. They just had birthdays.

"Mrs. Oslow? This is Della, down at the Odessa courthouse. You remember me? We lived down the street from you when you were just a little girl. That was before we moved from Midland to Odessa. Well, I just had to call and tell you. I think I just saw a ghost. Do you remember that . . ."

Chance found the address with little trouble. It also hadn't taken long to find out that the yearly taxes were up-to-date. But his hopes hit bottom when he pulled up beneath the shade tree across the street and stared blankly at the vacant lot. No house! And the only thing green for blocks and blocks was the lot full of weeds.

"Well hell," he muttered, "this is just perfect." He climbed out of his truck and walked across the street, jammed his hands in his pockets, and silently stared at what was left of a concrete block foundation and some porch steps. He supposed he was waiting for a miracle to occur, or at least, a hint of memory to surface.

Nothing happened. A little bit of hope died with the weeds wilting in the lot.

Then a man's angry voice behind him sent him spinning around. An inexplicable panic spurted through him. A feeling of having been here, standing as he was now, and listening to that same voice yelling at him, calling something . . . But just as quickly as the memory came, it went.

"What's your business here, mister?" the man asked.

The man approaching was a stranger. Chance saw evidence of too many beers hanging over his belly as the man hopped the curb and stopped. He was big and heavy. He wore jeans a size too small, a T-shirt that could have used a washing, and a week's worth of whiskers.

"I was told that this was the McCall property," Chance said, watching the man's face closely. He got a reaction, but it was not what he'd expected.

"What's left of it," the man said. "What's it to you?"

"Just trying to locate some relatives, that's all."

The man nodded. "Don't know why you're lookin'," he drawled. "I got too damned many to suit me." He jabbed his thumb back over his shoulder at the gaggle of kids playing in the yard across the street. "More than half them brats is mine, along with an out-of-work brother-in-law, and my old lady's mother. Shit! I oughta just light a shuck for parts unknown. Know what I mean?"

Chance shrugged. This was getting him nowhere. "So, you lived here long? Do you remember the McCalls?"

"Hell yes! How could you forget someone as hot as that bitch? She was up for grabs for anyone with the dough. I'da took her up on it myself, 'cept for the fact that we lived across the damned street. Can't exactly get a piece on the side with your old lady a'watchin'. Know what I mean?"

Chance's fury burned hot. It took everything he had not to shove his fist in the man's beefy mouth. But starting a fight wouldn't get him answers, and he might wind up in jail. It was a bad plan. He stuffed his hands back in his pockets and stared down at the cracked sidewalk. Maybe if he didn't have to look at the son-of-a-bitch, he wouldn't have to hit him.

"Can't say as I do," Chance answered. "Not married myself."

"Smart man," he replied. "Say, I didn't get your name."

Chance remained silent. He turned and stared at the overgrown lot. "What happened to the house?"

The man didn't seem to notice that his question never got an answer. His eyes lit up. "Oowee, that was one hell of an excitin' night, I can tell you."

Chance waited. The man hitched at his low-riding jeans, scratched an armpit, and walked toward the lot to kick at a stone.

"It was after midnight. I'll never forget. The McCall woman wadn't cold in the ground. She'd gone and killed herself a few days before." He turned to get Chance's reaction. There was none.

When Chance made no comment, the man continued with relish. "One of my kids was cryin'. Hell, one's always cryin'. Anyways, it woke me up. And the fire made it bright as day outside. The fire trucks was turnin' the corner when I run out on the porch. I figgered that damned McCall kid was still inside."

Kid! Somehow Chance knew the rest of the story before the man finished. But he had to hear.

"They sifted the ashes for two days before it dawned on me that the snot-nosed bugger'd had a pickup truck. And it was gone. It just stood to reason that he'd left in it, doncha' see? I called the cops myself."

Chance's belly twisted again. Cops! Please, God, he hadn't been running from them.

"But," the man continued, "they'd done already figgered that out. The kid's boss, a man named Charlie

Rollins who owned a gas station a couple a' blocks over, had cleared his name and told the cops that he figgered the boy just left town due to sadness or some such shit. Personally, I think he lit a shuck because there wadn't nothin' left to stay for. His old lady was dead and buried. Know what I mean?"

A flash of heat! Adrenaline spiked through him as his feet pounded on pavement! Fire snaked through windows and exploded in a shower of glass and debris. Red and yellow tongues of hell licked greedily at dry timbers.

Chance blinked slowly and took a deep breath. The images came and went so quickly, he knew that absorbing their meaning was next to impossible. He had to get away.

"Well, thanks all the same." He headed back across the street for his truck.

"Say! I didn't get your name," the man called.

Chance just waved and drove away, certain that the man was still staring. He was also certain that he'd stirred up another set of ghosts.

Dinner at the The Barn Door was a solemn affair. Ordinarily he would have enjoyed the thick, juicy steak and baked potato. Ordering from the menu had been difficult. It had more choices than the Triple T had horses. But, by the time the food had arrived, his appetite had disappeared. He'd never liked eating alone, and what he was trying to digest along with his food was causing him grief.

A visit earlier in the day to a local funeral home had

produced information that Chance was having trouble accepting. Leticia McCall had died May 7, 1980, and her son, an eighteen-year-old named Chance McCall, was the person responsible for her interment. There was also a note on the old records showing that a Charlie Rollins had paid for the burial in full.

A grim line curved the corners of his mouth. He felt regret for the loss of what must have been a close friendship. He'd obviously run away from Odessa, leaving at least one person behind who'd cared. And now Charlie was alone with no one to care for him.

Chance told himself he would make another visit to Charlie. It didn't matter whether or not Charlie remembered him. Chance would remember. That was enough.

His meal finished, he walked outside the restaurant and took a deep breath. The air was close, heavy with the lingering heat of daytime, not yet cool from the relief that always came at sundown. Chance was reluctant to go back to that hole-in-the-wall that passed for a motel room. He stepped out of the restaurant and looked around, searching for something that would help pass the time.

Country and western music drifted out of a little club somewhere close by. Chance left his truck where he'd parked it and decided to walk.

Garth Brooks's voice met him at the door of the bar as Chance pushed it open. He winced as the music vibrated his eardrums. The jukebox was turned all the way to meltdown. The air was smoky, the tables full. A small dance floor in the center of the room was a gathering place for a group of clinging women and groping men who seemed to be using the music as an excuse for foreplay. Thoughts of Jenny surfaced instantly and Chance wondered if this had been such a good idea after all. Remembering the woman he'd left behind was not just painful behind his zipper. It hurt the hell out of his heart.

"Beer," Chance ordered, and slid his elbows onto the bar. He rested one booted foot on the kick bar below. "Nothing fancy, just a bottle," he added, before the bartender could run through what was available.

The man nodded, grinned, and slid a tall brown bottle down the bar, slicing a wet trail through the assortment of napkins and peanut shells. Chance caught it in mid-slide and tilted it to his lips. It was sharp and cold. Several minutes passed as Chance savored the drink, then he turned around to check out the patrons. At this point, he had no thoughts of recognition. It had simply become a habit.

A bunch of women sitting at a table in the corner were looking at him with interest. Chance quickly shifted his gaze. He had no intention of giving them an opening. A couple of women gave him more than a welcoming smile as they danced past with their partners. *Jenny! I'd give a whole lot for one of your smiles right now.*

He frowned, turned around, drained the bottle of its last swallow, and set it back down on the bar. The bartender looked up, asking with a silent shrug if Chance wanted another. He shook his head and pulled out his wallet. Being in a place like this was only a reminder of the fact that he was alone and it was his own fault.

The bartender slid his hand across the bar and grabbed the money that Chance dropped onto the surface, then grinned as a picture fell into the dish of peanuts beside it. Before Chance could react, the bartender had picked it up and tilted it toward the neon light behind the bar to get a better look.

"Whooee, son. You like 'em young."

Chance frowned. It was the old picture of Victoria Henry that he'd found in his suitcase. Before he could respond, a hand slid into his back pocket and cupped his rear. A woman's deep, husky voice vibrated above the din of the music, as she leaned suggestively against his shoulder and took the picture out of the bartender's hands.

"Frank! You're just a dirty old man, that's what you are. That girl ain't someone he'd take to bed. That's his daughter. Logan Henry don't like babies, he likes women. Ain't that right, honey?"

Her hand clung to his backside in a movement of familiarity as she tilted her head back and gave him what Chance supposed was meant to pass as a sexy look. As far as he was concerned, she was way off the mark. And, from the look on her face, she'd just realized it, too.

"Oooh, honey!" she squeaked, and reluctantly removed her hand from his hip pocket, giving him one last squeeze as she did, "you're not Logan Henry, are you? But damn! You sure fooled me. I guess it's this light." She smiled as Chance took the picture out of her fingers and slid it back into his wallet.

"Nothing personal, okay?" she patted his butt to make her point.

He shrugged. Who the hell was Logan Henry? The girl's name was Victoria Henry. It was on the picture.

What did all this mean? Suddenly too many people were staring at him, and he didn't have a good feeling about it. He had to get out.

"If you're interested, I'm free later," the woman offered.

Chance smiled, but the woman knew the answer was no. She shrugged, stared at his backside once again, and said, "If you change your mind . . . you know where to find me."

He tipped his hat and left. It was none too soon. People were staring. He could hear the whispers. He walked to the pickup, suddenly anxious to get back to the motel, away from curious looks and prying eyes. Who the hell was Logan Henry?

The woman watched him leave and then dug into the front pocket of her faux designer jeans to pull out a quarter. She headed for the hallway between the restrooms, where a pay phone hung in plain view, dropped in the quarter, punched in the numbers, and waited.

"Hi, darlin'," she said, yelling to make herself heard above the music that had gone back into full swing, "it's me, Lorrie." There was silence as she listened. "You remember me. Lorrie, from Odessa? Yeah, that's right, darlin', that one." Well, the reason I'm callin' is . . . you don't happen to have a little brother, do you?" She listened again, her painted on eyebrows coming together over her nose as she frowned.

"Well, I was just askin' 'cause there was a man in here tonight with an old picture of Vicky. Yeah, I mean Victoria. Anyway . . . my Gawd, darlin', he's your livin' double, if you know what I mean. . . . No. I don't know where he went. I only saw him this once. . . . No, I don't know nothin'. . . . No, I won't say nothin' about this either. You know me. I promise."

She hung up the phone, rubbed her sweaty palms against her skin-tight pants, and shuddered. Whatever she'd just done by making that call, she wanted to forget. The man she'd called wasn't happy. Not one bit. A cowboy walked past the phone on his way to the men's room. She grabbed him by the arm and leaned forward, inviting his attention. It was all the invitation he needed.

Chance dropped onto the bed, relishing the feel of surprisingly clean sheets, and let himself air dry from the shower he'd just had. His wounds had healed, his scars were not so tender, but the wounds inside him were festering and he could feel it. This may have been the biggest mistake he'd ever made. He'd heard it said that you can never go home.

At first it had seemed the only sensible, honorable thing to do. How could he offer to share his life with a woman like Jenny Tyler when he didn't know what kind of a life he'd come from? What was so awful about his past that he'd never shared it? What secrets had followed him from Odessa to Tyler and made it impossible to tell Jenny he loved her?

And he did love her. He didn't have to get his memory back to know that. His body burned for her. His muscles grew taut with desire. Cursing softly beneath his breath, he shoved himself up from the bed and headed back to the shower. It was a good thing for the desk clerk that she'd taken his threat seriously. The room next to his had been silent for days. Tonight would have been his breaking point. He needed Jenny . . . desperately . . . in more ways than one.

A fist swung forward, smashing against bone and flesh. Blood spurted. There was a grunt and a thud, and dust swirled into his mouth and nostrils. A girl cried. Loud voices came from everywhere. Then there was silence.

A woman sat at a table, crying. A bottle of whiskey spilled onto the table as an amber river ran off the side and onto the floor. An argument ensued, soundless, but alive with motion and movement as she stretched her arm forward in supplication . . . and then she disappeared.

Heat blistered the back of his arms. Fire was everywhere . . . and he ran . . . and ran . . . and ran.

A siren screamed! Panic shot him out of bed as he stood, legs shaking, sweat pouring, heart pounding. Red lights pulsed through the curtains of the motel room, and then the sound passed, as did the lights.

"Sweet heaven," Chance whispered, wiping sweat from his face and neck with the end of the sheet. He dropped back onto the bed, trying to absorb what he'd been dreaming. The memories were already fading, and then they were gone. The only thing left was a feeling of impending doom. It was not enough to make him want to finish the night in sleep.

He pulled on his jeans, walked outside barefoot, and climbed into the back of his pickup truck. Leaning against the cab, he stared up into the clear night sky and at the curtain of stars blanketing the earth. How could that be so beautiful when his world was so lost . . . and ugly? But there were no answers up there, just as there were no answers down on earth. Not tonight. Not for Chance. He took a deep breath, closed his eyes, and thought of Jenny.

10

He moved quietly, *his face in shadow as he walked toward her bed with purpose in every step. Moonlight glow slid across his nude body, burnishing the muscles that rippled and tensed, as he neared where she was lying.*

He came out of the darkness. She could see his face, so beloved . . . so dear.

Chance!

She ached to touch him, to feel the power beneath those muscles, to hold that part of him that was so obviously ready for her. Her hands reached out, cupped. Breath caught in her throat.

His touch burned across her, his lips forging a trail of tension that began at her chin and hurtled down past her breasts. His tongue made a trail of its own, down past her rib cage, lingering just long enough at her navel to start a spiraling heat between her legs that made the bed tilt.

Her hands caught and held in the dark thatch of hair on his head as she hung on for dear life. He was taking her with him . . . to places she'd never been . . . and if she didn't hold on, she would never find her way back. She gasped and lost her hold on Chance. She reached behind her to hold onto the bed. It wasn't there! She fell backward and down . . . down . . . down. And heard him calling her name . . .

"Damn you, Chance McCall!"

Her cry broke the silence of the dream. Jenny bolted up in bed, gasping for breath, aching in places she'd never known could ache . . . in that way . . . for a man who was gone. For a man who came only in her dreams, and was driving her mad.

She moaned and catapulted herself out of the tangle of sheets. She walked to the window to stare outside at the long, black ribbon of roadway that stretched past the yard and into the dark night.

She swallowed once, tore the sticky nightgown off her body, and turned, naked and aching, to walk into her bathroom. She didn't need a light to find the cold tap. It wasn't the first time this had happened. But Jenny Tyler swore it would be the last. She splashed cold water on her face and neck without a shudder. Inside, she was already as cold as ice.

Marcus Tyler hung up the phone and buried his face in his hands. He knew that the call he'd made days earlier to a private investigator had been the right thing to do. But he was still apprehensive about how Jenny would react when answers came.

Questioning Henry had gotten him nowhere. The old man was as shocked by Chance's leaving as the rest of them, and as puzzled as to the direction he might have gone. But Henry was also just as convinced that he would be back. According to Henry, the man had demons to fight.

Marcus sighed and pushed himself away from his desk. He had his own demons to fight. His daughter had shut him out of her life, not that he'd had much of a place in it to begin with. But she'd shut everyone else out of her life, too. She existed, but she did not live. She was simply waiting for Chance to come home. He shuddered, wondering what hell he would have to face with her if that didn't happen. It didn't bear thinking about.

He snapped the lid of the Rolodex shut and walked out of the office. He had made an appointment at the investigator's office, and he was anxious to learn if there was any news.

Marcus had one clue: an old memory of an incident that had happened years ago, when Chance had been questioned about a man called Logan Henry, and a town in West Texas called Odessa. The look on the young man's face had held a world of secrets. And Chance's secrets were the obvious place to start.

Marcus walked through the impeccable rooms and hallways, looking at the comforts and expensive furnishings. He'd always given Jenny things. He'd just never managed to give her love. It showed, and he regretted it beyond words.

Her first reaction, upon learning that Chance was gone, had been hysterics. Marcus had been unable to reach her then. Juana had coaxed her to sleep, and to eat. Now, even she was having difficulties reaching Jenny. The girl had gone from hysteria, to anger, to cold indifference.

She'd gone days without talking, and then when she did, it had been nothing more than a sharp barb, a reflection of the pain she was carrying . . . alone.

Marcus cursed softly as he wandered through his house. It was his fault that Jenny had no one to turn to. And try as he might, he didn't know how to reach her. He didn't know how to help. Maybe finding Chance would be the first step. He hoped to hell the P.I. was successful, or that Chance would come home on his own. But he wasn't willing to lay odds on either.

"Marcus! I didn't know you were in the house!" Juana grabbed at her chest in surprise, juggling a dust cloth and a can of spray polish as she rounded a corner.

He grinned and held up his hands in surrender. "Sorry. I didn't mean to scare you. I was making some calls." He paused for a moment and then asked, "Seen Jenny?"

Juana frowned, began making the sign of the cross, and answered in a swift flow of Spanish that had Marcus waving in surrender.

"You know my Spanish is not that good, woman. Either slow down, or speak English." His blue eyes danced as a slight flush spread across her cheeks.

"Sorry. When I'm upset, my native tongue takes over, you know." She shrugged. "And to answer your question, your guess is as good as mine. She didn't come to breakfast. She missed lunch. I heard the kitchen door slam a while ago. I suppose she's out. She doesn't tell me anything anymore."

Her expression showed as much concern as he was feeling. They stared silently at each other, unable to get past the door their girl had slammed in their faces. Juana's face crumpled.

"I'm sorry," she said, as tears began to run, "I'm worried sick about her. What if that man won't come back? Oh Marcus, what if we lose her too?" She turned and walked away, leaving behind questions with no answers.

Marcus doubled up his fist and slammed it against the wall. The phone rang somewhere in the house, but he was in no mood to answer it. He grabbed his hat from the coat tree, yanked the car keys from the table, and left through the front door.

He knew a couple of people in Tyler who'd been casual acquaintances of Chance's. Maybe they could tell him something. Maybe one night Chance had inadvertently let something slip about his past that they'd remember. It was worth a try. And it sure as hell beat sitting around this house waiting for Jenny to ignore him. Yet he knew, as he drove toward Tyler, that it was no more than he deserved. He'd ignored her existence for years. He'd just now realized how much.

"If only her mother hadn't died . . . Oh hell!" he muttered as he turned onto the main highway. "That's an excuse and I know it! Jenny's *my* daughter. And I just stood by and let Chance McCall be the only man in her life who mattered."

Berating himself was not something he did by habit, but it did make him look at the last twelve years of Jenny's life anew. He could remember dozens of times he'd noticed Jenny dogging the young man's footsteps when Chance had first hired on. The many times Marcus,

himself, had called upon Chance to step in and care for
Jenny, when *he* couldn't be bothered.

And there were the later years when Jenny had been
growing into a woman. The only man she seemed to
notice was one who refused to let himself take what she
so obviously would have offered.

Marcus stepped on the gas. He didn't have a choice.
By God, he had to find Chance, or he'd not only lose
him, he would lose his daughter as well.

The dream last night had been the last straw. Jenny
had waited for days for the phone to ring, or a letter to
come in the mail. Neither had happened. After that,
she'd gone from withdrawal to anger. Anger with herself
for waiting, at Chance for making her wait . . . and anyone
else who'd happened to cross her path. The tension in
her body was tighter than a six-wire fence.

The lines around her mouth tightened as she neared
the stables. "Henry!" Her voice was sharp and strident.
He came running. "Saddle Cheyenne," she ordered.

"Hell no!" His voice was just as sharp. He loved his
girl too much to let her get away with this.

She glared. "Fine. I'll do it myself."

"Dammit girl. You ain't got no business ridin' that
stallion. Not in the mood you're in. You need all
your wits about you, and yours is gone with our fool
foreman."

Just the mention of Chance sent her resolve into
overdrive. She pushed past Henry, yanked a saddle and
blanket off a sawhorse, and dragged them toward the
stall where the stallion was stabled. The saddle bumped

against her legs as she alternately kicked and pulled it along. The saddle blanket itched and smelled of horse. She grabbed at the latch on the stall door.

"Well, hell. If you're so damned set on doin' this, let me help."

Silently, they saddled and bridled the anxious stallion, sidestepping his dancing hooves.

Jenny took the reins out of Henry's hands, walked toward the doorway leading the saddled horse, and never looked back. An impending sensation of dread overwhelmed Henry as he watched her mount. "Jenny, don't go," he pleaded. She wouldn't answer. "What the hell are you trying to do, anyway? Get yourself killed?"

She turned in the saddle. The look on her face stopped his heart. Her smile was bitter. The laughter lost . . . and hopeless. She kicked sharply against Cheyenne's flanks. The horse jumped, nearly bolting out from under her as it leaped forward.

"Goddammit, Jenny, come back!" Henry yelled. It did no good. She and the horse were soon out of sight.

He cursed loud and long, using every bad word he'd ever heard, in every language he'd ever learned. He cursed Marcus for not being here to stop her, and Chance for leaving her without a word. And when he'd run out of breath and curses, he sat down on a stump by the corner of the barn and waited.

The sun moved west as Henry watched. It dropped lower and lower to the horizon with still no sign of Jenny. He couldn't even look at his watch. Thinking about how much time had passed would make him crazy. Dusk was imminent. Hours had passed, that much he knew. And in his heart, he suspected the worst. Jenny had either had an accident or killed herself. He didn't know which and couldn't face either.

He stood up, legs stiff from hours of sitting, and hobbled toward the house. Marcus had to know what had happened. A search party would have to be organized.

"By God! Chance may be gone, but I'm not! If I have to do it myself, I will," Henry muttered, as he walked into the house without knocking. He was past manners. Juana saw the look on his face and burst into tears.

At first there was only the sun on her face and the wind in her hair . . . and the power of the horse beneath her as they thundered across the land. She let Cheyenne have his head, doing nothing to direct or control him, content only to maintain a seat in the saddle. With the passing of each minute, desperation gave way to indifference. The pain that had been building for days inside Jenny disappeared, but it left nothing in its place. Her mind was blank, and if Cheyenne had taken it into his head to buck or pivot then, Jenny would have flown out of the saddle and broken her neck, such was the speed of the horse.

A creek was just ahead. Jenny saw it but did nothing to change the direction of the horse's gallop. Unconsciously, she wrapped the reins around her wrists as her legs gripped the horse's belly. Its powerful hind legs bunched and kicked, taking the jump, clearing the narrow creek with feet to spare. Jenny came down in the saddle with a jolt but didn't lose her seat. Salt pooled in her mouth, and she realized she'd bitten her lip. It was of no consequence.

A small thicket of plum bushes and persimmon trees came into view, hanging persistently onto the sloping banks of a shallow pond while their roots grew long and deep toward the only collection of water for miles.

Cheyenne tossed his head, scenting the water, wanting to stop. Jenny yanked sharply at the reins and kicked. The horse reared in protest and spun sideways, but still Jenny hung on. It would have been easy to let go. She would have sailed through the air with ease, flung off by the momentum of the horse's protests. Yet she rode.

Time passed. Miles disappeared beneath the horse's hooves. Jenny felt nothing of the blisters that were forming on the palms of her hands from the death grip she had on the reins. She was completely unaware of the scratches on her face and the bits of leaves and twigs that caught in her hair during the narrow misses she had as the horse galloped beneath a scattering of trees.

And then a sound crept into Jenny's awareness. It jangled, and it heaved. It was the sound of the bridle's metal parts as Cheyenne sawed crazily at the bit, and the air the horse was trying to pull into its lungs in order to survive. Jenny had pushed it to the limit of its endurance, and still the powerful horse ran, giving what she asked of it, regardless of the consequences. Such was the nature of the beast.

"My God!" She leaned back against the stirrups, using her body weight to stop the big stallion. She had to. There was no feeling left in her arms. The horse came to a sudden and shaking halt. Jenny leaned forward and slid to the ground slowly. She landed on her back, with one rein still wrapped around her wrist too tight to come loose. She couldn't have been in a more dangerous position, lying weak and helpless, caught beneath the horse that had nearly killed the man she loved. Yet neither she nor the horse was capable of moving.

Cheyenne's big head hung, one rein trailing in the grass, the other around Jenny's wrist. His sides heaved as he stared glassy-eyed at the woman at his feet.

She moaned, staring sightlessly up as she opened her mouth, and pulled long, life-giving draughts of air into her lungs. Long minutes passed.

A screeching sound, high and far above her head, made Jenny blink. She looked up. A lone turkey buzzard circled, obviously waiting, hoping that she would never move again. Jenny shivered. What had she been trying to prove?

As suddenly as she asked the question, a voice answered, calling her name.

Jenny!

It came across the prairie, as plainly as if he were standing at her feet. She caught her breath and began to shake. Chance! All her life she'd leaned on him. Through every crisis her twenty-three years of living had brought. And now, when his world was crumbling around him, she was about to let him down. It took more courage than she thought she possessed, and strength she didn't know she had left, but she dragged herself to her feet. Somehow she managed to climb back into the saddle, but the loose rein dangled just out of her grasp.

"Cheyenne, I'm so sorry," she whispered, as she leaned forward and dug her free fist into the sweaty thickness of his mane. "I'm so sorry." Her voice broke. "Take us home, big fellow. Take us home."

She nudged his sweaty flanks with the toes of her boots, wrapped the mane tightly through her fingers, and stretched out across his neck. Sitting upright was impossible. Hanging on might be more than she could manage, but she was going to try. Somewhere Chance McCall was hurting, and God help the person who tried to stop her from finding him. She didn't know how to start or where to look, but she was going after him.

Jenny never knew when the Triple T came into view. She only knew that motion ceased. She looked up, saw the stables to her right and the foreman's quarters to her left. She was home!

Her fingers were numb as she loosed her grip in Cheyenne's mane. She swung one leg over the saddle horn and kicked the other foot free. Unable to stand, she fell to her knees on the ground.

It took a while, but when she finally could stand, she started toward Chance's quarters. Staggering weakly, she reached the porch and then turned and stared, wondering why the horse had followed. She looked down at the rein still wrapped around her wrist and would have laughed if she'd had breath enough. He'd had no choice. She'd pulled him with her.

"Now, boy. Now you're free," she mumbled as she unwound the rein from her wrist and let it fall into the dust alongside the other one.

She dragged herself up onto the porch, grabbed hold of the doorknob, and turned it. The door swung inward, revealing the long shadows of quickly fading daylight, slashing across the hardwood floor. Jenny's eyes turned toward the bed in the corner. She stared long and hard at the old metal frame and the blue, patchwork quilt coverlet, and then swallowed. Sheer guts pulled her toward the bed. She managed to get one knee onto the quilt before falling face forward across the bed, arms outflung, legs dangling off the edge, encompassing all she had left of Chance McCall.

The horse stood motionless outside the open door as Jenny cried herself to sleep.

"Damnation, it's about time you got back," Henry thundered.

Marcus got out of his car and came face to face with an angry man. His flesh crawled. Instinct warned him it wasn't ranch business that had sent Henry to the house in a cussing fit.

"What's wrong?" Marcus asked.

"Well, if you'da been here sooner, you'da known it for yourself. It's your daughter, that's what!"

It was just as he'd suspected. "Dammit, Henry, get to the point. What's—"

"She's gone. And for all I know, she's either broke her neck, or laying underneath that fool horse wishing someone would shoot them both!"

"My God!" Marcus whispered. "What in hell are you trying to tell me?"

"I *am* 'a tellin' you! Why don't you listen?"

Juana burst through the front door, waving her hands at the two men standing toe to toe, as near to blows as they'd ever been in their lives.

"*Pare!* Stop!" she cried. "I could hear you all the way in the back of the house. What is the matter with you two? Has this whole family gone mad?"

Henry turned and spat, then answered. "I ain't mad yet, but I'm about to be unless someone comes with me to the bunkhouse and organizes a search party."

Juana gasped as Marcus grabbed Henry by the shoulders.

"Dammit old man, if you don't spit out what you've been trying to say, I'll shake it out of you." The panic he'd been trying to suppress was heading for his heart. If Henry didn't say something and say it soon, he wouldn't be able to think.

"Jenny rode out hours ago on Cheyenne. She was in one hell of a black mood and I couldn't stop her. She's not back. The damned horse ain't either. Now that tells me one of two things . . . either she's—"

"Never mind," Marcus said. "I get the picture. Come on, Henry. We've got to go find her. It'll be dark soon. How many of the men are still on the ranch?"

"Not near enough," Henry mumbled, relieved that he'd finally gotten someone's attention. They headed for the stables.

Marcus couldn't think past the fear that was crawling up his throat. He'd wasted so many years of Jenny's life. She'd grown up without him, but he didn't want to grow old without her.

"Boss!"

Henry's shout came without warning. Marcus turned

and looked, following the direction in which the old wrangler was pointing. *No! Please God! Not Jenny!*

The horse was standing, head down, reins trailing in the dust. And he was alone! Henry reached him first and ran a searching hand across his shoulder and down his foreleg. His hand came away with grass and mud on the palm. He leaned down, lifted a hoof, and dug his thumbnail into the collection of mud, grass, and gravel packed in the crevices. It told him nothing except that the horse had been over some rough territory. He grabbed the horse by the bit, pulled its head up, and stared into its face.

"By God, I wish you could talk. You look like you've been to hell and back. And where along that road did you leave my Jenny?" Henry asked softly. He turned and stared at the look of panic spreading across Marcus Tyler's face. There was nothing to be said.

"Take the horse back to the stables," Marcus ordered, "and then send whatever men you can find here to me. We've got some planning to do. I don't want them all going in one direction, and there's no time to waste. We've got to find her before dark."

Henry nodded. He had pulled the horse around, and started to lead Cheyenne toward the corral when he noticed that the door to Chance's quarters was open.

His heart skipped a beat and then picked up the pace. He dropped the reins back to the ground and began to run. If what he suspected was true, he might have to go to church on Sunday after all. He'd prayed hard all afternoon, and it looked as if he was about to be called on his promises.

"What in . . . ?" Marcus saw the open door just after

Henry. He followed, hitting the steps one leap behind the old cowboy.

"Aw hell," Henry said quietly, coming to a sudden stop just inside the doorway. She was here!

Marcus ran past him and came to a sudden stop beside the bed. Was she real? He reached out and touched her shoulder. She moaned softly. Tears sprang to his eyes as he turned and stared at the old man who was watching them from the doorway.

Henry shrugged. As badly as he wanted to stay, it wasn't his place. She was Marcus's daughter. And it was high time he started acting like it. "I'll see to the horse," he said gruffly, then turned and walked out of the house.

Marcus knelt beside Jenny, running his hand across her shoulder and down her arm in a gentle movement. She mumbled something in her sleep. He leaned forward, trying to catch the words. It was then he saw the scratches on her face and the debris in her hair.

"Dear God, Jenny!" he whispered. "What happened to you?"

A stray hair clung tightly to her forehead, plastered there by sweat and mud. Marcus pulled it away from her face and smoothed it carefully, noticing for the first time how much like her mother she looked. A huge lump clogged the middle of his throat. He had a second chance and, by God, he wasn't going to screw that up, too.

"Jenny!" His voice was soft, as he called her from her sleep.

Jenny stirred. She heard her name, just as she had on the prairie. She struggled toward the sound, certain that he'd come home . . . back to her.

She moaned, calling his name aloud.

"Chance?"

But when she opened her eyes, it wasn't him. She stared up into blue eyes, so like her own, brimming with tears.

"I thought you were Chance." And then her breath caught on a quiet sob. "But Chance is gone."

Marcus pulled her into his arms and held her. He couldn't get her close enough. There were no words to be said. And when she wrapped her arms around him, buried her face against his neck and began to cry, his heart nearly burst. He'd never seen her cry. She'd never allowed it.

"It's all right, sweetheart," he said, as he patted her awkwardly on the shoulder. "I've got you back, and you're going to be okay. I promise. It'll all be okay, sooner than you think. But you've got to tell me . . . please say you weren't trying to . . . that you didn't intend to . . ."

Jenny interrupted. "I don't know what I intended," she said softly as she clung to his strength. "But I know what happened to me out there, and it saved me. Oh Marcus! Chance is in trouble. I don't know how I know it, but I do. He needs me. I've got to find him, and I don't know where to start looking."

That was all he needed to hear. Marcus leaned back and pulled a handkerchief from his hip pocket. "Here," he said. "Blow. I've got something to tell you that may help."

Jenny followed instructions and then listened, her eyes growing wide with hope as Marcus told her what he'd done. The private investigator had found Chance. He'd learned that much when he'd gone to Tyler earlier in the day. He had a city and an address, and it was what she needed to hear.

"You know that I have to go." She wasn't asking permission. She was stating a fact.

Marcus nodded. "Yes, Jenny, I do." He took a deep breath. "But I have something to tell you before you leave. I'm sorry I let you grow up alone. I'm sorry I wasn't always there for you when you needed me. But it won't happen again. I know I can't make up for what I've missed. But, if you'll let me, I promise to be a better father." He held his breath, waiting for the words that would make his world right again. And then they came.

"Oh Marcus, I've waited my whole life to hear you say that. And you've given me the most important thing I'll ever need in my life already. You've given Chance back to me."

"Now, Jenny," his voice was stern as he reminded her, "don't assume that just because you find him, it'll mean that all the problems will be over. Remember that there must have been a serious reason, or he'd never have left in the first place."

Determination enabled her to drag herself from the bed. "I don't assume anything, Marcus. I just need to find him. Everything else will fall into place."

"Okay! But you've got to promise me something before I give you his address."

She waited.

"Get a good night's rest before you start looking. He's not going anywhere, and you want to get there in one piece, okay?"

She smiled softly. "It's a deal. Walk me to the house?" She held out her hand.

Marcus grasped it tightly. He would have followed her anywhere.

The smile on his face stayed there till well past supper. And it was with much regret that he finally went to bed, allowing himself one final look in at his sleeping daughter, who'd been given back to him this day.

11

Chance tossed the disposable razor in the trash, glared at the nick he'd put in his chin, and stomped out of the bathroom. He was going to have to do some shopping today or else grow a beard. That razor had seen its last shave.

"For two cents, I'd pack up and head back to Tyler today," Chance muttered to himself as he walked past the rumpled bed. "To hell with ghosts and memories that want to stay buried. Maybe that's where they should be."

He shoved aside the curtain and stared outside. It was going to be another hot, sunny day. The only thing that seemed to vary was the degree and velocity of wind. Damn, but he missed the Triple T . . . and Jenny.

He'd had another dream last night, but this time it had been about Jenny. Something was wrong, he just knew it. Every instinct he had kept telling him to go back home. He shouldn't have left without talking to her. He knew that now. Hell, if he'd had any sense, he'd have brought her with him.

And then there'd been that phone call last night. It must have been around two in the morning when the phone rang, startling him so badly that he'd knocked it off the table before he'd been able to answer it. By the time he picked up the receiver, there was nothing but silence. It hadn't been a dial tone that buzzed in his ear, though, it had been the soft, almost undetectable sound of breathing. Finally, he'd hung up and then lain wide awake for hours, wondering who had called, and why they hadn't said a word after he'd answered.

He would have liked to believe that it had been a wrong number, or someone just fooling around. But his gut told him that it wasn't so. He suspected that the questions he'd been asking were starting to get results.

He let the curtain fall shut, patted his pocket to make sure he had his wallet and room key. He was hungry, having been awake so long. He set his Stetson carefully on his head, adjusting it to resist the wind gusts as he stepped outside and started across the parking lot, heading for the diner across the street.

His black boots made a slow, measured clop on the hot concrete. His blue jeans pulled across his muscular thighs as he increased his stride. The soft, well-washed, blue and white striped shirt clung to his chest in deference to the wind and heat, molding gently to the wide shoulders and powerful arms of a man who'd spent the last twelve years of his life using his muscles as well as his mind to perform his job.

Oh my God! It's him!

She'd spent hours last night calling every motel in town before she'd gotten results. She'd known the minute he'd answered that the phone call she'd gotten earlier in the day was true. But she'd had to hear his voice to believe it. And she'd recognized it instantly.

She caught her breath, pressed her fingers to her lips, and resisted the urge to shout for joy. The sun flashed in her eyes just as he walked into her line of vision, and she blinked rapidly, momentarily blinded by the bright rays. When he moved past her and stepped inside the diner, she started her car and turned to cross the street.

A car honked. She jumped, startled by the sound, and then waved an apology as she realized that she'd just pulled across traffic without even looking. The sight of him had rattled her that much.

It had been so long. Twelve years. And he'd changed. That was obvious. But, dear Lord, for the better. He looked magnificent!

Her fingers were shaking as she grasped the door handle and pulled. The wind caught her dress as she stepped out. She grabbed her skirt with one hand and her hair with the other. Her feet refused to move. She swallowed several times and looked down just to make sure they were still attached. She wasn't sure. She couldn't feel a thing. All she could do was remember.

He'd been barely eighteen, shirtless, with jeans

hanging loose on his slim hips. His dark, nearly black hair, badly in need of a haircut, was held away from his face with a red bandanna wound into a rope and tied around his forehead. She'd looked up through her windshield into eyes nearly as dark as that hair, and forgot to breathe.

March, 1980
Odessa, Texas

The bell rang at Charlie's Gas and Guzzle. It told Chance just what he didn't want to hear. Another customer had driven up wanting gas, and he had less than thirty minutes to fix a flat before the owner came back. A horn tooted, and he frowned, swiping the back of his forearm across his eyes and cursing softly as he looked up. It was some out-of-town honeys, way out of their league. What was a car like that doing in this part of town?

"Be right with you," he yelled, and dropped the tire iron. The flat would have to wait.

Charlie stuck his head out of the station office, started to urge Chance to hurry, and then walked back inside as he saw the boy already on the run toward the car. He didn't know what he'd do without him. He picked up the phone and continued to call in his gasoline order. The way business was going this month, he might be able to pay off that bank loan by the end of the year after all.

"Fill 'er up?" Chance asked, wistfully coveting the brand-new, candy-apple red Mustang. These girls didn't have to worry about who was paying their electric bill, or if there would be money for only two meals that day instead of three.

"Please," the driver answered, and several of the girls giggled and poked each other playfully.

They'd all seen the young man, bare to the waist, hot and sweaty in the afternoon heat as he pulled furiously at the tube he was trying to get out of the tire at his feet. He'd been all muscle and brawn and they'd been instantly entranced. His handsome face and shaggy hair had been pluses, too.

They were in the mood to be daring. That was what had sent them out of Midland toward Odessa. That was why they'd driven into a part of town in which their mothers wouldn't be caught dead. That was why they'd all urged Victoria to turn in at the gas station and ask for gas when the gauge registered full.

Chance grinned and winked at a girl in the back seat and muffled a laugh as she squealed and fell back against one of her friends. *My God! How old are these girls anyway?* The ones he knew were way past giggles and teasing. They knew what buttons to push to get what they wanted and had no compunctions about doing so.

He poked the nozzle into the tank and leaned one hand on the fender as he waited for it to fill. The pump kicked off with less than a dollar's worth of gas showing. He shoved the nozzle back into place, screwed on the gas cap, and flipped the door to the tank shut.

"Let me get that windshield," he said, and grabbed a squeegee and a rag.

Victoria was blushing three shades of red and just the tiniest bit of pink. The four freckles across the bridge of her nose were crying out for makeup. She knew it. But there was nothing she could do to quell the flutters in her stomach as the boy leaned across the hood of her car and ran the water-filled wiper onto her windshield. He was so cute! And from the way he was flirting with her friends, he knew it.

Her fingers gripped the steering wheel as he walked to her side of the car and repeated the same routine on the windshield in front of her. He leaned over to dry it as Victoria looked up. His dark eyes, filled with secrets, met her green innocent ones, and then he smiled.

She forgot she was blushing. She forgot she wasn't supposed to leave Midland or be in this part of town. She forgot there were four other girls in her brand-new car, an early graduation present. She caught her breath, and then tentatively, without blinking, returned the smile.

Chance stopped in mid-swipe, fascinated by the innocence of her face. Damn, but she was pretty! And then he remembered who he was . . . and what he was supposed to be doing . . . and finished the window in quick time. He leaned down, braced himself against the door, and stared at the girl again.

"Good thing you stopped, honey," he said softly, "you might not have made it home. You owe me ninety-three cents."

Victoria blushed and grabbed for her purse. "Here," she said, thrusting a dollar bill into his hands, "keep the change."

Chance whistled softly. "Pretty, and a big tipper, too."

The girls erupted into another fit of giggles as

Victoria turned on the ignition and shot out of the driveway.

Chance grinned and hurried back to fixing the flat tire.

The girls laughed and joked with each other all the way back to Midland. But late that night, when she was almost asleep, Victoria remembered the boy at the station and smiled. She was going back, and soon.

"Here boy," Charlie yelled, as Chance emerged from the washroom. "Payday."

Chance breathed a quiet sigh of relief. Unlike most boys his age, who had jobs after school and on the weekends for extra spending money, his pay went to cover bills and, if there was enough left over, to buy some extra food. They'd gotten their last cut-off notice this morning. He looked down at his watch. He had just enough time to get to the utility department and pay before they cut the electricity off . . . again. He hated it when that happened. Then he had to come up with what was owed, plus the late fee. His mother never seemed to be able to come up with the money for either.

"Thanks, Charlie. Gotta run. See you tomorrow."

He stuffed the money into his pocket, grateful that he'd been paid in cash. He wouldn't have had time to go to the bank and still make it to the utility department, and he suspected Charlie knew it.

It was late that evening when he started home with what was left of his paycheck in a brown paper sack. His mouth watered as the aroma of lunch meat and fresh bread wafted upward. It had been a long time since morning and breakfast.

His feet turned the last corner of the block as he headed for home. The shabby, two-bedroom house, with peeling paint and cracked windows, came into view. It sat alone on a corner, bounded by empty lots on either side. The old pickup truck he'd bought for a hundred and fifty dollars last year was sitting in the driveway.

That meant his mother was either home, or she was out with one of her "friends." The grass needed cutting. He'd have to ask that cranky neighbor across the street if he could borrow the lawn mower again. He knew what he'd say. Sure! Only he'd have to mow the neighbor's yard first. The hinges squeaked in protest as he yanked the screen door open, balancing his sack on one knee as he fumbled for his key.

"Chancey, is that you?"

The shrill, whining voice sent shivers up his backbone. He gritted his teeth, shifted his sack, and slammed the door behind him. She was home . . . and drunk . . . again. It was the only time she called him by that stupid name. The rest of the time she didn't call him anything. She didn't have time. What with the constant traffic of men coming and going, she didn't have time to do any talking. She was too busy screwing the town's male population.

Chance walked through the house, frowned at the assortment of clothing scattered on chairs and couch, tables and lamps, and wondered what the hell she'd been doing today. It was her day off from the job she had shuffling drinks down at Crosby's. He set the sack down on the kitchen table and was putting the food in the refrigerator when Letty McCall sauntered into the room.

"Honey? Didn't you hear your momma call?"

"Yes, Mom. I heard you," he said shortly.

"Well, why didn't you answer me? You could have frightened me you know. Might have been a stranger coming into my house. A woman can't be too careful, you know."

"Hell, Mom, you don't know any strangers. And if one happened by, you know where he'd be. He wouldn't be robbing us. He'd be . . ."

The slap cut across his cheek, stinging his conscience as well as his face. It was nothing more than he deserved. He knew what she was, but she was still his mother. And they were all each other had. He blinked slowly and licked at his lower lip. Those sharp red claws of hers had cut it.

Letty McCall took one look at the blood on his lip and burst into tears. Chance sighed, held out his arms and caught her as she fell forward, sobbing loudly.

"Chancey, please . . . I'm sorry. I didn't mean to hurt . . ."

"Hush, Mom," he said, patting her gently on the back. "I deserved it. It's been a long day. I guess I was just tired."

Her sobs quickly escalated into hiccups that gave way to a moan. "I need a drink," she mumbled, turning away, forgetting everything in the rush of adrenaline that surfaced at the thought of more cheap whiskey sliding down her throat.

"Shit," Chance said to himself. He slammed the door shut on the meager stash of food, and headed for his room.

It was his sanctuary, the only place in this house that was off limits to the men who came and went. And they knew it.

He'd claimed his territory the hard way after one of Letty's "friends" had wandered into it instead of the bathroom. It had amounted to one hell of a fight and the neighbors calling the police. Luckily for him, the patrolman who answered the call grasped the situation and simply hauled the drunk to jail to let him sleep it off. After that, word got around. Letty McCall's boy was to be left alone. Unfortunately, that rule did not apply to Letty.

It was getting dark outside. He knew that when the sun went down, another breed of people came alive in this town.

His belly grumbled, reminding him that it was empty. But his appetite had just vanished. He grabbed a clean pair of jeans and a T-shirt, and headed for the bathroom. He didn't have long to clean up from the grease and grime of the station and get out before someone would be knocking on the door. If he had to see the men who came knocking, then he'd have to fight. And he knew that it was futile.

A familiar glint of candy-apple red caught his eye. Chance turned away from the car he was servicing and stared. It *was* the same car. He hadn't been mistaken. But this time, only the driver was inside. He watched her park at the pumps and get out, stretch, and look around as if she couldn't see him servicing the other car. Her nonchalance was obviously an act, though. Tension radiated from every muscle in her body and she'd looked everywhere but at him. Eventually she'd have to. He was the only one on duty.

"You lost?" he called softly, and watched, fascinated by the way her long honey-blond hair fanned out as she turned. She smiled.

"No."

Her honesty surprised him. He'd expected more of the same giggling and simpering as before. And then he remembered. She hadn't been the one doing all the giggling. It had been her friends. She'd blushed. And she had exactly four freckles. At least that's all he'd been able to see.

"What'll it be?" he asked, as he handed the credit card back to his other customer and walked toward her.

Victoria caught her breath. It was like watching a cougar approaching and not being afraid. He moved slowly and steadily, his eyes fixed on his prey, with a fluidity of muscle and bone in perfect synchronization.

"Then, if you're not lost, you must need gas."

She smiled, and he forgot what he'd been about to say next.

"Yes, please. And I promise, this time, I really do need gas."

Shared laughter rang out in the empty driveway of the station.

"My name is Victoria Henry," she said softly, watching with renewed fascination as he filled her car's tank and cleaned the windshield.

He stopped as the sound of her voice flowed over him like hot molasses. He turned and, for a long moment, just watched the play of emotions running across her face. He'd been right. She was more than naive. She was greener than new grass, and he had no business even contemplating what had just crossed his mind.

"Hello, Victoria Henry," he said quietly. "I'm Chance McCall."

It was all the opening she needed. By the time Charlie got back from lunch, Victoria had wheedled out of him the fact that he, too, was graduating from high school in a few short weeks. That he lived alone with him mother. That he didn't know his father and never had. And that he'd worked for Charlie since he was thirteen years old.

Chance was stunned. He didn't know how she'd done it, but he'd just told her more about himself in a few minutes than he'd told any of his classmates the entire four years they'd attended Odessa High School together.

He supposed it was because she was so different. She had no secrets. She had nothing of which she should be ashamed. She was who she appeared to be: a beautiful girl on the verge of womanhood.

Charlie pulled into the driveway and grinned. He tooted his horn at the pair who were leaning side-by-side against the shiny red Mustang. He honked again when they jumped apart in startled guilt.

"I know what you had for lunch," Chance drawled, as Charlie came barreling across the driveway with a big smile on his face. "You're supposed to eat your Wheaties at breakfast, not lunch. You don't need all that pent-up energy this late in the day."

Charlie hooted. "That's not what I had, boy. And you know it." He grinned and leered.

When Chance almost blushed Charlie knew it was because of the girl standing beside him. He relented. The boy was obviously smitten and he'd teased him enough. "Go on with you," he said. "Go to lunch."

"Oh good. If you don't have plans, we can go together," Victoria said.

A panicked expression froze Chance in place. If she went with him, then he'd have to offer to pay for her lunch and he didn't even have enough money to buy his own. He'd planned on carrying out the garbage over at the Dairy Freeze in return for a burger and shake.

Charlie silently cursed himself for being unforgivably stupid. He knew what shape Chance's world was in. He'd helped the boy bail his mother out of the drunk tank more than once.

"Say boy," he said, before things got worse, "if you'll do me a favor on your lunch hour, I'll pick up the tab for you two at Henderson's Drug. They've got a special this week on burgers. I forgot to get the parts for Mabel Geraldine's car down at the auto supply. They know what I want. I called them earlier."

Chance stared at the innocent look on Charlie's face as relief overwhelmed him. The man was making up an excuse, and for the life of him, Chance couldn't be mad. If it weren't for Charlie, he'd have gone under years ago.

"No problem," Victoria said. "We'll take my car." And then she looked at the hesitant, almost wary expression beginning to spread to Chance's eyes. "But I'd appreciate it if you'd drive, Chance. I don't know Odessa well enough to find the place you'll need to go. Do you mind?" She held out the keys.

It was to his credit that his hands didn't shake as he

took the keys she dropped in his palm. Mind? He'd dreamed of owning a car like this one day. Driving it was just one step away from perfect.

"Here," Charlie said, holding out a ten-dollar bill. "When you eat this up, you'll have to quit. And as for the parts, just tell Pete to charge them like always."

Chance took the money and tried not to let it show how much the gesture meant to him. He'd make it up later, when Victoria was gone. "Thanks, Charlie. We'll be back later."

"You'd better," he teased, and watched Chance blush as Victoria slid beneath the steering wheel and then stopped about halfway across the seat. "I want you to close for me tonight."

And so it began. The routine varied, but at least twice a week, Victoria Henry made her way to Odessa, to Charlie's Gas and Guzzle, to see Chance. He knew one day that their relationship would end. That she would never . . . could never . . . live in the world in which he belonged. But for now, this taste of normalcy was sinfully addictive.

"Where you been keepin' yourself, Chancey?" Letty asked, her voice already slurred from liquor.

"Busy," he answered. He had no intention of going into details about his personal life with his mother.

"Don't be smart with me, boy." Her eyes watered as she tossed back a double shot of bourbon and she sighed as it burned all the way down.

The booze kicked in just about the same time Chance slammed the door shut behind him. She didn't ask where he was going, and it wouldn't have mattered if she had. He wouldn't have told her.

He was almost thirty minutes late. What if she didn't wait? What if . . . ? He breathed a sigh of relief as he turned the corner and saw the shiny red car parked in front of the theater. She was there!

Victoria bit her lower lip as she saw him coming around the corner. He was almost running. Obviously the pickup was on the fritz again. It was a constant problem.

"Hi," she said softly as she stepped out to greet him. He smelled so good she wanted to taste him, but kissing in public wasn't something she'd been raised to do, so she simply stared instead.

He was wearing nearly new blue jeans, a snow white T-shirt, and the same old, curled-up at the toes, black boots. His hair was still damp from his shower, but barely combed, and it hung just above the neckline of his shirt in dark rebellion.

His glance grazed her face, slid down, and lingered at the generous curves below her collar. He resisted the urge to run his fingers down the slender legs emerging beneath her shorts, just to see if they were as silky as they looked.

"You ready?" she asked, tucking her arm beneath his elbow, and starting toward the theater.

"I'm always ready for you," he teased, delighting in the blush he knew would sweep across her face and neck. He wasn't disappointed.

The movie was all they'd expected. It provided everything they'd come to experience. Darkness and anonymity. A proving ground for the touches she needed, and the kisses he hoped to secure. A place where whispers and private moments remained just that. It was with no small amount of regret that they realized the show was over, and the theater was emptying.

Chance slipped his hand in hers as they exited the building, and started walking her toward her car. It was late, almost midnight. He knew she had a curfew. He couldn't imagine what it would be like to have someone care where he was, or who he was with. He also knew that her parents didn't have the faintest idea in hell that their daughter was out with a boy from the wrong side of town.

"I guess you'd better be going," he said, as they lingered beside her car, each reluctant to be the one to break the closeness of the evening. "I don't want you driving too fast on your way home, just to meet your curfew."

Victoria smiled and leaned against him, taking advantage of the darkness to wrap her arms around his waist. She nuzzled her chin against his chest. "I like it when you worry about me," she whispered.

"I always worry about you, Victoria," he said. "I worry what's going to happen when you realize that you're tired of playing this game of hide and seek with your folks. And I worry how I'm going to face it when I know you're not coming back."

The low, even measure of his voice struck a chord of concern in her own heart. "It's not a game, Chance. Don't you ever say that to me again. And I wouldn't be 'playing this game' if you'd just agree to come meet my family like I've been asking you to."

He frowned. Meeting hers would mean that she'd have to meet his. It was unthinkable.

"I know your mother has problems," Victoria said, and hugged him gently to ease her words. "You don't have to spell out the extent of them for me to get the picture."

"Problems? I don't think I've ever thought of them as problems. She's not . . . she's just . . . hell, Victoria. She's just not your type, that's all."

"She can't be all bad, honey," Victoria whispered. "She had you."

Chance hugged her tightly. The praise was special because it was so rare in his life. But holding Victoria against him was causing a problem to arise that Chance couldn't deny.

Victoria moved gently against his lips, aware of his condition, secretly satisfied that she'd been the one to cause it. But it was impossible to act on it. She had less than an hour to get home.

"I'd better be going," she said softly.

Chance groaned, kissed the top of her head, savoring the smell of shampoo and perfume so he'd remember it when she was long gone. "I know. Remember what I said. Drive careful."

"I promise. And I wish you'd let me take you . . ."

"We've been through all this, Victoria," he said as he all but shoved her inside her car. "You're not taking me home . . . ever. You don't belong on my side of town. I won't have someone ever say that I dragged you down to my level. Go home, girl. Go home, now."

"Okay, okay." She frowned as she slid in behind the steering wheel. She looked up at the tall dark man staring down at her with a fierce expression on his face. "You know what? I just realized something. I think you and my father would get along just fine. You know why? You're just alike. I've never met any two men more hard-headed."

She blew him a kiss to soften her words, and then drove away. Chance watched until her taillights blended into the busy traffic, and he could no longer see her. He stuffed his hands into his pockets and tossed his head back, savoring the clean, fresh breeze that wafted through the street, taking away the scents of the city. He started for home.

Every light in the house was on. Chance could see it a block away. *Oh hell!* he thought. *Either she was having a party, or she had passed out again.* He hastened his steps, drawn back into his sordid world just by proximity.

He burst through the door, ready to do battle if need be. There was no need. Whatever battles had been waged were long over. From the look of the place, Chance supposed it had been a battle of the sexes. Letty was passed out on the sofa, clothing awry, an empty bottle lying just out of reach of her hand. A twenty-dollar bill had been tossed across her breasts.

Tears threatened to erupt and then froze as hard as his heart. Chance brushed the money onto the floor, kicked the bottle out of reach, and bent down and straightened his mother's clothing. A grim line formed between his eyebrows as he scooted his arms beneath her and lifted her to his chest. As usual, he was always surprised by how light she was.

Her bed was still made. Obviously they'd never made

it to the back of the house. He laid her down, pulled off her shoes, and pulled the bedspread over her legs. He turned on the small table fan, positioning it so that she would get the maximum effect of the feeble breeze.

She moaned once, muttered a name Chance didn't recognize, and then turned onto her side and curled up like a small child.

Chance stood back, looking at the woman who'd given him life, and wondered, not for the first time, how she'd come to be in this place . . . in this condition . . . and why she'd come here alone.

He walked through the house, turning out lights and locking doors and windows, and then headed for bed. The twenty-dollar bill still lay where he'd tossed it, the empty bottle and glasses making new stains on old territory. He pulled off his boots, slipped his shirt over his head, and dropped wearily onto his bed, suddenly feeling too tired and old for his years to bother with undressing further. He stretched out on his back, crossed his ankles, stared up at the water stain over his bed, and waited for morning.

12

"*But I want you* to take me to my prom, not some old boy my parents pick out."

Chance's lips thinned as his chin jutted in stubborn defiance. He and Victoria had been arguing this same subject for days. There was no way he could afford to take anyone to a prom. He hadn't even gone to his own. It meant renting a tux, buying flowers and, even more importantly, what would he drive to get there? Victoria Henry wasn't going to *her* prom in *his* pickup. Even if it was running. Even if she'd agree. And he damn sure wasn't being picked up and driven in her car like a gigolo.

"Victoria! Dammit, honey. We've been all through this."

"Yes, *you* have," she said. "And I've listened, every time. But you haven't listened to me. I don't care what you drive. I don't care what you wear. I don't need flowers." Her voice softened as tears flooded her cheeks. "I just need you."

"Oh hell," he muttered. "You don't have to cry. Please, honey. Don't cry!" He looked around nervously, convinced himself that they were alone in the station office, and pulled her into his arms. "You once accused me of being hard-headed. But I don't hold a candle to you, girl. I'll take you to your damn prom. I'll wear a tux. And you'll have a corsage. Just quit crying." His voice softened. "Please."

Victoria sighed, wrapped her arms around his waist, and sniffed. "Thank you, Chance. I don't mean to be selfish. I just don't want to attend an important event like my prom with anyone but you. If that's bad, then sue me."

He grinned, and then looked up and caught his boss waving at them through the window. He'd never hear the end of this.

"Come on," he urged. "You've got to get out of here before I get fired. Charlie's back from lunch and I've got work to do."

"Okay," Victoria said, tilting her face up for her kiss.

Chance looked back through the window. Charlie was still there, waving ... and grinning. He looked down at Victoria's waiting lips and cursed softly to himself. She was worth it.

He bent down, tasted the soft, supple curves of Precious Pink he'd watched her applying minutes earlier, and knew that it was not enough.

"You in over your head, boy?" Charlie asked, as they both watched the red car dart out of the driveway and move into the flow of traffic.

"Probably," he answered. "I just agreed to go to a damn prom."

Charlie Rollins remembered his own, remembered his daughter's high school years, and knew that Chance deserved a memory worth keeping, too.

"Well, if you're goin', you'll be needin' somethin' to drive. You close for me every night this week, and you can drive my Olds."

Chance turned and stared. Charlie's blue eyes got brighter and he fidgeted with the rag hanging out of his hip pocket.

"You don't have to," Chance finally managed to say, moved beyond words by the generosity of a man who was, by all rights, only his employer.

"I know that," Charlie snapped. "That's why I offered."

Chance held out his hand. "It's a deal."

Charlie grinned. "Damn, but I like a good deal, don't you, boy?"

Chance laughed. "Yeah, Charlie. And thanks to you, I just got one."

Chance breathed a small prayer of thanksgiving that his mother had to work tonight. He didn't want to explain what he was doing with his boss's car, or why he was wearing a rented tux, or why he'd gotten a haircut. He glanced at the clock over the refrigerator, pulled nervously at the bow tie he'd finally managed to fasten, and opened the refrigerator door. The corsage was still there! A cluster of pale pink miniature carnations haloed with something the florist had called baby's breath.

He hoped it would do. All Victoria had said was it needed to be pink. He grabbed the box off the shelf, checked his pocket for money and keys, and headed for the door. It was time!

The drive to Midland didn't take long. But it might as well have been to the moon. The farther Chance drove from Odessa, the more he realized that he was in over his head. He'd never, not once in all his eighteen years, let a girl get to him like Victoria had. And to top it all off, they'd never even gotten close to making out. He frowned at the thought. Somehow, making out wasn't a term he could associate with the tall, blond girl with flashing green eyes. Making love . . . maybe. But making out?

The address she'd given him meant nothing. He didn't know front from back in that town. He just kept repeating the directions she'd given him as he drove into town.

Turn right at the station just past the . . . Go two blocks north and then take a left at the . . .

Finally, he turned onto a residential street and breathed a sigh of relief as he saw a familiar red car parked in front of an elegant, two-story, frame and rock home. He pulled into the driveway. Her parents weren't supposed to be here. He was to meet them later at the prom where they were serving as chaperons. He took a deep breath and knocked. *The things I do for you.*

It swung back almost instantly. She must have been watching out a window. The smile on her face was no less breathtaking than the dress she was wearing. It was strapless. And other than thinking she looked like she'd just stepped off a cake, Chance would have been unable to describe it. The layers and layers of frothy white lace, tipped with the palest of pink, brushed against each other with a swish-swoosh as she walked toward him. The skirt of the dress yielded and then seemed to float around his legs as he walked into her embrace and kissed her softly on the cheek. This Victoria made him nervous. She looked like a princess, and he felt like a damned frog.

"For me?" she asked, pointing to the corsage.

"Oh, here," he said, suddenly embarrassed. "I don't know where you'll wear it, though. If you'd told me you wouldn't have a . . . I mean if I'd have known that the dress didn't have a . . ."

Victoria laughed. "Chance McCall. I think you're embarrassed. It's got to be a first. And it's good for you, my man. You're entirely too worldly for me. Come on. The dance won't wait . . . and neither can I."

Before he knew it, they were in the car with the corsage pinned at her waist. Silly smiles, stolen kisses, and a pounding heart, got him to the prom under Victoria's directions. He parked Charlie's car, vaulted from his seat, and hurried around to the passenger side to help Victoria and her skirt make as graceful an exit as possible from the car.

"You look so good," Victoria said softly, as she pulled at a crook in his tie. "All tall, dark, and handsome in this tuxedo. I'm going to have to fight the girls off of you all night, and you know it."

He grinned. "I may have to fight, but I doubt it'll be girls, honey. You're the one who looks good enough to eat. Now come on, let's get this over with. I don't know how or why I let you talk me into it."

"Hush. Come on. Let's go get this meeting with my parents over with so we can enjoy the dance."

The smile on his face disappeared. He didn't have a good feeling about this. And, looking back later, Chance knew he should have followed his instincts.

"Oh my God!" Margaret Henry muttered through a fake smile, as she nodded at an acquaintance and then stared at the couple coming through the door.

She'd known her daughter had been making a lot of trips in her new car, as she'd been paying the gas bill. But she'd never imagined that it would be to another world. That's where boys like that one came from. In Margaret's day, it had been called, "the wrong side of the tracks."

Her eyes missed nothing of the unconscious swagger and dark, knowing eyes that'd seen more of the world than Victoria even knew existed.

"What?" Logan Henry sighed. He hated occasions like these, yet he knew that their standing in the community demanded that they attend them. Especially this year, when their only child was a graduating senior.

"Victoria!" Margaret hissed. "She's just walked in with her surprise. I told you she'd been up to something. But you assured me that it was nothing. You told me to leave her alone, let her try out her wings. Well Logan, I hope you're satisfied. It looks to me like your little chicken has flown the coop. I think a fox has been in the hen house."

"My God, Margaret. Your metaphors boggle the mind. What the hell are you . . . ?"

He turned and looked in the direction of his wife's anger. Every sin he'd ever committed had just come in the door to haunt him. Logan forgot to finish his sentence. He didn't hear Margaret's answer, or the music that had already begun to blare. He saw no one except the tall, dark boy who'd just walked in on his daughter's arm.

"No!" It came out. Unexpected. Unpreventable.

Margaret turned and stared. "Not now!" she hissed. "Don't you dare make a scene! This is Victoria's night. She won't forgive you . . . and neither will I if you ruin this for her. Do you hear me, Logan Henry?"

He watched, horrified, as they came toward him.

"Mother . . . Daddy . . . I want you to meet my friend, Chance McCall. Chance, these are my parents, Margaret and Logan Henry."

"Mr. and Mrs. Henry," Chance said, "it's a pleasure to meet you." His gaze slid from Margaret's face then back to Victoria's. "Victoria, you have much to be grateful for."

"Why?" she asked.

"That your father had the good sense to marry someone as beautiful as your mother. You two look more like sisters than mother and daughter."

In spite of herself, Margaret Henry blushed. It had been years since she'd heard a compliment as ingenious . . . and as nicely put. She smiled, just a bit. It wouldn't do to get too familiar with someone who'd have to go, but she could see what had drawn Victoria. The boy had magnetism. A *lot* of magnetism.

"Thank you," she said, answering Chance's compliment. "You know, we haven't met you before, have we?

But . . . you really remind me of someone. Are you from Midland? Who are your people? Maybe I've met your mother and just didn't—"

"Mother," Victoria broke in, "you don't have to learn someone's family history every time you meet." She turned and smiled up at the closed expression on Chance's face, hoping that it would soon disappear. She'd seen it come and go more than once during their relationship.

"It doesn't matter," Chance answered shortly. "She has a right, Victoria. If I were her, I'd want to know who someone as special as you are is with, too."

Margaret winced. She didn't want to like this boy. But it was becoming more and more difficult. She turned to her husband, hoping for a sign of support from him. It was obvious from the look on his face that she'd get nothing here. He looked like he was about to have a heart attack.

"And no, ma'am," Chance said, "I'm not from Midland. I'm from Odessa."

Logan Henry inhaled sharply. He'd known it! But hearing it confirmed made it all the worse.

"And as for meeting my mother . . . I doubt it unless you've ever been in Crosby's bar and ordered a drink."

Complete and total silence met his answer. He stared into their eyes, waiting for the shock to appear, for the argument to ensue. To Margaret Henry's credit, neither happened. And it took everything she had to assure herself that it did not.

"Well!" she finally said. "I'm sure your father appreciates the extra paycheck. Jobs are hard to come by nowadays. I've heard—"

"I don't know my father, Mrs. Henry. Never had the pleasure." The slow drawl was thick with old anger.

Margaret saw something other than defensiveness in the boy's eyes. She saw a wall of pain.

"I'm sorry," she said quietly. "None of this matters except that you and Victoria have a wonderful evening, you hear? Victoria, you look absolutely beautiful. And that corsage is exquisite, if I do say so. You have good taste, Chance. It's lovely."

Chance blinked. The expected thunderbolt didn't flash. The uproar he'd been bracing himself for didn't erupt. He suspected that he'd just met what was known as "a real lady." He sighed once, quietly, and smiled down at the look on Victoria's face.

"Yes, ma'am. I chose Victoria, didn't I?" He grinned slightly. "Or she chose me. At any rate, may we be excused?"

Victoria sailed away on his arm, beaming with delight that the long-dreaded meeting was over, and that nothing untoward had occurred.

"See," she said, as she slipped into his arms, "you worried about nothing."

Chance turned her around, moving in step to the slow waltz beat as her parents faded from sight. But the look on her father's face did nothing to assure him that Victoria's statement had a word of truth. In fact, now that he remembered it, Logan Henry had said nothing at all. It had been his wife who'd done all the talking.

Logan Henry stared across the crowded dance floor and into Chance's eyes. A strange signal passed almost undetected, but it was there.

Chance's flesh crawled. The look was intense and full of hate. "I don't know, honey," he said. "I think your father'd like to put out a contract on me, and ship you off to Europe."

Victoria leaned back in his arms and laughed. "You're imagining things, Chance. Hold me closer and don't skip a dance. This is the first time I've been able to be in your arms in public and I don't intend to waste a moment."

His heart twisted at the poignancy of her statement. She was right, and it shouldn't be so! Chance knew that he was out of her league, but for the life of him, he didn't want to give her up.

"Then come here, honey. It will be my pleasure to hold you, all night long."

She shivered at the implied promises.

He slid one arm around her waist, pulled her tight against his lower body, wrapped her other arm around him, and together they melded into the swirl of dancers clad in finery and expensive lace. It was a night to remember . . . and one he would pray to forget.

"Will you quit staring at that boy," Margaret whispered. "You're going to make Victoria nervous."

Nervous! Hell, they didn't know the meaning of the word. Logan Henry didn't know what to do, but as the clock wound its way toward midnight, he knew he had to make a decision. Ever since he'd seen his daughter come into the dance with that boy, he'd had visions of his prom night, and what happened later, in the back seat of a car. This couldn't happen to her. Not with him! Not ever!

His stomach roiled. Sweat was running down the middle of his back. A slow, burning rage was building. His anger was getting out of hand. He knew it but couldn't seem to stop it. Just watching the way they clung to each other on the dance floor made his blood pressure rise. He turned and glared at his wife's impatience. *If she'd just shut her mouth, maybe I could think.*

And then he looked up and felt his belly heave. They were nowhere in sight!

"Margaret! Where the hell did they go?" Logan asked.

She shrugged. "Victoria waved as they danced past a while ago. I think they may have decided to leave a bit early. She was making snacks at the house when we left. They may be planning to go home and get a bite to eat. If we give them a thirty-minute head start, it won't be too obvious, and then we can go home and join them. What do you think?"

"I think you're crazy." He started through the crowded dance floor, threading his way among the couples like a man gone mad, pushing and shoving, ignoring the cries of dismay and concern.

Margaret was appalled. She didn't know what had gotten into her husband, but she knew it would take months to live down his rude behavior. She hurried after him, trying to excuse his boorishness by claiming he was ill.

"Here, Chance," Victoria said, as they exited the hot ballroom and breathed the cooler night air, "take off your jacket, and that tie. You've suffered long enough for me."

It didn't take a second urging. He grinned and complied. The tie was stuffed in his jacket pocket and both were tossed into the car.

"I have some sandwiches and snacks at the house," Victoria said. She threaded her arms around his neck and tilted her head back, offering herself to the boy in her arms. "That is . . . if you're hungry."

"I'm hungry, all right," Chance said, "but not for food, honey. For you."

He pulled her into his arms, turned her around until he had her pinned between the car and his aching body, and lowered his head, capturing the sweetness of what she was offering. She moaned quietly and moved against him, relishing the ache that was building between her legs, aware that he wanted more from her than kisses. The thought was intoxicating . . . and frightening. And then their world fell apart.

"Turn her loose, you son-of-a-bitch," Logan Henry yelled, and pulled roughly at Chance's arm.

His hand swung out as he pushed between them and unintentionally clipped Chance on the side of the jaw. Caught unawares, Chance staggered, unable to regain his balance, and fell backward onto the blacktop parking lot.

Victoria screamed. "Daddy! Have you gone crazy? He was only kissing me. Leave him alone."

But Logan was past reason. Just the sight of the two, entwined in each other's arms, pressed so intimately together, had been the last straw. Visions of bare arms and legs and cries of joy had overridden all sense of propriety. He would stop this relationship now. For all he knew, it might already be too late to undo some of the damage. If this boy had made love to Victoria, he'd kill him.

Chance was shocked . . . but not surprised. His street instincts had seen this coming. More than once during the night, he'd sensed the man's antagonism across the crowded floor. And he'd known that his relationship with a girl like Victoria could cause trouble, for him as well as her.

The two men stared at each other, silently assessing each other's determination. Chance sighed. He would not fight her father. It would serve no purpose other than to emphasize the distance between their worlds.

"Chance!" Victoria stumbled as she tried to get past her father and help him up. She was beyond embarrassment. Fear for the boy she'd come to love was uppermost.

"Get away from him," Logan snarled. He shoved his daughter aside, intent on keeping them apart at all costs.

Her foot caught in the hem of her dress. She fell forward and, as she did, the back of her father's hand caught her across the face. The slap reverberated in the night like a gunshot.

Margaret Henry arrived in time to witness what looked like a slap. Her husband had struck their daughter? She couldn't believe what she was seeing.

"Logan! Have you taken leave of your senses?" she cried, frantically looking around to ascertain that they were unobserved. That he had lowered himself to brawling was not to be believed. That he had laid a hand on their daughter was unforgivable. She hurried to Victoria's side.

Fury exploded as Chance came to his feet. "You bastard," he said harshly. "Letting you shove me around was one thing. But you shouldn't have put a hand on Victoria." His arm came up and his fist shot out.

Logan's head snapped back and blood spurted. He blinked, startled by the intensity of the blow. His tongue slid across his lower lip, tasting blood seeping from a cut. He smiled. He should have known the boy could fight. His entire life had probably been one long battle.

"Oh my God!" Margaret moaned, and pulled her daughter out of the line of fire. She could only stand and watch as the two men, one older and stronger, the other younger and more determined, began to exchange blows. Silently, one after the other, back and forth, in the shadows of the parking lot.

Chance's breath escaped in one harsh grunt as Logan Henry's fist connected with his stomach. He staggered once, leaned over, and spat. It kept what wanted to come up, down. The sorry son-of-a-bitch was enjoying this, Chance thought. He could see the glow in Logan Henry's eyes. He grabbed hold of his knees, regained control of his breathing, and came up swinging. The intensity of the blows they were exchanging surprised both men. This was no longer about Victoria.

Logan's belly hurt. His eye stung where a fist had unexpectedly struck. Tomorrow he'd have a fat lip. His breath was coming in harsh gasps but, for the most part, he'd been unaffected by the fight. The boy, on the other hand, was not faring so well. And even in his fury Logan knew he'd gone past the limits of reason. He'd hammered the boy about the face and stomach until he was ashamed of himself.

A grudging sense of admiration slipped into his conscience. If the crazy fool would just stay down. But each time he fell to the blacktop, Chance would lift his head, take a long drink of air, and stagger back to his feet, daring the older man to do it again. And he did.

One eye was cut badly, and bleeding profusely. Chance could feel the blood running down his neck and onto his shirt. His knuckles were so swollen he couldn't make a fist. It hurt to blink so he didn't. And he knew that he'd probably be eating soup for the rest of his life. The last blow he'd taken in the belly had cracked a rib. He'd heard it before he'd felt the pain. It would be so simple to just stay down. He could see the look on her father's face. He wanted it to end. But something inside Chance wouldn't let himself be the one to quit. Something kept pulling him up to take another . . . and another . . . and another blow.

Victoria's sobs penetrated Logan Henry's consciousness. A slow horror began to invade his mind. *What in God's name have I just done to my own . . . ?*

"Daddy! Please! You've got to stop. You don't understand." She tore away from her mother's arms and flung herself between Logan and Chance. "I can't believe you've hurt someone this badly that you don't even know." Tears thickened her speech as she pummeled her father's chest with shaky fists. "He's a good boy . . . and a good student. He has a job. I know all about him . . . and his family. You've got to stop this, Daddy. You don't understand . . . I love him!"

Red rage fused behind Logan Henry's eyes as sanity disappeared. *Love! Oh my God! I was right! It is too late!*

"I'll kill the bastard," Logan snarled, and started to push his daughter aside. "He had no right to touch you. Not him!"

Victoria slapped her father. It startled everyone involved, but no one more than Chance.

"You filthy-minded . . ." Words failed her. "Chance has done nothing for which he should be ashamed," she cried. "He's never done anything to me, except treat me with constant respect and love. And no . . . we haven't made love. But I wouldn't have stopped him if he'd tried."

Chance groaned. *My God! Victoria!*

Logan's breath caught in the back of his throat. He turned on his daughter, grabbed her by both arms and began to shake her. He didn't believe her. Her hair tumbled around her face and the pink corsage fell to the ground.

"You fool! Goddammit, don't ever let me hear you say that again. You can't love him."

"I'd like to know why not!" Victoria shouted.

Chance staggered to his feet and reached out a hand to help her. But it never connected as Logan Henry's words shocked and then put everyone present in a momentary state of suspended animation.

"Because he's your brother!"

Margaret Henry moaned and closed her eyes. She wasn't hearing this. And then, slowly, she opened them and stared at Chance. The truth hit her first. It had been staring at her all night. She wanted to vomit.

"No! You're lying!" Victoria screamed, and fell back into her mother's arms.

Chance's breath escaped in a slow hiss. He stared up at the man who loomed over him with hatred oozing from every pore.

"You're a damn liar," Chance muttered, trying to talk around the pain. "My mother has been with so many men, even she couldn't tell you who's responsible."

For the first time, a glimmer of guilt hit Logan. He tried to speak and then swallowed. To save Victoria, they had to believe him.

"When I met her . . . I was the first."

Margaret Henry gasped and met her husband's eyes. The truth was there. She shook her head and walked away.

Logan cursed soft and long. He watched the end of his marriage disappearing into the darkness.

Chance staggered backward and leaned weakly against Charlie's car.

"I don't believe you," he whispered. He didn't want to. It meant that Victoria was . . . That more than once they'd almost . . .

"You have to," Logan said. "You can't love Victoria. Not in that way."

"You beast!" Victoria cried. "You're just doing this to keep us apart."

"No, honey." His regret was overwhelming. "I wouldn't destroy myself just to hurt you . . . now would I?"

She stared at the truth in her father's eyes and moaned. She turned, reached toward Chance, and then let her arms drop to her side as shock overwhelmed her. She swayed.

Their reactions were instantaneous as both men tried to catch her. She staggered backward, horror thickening her voice as she cried, "Don't touch me, either of you! I don't want Chance for a brother. I love him. I wanted to marry him! And now . . . because of you . . . I can't. I'll never forgive you," she said. "Never!"

Logan winced as Victoria ran out of sight. He turned to Chance. He had to make the boy believe him. His daughter's future depended upon it.

"Letty was seventeen. I'd been married less than a year."

Chance stood transfixed, listening to the man turn his world upside down.

"I didn't mean for it to go as far as it did. But she was so damn pretty . . . and Margaret hated sex. I needed . . ."

Chance staggered forward and set his fist against Logan's chest. "You sound just like every man who's come knocking on my mother's door. They all need something. And they want it from her."

The pain in the boy's voice was impossible to deny. For the first time in his life, Logan Henry was ashamed of what he'd done, and he didn't like the feeling. That made the rest of his story harsher than he intended.

"Yes, and she gave it out, willingly. She was hot, and I wanted it, but I knew it was a mistake. When I tried to break it off with her, she got hysterical. The next thing I know, she's telling me she's pregnant. We had a terrible fight. I told her that a baby wouldn't keep me with her. Nothing would do that. I didn't love her. I didn't want her. I gave her ten thousand dollars. Told her to get rid of the baby and get out of my life."

The pain swelled inside Chance's heart. He'd always known that he'd been unwanted. But hearing it said aloud, in such a manner . . .

"Maybe she did," Chance said. "Maybe I'm some other man's kid. Didn't you ever think of that?"

"Yeah," Logan said. "And I tried to tell myself that the day a letter and a picture from Letty arrived in the mail. Your baby pictures and mine were so alike, even I couldn't tell them apart. I was furious with her for tricking me. I thought she'd gotten rid of . . ."

It dawned on Logan how careless his opinion of Chance's life had been. How selfish and cruel he'd been in wanting to end another life just to make his easier.

He flushed, unable to meet the look in the young man's eyes. "Anyway, I found out she'd used the money to buy a house, and had you instead. I never spoke to her again. Oh . . . I saw you once or twice later . . . by accident, but she didn't know it. I knew who you were, and I knew what I'd done to her. But, dammit . . . there were never any promises between us. And she knew I was married. At least she did by the time she got herself pregnant. It wasn't my fault."

Chance's skin crawled. He'd spent his entire life in a

house that this son-of-a-bitch had paid for. He wanted to throw up.

"Look," Logan said. "I always knew where you were. I should have said something sooner . . . maybe paid to—"

Chance doubled up his fist and then took a step backward. This had to stop. He spat blood in the dust at Logan's feet and pointed a shaky finger at him.

"I don't want anything from you. Not now, not ever. Don't think just because you've been caught, that it's going to cost you. Believe me, living down the fact that you're my father is going to be harder for me than for you. I always told myself that he was probably just some 'good old boy' having himself a Saturday night fling. I don't want to face the fact that the man who spawned me is a genuine bastard. You leave *me* alone! *I'm* the one who doesn't want to be bothered. Not by the likes of you."

He turned and staggered, then caught himself by holding onto the fender. Somehow, he managed to crawl into Charlie's car. He didn't see the look of pain sweeping over Logan Henry's face. And if he had he wouldn't have cared. Everything inside Chance was cold and dead.

Chance turned the corner of his street and stopped his pickup truck, letting it idle as he tried to get up the courage to go inside his house and face his mother.

He'd returned Charlie's car and retrieved his old truck without detection. It had taken all of his strength just to walk from one vehicle to the other. Every bone in his body ached from the beating he'd taken tonight. The tuxedo he'd rented would probably have to be burned. They'd never get out all this blood. But the tux was the least of his worries. Confronting his mother would be the hardest thing he'd ever done in his life. He had to hear the truth from her lips before he'd be completely and totally convinced that what he'd learned tonight was true. Then, and only then, could he face the world knowing that Victoria Henry would be off limits forever.

As luck would have it, Letty McCall walked into the kitchen and turned on the light as Chance walked in the front door.

"Dear Lord," she whispered and stepped forward. "Chance, what happened to you?"

The pain inside him was so great that his answer came out without thought. "I met my father," he drawled. "Hell of a guy."

Letty staggered. Her face paled and she reached out. He stepped back, unwilling to be touched. As badly as he'd been beaten, the pain inside him was worse.

"What are you saying?" Letty whispered. "Where did you go tonight? How do you know . . . ?"

"You want to know where I've been?" Chance shouted, and then winced at the pain in his jaw. "I'll tell you where I've been. The same place I've been for the last few months. With a girl. And do you want to know who she is, Mother?"

Letty shook her head. The look on her son's face was scaring her to death.

"Well, I'm going to tell you anyway," Chance said, and jabbed his finger into his mother's shoulder. "For the past few months I've been busy falling in love with my sister. Isn't that a hoot?"

"No. . . . Dear Sweet Lord," Letty moaned, and covered her face with her hands. "Are you sure it—"

"Her name was Victoria Henry, Mom. Does that ring a bell?"

"Logan!" The name came out in a whisper. Letty sank down into a crouching position on the cracked linoleum.

It was all he'd needed to hear, and what he'd feared most. The bastard had been telling the truth! Chance's heart turned to stone. Every instinct he had told him to get out before he said something he'd later regret, but the pain he'd been dealt made him want to hit back.

"So! It's true. You screwed the bastard, got yourself pregnant, and then tried to trick him into marrying you."

"Chance! You don't understand. I loved—"

"Don't even say it," Chance said. The hurt inside him kept growing. "Don't tell me anything about that man. I don't want to hear it. I just want to know one thing. Why the hell didn't you do what he wanted you to do? Why didn't you get rid of me, Mom? Why did you keep me and then drag us both through all this hell?"

Letty began to cry. Her head dropped to her knees as she curled herself up into a tiny ball.

Chance was too far gone to recognize her distress. He turned and started out of the house.

"Where are you going?" she begged. "Come back. You need to let me doctor those—"

"I don't need anything. Not from you. Not from anyone. And I've spent the last night I'll ever spend underneath a roof that Logan Henry paid for."

He walked out of the house, ignoring his mother's pleas to come back, and crawled into the back of his pickup truck. It might be dirty, and it was damn sure hard. But it wasn't as dirty as he felt inside, and not nearly as hard as the knot in his gut.

He needed to cry, but the tears wouldn't come. There were too many aches to let him focus on the one in his heart. It was only after the sun awakened him the next morning that the tears fell. And then they were not for him. They were for what was left of his mother, who'd ended her life as his had begun: without thought.

13

Charlie Rollins was running. The first customer he'd had when he opened up had been his last. The gossip had spread through Odessa fast. Bad news always did. The man who'd wanted gas had also wanted a reaction from Charlie. He knew the McCall boy worked for him. People were saying that the kid had been beat up bad and his mother was dead. People were saying that Chance had killed her by accident during a fight. People were talking. Charlie was running.

A police car was still outside the house, as well as an ambulance and the coroner's car. A sick feeling grew in the pit of his stomach. Chance was like a son to him. And growing up in a place like this, with a mother like Letty . . . it didn't bear thinking about.

He ducked under the taped off area around the house that indicated the place was still under investigation, and started toward the door.

"Hey! You can't go in there!" a policeman yelled.

Charlie kept on walking.

"Didn't you hear me?" the policeman repeated. "I said you—"

Chance walked out of the door . . . alone. Charlie stopped in mid-step and swallowed.

His face! What had happened to this boy? Yesterday he'd been a kid, excited about going to a damn high school dance. Today, a cold, hard man was all that was left of the Chance that he'd known.

Chance looked up. Charlie was standing just a few feet away. The pain that had frozen in his eyes began to melt. He shuddered and started to speak, but the words wouldn't come.

"Dammit, boy. Come here," he said. Chance walked into his arms.

The comfort was awkward, as it always is between men, but the feelings were sincere and Chance could feel it. He wrapped his arms around the smaller man's shoulders and hung on. Words wouldn't come. Only the pain flowed, and with it came the tears that he couldn't spill last night.

"She's dead, Charlie. It's my fault. I might as well have put a gun to her head and pulled the trigger."

"I don't understand," Charlie said, as he pulled away and drew Chance down to sit on the curb. "What happened? And what in hell happened to you? Did she do that or . . . ?"

Chance smiled through his tears and scared the hell out of him. Charlie'd never seen so much hate and bitterness in one man in his life.

"Oh hell no," Chance said softly. "My mother didn't do this. My father did."

Charlie's mouth dropped. "Your . . . But I thought . . . What made him . . . ?" He cursed and spat. "Who is he? I'm gonna take a bat to the son-of-a-bitch and he's gonna know the reason why." He jumped to his feet and began pacing a circle in front of Chance.

"Who is he? That's going with me to my grave, Charlie. He doesn't deserve to be named."

Charlie felt the boy's pain as vividly as if it were his own. "Did he hurt your momma, too?"

Chance smiled. The same sick feeling of dread slipped over Charlie again. This boy was ready to kill. He could smell it.

"Yeah, he hurt my mother, a long time ago. I guess me and every other sorry man walking just finished her off."

Charlie knelt down in front of him. "I don't want to hear you talk like that. You, above all others, have stood by that woman when she didn't deserve it. And don't argue with me about that. You know I'm talking the truth."

Chance shrugged.

"I don't know what happened between you and your momma last night, but I know you wasn't to blame. I know you better than that."

Chance looked up. Charlie Rollins was the only man who'd ever believed in him. But for Charlie, he would have been on the streets years ago, searching for happiness in a bottle, and looking for an easy way out of the constant poverty—just as Letty had done.

"She's dead because she swallowed a bottle of pills and chased it with a fifth of whiskey. And she did that because of what I said to her. I'll never believe anything different."

"I can't change your mind," Charlie said. "Only time will do that. But I can help you make the necessary decisions."

Chance stared. Decisions?

"Her funeral for one, and where you're gonna live for another."

It was the word *funeral* that tipped the scales. Chance staggered to his feet and just made it to the tree across the street before his stomach heaved . . . and heaved . . . and heaved. And then Charlie's arms were around him, pulling him away from the end of his world.

"Dear Lord, we inter this precious woman to the earth from whence she came. Ashes to . . ."

The minister's voice droned as Chance blocked out every sound save the one of clods of earth falling onto the lid of the coffin that would be his mother's final home. Thoughts of his mother and heaven together were incongruous. They'd lived in hell on earth. It only stood to reason that they'd spend eternity in the same place.

He stared, dry-eyed and hollow, listening to the sounds of the minister's voice but unable to absorb the words. Everything around him was surreal . . . larger than life. It was like watching himself in a play. Any minute now someone would yell "cut," and things would be back to normal. But no one yelled. And no one cried for Letty McCall.

The only people in attendance other than Chance were Charlie Rollins and his wife, three drunks from

Crosby's bar, the night shift bartender, and a trucker who'd been passing through. Letty's funeral was not a social success. It figured. Neither was her life.

"Boy," Charlie said to him after the short ceremony, "me and the wife have talked it over. We want you to come stay with us until you decide what you want to do. It ain't like we think you can't manage on your own. You've been doin' that anyway. We just—"

"Thanks, Charlie," Chance said quietly. "But I don't think I'll be staying in Odessa. This is the last place I need to be." Thoughts of running into Victoria made him sick. Thoughts of killing Logan Henry were too vivid to ignore. If he stayed, he'd only wind up in trouble.

Charlie nodded. He'd suspected as much. But losing Chance was like losing his own son.

"I understand, boy. Really I do. But you've got to keep in touch. I won't let you go without that promise."

Chance tried to smile, but it didn't quite reach his eyes, and his mouth hurt too much to push the issue. His face was just beginning to heal. It had taken two days before he could swallow without tasting blood. He'd get well—Charlie had taken him to a doctor for that assurance. But the secrets inside him would fester . . . and fester . . . and he'd never heal. Not from those. Never from those.

Just thinking of Victoria brought on guilt and sadness. Remembering his mother made him sick. What he'd said to her had hurt her enough that she hadn't wanted to live.

"I won't make promises I can't keep, Charlie. You know me better than that."

"Well hell, boy, then take care of yourself. I'll miss you."

Chance hugged the man and suffered a kiss from his wife, but the words went in one ear and out the other. He was as dead inside as the woman they'd just put to rest. He watched the mourners leave. Finally, they were gone. He stared down at the dirt at his feet and tried not to think of his mother buried beneath it.

"What are you going to do?"

The words rang in his ears. He looked up, unable to believe the gall of the man beside him.

"You have no business here," Chance said, and stuffed his hands in his pockets to keep from putting them in the man's face.

Logan Henry frowned. This was worse than he could have imagined. After their fight, he'd never envisioned that even more of this boy's world would collapse. It had taken harsh, accusing words from his wife, and a daughter near death, to make him realize that every ounce of blame lay on him.

"Do you need money?"

Chance stepped forward. "Now you ask? Now that she doesn't have to lay on her back to get the money to feed us? Now that she won't have to turn another trick to keep the gas from being turned off in winter?" He took a deep breath and pointed down. "You ask her if she needs any money. I don't want a damn thing from you!"

Logan was hurting too. And when he hurt, just like Chance, he lashed out at whoever was available.

"Stay away from Victoria," he said.

Chance sneered. "I'm not the low-life you are, mister.

I wouldn't do that to her. You just keep your hands to yourself. You hit her again . . . I'll know it."

Logan flushed. "I didn't mean to hit her. It was an accident. I've never laid a hand on her in my life." And then he took a deep breath and let the words fall out before he changed his mind. "She tried to kill herself."

Chance turned pale. "My God," he mumbled, as his knees went weak. "Is she . . ."

"She's alive. And she'll be fine. It was the shock . . . I think." His voice shook. "I've got to find a way to make it up to her," he said. "In time, she'll understand. She has to."

Chance saw the guilt that Logan Henry was bearing. He wanted to enjoy the fact that the man who'd ruined his mother's life was in pain. He needed the satisfaction of knowing that he wouldn't rest easy again in this lifetime, but all he could do was weep.

"Victoria may never understand why you were such a bastard," Chance said, as a single tear ran down his face. He stared at the mound of earth that was quickly drying to a hard shell over the only family he'd ever known. "*She* didn't."

Logan looked at the grave and wanted to take back the last twenty years of his life and do them all over again. But it was too late . . . for everything.

"Where are you going?" he asked, as he watched Chance walk away.

"I'm leaving you here to face your ghosts," Chance said. "And I hope you rot in hell alongside them."

The moon was up, shining a weak, quarter glow on the overgrown yard and the rusty pickup parked on the street in front of the house. Chance walked through the rooms, occasionally opening a drawer, looking in a closet, making certain that he'd taken everything he would possibly need.

Only yesterday one of the neighbors had knocked on the door and callously inquired as to what Chance intended to do with his mother's things. Chance had slammed the door in her face. He already knew what he was going to do with their things. What he couldn't take, he wouldn't leave behind.

His suitcase was packed. Several things he'd simply left on hangers and dumped in a pile in the seat of the truck. He had his wallet, what little money he'd saved from his last paycheck, and his high school yearbook. It was a strange combination of choices, but understandable when he thought about it. They were the only things of value that he owned, that Logan Henry hadn't indirectly provided. He wanted nothing from the man.

A strange anxiety seized him. It was time! Suddenly he couldn't get away fast enough. He grabbed the can he'd brought from the station and began walking through the house, methodically pouring a thin, steady stream of gasoline on and over everything. Walls and floors, furniture and clothing; nothing escaped his treatment.

He walked out of the house, tossed the empty can into the back of his truck, and stood for a moment in the shadows of the yard, watching the house take its last breaths. He shuddered, dug into his pocket, and pulled out a book of matches. They were from Charlie's Gas and Guzzle. He stepped up onto the porch, kicked the door open, and yanked the safety match across the pad. It flared instantly. Chance gave it a toss and then ran.

The air inside the house ignited before the match ever hit the floor. Chance reached the pickup just as the first window blew, shattering glass and wood across the front yard. He started the truck, put it in gear, and accelerated. The glow of the flames was bright in the rear view mirror over the dashboard. The hair on the back of his arms smelled singed where he'd come too close to the flames. Chance McCall had just burned every bridge connecting him to Odessa. He headed out of town with the sound of sirens fading away behind him. It was time to leave. He never looked back.

"Hey, good lookin'," the waitress teased, "what'll it be this morning? We've got a special. Pancakes and sausage, all you can eat for two ninety-nine."

Chance nodded. She was becoming a familiar, almost comfortable part of his life, even though he still didn't know her name. He wondered how many other good people were still in this town that he'd never had the pleasure of meeting.

The town had become almost familiar, too. He'd gotten used to its flatness and even welcomed the wind, knowing that by evening it would be nothing but a cool reminder of the dying day. Every morning he awoke with a feeling of anticipation, hoping that this would be the day that his problems would be resolved and that he could go home to Jenny. But every day turned into the next and then the next, and he was starting to worry. Maybe he should just call it quits and go back.

He fiddled with the steaming cup of coffee in front of him, waiting for it to be cool enough to drink. The early morning sun bounced off the windshield of a car that had just pulled up in front of the diner. It flashed directly into Chance's eyes. He blinked, tilted his head to get away from the sun's rays, and then stared at the woman getting out of the car.

She was tall and blond, about his age, and wore her years and her money well. The stiff breeze outlined the long legs beneath her dress as she fought the wind gusts and her skirt. Her other arm was wrapped around her hair, trying to hold it in place. Neither was succeeding. Chance started to smile at her struggles and then he saw her face.

Coffee sloshed over the side of the cup. A pain shot through his head, single and swift. Just as suddenly as it had appeared, it was gone. A sense of dread began to take hold. He'd felt it once before, when he'd learned that Letty McCall had committed suicide. He held his breath, resisted the urge to bolt, and watched the woman walk into the diner. She was heading for his booth.

"My God! I thought you were dead! You left without a word . . . and never came back. I thought you were dead!"

Her voice shook as she slipped into the other side of the booth and slid her fingers across his hand. The look on his face made her jerk back in surprise. He looked as if he didn't know her. "I'm sorry if I've made a mistake. But . . . you are . . . your name *is* Chance McCall . . . isn't it?" she asked.

Chance took a deep breath. He'd come to Odessa for

this reason. He'd wanted to locate someone who knew him. It was the only way he'd ever be able to find himself. But now that the opportunity was here, his fear of knowing the truth increased.

Victoria couldn't understand this distance between them. Yes, one relationship had ended between them, but there was still another that she desperately wanted to salvage.

"I'm Chance McCall," he answered.

"I knew it," she cried. "I couldn't be that wrong about someone I knew so well."

Chance didn't want to hear this. Thoughts of Jenny overwhelmed him. What if he'd left a wife behind . . . or children? He'd never considered that possibility. The idea of not being able to claim Jenny Tyler made him sick.

Victoria was stunned. She hadn't expected a cold shoulder. Not from Chance. They'd shared so much as victims of the same twist of fate. Surely he wasn't blaming her, too?

"Chance? What's wrong? Don't you recognize me? I know it's been twelve years, but I can't have changed that much." She tried to smile, but it died when she saw the look in his eyes.

"I'm sorry," he said, "but I don't know you. Should I?"

"Yes, dammit," she said softly, and waved away a waitress who'd started toward their booth. "You *should* know me. I'm Victoria!" And then she hesitated before adding, "I'm your sister!"

The pain behind his eyes surfaced upon impact. Beads of sweat appeared on his forehead as he pulled himself up from the booth. A persistent feeling of doom lent strength to his legs as he walked away. He stepped out onto the sidewalk, threw his head back, and drew long, slow breaths into his lungs. *A sister? I have family? Why don't I believe her? Yet what could she possibly have to gain by lying?* And then another thought struck him. She said her name was Victoria? The girl in the picture was Victoria. He'd left the picture in his room.

Getting that picture suddenly became all important. He didn't think, he just reacted. He started across the street, heading for his room at the motel.

"Chance! Wait! I don't understand," she called. "You've got to let me explain." She was behind him. He could hear her running to keep up.

He unlocked the door. The school yearbook was on the table, and the picture beside it. He grabbed the picture and turned to her. "It's you, isn't it?"

Victoria was out of breath and nearly out of patience. She hadn't slept a wink since Della had called her from the courthouse. She'd talked way into the night with her husband, Ken, before deciding that this meeting must take place. She wanted to shout in frustration when it dawned on her that he was sincere. She took the picture out of his hand and stared.

"My God! You've had this all that time? Yes, it's me," she said. "But I don't understand. You have this picture, yet you pretend not to know me?" Her voice was thick with hurt.

There was nothing to say but the truth, and hope to hell that it made things better.

"I'm not pretending," he said. "A few months ago I was injured. When I finally recovered, everything was back in place except my memory." He took a deep breath and then blurted the rest of it out in a rush. "I've even had to take someone's word that I'm Chance McCall. I don't remember. The doctor kept telling me to be patient. That it would all come back when it was time. But time was running out. There's a woman I love very much, who deserves more than bits and pieces of a man. I came back, hoping that this place or someone I found here would trigger the memories. Until today, I'd just about given up."

It hurt her to hear him say that he loved another woman. Once he'd said the same to her. And then her conscience and reason surfaced. Jealousy didn't belong in their relationship anymore. "So, do you remember me now?" Victoria asked.

"No. But you're the first person who's remembered me. I was beginning to think I hadn't mattered to a living soul. I guess when you recognized me, I got rattled. Sorry I ran out on you."

He waited, willing her to accept him. There was nothing else he could say or do to make it easier for both of them.

But Victoria knew what to do. "Oh, Chance. You mattered. You always did. Come here. I've waited twelve years to do this." She gave him a quick hug.

Her touch was gentle, and unobtrusive, and for some reason, familiar. Chance took a deep breath. "My sister?"

For a moment, Victoria remembered more, but now was not the time. It would be better if he remembered that on his own. And it might be better if he didn't remember that at all.

"Yes, darling. Your sister. Welcome home."

His arms slid around her shoulders. He closed his eyes and finally relaxed.

Jenny Tyler drove into Odessa with a new understanding of the man she'd known as Chance McCall. This country he'd come from was so different from hers. Here it was all flat and open, with nowhere to hide. Nowhere except inside one's self, and Chance had been good at that.

She pulled up to the pump at a gas station and parked. An attendant hurried out, wearing greasy coveralls and a smile.

"What'll it be, miss?" he asked. "Fill 'er up?"

Jenny nodded.

"How ya'll doin'?" he asked.

Jenny smiled. People were certainly friendly here. It made her feel just a tiny bit better. The hole in her heart was badly in need of patching, and a friendly face helped.

"I'm doing fine," Jenny said. "Maybe you could help me locate an address. I'm looking for a motel."

"You bet," the man answered as he finished wiping the windshield. "There's the usual chain motels. And there's a couple that come to mind that are privately owned. There's the Best Western Garden Oasis or maybe the Parkway Inn. Want me to tell you how to get there?"

"No," Jenny said. "I already have an address. I just need directions. Here it is," she said, and handed the scrap of paper out the window.

The man frowned, looked at Jenny and then back at

the paper. "I don't think you'll be happy staying there, miss," he said. And then he hesitated, obviously loath to criticize his own hometown, before his better judgment overcame his pride. "In fact, I'd like to ask you to reconsider your choice, miss. This place doesn't exactly cater to your type of clientele. They go more for the 'hourly' customers, instead of the overnight ones, if you get my meaning." He almost blushed as Jenny smiled.

"Thank you," she said. "But I don't intend to stay there. I'm just looking for a friend. This was the last address I was given."

"Oh!" He nodded, satisfied that he'd given her sufficient warning, and handed back the paper. "Well, then you'll be wanting to take a left at the next stoplight. That motel is about nine or ten blocks down on the left-hand side of Second Street. Good luck to you. And you owe me twelve-fifty for the gas."

Jenny paid and drove away. Anticipation was mounting. She knew it might be a bad time to catch Chance. But she didn't care if she had to wait all day. One way or another, she was going to see him . . . and soon.

Her excitement gave way to a growing fear that if and when she found him, he might be angry, even furious, that she'd followed him. But she didn't care. She had the right.

The motel was exactly where the attendant had claimed it would be. And the reputation at which he'd hinted was obvious. She'd never seen such a seedy, run-down place. It was hard for her to believe that Chance had chosen it.

She turned in and parked by the office. There was a truck in the lot that looked just like his. Her heartbeat accelerated. She took a deep breath, grabbed her purse, and started toward the office, then turned back and locked her car. It was instinctive.

The row of dead bugs lying against the outside wall of the building did nothing to assure her that there were not countless live ones running about inside. She pushed the door open and walked up to the counter.

"It's twenty dollars," the desk clerk said. "It don't matter whether it's for an hour or all night. Twenty dollars."

Jenny stared. She hadn't seen horn-rimmed glasses in years. And that particular shade of peroxide-blond hair must have been painful. It was the only way to describe the translucent white fuzz teased in all directions. And then she remembered her manners.

"I don't want a room. I want to know what room Chance McCall is in."

"Oh, I'm sorry," the clerk answered, "but we aren't allowed to give out that information."

Jenny's eyebrows rose, and she stared, persistently, watching the woman's gum that slipped from one side of her mouth to the other as she chewed.

The clerk fidgeted. She didn't know how to argue with someone who wouldn't talk. Finally she added, "It's nothing personal, you understand. I'm sure you're a real nice lady and all, but I have to answer to paying customers. They have a right to privacy, you know."

Still Jenny said nothing. She stepped up to the counter, stared at the wall of keys hanging in plain view, and noted that only one was missing, twelve B. It was a place to start. If she had to, she'd knock on every door in the place until she found him. She'd been afraid for too long, and come too far to be stopped now.

"Never mind," Jenny said. "I'll find him myself."

"Now you wait a minute," the woman called. "I might just have to call the police."

"Go ahead," Jenny said. "Call them. And then call Chance McCall and tell him that you just had Jenny arrested. And then . . . I suggest you get out of town while you can. He won't be happy."

The clerk remembered the man in twelve B. She'd already been witness to his temper. She had no intention of suffering the same fate again.

"Fine," she said, and turned away. "Just don't blame me if something happens to you. That man ain't friendly. Not one damn bit."

Jenny smiled to herself. That was her Chance. He was still here. She hurried down the cracked walkway, searching the numbers on the doors as she ran. Some numbers were missing, some were hanging by a hint and a promise. One door was open . . . standing ajar. Twelve B! This was the one.

"Chance?" she called as she pushed the door all the way open.

For the longest time, she stood frozen, staring at the tall couple entwined in each other's arms, one blond and female, the other dark and very familiar looking. A pain hung suspended just behind her heart, making it very difficult to catch her breath. Her legs began to shake, her eyes filled. But it wasn't despair that erupted. It was anger. In pure, unadulterated, Tyler form.

"You must be real desperate, honey." She enunciated with venom in every syllable. "It's not even Saturday night and you're already at it."

Her accusation sent the couple spinning around, surprised by the sound of a woman's voice. Victoria stepped back in shock at the sight of a furious woman standing in the doorway. But Chance grinned. He started toward Jenny with arms outstretched.

"Jenny! How did you—"

"None of your damn business, Chance McCall. How dare you? How dare you run off without a word? How dare you do this to—"

Chance caught her and pulled her into his arms. He mashed her face against his chest and began to laugh. "I missed you, Jenny. I don't know how in hell you found me, but I've never been so glad to see anyone in my entire life."

Victoria watched the couple's greeting with a trace of envy. She knew that she'd just met the woman who'd claimed her brother's heart, and it was up to her to smooth out this misunderstanding before it got worse. Chance had suffered enough at the hands of her family. If she had to, she'd spend the rest of her life making certain that it never happened again.

"Damn you, Chance! You left me. You didn't even have the guts to tell me you were going, you just left." Jenny's words were muffled, her voice accusing. She was struggling hopelessly against the firm grip in which she was being held. Her fists hammered against his chest. "And now, I find you wrapped in some floozy's arms. Why is it always someone else? Why do you—"

"I'm sorry," Victoria said, as she walked up beside the couple. "I think it's my time to make an exit. Please," she said, gently touching Jenny's back. "It's not what you think. He's my brother!"

Jenny's struggles ceased. "Brother?"

"I guess so," Chance said softly, and pressed a kiss on her forehead. "I have to take her word for it. Just like I took yours, Jenny. Do you understand?"

Jenny's breath exited her body in a whoosh. Suddenly the adrenaline that had sent her flying into the room in a frenzy left her weak and shaking. She nodded. It was then she realized that he still had no memory.

"I'll see you tomorrow, Chance. And Jenny . . . I look forward to meeting you when we're all under less . . . stress?" Victoria smiled. "I'll see myself out."

The door shut behind her. And then they were alone. Jenny was right where she needed to be. In the arms of Chance McCall.

14

Jenny began to cry. Not loudly. Not at first. The tears slid out of the corners of her eyes and down her face. It was Chance's groan of regret that sent a sob bubbling up. When he wrapped her in his arms and lifted her off her feet, she finally gave in to the pain.

"You left me," she sobbed, pounding weakly against his chest with her fists.

"I know, baby," he said softly. "And if I had it to do all over again, I'd bring you with me."

"You didn't call. You didn't write." She tried to push away from him, but his grip tightened. She gave his chest one last thump and then collapsed into his arms.

"I know, Jenny," he answered. "If I could change that, I would. But I can't. All I can do is ask you to forgive me. Okay?"

She moaned as he pressed against her, reminding

them both that their bodies were awakening to a deeper need.

"Please, Jenny. As God is my witness, I did it for you. For us. I couldn't think of a way to tell you how I felt without compromising you with a past I didn't remember. Do you understand?"

"No," she said. "But I'll accept it as long as you promise you'll come home with me." Her voice lowered, her hands touching him constantly as she continued. "I nearly didn't survive this stunt, mister. I can't bear another."

There was something about the way she said it that made Chance know there was more to her statement than just physical longing. He tilted her face up and stared deeply into her eyes, for the first time since her arrival really looking at the woman in his arms. It was then that he saw the tiny cuts and scratches on her face, and the healing bruise on her lip. His stomach turned. Something had happened to Jenny and he hadn't been there to help. She'd been hurt and suffered . . . alone.

"What in hell happened to your face?" His voice was dark, his tone ominous. He pinned her against the wall, turning her face in first one direction and then the other, searching the surface for every telltale mark.

Jenny shrugged. She felt his body tensing, and knew it would only be a matter of moments before he got it out of her. She'd never been able to keep a thing from him.

"What happened, sweetheart? Did you have a car wreck?"

She shook her head and tried to bury her face in the

curve of his shoulder. He grabbed her by the chin and turned her, firmly, but gently, back around to face him.

"Did you fall . . . or have you . . . ?" Suddenly a thought occurred, and it was one he didn't like. One that sent cold chills through him.

"Jenny, look at me! Did you ride that goddamned horse?"

She didn't even have to answer. He could see it in her eyes. "What were you trying to do, kill yourself?" She hesitated a fraction of a second too long for his peace of mind. He held her, desperate for her denial. "Tell me that's not the truth! Tell me I didn't do that to you! Please . . . Jenny!"

The torment in his voice shamed her. She threaded her fingers in his hair, pulled his face down to hers and whispered, "I promise, Chance. I wasn't intentionally trying to hurt myself. I was just at my wits' end. I didn't think. I just reacted."

"My God!" he whispered. "If anything had happened to you . . ."

He took instant possession of her lips, smothering her sigh of relief. She was soft, compliant, and at the same time on fire. He could feel it as she moved beneath him, giving him access to any or all of her that he desired. It was so giving, and so loving a gesture, he didn't even try to resist.

"I want to make love to you, Jenny. If I've learned anything these past few days, it's that I don't have to have my memory back to know I love you."

A sob caught in the back of her throat. She'd waited a lifetime to hear those words. "Thank God for small favors," she whispered. And then Chance descended.

They tore at the clothing that lay between them, buttons, snaps, zippers . . . unbuttoned, unfastened, undone. A sob drifted through the quiet, and then a whispered endearment, a gentling of the emotions that had flared.

Jenny had one swift moment of panic, knowing that there was still a secret between them of which Chance was not aware. He thought that they'd been lovers. In Jenny's heart, it had been so. But their bodies had never shared what was about to happen. Jenny had no intention of revealing prematurely what would soon be obvious enough. By then, she hoped and prayed that Chance would be too far gone to care.

Chance slipped the blouse from her arms, letting it fall to the floor below. His fingers slid across her skin and then around, unfastening the catch on her bra with one smooth, slick, snap. He held his breath as her breasts spilled into his hands, willing himself not to think about the growing passions of his own body. Jenny was driving him into a need he couldn't control. She sighed and moved beneath his touch and sent his senses reeling.

"Jennifer Ann, I'm about to love you in a way you've never known. In a way you'll never forget."

You have no idea how true your words are, Chance.

The last of their clothes fell to the floor. Chance lifted her into his arms and carried her to the bed. He laid her down and then almost lost what control he had left as she coiled herself around him like the tendril of vine. Her arms and her legs, her hands and her mouth . . . they encompassed and completed him.

Chance moved across her body, pressing her down

into the mattress, reveling in the feel of silky skin and body heat, the moans of satisfaction as his mouth moved across her face, her neck, her breasts, and then her stomach. His hands began a foray at the back of her knees and around, sliding up and down, around and behind, slowly, sensuously, seeking, touching.

And then his mouth and his hands met at the core of Jenny and she felt the need to tell him, to say that the joy he was giving her was more than she'd dreamed, and still not enough. But coherency was impossible. Her body moved of its own accord, a puppet to the sensuality that Chance had unleashed. She moaned, she begged. She arched up to meet the touch, and then dissolved as her nerves came alive beneath the strokes of his fingers. His name became a chant, a cry for completion.

Chance couldn't think. He could only feel. Jenny's body was hot beneath his mouth and hands. She moved against him in a fevered need. His blood thundered, his heart pounded. Every muscle in his body was rock hard and tense. She slid her hands downward and grasped his shoulders to urge him up. His breath came in thick, tortured gasps as he tried desperately to control himself as he moved above her.

"I love you, Jenny. Never forget . . ."

What she did next drove everything else from his mind. There was nothing left but sensation . . . and Jenny.

Her hands caressed his hard aching manhood as she opened beneath him. She guided him down, and then lifted herself up, an offering he could not refuse.

He plunged . . . and then froze. For a heartbeat he

thought he'd imagined the resistance. But the swift look of pain that came and went on her face told him he hadn't imagined a thing.

"What the hell . . . ?"

There was no time for answers. Jenny began to move beneath him, and he forgot the words. He forgot everything but the wild, wet heat and her hands on his back. The feel of her mouth and her legs wrapped around him. And then Chance . . . and the bed . . . and the world rocked on its axis.

Jenny felt it coming. It was more than she'd imagined. The feeling was spiraling from somewhere around her heart downward, building in intensity as it coiled low in the pit of her stomach.

The iron hard thrust of Chance's body as it moved in and out, over and over, was focusing the feeling into one, huge, aching need.

And then, before she had time to prepare, it was there and she fell. She fell up and then down, lost in the black space of a little death that had come at the hands of Chance McCall. She called his name aloud, once, and then the fall ended as he caught and held her, tightly, and securely, and loved her all the way back down.

He was so quiet. It had been almost an hour since they'd fallen into each other's arms, replete from the intensity of their lovemaking. Not a word had passed between them.

Jenny knew that a reckoning was due. She'd seen the knowledge that she'd been a virgin nearly pull him undone. And then everything had vanished but the passion between them. Then there had been room for nothing else. Now was a different story.

She ventured a quick glance upward. Her heart stopped. He was staring at the ceiling overhead with a look of total disbelief on his face.

"Chance?"

"What could you possibly have to say that will explain that away, Jenny?"

"You have to understand . . ."

"What kills me," he whispered, "is wondering what other damned lies you've told me that I've yet to uncover." He rolled her over on her back, pinning her down with his body and a stare.

Jenny pushed herself out from under him, leaped out of the bed, and pointed at him in accusation.

"Lies? There were no lies between us. You *were* the only man who'd ever shown me passion. You *were* the only man who'd ever made that kind of love to me. But, unfortunately for me, it was one-sided. You made me take, but you wouldn't let me give. I hated you for what you made me feel alone, when all I wanted was to share what I'd saved for you!" Her dark hair tumbled around her face, hiding her tears.

Chance was dumbstruck. "Why, Jenny? Why did I do that?"

"I don't know," she moaned, and buried her face in her hands.

Chance pulled her back down beside him, cradling her as he whispered, "I'm sorry, baby. And I guess it doesn't matter whether this was the first or the fortieth time we've made love. I just know it won't be the last. Ever since I left the Triple T, you've been in my thoughts all day, and my dreams all night. In fact you should be getting worried now, lady." He pulled gently at a curl beside her ear.

Jenny wrapped her arms around his chest and sniffed. "Why? What do I have to be worried about?"

"I'm seriously considering the idea of never getting out of bed again," he drawled. Before she knew it, he'd lifted her up and then lowered her down, moving within her in a gentle, teasing manner.

Jenny's mouth formed a perfect O as she slipped over him in one smooth motion. His hands held her down on him, unwilling to release her, yet unable to resist the plea in her eyes. Relenting, he let her move just once, testing, teasing, and then it was no longer a game. Just as he'd feared. Just as he'd hoped.

Chance watched her body above him until he could no longer focus, until he could no longer feel the silken heat around him. All he could do was hang on as his body erupted, spilling into the woman who'd given herself to him.

Fire danced across the wall in front of him, trapping him with flames that licked and singed. A woman's laughter turned into screams. His breathing became labored as he ran. A finger pointed accusingly, but he couldn't see the face behind the hand. Someone called his name, aloud! Over and over. He turned, trying to see, trying to help . . .

"Chance, please!" Jenny was shaking him gently, trying to pull him out of the nightmare that obviously held him in its spell. "Wake up! You're dreaming!"

He sat straight up in bed, coming awake instantly, drenched in sweat. The room was dark, the shadows on the walls coming from the neon lights that slipped through the loosely woven curtains. Curses fell from his lips, slowly and methodically, as he staggered from the bed and headed for the bathroom. *God in heaven, would this never end?*

Jenny was shocked. She knew that he'd been suffering, but not to this extent. The fact that he'd gone off on his own began to make sense. For the first time since he'd left the ranch, she almost understood his need to know his past.

Oblivious to her nudity, she quickly followed him into the bathroom and stood in the doorway as he leaned over the sink and slapped water onto his sweaty face.

"Can I help?" she asked.

Her voice was quiet. It settled the boiling intensity in his gut almost instantly.

"I'm sorry," he said. "It's just more of the same as far as my mind goes. I can't remember a damn thing during the day. But when night comes, and I try to sleep, I think everything stored in my memory tries to come back at once. And I don't have a point of reference to keep it all sorted. It's like watching thirty years of living fast forwarded into thirty seconds." His voice deepened as he grabbed for a towel. "Scary as hell."

"Sounds to me like you need a change of scenery." She waved her hand at the faded wallpaper and rusty spigot in the bath.

"No, Jenny. What I need is you." The fact that they were standing mere inches away from each other, stark naked and available, overwhelmed him. "Come here. I think we could both use a cooling off period." He pulled her into his arms and walked them into the shower.

As usual, the flow came out one measure stronger than a trickle. Yet Jenny gasped as the shock of the cold water hit the middle of her back . . . and then gasped again as Chance's hands followed the water's path, turning her slowly, around and around, letting the water catch her cheek, run down her neck and across her breasts, and then slide between their bodies and down the front of their legs. Everywhere the water went, Chance was sure to go.

She'd witnessed his pain as he slept, and was witnessing another pain that was growing as their bodies touched. He was fully erect, pulsing gently against her leg as his hands continued to work their magic on her body. But, this time, it would not be Jenny who received. It would be Jenny who gave. Passion was heavy in his eyes as she reached down and cradled his manhood in her hands.

"Let me," she said.

Chance's breath caught. He tried to speak. Nothing escaped but a moan. Jenny's hands were moving . . . too close . . . for comfort. Her lips slid across his chest, catching droplets of water just before they ran down past his waist, using her mouth and her tongue to torture his senses. Between her hands and her lips, Chance was a lost man.

Jenny's mouth slid down his body and finally covered him. He could do nothing but concentrate on breathing, because what she was doing with her hands and her mouth threatened to stop his heart. All sensations intensified. There was nothing in his world but water buffeting his face, his hands wrapped in the shower curtain as he struggled to stand, and her touch. Then it came—the feeling, the need.

"Jenny!" The word was one, long, cry. It came in the form of a wave that rushed through his body. He moaned, shuddered, and dropped to his knees.

Jenny wrapped her arms around him and clung. The shower continued to sluice. Chance tilted her face away from the water, circling his thumbs across her temples in wonder at the intensity of her giving spirit.

"I love you, Jenny. More than you can ever know. I don't know what's going to happen tomorrow, but I don't care, as long as you're beside me."

"Oh, Chance, for the last twelve years of your life I've been beside you . . . every waking hour of your life. And I've been trying to tell you for years that I'd be willing to do it for the rest of mine."

"My God!" He pulled her up and out of the shower. "And to think I almost lost this."

"You up for more of the same?" Jenny teased as Chance turned off the water.

He turned and stared, mouth slightly agape as he grabbed a towel and began drying her off. "Lord have mercy," he said. "I've created a monster."

"Yes, you have," Jenny said, "an insatiable monster. And this time it's your turn to do all the work. I think I'll just lie back and relax, and enjoy the show."

Chance grinned. "You can try to relax, baby," he promised, "but I don't know how relaxed you're gonna be when I'm through with you. If I don't wind you up tighter than a spring, I'll just have to start over and do it again until I get it right."

"Wipe that smug grin off your face. One thing you don't have to worry about is getting it right, and you know it." Jenny glared. "All I can think of are those Saturday night women you practiced on."

"I have to plead innocent to those women you keep mentioning," Chance whispered, as he laid her down on the bed. "You remember. I don't! All *I* remember is waking up in a hospital and seeing your blue eyes staring down at me with enough love to stop a war. It scared the hell out of me then, and it scares me now, but I'd be a whole lot more frightened if I thought I'd never see them again."

"I'm not going anywhere," Jenny said, threading her fingers through his hair.

"You're telling me," he said as he covered her body with his own.

Chance woke first. He could tell by the sun's rays halfway up the wall, that they'd overslept. He was hot. Possibly because Jenny was stretched out, full length, head to toe, on top of him. Her legs were wrapped on either side of his, her breasts pushing against his chest, her arms dug in beneath his rib cage, holding on for dear life. She'd fallen asleep in his arms. Chance smiled. A man could get used to this.

The phone rang. Startled, Jenny raised up, stared into his laughing face, and then moaned and dropped back onto his chest as he cradled her with one arm and grabbed the phone with the other.

She listened to the rumble of his voice beneath her ear as he talked. His hand absently stroked the ridge of her backbone and Jenny shivered, remembering the depth of loving that had passed between them last night. In fact, she wondered if she'd be able to walk. She was sore in places she hadn't even known existed.

Her mind wandered as he talked, and then began to focus as she realized he was talking to the woman he'd called Victoria. Her entire body tensed. Maybe that lady was his sister, but until Jenny had some kind of proof, she wasn't willing to give her an inch.

"Okay," Chance said, as Victoria ended her apology. "No big deal. We can do the sight-seeing tour tomorrow. Jenny and I need to do a little of our own first, anyway. Call me whenever you're ready to come over. We'll be waiting."

"What?" Jenny asked, as Chance hung up the phone.

Chance grinned. He heard the tension in her voice. She'd never been a good poker player.

"Victoria can't come today after all. Her husband's leaving on a business trip and she needs to get him to the airport and then find a sitter for her children before we do any sight-seeing. She was going to show me some of the places I used to know, hoping that one of them would trigger a memory. I told her that tomorrow was soon enough. I've waited this long. One more day can't matter."

"She's married? She has children?" The relief was obvious in her voice.

"Yes, Miss Nosey. At least that's what she claims. I have no reason to doubt her."

"Well! Good! Then, that settles that!"

Chance laughed.

Jenny tried not to blush, but her conscience got in

the way, and it came sweeping over her in spite of her resolve.

"I'm hungry," Jenny said, trying to change the subject.

"Me too," Chance said, as his laughter dissolved into one last smile. "But I suspect you need to take a long, hot soak before we do anything. You never could do anything by half measures, woman. Last night just proves my point." He rolled her off of him and then got out of bed.

"Where are you going?" Jenny asked, watching his big, nude body with interest.

"To run you a bath, darlin'," he said softly. "I'll wager you feel like you've just ridden horseback for three days running."

Jenny blushed.

"Am I right?"

"Do you always have to be right?" she asked, trying to whitewash her condition with an accusation.

"Only about you, Jenny Tyler. Only about you."

She sighed. "Then run the damn bath. I may never walk again."

Chance smiled gently and then grimaced. "I'm sorry, honey. I should have been more careful. But I can promise you . . . you'll not only walk . . . you'll ride again. And sooner than you think."

He laughed as she blushed once more, then disappeared into the bathroom.

The meal was behind them. It had been rich and satisfying. Pancakes, sausages, twelve kinds of syrup, and enough coffee to wash it all down.

Chance smiled at the satisfaction on Jenny's face as they drove down the street.

She looked around at the neat, tree-lined streets and immaculate landscaping, as they passed houses and businesses. The persistent presence of lawn sprinklers told her that Odessa residents refused to give in to the fact that it often didn't rain more than fourteen inches a year. Their lawns were immaculate . . . and green.

It suddenly occurred to Jenny that Chance wasn't just driving. He obviously had a destination.

"Where are we going?" she asked.

The light in his eyes dimmed and his mouth thinned as he answered, "I want you to meet someone. It's taken a bit of detective work, and I still don't remember it, but it seems I owe a lot to this old fellow we're going to see."

Jenny nodded, scooted a bit closer to Chance, and rested her hand on his thigh. Whatever it took, she was going to help him put his life back together.

The retirement home was the same, still a sad place. But the yard had been mowed, and the shrubbery trimmed. He parked, took a deep breath, and helped Jenny out of his pickup truck.

"This isn't a happy place to be, Jenny. But honestly, I don't think Charlie Rollins knows it."

"Is he . . . ?"

"He has Alzheimer's disease. I know it will progress to the point that he's virtually helpless, but right now, he's just a little bit lost in the past."

"Oh, honey!" Jenny hugged him. It was instinctive. Sympathy for Chance, and the man she had yet to meet, overwhelmed her.

"Come on," Chance urged. "This time, the visit won't be so bad."

"Why not?" Jenny asked.

"Because I've got you with me," he said.

The smile in her heart stayed with her all the way past the reception desk and the wheelchair bound residents who lined the walls of the room. The invasive odors of the home slipped into the back of her mind as she focused on the intensity with which Chance moved. If this man meant that much to him, he was going to mean the world to her, too.

As usual, the room was immaculate. The lights were on, the window shades up, the curtains tied back. But, this time, no little man came rocketing out from under the bed. He was sitting in a chair, staring blankly out a window.

Chance took one look and decided that this was not one of Charlie Rollins's good days. He started to ask Jenny if she'd rather wait outside, when she walked past him and knelt in front of the old man.

"Hello, Charlie," Jenny said. She brushed her fingers across the hands lying limply in his lap, and lightly traced the gnarled knuckles.

Before either of them knew it was happening, Charlie clasped Jenny's hand and held on. He turned his watery eyes her way and blinked several times in succession. Jenny knew it was not to clear his vision. He was desperately trying to clear his mind.

"Chance came back to see you, Charlie. He told me I could come along and meet you, too. He says you're very special."

Chance walked around, pulled up a chair, sat down in front of Charlie, and patted his knee.

"How you been doing, Charlie? Did you get Mabel Geraldine's car fixed?"

Charlie blinked. And then he smiled. Just a bit, but it was still there.

"Yeah," he answered. "I think so. Is that you, Chance?"

Chance's stomach churned. *My God! He knows my name!*

"I'm here, Charlie."

He nodded. "Good," he said. "I'll be wantin' you to close for me tonight."

"Sure thing," Chance said. His voice thickened with emotion as it dawned on him that he must have worked for Charlie. Until this moment, their relationship had been a mystery. He knew that Charlie had paid for his mother's funeral. This explained a lot.

"Oh, Chance," Jenny whispered. Tears pooled.

"This your girl?" Charlie asked, and patted Jenny's hair.

"It sure is, Charlie. What do you think?"

"I think she's pretty," Charlie said. "But she's not like I remembered. . . . I just can't seem to remember . . ."

"It's all right," Jenny said. "Would you like me to brush your hair? When I don't feel good, I always like for someone to brush mine."

Charlie thought a minute and then nodded and smiled. "That'd be just fine, missy."

Chance held his breath, willing Charlie not to lose his tenuous hold on reality, praying that this visit would be one to remember. Chance had no intention of going back to Tyler and forgetting that Charlie was here. But he knew that each time he returned, Charlie Rollins would be farther and farther away. The thought overwhelmed him with sadness, knowing something precious had been lost.

Jenny picked up the brush from the dresser, walked around behind Charlie's chair, and began to stroke the bristles through the short, snowy stubble. Slowly and methodically, she worked the brush all the way around his head, patting the hair back in place with her fingers after the brush passed through.

Chance watched, mesmerized by the gentleness of the woman who'd stolen his heart. As long as he lived, he knew he'd never forget the sight of Jenny lovingly grooming the old man's hair.

"Does that feel good?" she asked, careful not to chatter or speak loudly, certain that the less Charlie had to decipher, the better off he would be.

He nodded, started to smile at Chance, then lost his grasp of reality in the blink of an eye.

Chance watched a tear roll down Charlie's weathered face. Another followed. He wanted to haul the old fellow up from the chair and hold him like a baby. But something told him not to move. He nodded for Jenny to stop, and patted his knee, offering her a place to sit since he was occupying the only other chair.

Jenny put down the brush, complied with Chance's silent request, and leaned back against his chest, relishing the feel of his arms as they enveloped her. She sensed that Chance was holding her because he couldn't hold Charlie.

"I'm sorry, sweetheart," she whispered quietly, as they watched the tears flowing unheeded down the old man's face.

"Oh, God, Jenny. So am I. So am I."

15

Logan Henry hadn't slept in days. Not since the call from Odessa. Not since an old girlfriend had asked him if he had a little brother. Not one dreamless hour since. Rationally, he knew there were any number of explanations for the case of mistaken identity. But instinct told him that rationality had nothing to do with secrets coming home to roost. He couldn't get past the "what ifs."

He'd made it to bed every night. And his eyes *would* close. But the minute the light was shut out of his world, the memories came flooding in, ghosts and all. He'd tried getting drunk. It had done nothing but add a sick hangover to his hell. He'd tried getting mad, but the anger never got past the guilt. All in all, Logan Henry was one pissed off good old boy.

Finally, it was getting pissed off that had motivated him.

He'd lost his home, his wife, and very nearly his daughter. He'd stood and watched a house burn, thinking the kid had burned with it. He'd spent the last twelve years of his life trying to forget the fact that he'd fucked up. He wouldn't relive this again. Not by a damn sight!

He stormed out of his house, crawled into his car, slammed the door shut, shoved the key into the ignition, and left a cloud of dust and gravel as he rocketed out of his front yard. The low-slung ranch house faded from view as Logan pulled onto the highway and headed for Victoria's house. He needed some answers. If what he feared was true, more than likely she would know.

"I'm sorry I had to change our plans," Victoria said, and absently doodled on a note pad by the phone, tracing and retracing the numbers she'd just called as she talked. "Yes, Ken is going to be gone for several days. The Chuck Wagon Gang has a convention to feed in Vegas. It'll take a lot of preparation plus traveling time. He'll be gone several days." She grinned. "He loves this so much, I never mind. The Gang is great. They do a lot of good for our community . . . and I think it does them just as much good. I know Ken comes back tired but exhilarated. So, I'll have to rethink the baby-sitter situation and give you a call tomorrow." She paused, smiled softly, and drew a heart around the set of numbers. "Thanks," she said. "I knew you'd understand." She smiled again, gently, openly. "I'm looking forward to it, too."

"What the hell are you looking forward to if your

husband is out of town?" Logan Henry barked, as he walked into the kitchen.

"Daddy! My God! Don't *ever* do that to me again!" Victoria gasped, and dropped the phone receiver onto its cradle. "You scared me to death!" Then she glared. "Don't you ever knock? This is not your house, it's mine. You're always welcome here, but I swear to God, if you do this again, I'll ask for my key back. Then you'll have to wait at the door like everyone else. You know Ken only gave that to you in case you had to pick up the twins unexpectedly. It does not give you the right to walk through my life without notice!"

Logan shrugged. "I asked you a question, Victoria. Who were you talking to?"

Her pulse quickened, but she'd long been accomplished at hiding her feelings. She arched her brows, stared him straight in the eye, and said, "Not that it's any of your business, but it was just a friend. How would you like it if I used my key to your house and just walked in some morning early . . . or better yet, late some night. Should I ask who the woman in your bed is, or should I pretend I simply don't notice?"

He flushed. "You don't have any right to dictate to me, missy! Don't you forget that I'm your father!"

Her anger matched his. "I'm not about to forget anything, Daddy. I hope you don't either. I would hate to think that there may be more of us cropping up out there from time to time."

"What the hell are you talking about? More of who?"

"More babies, Daddy! I hope you're using birth control now. It can get so messy when unexpected *things* crop up." Pain and sarcasm mingled in her accusation.

"You're never going to let me forget that, are you?" He stared blindly at the thin, nearly transparent scars on her wrists. But pride kept him indignant and upright.

She sighed, dropped the pen onto the cabinet, and hugged him. It was useless to be angry with a man who never saw anything but his side of a story.

"I'm sorry. I don't know what even made me bring it up. And yes, I'll let you forget anything you want, Daddy, if you'll promise not to walk into my house unannounced again."

He muttered and returned her hug. He hated to admit it but, except for his twin grandsons, Victoria was the only person who still loved him. He was under no misconception about his son-in-law's opinion of him. Ken Oslow was the one who'd had to pick up the pieces of Victoria's life at a time when it had been touch and go if she'd ever had one. He knew all there was to know about Logan Henry and his past sins, and Logan hated him for it. Hated him, and at the same time, was thankful that the man had done what no one else could do. He'd given Victoria back to them.

"So! If you'd needed a baby-sitter, all you had to do was call me. You know I'm available. It's not like the boys are trouble anymore. Except for being loud and messy as hell, being ten years old is a lot better than ten months old."

"I didn't want to bother you," she said, and dropped the subject. There was no way she could bring herself to use her father like that when she was about to deceive him in the process. Victoria didn't have it in her to be that devious. On the other hand, she had no intention of informing her father that Chance was back in town, not when Chance didn't remember anything of the past. The only way she could protect him was to keep her father as far away as possible, at least until Chance was ready to face him.

Logan nodded, pretended to drop the subject, and stared long and hard at the number on the pad that she'd outlined with a heart. It seemed familiar. He made a mental note of it, hugged his daughter, kissed her good-bye, and made an exit as hasty as his entrance.

"See, Monroe! I told you it was Chance. Don't ever tell me I don't know someone whose diapers I used to change!"

Chance's mouth dropped open. Jenny started to smile. The tiny little woman who'd been standing just outside the door of the retirement home enveloped him in a hug that ended almost before it began. She dropped her arms, stepped back, and shook her finger in his face.

She was a little bit of nothing dressed in green and white seersucker. The man at her side was wearing blue jeans with a shiny white crease, and a white, long-sleeved shirt. The buckle on his belt was almost as big as he was, and the straw cowboy hat on his head was broad enough to provide shade for the both of them.

"Where have you been all these years? When I saw you coming out of Charlie Rollins's room, you could have knocked me over. We came to visit a friend, and I told Monroe, 'that's Chance McCall or I'm a monkey's uncle.' 'Course, in my case, it would be a monkey's aunt." She took a deep breath. "Why did you just disappear like that, boy? What's it been, ten . . . fifteen years?"

She didn't give him time to answer.

"You know we would have helped you out. Yes, we'd moved from the neighborhood. And I know that later, your momma took a . . ." she hesitated and blushed, but it did not deter her from finishing her statement, ". . . turn for the worse . . . with her drinking. But if you'd just let us know . . ." Tears came to her eyes. She crinkled up her little nose, dug a tissue from her handbag, and blew. "I didn't even know about the funeral until it was over. We were so sorry."

"Now, Susie," the old man said, "set back and let the boy breathe. You always did smother him." He smiled at Chance and Jenny, and hugged his wife by way of apology for the criticism.

The elderly couple stood side by side, obviously waiting for Chance to speak. He was dumbfounded by the fact that this old couple not only knew him, but liked him. And from the sound of it, they had known him for a long time. *Diapers! My God!*

Jenny took one look at the shock spreading on Chance's face and decided it was time to intervene. She slipped her hand through the crook of his arm and smiled.

"You'll have to excuse Chance for being a little slow about recognizing you. He suffered an accident a few months ago and his memory hasn't fully returned to normal. Sometimes people who should be recognized . . . just aren't. You understand, I'm sure."

"She's right," he said. "It's daunting to meet someone who's seen my bare backside and not remember their name."

Monroe laughed and Susie blushed.

"Well, I'll say!" Susie said. "Can't remember a thing?" She frowned . . . and then her face lit up at the thought. "So, I guess I should start all over."

Chance grinned. He sensed the beginnings of another monologue and held up his hand. "Why don't we all go over to that bench under the shade tree there? It'll give us a place to sit while I catch up with another piece of my past."

The four of them sat down. For one long moment, they all stared silently at one another, and then, as one might have expected, Susie was the one who rejuvenated the conversation.

"Is this your wife?" she asked.

Jenny grinned and watched Chance squirm.

"No, ma'am, it's not. At least . . ." he turned and gave her a look that made her heart race, "not yet. Her name is still Jenny Tyler. I'll do what I can as soon as possible to fix that."

Susie nodded. "Well, fine then. I'm Susie Belton, and this is my husband, Monroe. Although it seems strange to be introducing ourselves to someone we lived next door to for almost nine years. I used to baby-sit for your momma, Leticia. You were like a grandson to us. I made cinnamon rolls at least once a week." She looked over at him and patted him on the knee. "You always liked my cinnamon rolls."

A feeling of peace enveloped him. If his head didn't remember these people, his heart did.

"This is really wonderful, running into you folks like this," Jenny said. "I know Chance will be even happier when he's fully recovered and can look back on this day. Maybe if you'd give us your address . . . ?" She looked at Chance, her eyes asking permission that he silently granted. "He'll want to write when we get home."

Susie beamed. She liked this pretty, dark-haired girl. It was obvious she had a good head on her shoulders. Not like that poor, misguided woman who'd given birth to Chance.

"We'd be proud to do just that," Susie said. Her hands shook as she dug in her purse, trying to find a bit of paper.

"It would mean a lot to me, Mrs. Belton," Chance said. "You can't know how grateful I am that we found each other today."

She nodded as she wrote, and then added, "I can imagine that it must be frightening not to know things about yourself. Just look at poor Charlie." And then her voice got quiet. "But there is another way of looking at this. I've never heard of a more perfect opportunity to start over. If your past wasn't what you'd wanted, think of the options. Everything is fresh and new. You don't have any old memories hanging around in your head, telling you that you failed at this, or were incompetent at that. You can get up every morning with a whole new attitude on life."

Emotions flooded Chance. He sat, spellbound by the elderly little woman's wisdom.

"Where were you when I needed to hear this months ago, Susie Belton?" he asked.

She leaned over, patted his chest around the region of his heart, and smiled. "I was in here, Chancey. I was in here all the time."

Chancey! The childish nickname made his stomach tilt. A funny little pain skipped through his head. He caught her hand and held it against his chest.

"I will remember. One day all of this will come back to me. I'll remember how special you were to me then, and how much this means to me now."

Monroe shifted in his seat and patted his tiny wife on the shoulder. He smiled at Chance and Jenny and then stood.

"Come on, Susie Q. Time's a wastin', and we've spent enough of their day already."

Chance stood and started to shake the old man's hand.

"I always used to get a hug," Monroe said gently.

Chance hesitated, but it was momentary. Something about the elderly couple made this public display of affection easy.

"It would be my pleasure, sir," Chance said. His voice was quiet, but his grip was firm as he embraced the old man.

Jenny's eyes teared. There was no other way of expressing the emotion that swept over her at the sight of Chance being loved by these people. She could only imagine his joy. Even if he didn't remember, he could feel the love.

Monroe Belton took his wife by the hand. Despite their ages, they smiled at each other like teenagers as they walked to their car. After he'd seated her, he leaned over and gave her a peck on the cheek before turning and waving good-bye.

Jenny smiled and waved. She felt Chance grab her hand and squeeze. They stood quietly and watched the couple drive away.

Chance was shaking. Emotion was overwhelming him.

"Oh, Chance . . . that was just wonderful! Aren't you glad . . . ?"

"I want to make love to you, Jennifer Ann. Very badly. Right now. For a long, long time."

His fingers tightened around the palm of her hand. She stared into his face. His eyes were burning with need. The high, sharp angles of his cheekbones were brushed with swatches of heat. That arrogant nose and stubborn chin became even more defined as he waited for her reaction.

"I'll drive," she said, and beat him to the truck.

Jenny sat on the side of the bed and watched as Chance knelt at her feet. He pulled off her shoes.

She leaned forward, kissed the top of his head, and framed the sides of his face with her hands. He looked up and the breath caught in her throat. His hands slid over the bottoms of her bare feet, and then moved upward with intent.

Chance moved with them. And then she was on her back in the middle of the bed with Chance astraddle her legs, very slowly and methodically removing every stitch of her clothing.

The button slid out of the buttonhole. The zipper rasped harshly into the sudden silence of the curtained room. The air conditioner kicked on, and the hum blended with the rhythm of Jenny's heart. Loud and hard.

Chance hooked his thumbs in the belt loops of her

slacks, leaned back on his boot heels, and skinned them off of her as slick as water down glass. Jenny moaned once, very quietly, and swallowed as his fingers started up the buttons on the front of her blouse.

"Chance . . ." she began.

"Sssh." He leaned down and planted a lingering kiss on her lips, then withdrew and left her wanting more.

A button would go sliding through its hole, the blouse would slide back and, inch by inch, more and more of Jenny was revealed. Chance burned. He couldn't think past this overwhelming need to claim what was his. To brand, with his body, this woman who lay beneath him, and lose himself forever in the strength of her love.

The blouse lay open, revealing a bit of elastic and lace marking another boundary through which Chance must pass. He leaned forward, slid one hand across her rib cage, and feathered his fingers across the lacy cups, letting his thumbs linger longer on the hard nubs throbbing beneath. His hands shifted, moving around and under her, arching her back, moving her up to meet his mouth as the blouse and bra fell away, leaving her bare to his lips.

Jenny shuddered, dug her fingers in his hair and moaned as Chance completely covered the tip of one breast with his mouth. The stroke of his teeth and tongue on the super-sensitive skin produced an answering ache below her waist. Just when she thought she could bear no more, he left that breast and moved to the other, starting all over again, the continuous coil of need.

She slid like hot oil across his body, at once soothing

and burning. Chance blinked, concentrating on the last bit of lace that separated them. He slid his palms down the back of her briefs, cupped her hips, and lifted. The nylon and lace came away as his hands moved out and down.

"Jenny! You are so much woman. I want . . . I need to . . ." He shuddered and moved like heat lightning. Too frightening. Too fast.

Jenny gasped as he stood over her, balancing himself on the mattress as he unbuttoned his Levis, one button at a time. She watched his swollen member emerge, as denim gave before passion. And then he came back down to her, bare skin against bare skin, knees on either side of her legs, and slowly stretched until he was lying full length atop her, not moving, not taking what she was waiting for him to claim.

Chance closed his eyes. He wrapped his fists in the dark tangle of hair caressing her shoulders, buried his face in the curve of her neck and inhaled the essence of Jenny. He was letting her feel the full measure of his body.

Jenny had never felt so safe. This man was so big and so strong. But he was telling her in the only way he knew how, that regardless of his size and strength, he was helpless in her hands. Jenny wrapped him in her arms, relishing the feel of his massive body pressing her lower and lower into the mattress.

"Please," she asked.

It was what he'd been waiting for.

He slid up, just a bit, just enough to fit. His mouth opened, carefully, competently, and took from her lips what he needed to survive.

The pressure of his mouth drew breath from her lungs, constantly searching for unexplored territory beneath his tongue. And when he was satisfied that he had mapped it all, he withdrew and rolled gently to one side, cupped her closely to him, fitting her length to his, and slid his hand down across her breasts, feathered it across her stomach, and gently parted her legs with a whisper and a touch.

"Chance?" Jenny was almost beyond words. But the look on his face and what he was doing with his hands made her forget what she'd been about to say.

"For you, Jenny. For you. Let me do this for you."

His husky whisper rasped across the silence. She closed her eyes, gave herself up to the man with the golden touch, falling away into nothing as heat burst and spilled between her legs.

And then she was weak and shaking and wrapped in his arms, as he buried his face in the valley between her breasts and whispered things to her that started the need all over again.

He rolled over and across her, nudging her legs apart with a knee before he stroked his swollen manhood up and down the satin skin on the inner sides of her thighs. It was not where he wanted to be. He needed to be inside, where it was tight and hot. It was time.

Chance stared down and lost his hold on reality as he slid into her in one, slow, endless, movement.

Jenny groaned unceasingly and tried to move against that part of Chance that was pinning her down. He'd taken possession, but he would not consume. She was impaled and throbbing, with nowhere to go.

"I want it to last forever," he whispered. His lips

were firm, pressing tightly against the ridge of his teeth.

"Chance!"

Her fingers dug into his back and then her plea was answered. He began to move. At first, the thrusts were controlled. Slow, even motions of perfect symmetry. But the pull was addictive, and the fit was tight. His body betrayed his convictions as Jenny's legs wrapped around his waist. He slid deeper than he'd been, and couldn't find his way back to sanity. Suddenly his need was too great, and Jenny's sweetness too compelling. He shuddered, over and over and over.

Finally, his heartbeat steadied along with his consciousness. He found himself lying full length atop Jenny, almost smothering her with his weight.

"Damn, honey!" he muttered, and rolled away as quickly as he could manage, "I'm sorry. Are you all right?"

"Nothing lasts forever," Jenny mumbled, and stretched like a cat, one leg, one arm at a time. "That's why we've got to keep doing it over and over and over . . . trying to get it right."

Chance couldn't believe what he was hearing. He'd nearly killed himself and she was already reminding him about next time. He stared up at the ceiling, buried his face in his hands and smiled. It wasn't enough. The smile grew as a chuckle slipped up his throat. And when it came out, it was a laugh. Another and another followed until Chance sat up in bed and roared with laughter.

Jenny blushed. Just once. And then she smiled like the proverbial cat who'd just eaten the whole damned hen house.

Chance turned around, saw the look on her face, and started laughing again. Jenny took his pillow and swung. It caught him full in the face and knocked him off of the bed.

"Are you all right?" Jenny asked as she leaned over the bed and looked at the big man on the floor. It had been a spur of the moment action she didn't want to regret.

He was still laughing. "Hell no, lady. I'm not all right."

He took a deep breath, groaned and crawled back onto the bed. He slung the pillow to the floor, pinned her arms above her head, and growled softly before he descended. "I may never be all right again. But I'm damn sure never going to be bored."

And then no one laughed. Finally, long hours later, they slept.

"The phone's ringing!" Jenny made a run for the motel room. She fumbled with the key and then muttered a none too silent curse as the door swung inward at the same time the phone stopped ringing. "Well, damn!"

"Jennifer Ann! You've been hanging around ranch hands too long. You're beginning to sound like them . . . and me." Chance grinned and kissed the top of her head as she tossed her purse onto the bed and flopped down in disgust.

"It might have been Marcus," she said. "I should have called him this morning before we went to see Charlie. But I didn't think. Thanks to you, I also didn't think after we came to and decided to get some lunch . . . or dinner. Whatever you call this mid-afternoon meal."

Chance's eyebrows rose. "Marcus? So you two are back on speaking terms again?"

Jenny smiled. "That's right! I didn't tell you. Oh, Chance . . . I think Marcus and I have finally come to some kind of understanding. He really loves me! Did you know that?"

The poignancy in her voice overwhelmed him. To think that she'd grown up not knowing that. Although Chance didn't remember, it explained what he'd sensed of her dependency and devotion to him. If he'd been the only man in her life, then it was understandable why she'd given him so much love. There was no one to claim a part of Jenny but him.

"Yes, sweetheart," he said, and sat down beside her. He slid his arm around her in a hug. "Even I saw that much. And I should have been the one to call him when you arrived. I knew how concerned he would be. But you sort of took me by surprise." He grinned at her look of defiance. "Come on. We'll call him now."

Jenny dialed, waited, and then blurted everything out in a rush as her call was answered.

"Juana! Is Marcus there? Yes . . . I found him!" She turned and grinned at Chance, patted the bed beside her, and leaned against him as he sat down. "Yes! He's here . . . with me. Right now." She waited. "Juana went to get Marcus. She thinks he's outside talking to Henry."

She frowned. "If he's outside, then it wasn't Marcus who called. I wonder who it was? You've already talked to Victoria today. Who else have you met since you arrived who might have been calling?"

Chance frowned and shrugged. "No one." The thought was disconcerting. There was always, in the back of his mind, the fear that some secret was yet to be uncovered that would blow his world apart. And now, with his love of Jenny so new and fresh in his heart, the fear that something would happen to ruin it made him sick.

"Marcus!" Jenny's face lit up. She slid her hand across Chance's leg and held on, as if assuring herself that what she was about to say was true. "I found Chance. He's here . . . and he's okay." She listened. "Yes. Yes . . . I promise. I'm okay, too. If you don't believe me, then ask the man." She handed Chance the phone.

"Marcus?" He smiled. It was too good to be true. Twice in one day people seemed happy to see and hear from him. "Yes sir. I'm fine. And yes, I've been properly chastised for not telling anyone about this trip."

Jenny listened and leaned against his chest as Chance hugged her a little bit tighter.

"Oh . . . and Marcus . . . you remember what we were talking about just before I left? Good! Then I still have your permission?" Chance grinned at the look on Jenny's face. There was something she didn't know and it was eating her alive. "Okay. You bet, sir. Yes, we won't be here much longer. Not more than a day or two at best. We'll call before we start home. Here's Jenny."

He handed the phone back to her.

"What was Chance talking about?" she asked. "But . . . Just . . ." She sighed. "Okay, fine. Yes, I love you too." She grinned and nodded and then disconnected.

"What did he tell you, honey?" Chance asked.

"He said for me to hold my horses. That I'd find out what I needed to know when it was time."

Chance grinned. His love for this woman was overwhelming. He wrestled her to the bed and pinned her down.

"What do you think, Jenny?"

She gave him a clear blue stare. "I think it's time."

She was flat on her back, arms pinned above her head, her legs locked beneath his weight, unable to do more than breathe. And what he said next took that away, too.

"I love you, Jenny."

Tears shot into her eyes. So sudden, so unexpected, she didn't even have time to think. "I love you, too, Chance," she answered softly.

He took a long, deep breath. The muscles in his arms corded as he held himself suspended above her. A knot formed in the back of his throat.

"I can't face the rest of my life without you, Jenny. I can't face the fact that you could get hurt again and I wouldn't be there to help. I can't face another morning without you in my arms."

"So what do you think we should do about this?" she asked, wrapping her arms around his neck.

"I think . . . that maybe . . . just maybe . . . if you marry me, everything else would be all right."

He waited, empty and unsure.

"I think you may be right," Jenny said softly. And pulled him down to her kiss.

Chance felt he would burst from joy. He wrapped her in his arms and rolled them over until Jenny was on top of him. He couldn't remember the past, but for the first time since he'd awakened in that hospital room, lost and afraid, he felt whole.

There was no longer a vacant spot in his soul. Jenny Tyler had filled him, completely.

Logan Henry slammed the phone down in disgust. No answer! That meant he would have to wait and either try again, or . . . His eyes narrowed. A thought occurred to him. What was it Victoria had said about canceling plans? That meant that there were plans to be remade. If he couldn't get answers one way, he'd get them another.

16

"*What did they say?*" Henry asked when Marcus hung up the phone. "Are they all right? When are they coming home?"

Marcus smiled. "She found him! They're both fine. They'll be home soon, within the week I'd guess."

"*Madre de Dios*," Juana muttered, making the sign of the cross, then promptly burst into tears.

Henry snorted. "Women!" And then he added, "Marcus, did Jenny say how the boy was feeling?"

Marcus smiled again, only broader. "Didn't have to," he said. "I could tell for myself that he's feeling fine."

"What makes you think that?" Henry asked.

"Because he more or less asked for Jenny's hand in marriage. That's how I know."

Juana's tears freshened, only now she was laughing and crying, all at the same time.

Henry scowled. He'd like to have had the luxury of venting his emotions in the same manner, but had to settle for a gruff comment instead.

"'Bout time," he said. "Damn kid's been in love with her for more years than I can count."

Marcus stared at him. "You mean this has been going on for that long? Why in the world wasn't I told?"

"Wasn't anything to tell," Henry said. "I said Chance loved her. I didn't say he ever did anything about it."

Understanding dawned. "Juana, did you know about this, too?"

She nodded and began a tirade in Spanish that she promptly had to rewind and begin again in English.

"He is her world. Where he goes, Jenny is always there. She laughs when he is happy and cries when he's sad. I warned her over and over not to expect too much from a man with secrets. She wouldn't take no for an answer. It seems the man has finally faced that."

Marcus nodded. He was beginning to understand the depth of his daughter's love for this man.

"Well, one thing's for damn sure," Marcus said. "I won't have to traipse any more fools through the Triple T, trying to find one Jenny likes. No wonder she didn't seem interested." He grinned. "Thought I was doing her a favor. She probably wanted to strangle me."

"Not half as much as she wanted to do away with that Turnbull fella," Henry said.

They looked at each other, remembering the panic that had erupted when the horse had nearly killed Chance and Jenny. And then the fear they had all gone through, thinking that Chance might not survive.

Marcus rubbed his hands together. "Well, that's all

behind us. They'll be home soon. And if my guess is right, we'll be planning a wedding. Damn, but Jenny's going to be the prettiest bride! I'm going to throw the biggest reception Texas has ever seen. Juana, start making some calls. Check on catering prices. See if the church . . ."

"Don't you think you should wait for Jenny?" she asked. "After all, it *is* her wedding."

He sighed. "You're probably right. But, just in case, make a few calls, anyway. Never hurts to get an idea of what's available . . . don't you think?"

Henry and Juana looked at each other, shook their heads, and burst out laughing. Marcus Tyler might have come to a better understanding with his daughter, but some things never changed. He still wanted to run the show.

Chance pulled Jenny's car into the motel parking lot. After their phone call to Marcus, he'd left Jenny in the shower and had gone to gas it up for her. She'd convinced him that three people sight-seeing would be more comfortable in her car than his truck. He was looking forward to tomorrow's outing. If he was lucky, Victoria would be able to answer whatever questions he had left about his past. Then he could rest easy and he and Jenny could go home to the Triple T.

He slipped the room key in the lock, opened the door, and then froze. Jenny was standing in the middle of the bed, dressed but for one shoe that she clutched over her head in a position of readiness to attack. Her face was white as a sheet, her eyes wide and panicked.

"Jenny! What in hell . . . ?"

She bit her lower lip and pointed.

"What, honey? I don't see anything." He started toward the dresser.

"Look out, it went back there! I saw it!"

"Saw what, darlin'?" He couldn't imagine, but from the look on her face, it must have been a lion.

"The mouse. It was in the closet. I picked up my shoe. It stared at me!" She shuddered and did a nervous little two-step in the middle of the bed as Chance walked toward the dresser.

"There it goes!" she screamed, pointing at a tiny ball of fur that shot out from behind the dresser just as Chance moved it.

Luckily for Chance, he ducked to swat at the mouse just as Jenny chucked the shoe. It missed him, hitting instead the corner of the door, just as the mouse exited into daylight and safety.

She screamed, buried her face in her hands, and sank down onto the middle of the bed.

Chance stared. This was a Jenny he'd never seen. He wanted to laugh, but sensed that hilarity was not a wise move at this time. He decided to retrieve her shoe instead.

"Here, darlin'," he said, crawling onto the bed. He fished her bare foot out from under her, and put on her shoe.

"Thank you," she said, and looked up at him with tear-filled eyes.

"You're welcome," he said, and brushed a lock of hair out of her eyes.

"Chance?"

"What, darlin'?" he asked, gathering her into his lap.

"Can we please move to another motel?"

He couldn't help himself. The laugh came, and with it, the knowledge that no matter how long he loved Jenny, she'd probably always be full of surprises.

"We sure can," he said. "I should have thought of that myself when you got here. This isn't the kind of place you should be in."

"Thank you," she said, and curled her arms around his neck.

He could feel her shaking. "You're welcome, again," he said. "Do you want me to pack everything up for you while you wait in the car?"

She nodded.

"I can't believe you're afraid of mice, Jennifer Ann. You've fought bigger battles all your life." His voice was teasing as he tried to get her in a better frame of mind. "You rode that crazy horse and nearly killed yourself, and you're afraid of a little, bitty, furry critter no bigger than—"

She shuddered again. "Don't talk about it, I know it's silly. But I can't help it."

"It's not silly, sweetheart. It's just surprising. Remember old Melvin Howard? You nailed him so hard . . ."

Jenny crawled out of his lap and grabbed him by the shoulders, nearly dancing with excitement. "Chance! Chance! Do you know what you just did?"

"What?" Maybe he should have tried to kill the mouse and not chase it away.

She threw her arms around his neck and propelled them both backward onto the bed. "Oh, Chance! You remembered something that happened to me when I was thirteen years old. Melvin Howard made a pass at me at the bus stop and . . ."

The flesh crawled up the back of his spine and raised goosebumps on his forearms. His voice lowered to just past a whisper as he stared into the past. "It was raining . . . wasn't it?"

Jenny began to cry. "Yes, darling. It was raining. And you were so mad. I thought you were mad at me."

"My God!" Chance muttered, and pressed his face against her shoulder. It was the first, but he sensed it would not be the last memory that would slip back to him. It was happening! He was really going to regain himself.

"Come on, Jenny. Let's get you out of here, and then we're gonna celebrate. I know a great place to eat. It's called The Barn Door."

She frowned at the rustic sound of it.

"It's great! Take my word for it, okay? And we can break in the new bed at the motel later on. Remember, we have to keep practicing and practicing until we get it right."

The image he painted in Jenny's mind did just what he'd intended. It got her mind off of mice and onto him. He seated her in the bed of his pickup, left the door to the room open, and packed all of their belongings, with Jenny giving orders from the back of the truck.

A feeling of warmth flowed over him as he packed her toilet kit. If he wasn't mistaken, he'd just found a packet of birth control pills. He smiled, thinking of the day when they would not be necessary.

Finally he was through. "Wait here," he said. "I'll check out, and then you can follow me to the new motel.

I've seen several nice ones, but one caught my eye the first day, as I came in on Interstate 20. I think staying in a Garden Oasis would be a welcome change from this place."

"Garden Oasis . . . in West Texas?" The smile was back in her voice.

"You can find all kinds of things in West Texas, darlin'. Even an oasis . . . if you know where to look. Are you willing to follow me and find out?" He grinned, admiring the look he'd just put on her face.

"I'd follow you anywhere, Chance McCall, and you know it. I followed you here, didn't I? I think I can manage to make it a few blocks farther . . . especially if it's an improvement over this place."

"Say, Jenny, did you bring a swimsuit?"

She shook her head.

"Then I'll make sure that the Best Western Garden Oasis has a pool. I always did want to go skinny dipping with a pretty girl."

"Not in public, you fool."

On his way to the motel office it dawned on him that she hadn't refused to go skinny dipping with him. She'd just refused to do it in public. He smiled. Loving Jenny was never going to be dull.

The desk clerk frowned as the crazy man from twelve B walked in. He would come right in the middle of "Days Of Our Lives." It was her favorite soap and Lawrence was about to pull another dirty stunt on Carly. She kept one eye on the television and the other on the man who was waiting impatiently at the counter.

"What can I do for you?" she asked.

"I want to check out."

She turned and stared, her soap forgotten. "Oh . . . then I guess you're ready to leave Odessa?"

He didn't answer.

"So, where'll you be heading now?" she asked, as she fumbled through her files to total his bill. Again, silence answered her question.

She pulled her glasses down the ridge of her nose with one obviously fake fingernail and frowned. "I'll have your bill figured in just a minute. Let's see, part of the time you had two in a room so that makes . . ."

"There are roaches . . . and mice . . . and I only got clean sheets every third day. You rent rooms by the hour . . . and you're worried about the fact that for two nights I had my fiancée in the room with me? I . . . don't . . . think . . . so."

His words had the desired effect. "Here's your total, sir," she said quickly. "Do you want to put this on your credit card or pay in cash?"

"Just use the card number I gave when I checked in," he said. "Do I need to sign anything?"

She shoved a hand-written bill toward him. "This'll do it for me. You have a nice trip, now. And come back to see us real soon."

Chance resisted the urge to say, Not in this lifetime, lady!

The desk clerk breathed a sigh of relief as Mr. Twelve B finally exited her life. When she turned around she realized that she'd completely missed Lawrence's latest dastardly deed.

"Well, shoot," she said, and slumped back into her chair.

Logan Henry cruised the street in front of the motel that matched the phone number he'd called earlier. The parking lot was empty. That didn't surprise him. It didn't normally have customers until the sun went down. He should know, he'd been one of those customers more than once. That had been in earlier days when half of his night had been spent laying women and the other half drunk, trying to forget their faces.

He shook off the memories, and headed for the office.

The desk clerk frowned as the bell jangled over the door again. If she missed this entire episode, she was gonna be pissed.

"Can I help you?" she asked sharply.

"Maybe," he said, leaning over the counter. Logan toyed with the idea of flirting to get his answers and decided on bribery instead. He'd never been that desperate for a woman in his life. "I'm looking for a little information."

Her eyebrows rose as she watched the big man's hand sliding toward his pocket. She smirked and sidled up to the counter. "I'm just full of information," she answered, and then stared pointedly at his wallet.

This one would be easy. Money always got results. "I'm looking for someone," he said. "A man, maybe six feet or more. He'd have dark hair and eyes." He started to give her some further description when he realized that he had no idea what in hell his own son looked like now. The knowledge was unsettling. "Well, have you seen anyone fitting that description . . . say in the past few days?"

Something about the man's face reminded her of Mr. Twelve B; and that in turn reminded her how scary the sucker was when he got mad. Even if he was gone, she didn't think this guy had enough money to pay her to make twelve B mad. She didn't want him coming back and accusing her of anything. A lady had to be careful nowadays. "Not much of a description," she said, and pushed herself away from the counter. "It'd fit just about half the male population of Odessa. You want a room?"

Logan Henry couldn't believe it. He pulled out a wad of twenties and began peeling them off, one at a time. "Dammit! Are you certain you don't remember anything?"

She fidgeted at the sight of all that money, but the memory of the big man who'd resided in twelve B outweighed her greed. She turned beet red, shoved her glasses up against her face, and pointed at the door.

"What kind of a place do you think this is? And better yet, what kind of a woman do you think I am? I can't be bought, mister. By God! I'm not for sale."

Her breast was heaving beneath her hot pink jumpsuit as she watched the man leave her office. The announcer's voice on the television behind her caught her attention and she turned in fury as she heard, "and so are the days of our lives."

"Well that just figgers," she drawled as she slammed her butt down in the chair, and dialed the phone.

"Georgie," she asked, "did you watch 'The Days'

today? Well, thank God! I've had such an afternoon, you wouldn't believe. I missed everything after Lawrence was about to . . ."

Logan Henry slammed the car into reverse and backed out of the parking space. His driving mirrored his mood as he left tracks of his tires on the pavement. The smell of hot rubber sifted through the air, and then the constant Odessa wind moved it away.

Chance was too quiet. Jenny'd noticed it happening right after they'd called Marcus. He'd managed to laugh and respond to all her remarks at the proper times as they took a room at the Best Western Garden Oasis. But the more time passed, the quieter he became. Finally, Jenny could stand it no longer. If she was the cause, she had to know.

"Are you mad at me?" she asked. " 'Cause if you are, you'll have to tell me what I did wrong. I know being afraid of a little mouse caused a lot of upheaval, but honestly Chance I just can't help . . ."

Chance scooped her up from her seat in the middle of the bed and cradled her against his chest. He stared long and hard at the uncertainty behind those somber blue eyes.

"Jennifer Ann, if I ever hear you say anything so stupid again, I'll wring your little neck. I'm not real up-to-date on what my past personality has been . . . but if I was that goddamned picky about my life, I don't want it back." He hugged her to soften his words. "No, I'm not mad at you. And I'm sorry if you thought I was . . . even for a minute." He leaned down and kissed her

gently, lingering longer on her full lower lip than absolutely necessary.

He stepped backward, lowering them both into a
chair. Jenny settled comfortably across his lap and
leaned her head against his shoulder. She picked
absently at a shirt snap as she waited for his explanation.

Chance sighed. He nuzzled the top of her head,
inhaling the fragrance of her shampoo, smiling to himself
at the way she curled into his lap like a contented cat.
My Jenny! The thought was intoxicating.

"So?" she persisted. "You're going to have to communicate. That's what caused all this separation to
begin with. You keep secrets."

The tone of her voice told him more than words
could ever have done. He'd hurt her . . . many times.
But that was then, this was now. She'd never be victim
to secrets again. At least, not from him.

"Who called me, Jenny? It wasn't Marcus. We talked
to him. And I called Victoria a few minutes ago and let
her know our new location and phone number. The call
we didn't answer wasn't from her either. There's no one
else who knows I'm here."

"So?"

"So, who's still out there watching me . . . that I don't
remember? What if there's a part of me I don't know about
that could hurt me, or us? We still don't know everything
there is to know about my past. What if I've done—"

"Just shut up, Chance!" Jenny said sharply. "I don't
want to hear anymore of these 'what ifs.' If you don't
know yourself any better than that, then you're just
going to have to take my word for it. I can tell you
that I'd bet my life you've never done anything of

which you should be ashamed. You're not that kind of man!"

The fierce look of protectiveness was back. He'd seen it when she'd come storming in the door of the motel and caught him hugging Victoria. And he'd witnessed it when she'd stepped in and assumed control of the conversation between him and the Beltons, when they met outside the nursing home. He'd been so stunned by their appearance, he'd been speechless. It hadn't taken Jenny long to come to his defense. She might be little, but she was mighty, and she was all his.

"You know what, honey?" he said.

Jenny saw that familiar grin spreading across his face and knew he was about to tease her. It always happened when she got too intense, and that was often.

"What?" she muttered.

"You make a better lover than a fighter. You're just the least bit undersized to be trying to whip the butts of everyone who bothers me."

Jenny wanted to argue, but she knew when she'd been bested. It was time to change the subject.

"I only have one thing further to say," she said.

Chance caught the intent look on her face and knew a barb was coming. "What's that, my little mighty mouse?"

She glared, daring him to mention her and mice again in the same breath. "Either take me to bed, or feed me."

He burst into laughter, dumped her off his lap, and then pointed to the door. "Get yourself out the door, woman. I've got to feed myself before I take *you* to bed again. If I don't you'll kill us both."

Jenny had the grace to blush. "Well," she shrugged, "we have to kill time somehow until Victoria comes tomorrow. I just thought—"

"Get your purse, Jennifer Ann," Chance said, laughter still evident in his voice. "You think entirely too much."

It was getting late. The sunset was as magnificent as usual, but Logan Henry didn't see it. He was too busy searching for a gas station. The one he finally found was self-service, and he cursed to himself as he crawled out of his car, longing for the good old days when all you had to do was drive into a station and yell, "fill 'er up." Nowadays he had to hunt for a station that still offered such services and pay more for the gas. Not that money was a problem, it was just the principle of the thing.

He turned to survey the busy intersection, wondering where he ought to go for his evening meal. Ever since his wife had left him, he'd eaten out more than in. Cooking was not one of his skills. He had a housekeeper, but she didn't like to cook and did so only when asked. Today he hadn't thought to ask. He looked at his watch and sighed. It was too late to ask now. She was probably gone already.

A car honked at the gas station across the street. He turned in reflex at the sound, and then stared in shock at the tall, broad-shouldered man who was putting gas in a red pickup truck. The face was more than familiar. It was like looking at a mirror image of himself . . . only thinner . . . and younger. The man turned and smiled, obviously talking to someone else inside the truck. *Oh*

Jesus! Logan thought. *It's got to be him. I was right! And, he's not alone! Where in hell is Victoria?*

His stomach churned. Sweat popped out and ran down the back of his shirt. Then a big eighteen-wheeler pulled up to the stoplight and stopped directly between the two stations, obstructing his view. Another pulled up behind it, and Logan cursed in fury.

"Move, dammit," he muttered aloud, and then winced at the frown he received from an elderly lady getting out of a BMW at the pumps just ahead of him. "Not you, ma'am," he apologized, "I was talking about . . ." It didn't matter. What in hell was he thinking? He didn't have to apologize to a total stranger. But he did have to know the identity of that man . . . and who he was with.

He started across the street. He didn't think. He just ran. A car came to a screeching halt only inches away from him. The driver honked, and Logan shrugged and started again. The light changed, and the traffic began to move. He was caught between a rock and a hard place. Either he got the hell out of the street or became the latest spot of roadkill on Highway 80.

He jumped back onto the curb just in time, watching in frustration as the traffic began to move. The two big eighteen-wheelers ground their gears, jerked and screeched, and slowly moved across the intersection. Logan held his breath, waiting, staring intently across the street through the dusky evening.

"Well, hell's fire!" he yelled, as the space between the stations cleared. The red pickup was no longer anywhere in sight. The man and his companion had disappeared.

The woman in the BMW turned and glared. "Listen,

mister!" she said, "you'll live a whole lot longer if you'll just calm down and wait your turn. Take it from one who knows."

She set the nozzle neatly back into the pump, retrieved her purse from the front seat of her car, and went into the station office to pay.

Logan didn't know whether to laugh at the incongruity of their misguided conversation or curse in frustration. The answer to his sleepless nights had been right across the street, and he'd lost it.

He didn't know where the red pickup truck had gone, but he knew where *he* was going. Gas flowed, money changed hands, and Logan Henry headed out of town, racing nightfall.

"Grandpa!" the twins yelled in delight as they opened the door.

Logan grinned, caught the two blond-haired ruffians in mid-flight, and wrestled them both to the living room floor.

"Where's your momma?" he finally asked when they stopped squealing and laughing.

"I'm right here," Victoria said, as she walked into the room. "Kenny! Mark! Get off your grandpa right now! What have I told you two boys about wrestling in my house?"

Logan grinned in apology for what he knew was an infraction of Victoria's long-standing rule. "It was my fault," he said.

"It always is," she answered. And then she changed the subject. "Have you had dinner? I just got home. I haven't had time to fix anything. yet. It'll be no trouble to add another steak to the grill."

"Where've you been?" he asked. Too sharply. He knew it the moment the words came out of his mouth. He tried to soften the implication, but it was too late.

"Give it a rest, Dad," Victoria said. Anger was thick around her.

"I didn't mean it the way . . ."

"Yes you did. If you have any respect for me at all, at least don't lie to me about that!"

"Mom! What's wrong?" Kenny asked. "You and Grandpa are always fighting. Why? Don't you like each other?"

Mark echoed his brother's question by punching his grandfather's leg, trying to start the game all over and break the tension.

"Of course I do," Victoria said. "Both of you, go wash. Now! Then you can help me with the grill."

"Yea!" they yelled in unison, and ran from the room, each in a desperate effort to be the first through washing up and the first back to the grill.

Victoria rolled her eyes and headed back to the patio.

"Come on," she called over her shoulder, "you can start the charcoal. I always make a mess."

"Victoria?"

"What?" She turned, surprised that her father was still standing where she'd left him.

"*Do* you like me?"

The question broke her heart. How long was this thing going to stand between them? Even when they both tried to ignore it . . . even when they each managed to forget it for a span of time . . . something kept reopening the old wounds . . . and reviving the old anger.

Victoria felt guilt at concealing her knowledge of Chance's return. For years, she'd yearned for a reconciliation among them all but feared that it was nothing more than a dream, because Chance's whereabouts were unknown. She imagined a time when he would be welcomed as a brother, a beloved addition to their family. And now, when it was so close, it seemed as impossible as it had the day all their worlds had fallen apart.

"Daddy!" Her voice broke, and she walked back into his arms. "I'm sorry," she said, swallowing tears. "I didn't mean to jump on you."

He hugged her tight. "And I didn't mean to imply anything." His conscience tugged. "Well hell, I *did* mean to imply, but I'm sorry, anyway."

Victoria laughed. He was impossible, as always. But when it mattered, he was honest. He might not have many scruples, but he had a conscience that wouldn't let him be a total heel.

"Come on," she said. "Let's get this show on the road. I'm starving. Ken is coming home day after tomorrow, and I can hardly wait. He and the boys had to postpone their trip to Big Bend National Park. They've been driving me crazy. When he returns, I'm going to go to bed and sleep for a week."

Logan smiled, followed her onto the patio, and dutifully began building a fire in the grill. But the thought kept rolling around in his head that she never had answered him. He still didn't know where she'd been. Or if she'd been there alone.

17

The phone rang. Victoria rolled over in the darkness and grabbed the receiver before a second ring woke the boys. It had taken forever to get them to bed. They were too wound up from their grandfather's unexpected arrival at dinner time and the wild game of touch football that had followed.

"Hello," she said. Her voice was low, and relaxed. "No, I wasn't asleep. I've been waiting for you to call."

"I miss you, Vicky," Ken Oslow said, listening to the sleepy tone in his wife's voice.

"I miss you, too, honey," she said. "You being gone now couldn't have come at a worse time."

"Are the boys giving you fits about the postponed trip . . . or is it more?"

She sighed. "It's more. I wish you were here. I need moral support. I feel so guilty about not telling Daddy that Chance is back. But, it's as I told you last night,

Chance really doesn't remember us. Not anyone or . . . anything."

"Are you sure?" Ken couldn't disguise the bit of jealousy that crept into his question. He'd spent too many years trying to get over the fact that his wife's first love had been her half-brother. Innocent as their relationship had been, it had still been emotionally deep, and he knew it. Victoria had hidden nothing from him. That honesty was what had saved their own relationship, and ultimately, made their marriage last.

Victoria heard the doubt in his voice. Her heart went out to the man who'd loved her past understanding. When most boys would have turned their backs on a girl who'd tried to commit suicide, he'd been the glue that had put her life back together. And when she'd finally healed, both in body and spirit, she had realized how deeply she'd learned to love the tall, sandy-haired young man with the gentle smile and soft brown eyes.

"Yes, I'm sure," she said. "In fact, I think I scared him to death when I first confronted him. He's really been through a bad time from his injuries. And I never realized until now how much we all rely on bits and pieces of our pasts to make us who we are. Think about it! How can you focus on tomorrow when you have no anchor from yesterday? Know what I mean?"

Ken listened, and in his mind he understood. It was just his heart that was having difficulties.

He was quiet a bit too long for Victoria's peace of mind.

"Ken?"

"What, honey?" he asked.

"You would like him."

Another silence lingered and then she heard his sigh.

"If he's anything like you, I probably would."

Victoria laughed. The sound surprised him.

"What's so funny?" Ken asked.

"Chance is the spitting image of Daddy."

"Good Lord! I hope that's in looks only."

She laughed again. "It is," she assured him. "I wouldn't have . . ." She stopped herself.

"You mean, you wouldn't have fallen in love with him in the first place if he'd been anything like Logan. Isn't that right?"

"Yes. That's exactly what I started to say. He's kind, and thoughtful. And full of fun. At least . . . he used to be, before my family ruined his life."

Ken sighed. "Now Victoria, don't dredge up old guilt. You're not responsible. I told you once, and I'll say it again, the sins of the fathers may fall on children's heads, but the children don't cause the sins to occur in the first place."

"I know." She hesitated, wanting him to change the subject. "It's too late at night to get this serious."

Ken understood. As always, he knew exactly what to say to lighten the mood.

"Logan's gonna hate the fact that one of his wild seeds took root and grew up so much in his image that he couldn't deny it."

Victoria smiled. "As usual, you're right. And the sad fact is, that's what Chance hated the most. When he found out the truth, denying it was impossible. He was younger, of course, but even then the resemblance was there. How do you deny your own face?"

She thought back to that time, and wondered again,

as she had so many times before, why she'd never seen it then. The only answer she'd ever been able to live with was that she hadn't been looking for it.

"He should be glad he doesn't look like you, honey," Ken said. "I don't think a pretty face like yours would be becoming on a man."

She turned her face into the pillow and giggled, trying not to alert the boys to their father's call. That would have them both up and out of bed, begging to talk.

"I'll call you tomorrow night, honey, just to find out how your day went," Ken said.

"Good. And then when you get back, I'm inviting Chance and Jenny out and you can meet . . ."

"Who's Jenny?"

"Oh, that's right! I forgot to tell you. She's his girl-friend . . . or fiancée . . . whatever the case may be at this time. And . . . I like her . . . I think. We haven't spent any time together, but I'm looking forward to it."

"He has a girl? Good! I'm liking him better already."

"Oh Kenny," she whispered, "you'll always make me feel special. You act as if you're still jealous. After all these years, and our ages, and babies, I'm not as . . ."

"You're beautiful. You always have been. You always will be. You're my girl, Vicky. Don't ever doubt it. I love you."

The words of support were just what she needed to hear.

"I won't, darling," she said. "And sleep tight. I love you too. I'll look forward to your call."

They disconnected. Victoria could actually feel the last, lingering, little wish of "what if" slip out of her heart forever. If Chance hadn't been her brother, she would still have regretted not knowing and loving Ken Oslow. He was one of a kind.

Logan Henry did something he shouldn't. He knew it the moment he left his daughter's house and turned toward Odessa instead of his own home, but the need to know kept driving him crazy.

Before he had time to change his mind, he was driving toward the old motel, almost certain that he'd find a red pickup truck parked in the lot. His stomach grumbled, reminding him that he'd eaten too much and then played too hard with the twins. It was difficult to face the fact that he wasn't so young anymore.

The motel came into view. He slowed down, stared into the shadowy parking lot, and then cursed. There were several cars and two pickup trucks. But none of them were red.

"Damn!" He slammed the steering wheel with his fist and gunned his car down the street.

A police car cruising past flicked his lights at him, telling him in as nice a manner as possible, without pulling him over, that he'd better slow down or else. He eased up on the gas. What he didn't need now was a ticket. But, he convinced himself, what he did need was a drink. He turned down another street, cruising the strip until he found the establishment he'd been looking for.

The New Brewery was a popular watering hole. The parking lot was crowded, which meant the interior of the place would be the same. That was fine with him. Noise and booze were just what he needed to get his mind off the demons taunting him.

"Hey, there," he said, in answer to a woman's wave of recognition. Tonight might prove fruitful in more ways than one. He grinned, ordered a drink from a girl who came sailing by with a tray full of glasses, and slipped some money in her hip pocket for good measure. He felt better already.

Jenny leaned back in her chair, looked at her empty plate, and sighed. "I've never been so full in my life. This was too good. I ate as if I hadn't seen food in a week. Did I embarrass you?"

"Honey, the only way you'll ever embarrass me is . . ." He leaned over and whispered in her ear, delighting in the flush of red that swept across her cheeks, obvious even in the dim lighting.

"Well now," she said, giving him back as good as he gave, "I think I can manage that." She wagged her finger beneath his nose, "but I need to work off some of this food first. Let's either go for a walk or . . . I know . . . Let's go dancing! Do you know that I've never danced with you?"

He rolled his eyes and sighed. "No, darlin', you know damn good and well that I don't know that. And, as usual, I'm at your mercy. What if I can't dance? Did you ever think of that?"

"I don't believe it for a minute," Jenny said. "You spent too many Saturday nights somewhere besides in my arms. Besides . . ."

She grinned. He felt it coming.

". . . you're too good in bed not to be good on your feet."

Chance leaned back in his chair and roared with laughter. Several people turned and smiled. Jenny ignored them, waiting for Chance to deny what she'd just said. But he didn't.

"Where do we go?" she asked him.

"Where do you want to go, miss?" the waiter asked, as he walked up and handed Chance the check.

"Dancing." Chance grinned. "The lady wants to go dancing."

"There's a lot of good places available," the waiter said. "There's Cheers, and Chelsea's Street Pub, and The New Brewery, and . . ."

"The New Brewery. That sounds like a possibility," Jenny said. "The New Brewery, for new beginnings."

"The Brewery it is. Now tell me how to get there. I've got to take a woman dancing."

"This is great!" Jenny said, as they walked into the dimly lit din. The music was blaring, the floor was packed, and the crowd was lively.

"Yes, if we can find a table," Chance yelled into her ear.

"Need a table?" a waitress asked.

"Ask and ye shall receive," Jenny said.

"I don't think that refers to tables in bars, darlin'."

They followed the waitress to a corner of the room. She took their order and then disappeared.

Jenny looked around, absorbing the ambiance. It was the same, world over. Where country music was playing, the couples were in each other's arms. They were smart enough to realize that up close and personal was a whole lot better than dancing apart.

"Seen enough?" Chance asked.

"Cowboy, either hold me, or cut me loose and let me roam," Jenny said. Her feet were already tapping in time to the music.

"You don't roam for anyone but me, darlin'," Chance said as he swung her into his arms and into the two-step rhythm of the song.

The music played on. The couples danced. Jenny and Chance were lost in the loud and noisy chaos of the night, and in each other.

After more than two hours passed, Jenny was finally winding down from her dancing high. Chance was tired, but not tired of holding Jenny.

Dancing with her had been another revelation. He hadn't known that fleeting touches of his hand across her curvy backside, her breasts brushing gently against his chest as they swayed in time to the music, or the intermittent contact between their thighs, could be such a turn-on. But he did now.

He didn't need her naked and begging to make him want her. He didn't even have to have her alone. Here they were, surrounded by a maelstrom of milling couples, dressed from neck to ankle in jeans and shirts, and he was hurting like hell.

But something was bothering him, and it had nothing to do with Jenny. For a long time, he'd had the strangest sensation that he was being watched. And it wasn't a clinical kind of observation. It felt personal—an "I know who you are," sensation.

Logan sat in a chair against the wall, holding the same drink he'd ordered when he first arrived. He was all but frozen to the spot, staring at the tall man with the pretty, dark-haired woman who kept passing his table as they circled the small dance floor.

The pain in his chest kept reminding him that he hadn't died on the spot. *Hell!* he thought to himself, *I thought you were through with me, didn't I, boy?*

And then he caught himself. This person was no boy. The boy had become a man . . . and quite a man at that. He slammed the drink down on the table and it sloshed all over his fingers, making the couple beside him stare and frown in disapproval.

"What are you lookin' at?" he growled, and waved at the waitress who quickly replenished his order.

What really made Logan Henry sick was that he was looking at the one thing he'd always wanted. A son. He'd known for such a long time that he had one but had refused to claim him. He had let the boy fend for himself in the worst possible atmosphere, and he'd done the boy's mother an injustice. In his heart, he knew it. He just couldn't bring himself to say it. Not to Margaret, his ex-wife, and not to Victoria. And especially not to the one who'd needed to hear it most, his own son.

When he'd first seen Chance walking through the throng of dancers, he thought he'd imagined it. He couldn't be so lucky as to have the object of his search actually walk in and sit down in the same room with him. But having his fears confirmed, that the man was here, didn't make them better. It only made him wonder why Chance McCall had come back to Odessa.

Now he had new fears. What would this do to Victoria? Once he'd nearly beaten the boy to death. He'd later regretted it, but it had been too late. Now he feared another confrontation, but this time, he wouldn't be beating anyone. This man, his son, was taller, broader, and a damn sight younger than he. What was making him furious was that the bastard could become king of the hill, and Logan Henry wasn't ready to step aside for any man.

"Chance?" Jenny asked as the last notes of a song faded away.

"What, darlin'?" He leaned down to catch her question.

"Who's that man?" She pointed toward the opposite side of the room.

"What man?" Then, through the dim light, Chance caught the stare. It was fixed and threatening . . . and familiar. A sensation of déjà vu crossed his mind.

Logan knew they'd seen him. It was time. Maybe it would take nothing but money to get rid of the problem. He stood up and started across the dance floor, blind to everything but the couple against the other wall, and walked straight into a waitress carrying a full tray of drinks.

The tray went flying, and the drinks followed. Three tables and the patrons seated there were drenched. The uproar that followed engulfed Logan Henry.

"Come on, honey," Chance said. "I don't know what his problem was. Maybe he was just looking for a fight. If he was, he found what he was looking for."

He hustled Jenny quickly out of the club before the little fracas got bigger. Besides, he still had a problem to work out, and it was growing by the minute. He shifted uncomfortably in his seat, trying to ease the pressure behind his zipper, and then grinned as Jenny slid her hand up his thigh.

Chance walked out of the bathroom, a bath towel wrapped around his waist, and then stopped in his tracks at the sight of Jenny lying stretched out in the middle of the bed, wearing nothing but a smile.

"What are you doing, darlin'? Is this supposed to be a hint?" He was almost afraid to hear her answer. As far as he was concerned, Jenny was a law unto herself.

"Ummm . . . I'm about to embarrass you," she said. She crawled out of the bed, and yanked the towel from around his waist.

He grinned. "Well, you've done it," he said. "Just look at me blush."

Jenny stared, fascinated in spite of herself at the rising evidence of his embarrassment. "You don't look like you're blushing to me," she said. "It looks to me like you're too full of pride for your own good. You know what they say, 'pride goeth before a fall.'"

"Then catch me, darlin', before my pride falls."

Jenny's hands snaked out, and Chance groaned.

"Not again, you don't," he warned. He scooped her off her feet and deposited her on the bed.

Jenny's hands stopped their search as Chance slid between her legs. Her eyes widened. But there was no time to talk as Chance took Jenny dancing.

Chance swore. He turned and swung, but there was no one there. The voice taunted, just beyond the circle of light from the fire burning inside the house. "Bastard!" *the voice called.* "I didn't want you! You weren't supposed to be born!"

He tossed and moaned, trying to argue, needing to stop the taunt. But it remained just out of reach, and just out of sight. And then, as always, the woman's voice crying, and the girl's voice begging. And the blood . . . everywhere. Then the sirens . . . and the flashing lights . . . and a pain exploding inside his head that sent him rocketing out of bed.

Jenny woke just as he moaned, and before she could stop him, he was out of bed, staggering in the darkness toward the bathroom.

She was behind him in a flash. In time to catch sight of the tears just before he rubbed them away. It sent her into a rage.

"I don't know who's hurt you!" she cried, as she yanked the towel from his hands and began drying his face on her own. "But I can tell you, as God is my witness, when I find him . . . or her . . ." Her threat ended on a sob.

"Jenny!" He gathered her in his arms. "Honey! Don't! I don't know what makes these come." He ran her hand across his face, tracing the last path of the tears. "I don't feel sad when I wake, baby. I'm not even aware it happens. The worst I can say is, this always leaves me feeling . . ." he shrugged, searching for the word to describe the emotion, ". . . empty."

He held her hand, turned out the light, and led them both back to bed.

"Come here, little warrior," he said, curling her spoon-fashion into the curve of his body. "Maybe if I hold you, the dreams won't come. And then we can both get some sleep."

"But—"

"Hush. Tomorrow's soon enough for worry. Just hold onto me . . . and rest."

Jenny complied. But she didn't sleep. She stared blindly into the darkness, curving her body protectively against him, as if warding off any further demons that might come stalking.

Logan walked into his house, flung his car keys across the room, and staggered down the hallway toward the bathroom. He winced as the bright vanity light over the mirror blinded his bloodshot eyes.

"You look like hell," he told himself, and leaned forward, staring long and hard at the evidence of his "good time."

He had a cut on his lip and a darkening bruise across his cheekbone. Victoria was going to have a fit. She'd rant and rail at him for setting a poor example for his grandsons. And she'd be right. When would this constant spiral of wrong decisions ever stop?

"When are you ever going to get it right, you fool?" he asked himself. He snorted, turned on the taps, and began to bathe his hot, aching face with cool water.

Later, as he lay in bed, waiting for sleep or morning, whichever came first, he thought back to the look Chance had sent him from across the room. It was strange, but it had not been what he'd expected. He'd expected hate, or anger. At least disgust or disdain. What he hadn't expected was to be ignored. Chance had looked at him as one would a stranger.

"Surely I haven't changed so much he didn't recognize me?" Logan muttered to himself.

But the answers wouldn't come. And neither would sleep. When daybreak finally arrived, Logan was sitting on his back porch, nursing a cup of hot coffee and the makings of a black eye. Hell of a way to greet a day.

Victoria sighed and checked her makeup in the rear-view mirror as she pulled out onto the highway. The babysitter she'd hired to come stay with the twins had been late. Chance and Jenny would be wondering what had happened to her. Anticipation jumped as she faced the idea of spending the day with Chance. Learning what kind of a man he'd become was exciting. She'd dearly loved the boy. She wanted to love the man . . . but as a brother. At last, that thought was firmly entrenched in her heart.

She fidgeted nervously as she entered the outskirts of Odessa, squinting at the bright sunlight that bounced off the hood of her car. She fished her sunglasses out of her purse, slid them up her nose and into place, and began watching for the right street. The Best Western Garden Oasis was definitely several steps up in accommodations from where they'd previously been. She grinned, remembering Chance's humorous explanation for the sudden move. Victoria sympathized. She had the same problem with snakes.

The motel sign came into view. She changed lanes and turned into the parking lot. Now all she had to do was find room 224.

Logan felt like the lowest kind of sneak. He couldn't believe he'd actually staked out his daughter's house and was following her into town. But he had, and he was, and there was no denying the fact that he was frantically trying to keep her in sight and remain undetected at the same time.

"This looked easier on TV," he said, as he dodged a delivery van that changed lanes in front of him.

It was the way Victoria had been acting that worried him. Ken was out of town, and she kept hiring baby-sitters. It was unlike her to be gone so much from the boys. And then there was the phone number to that seedy motel. Although the man had been nowhere around, it remained to be answered why she'd had the number in the first place.

Logan kept remembering that his daughter had once tried to kill herself over this man. And he remembered Chance, twelve years ago, by his mother's grave. The hate on his face, the torment he was obviously going through, could have festered enough for all these years that he'd finally decided it was time for retribution. What better way than to destroy everything that Logan Henry held dear?

It didn't occur to Logan that other people might not be willing to destroy one person to get to another. The conclusion he'd come to was simply a deduction based on actions that he would have taken.

"Oh, shit!" he muttered when he saw his daughter's car turning in to another motel.

He darted across the lanes of traffic, turned in several cars behind her, and parked out of sight, watching as she exited her car and began walking toward the rooms.

"This still doesn't mean anything," he said. "Dammit, she's my daughter. I've got to trust her."

But he sat in the car, feeling sick and sweating pro-

fusely, as he watched Victoria disappear into the lobby.
He knew that when she came out, if that man was with
her, he was ready to kill.

"Victoria! Come in," Jenny said. "Chance is just getting out of the shower."

Victoria smiled, taking note of the fashionable cut of
the pink slacks and matching blouse Jenny was wearing.
She took the offered chair, and then tried not to stare at
the obviously unmade bed.

Jenny saw the look. But her answer was not what
Victoria would have expected.

"He has nightmares," Jenny said. Her voice was
quiet, almost accusing.

Victoria blanched. An instant understanding passed
between the two women. Whatever else, they were both
staunch supporters of Chance McCall.

"I'm so sorry," Victoria said. "It's still hard to believe
that he doesn't know me. That he doesn't remember . . .
anything."

"Well, believe it!" Jenny said. "The first time he woke
up in the hospital, and stared at me with that frightened,
blank look, I wanted to die. But . . . some things bridge
memories. Love is one. And I think his memory has
started to return. Little bits and pieces of things are
returning at the most unexpected moments."

Victoria's stomach turned. When he finally did remember
everything, he might not be as happy to see her.

"I guess it's hard to see your own brother and realize
he doesn't remember all the childhood memories you
once shared," Jenny said.

Victoria twisted her hands in her lap. How much did she dare say and not give away what was not hers to tell?

"We didn't exactly grow up together," Victoria said. She took a deep breath and continued. "We sort of found each other . . . by accident." She looked up, caught Jenny's look of concern, and smiled. "In fact, at first, we didn't even know we were related."

Jenny was trying to understand what Victoria was saying, and pick up what she was omitting at the same time.

"That must have been . . . disconcerting, to say the least," she said.

"Devastating would be more like it," Victoria said. "And then Chance's mother committed suicide and I . . ." She broke off, unconsciously tracing the thin, white scar on her wrist, and staring out the window, momentarily lost in the ugly horror of yesterday.

Suicide! Chance hadn't mentioned that, and Jenny realized that she hadn't asked how his mother had died. She caught the absent movement of Victoria's fingers tracing the marks on her wrists, and tried not to stare. Dread for whatever else Victoria might reveal began to build.

"How old were you when you two met?" Jenny asked.

Victoria looked up. Long moments passed as she judged the wisdom of giving Jenny this much information. Finally, she spoke.

"We were both eighteen, just about to graduate high school."

"But how could you be the same age and . . ." Jenny stopped. "Oh!" The answer spoke volumes.

"Yes, 'Oh,'" Victoria said. "We're actually only half-siblings. Chance is older by only a few months. Daddy was married to my mother . . . and fooling around. Chance grew up unaware of his father's identity. And I grew up thinking I was an only child."

"I'm sorry," Jenny said. "This is something that you and Chance . . ."

"No!" Victoria cried, and clasped Jenny's hand. "You don't understand! It's not something I could ever tell him. It's something he must remember on his own." She shuddered, her eyes begging for agreement. "You have to promise me not to say anything about this."

"I promise," Jenny said.

"What are you promising, girl?" Chance asked, as he breezed out of the bathroom.

Both women stared in appreciation of the broad, tanned span of shoulder and muscle across his bare upper half. He was dressed in blue jeans and boots, his hair damp and neatly combed, carrying his shirt.

"Not to ask for seconds at lunch," Jenny said, knowing that the mention of food would make Chance think they'd been discussing last night's restaurant and menu. She was right.

"I hope not," he said. "Did she tell you how much she ate last night? For a little bitty thing, she can pack it away."

"Hush, smart ass," Jenny said, ignoring his look of glee. "Put on your shirt and quit trying to impress us with your feeble display of muscles."

Victoria grinned, enjoying the play of love talk between them. She felt good inside. This woman loved Chance enough to weather whatever happened, just as Ken loved her. It was going to be all right.

"Oh Chance!" Victoria gasped, as she watched him turn around, trying to catch the sleeve of his shirt as it dangled down behind. "What happened to your back?"

The freshly healing scars from the injuries he'd suffered were shining pink against his firm, tan back. Victoria stood and walked over to him. Her finger traced a path down his back and around his rib cage. She realized, for the first time, how severely he'd been injured. She'd known he'd been close to death, but seeing it so blatantly revealed made her feel sick. What if he'd died? Tears sparkled in her eyes. She blinked furiously, trying to overcome the sudden burst of emotion at the thought.

"That's because of me," Jenny said. Her voice was quiet and full of pain.

"No, darlin'," Chance said, pulling her into a hug. "I don't have to remember anything to know that it was for you . . . not because of you. There's a world of difference."

"He's right, you know," Victoria said, smiling through her own tears as she watched Chance comforting Jenny. "A man will do a lot for the woman he loves. I should know. Ken did the same for me."

Victoria changed the subject, suddenly anxious to get outside and into the fresh air, away from too many old emotions and memories.

"Come on, you two. Chance, get your shirt on. We've got a city to see."

In no time, they were ready to leave, and had started out the door when Jenny remembered her sunglasses. In the constant bright sunlight and near cloudless skies, she would be miserable without them.

"I need my shades," she said. "You two go on, I'll catch up with you at the car. Can't be getting squint lines at my tender age."

"Okay," Victoria said. "We'll be just outside. I insist on taking my car. It'll be easier, since I'm the tour guide and driver. Deal?"

"Deal!" they agreed.

Jenny went back into the room, and Chance and Victoria walked outside, laughing and talking as they made their way to her car.

Logan saw red. It flooded his vision, blurred his thoughts, and sent adrenaline flowing in overabundance. The car door flew open and he jumped out, roaring in anger at the attractive couple who'd just exited the motel lobby, arm in arm.

18

Victoria heard Logan coming before she saw him. She looked up in shock, then reacted by grabbing Chance's arm and pushing him back. She started to run toward her father, convinced by the look on his face that he was out of control. She had to stop him and explain before he did something unforgivable and irreparable. Chance would be caught unaware, not knowing who this man was or why he was coming at him.

Victoria was not mistaken. Logan Henry was ready to kill.

"No, Daddy! Stop!" She grabbed her father by the shoulders, setting herself between the two men, stopping his advance.

Shouts flew out of his mouth and curses spilled from angry lips as Logan tried in vain to get past his daughter's restraint.

Chance stared at him and realized it was the man

from the club last night who had charged across the parking lot like a madman.

And Victoria was calling him . . . *Daddy?*

The world spun. Chance staggered from the onrush of images that flooded his mind. People's faces suddenly had names . . . incidents were recalled in the flash of a heartbeat . . . and in that moment, in the heat of their argument, Chance saw his past . . . and remembered!

What he remembered nearly made him gag. Overwhelming, uncontrollable fury sent him forward. He yanked Victoria away from the man, blocked the punch that was coming his way, and pinned Logan Henry against his car in the space of seconds.

"You won't ever . . . not ever . . . hit me, or anyone I care about . . . ever again," Chance said.

The threat was quiet and obvious and real. In spite of his anger, in spite of his fury at the sight of his daughter side by side with the man who could ruin them all, Logan Henry shivered. He was trapped by the devil, and he knew it.

Chance's eyes were dark and wild, his face contorted, like a predator ready for the kill. Logan's arms grew numb from being pinned over his head. A vein in his temple began to throb, sending a thunderous pain shooting behind his eyeballs. He tried to speak, but the words wouldn't come.

And then he and Chance were torn apart by a small whirlwind who shoved between them, shouting and pushing them aside in fury.

"Don't touch him!" Jenny screamed.

Logan stepped back in shock. Who was this woman? And what did she have to do with Chance and Victoria?

"Jenny," Chance was trying to get her under control. "Jenny! Listen to me! Get back before he hurts you." All he could remember was another time . . . and another woman falling to the ground at this man's hands.

Jenny stopped, her breasts heaving, her hands curled into fists.

Chance was shaking with rage. The adrenaline that had coursed through his body had overridden his nervous system. He didn't know whether to just strangle the man and be done with it, or walk away. Neither seemed satisfactory. One would be too quick, the other lacked justice.

Jenny turned and threw herself into Chance's arms, holding onto his strength. It was all she could do. When she'd come out of the lobby and seen the two big men in the first stages of a fight, all she'd thought was, *Chance can't be hurt again.* If he suffered another blow to the head . . .

"Are you all right?" she asked, her voice muffled against the front of his shirt.

Chance took a deep breath and closed his eyes. The feel of her in his arms was beginning to calm his rage. She was shaking. At least he thought it was her. It could have been the thunder of his own heart. *My God! I remember! I remember!*

Victoria touched Chance's arm in a gesture of appeal and then began to berate her father for his actions.

"Have you lost your mind?" she cried. "Look at you! You look like something the cat's dragged up that the dog wouldn't eat. You come out here . . . in broad daylight . . . in a public place . . . and try to start a fight. And what's worse, for no reason!"

"What the hell is he doing here?" Logan snarled, pointing toward Chance. "I see you two coming out of a motel . . . what am I supposed to think? Better yet, what would Ken think?"

Victoria was livid. "Ken thinks you're a bastard, Daddy. He always has. I've defended you for years. It seems I should have listened to my husband."

Logan was dumbstruck. "Bastard? How dare—"

"Oh shut up!" she cried, and turned to Chance and Jenny. "I'm sorry . . . so sorry." Embarrassment and shame made her want to cry.

Jenny spun out of Chance's arms. She took it upon herself to answer Logan Henry's question and accusations.

"I'll tell you what Chance is doing! He came out here to find himself . . . and his memory. If you're part of his past, I can see why he wanted to forget." Her eyes were wild, her body shaking as she pummeled the man with words of accusation. "For the past twelve years, Chance's whole past was a secret to me. But I didn't care! I loved him for who he is . . . not who he was. Three months ago, he saved my life, and nearly died in the process."

Logan felt sick. Everything he'd supposed had been wrong. As usual, he'd put his foot in sideways and had it stuck up his own ass.

"But I—"

"I'm not through talking to you," Jenny said. "When I am, you get out of my face, but not until."

"Jenny," Chance said, starting to grin. "Honey! I *am* big enough to take care of myself . . . don't you think?"

Jenny ignored him. He'd figured on as much and

stood back, letting her have her say. There'd be no stopping her till she did.

"He was so close to dying . . ." Her voice broke, remembering how frightened she'd been. And then she got her second wind and started back in on Logan. "But he didn't! The only problem was, when he finally woke up in the hospital, his memory was gone! Do you hear me? Gone!" Jenny thumped him on the chest with her forefinger, jabbing sharply with each word to emphasize her point. "He had to take everyone and everything on trust. There was no constant in his life."

"I had you, Jenny. You were my constant, darlin'." He came up behind her, slid his arms around her shoulders and pulled her up against his chest, holding her gently but firmly.

He wasn't entirely sure it was safe to turn her loose yet. Jenny was a fury when threatened. He didn't give a damn about Logan Henry, but he didn't want Jenny to soil herself on the man.

Logan didn't think it was possible to feel worse, but he soon discovered that he could. Victoria was giving him a look he hadn't seen in years. It was somewhere between despair and disgust. Chance had already made it plain that his feelings hadn't changed. And this little thing, this woman who was being barely restrained, wanted to whip his ass.

"You have to understand," Logan finally managed to say. "It was what happened in the past that made me think . . ."

Jenny was furious. "I don't have to understand anything but that you tried to hurt Chance. Just who the hell do you think you are, anyway?" she asked.

"He thinks he's my father," Chance said. His words hung in the air, silencing the others.

Jenny turned and stared at Chance. She was speechless. She looked back at the older man, seeing for the first time the resemblance. But for twenty pounds and the difference in years, they were nearly identical in features and build.

"Well, Good Lord!" Jenny said. And then her eyes lit up and her face beamed. "Chance! You remember, don't you?"

He hugged her. "Yes, darlin', I remember everything . . . and everyone."

"I *am* your father," Logan said. "Whether you like it or not. Whether you choose to acknowledge it or not."

"I never had a choice, you son-of-a-bitch," Chance said. "I didn't even know you existed until it was too late. And then the way I found out . . . by accident. If it hadn't been for Victoria . . . and me . . . you'd never have acknowledged it, and you know it."

Chance saw the pain on Victoria's face. For the first time in twelve years, he came face to face with the girl he'd left behind.

She smiled in silent recognition of what had been. It was time for what was to come.

A weight lifted, lightening the load of guilt Chance had carried for too long.

"I admit I made some mistakes," Logan said. "But I tried to rectify them. I offered to help you—"

"On the day I buried my mother," Chance snapped. "What did I need with your help then? Between the two of us, we'd already killed her."

Jenny groaned. What she was hearing made her heartsick for Chance.

"What happened wasn't your fault," Logan said. "She . . ."

"What do you know about it? I came back from that dance beat all to hell and she wanted to know what was wrong. Do you know what I told her? I told her that I'd just met my father. That this was how glad he'd been to meet me."

Jenny's heart was breaking. The horror Chance had lived through would have ruined a lesser man. For the first time, she began to understand the reason for Chance's reticence over the years, and his refusal to acknowledge that he'd loved her. How could he have loved anyone? No one seemed to have ever loved or wanted him . . . except possibly Victoria.

Jenny saw the look that passed between Chance and Victoria. She knew that once something had happened . . . something that obviously almost killed them both. She remembered the scars on Victoria's wrists, and the hints Chance was making now about the relationship that had once existed between them. She wrapped her arms around her middle and tried not to shake. She just couldn't lose Chance. Not now. Not when they'd finally found each other.

"As for guilt," Chance continued, "I may as well have put a gun to her head and pulled the trigger myself. We had one hell of a fight, and the next morning she was dead. I've lived with that fact every day of my life since."

"I told you I was sorry. I don't know what else to say." And then he remembered. "About your house . . . the one that burned. I've been paying the taxes on the property. I thought that maybe sometime you'd want to sell it and—"

"I don't want a goddamned thing from you." Chance's voice was soft and low. "That's why I burned the place to begin with. I'd spent my last night under a roof that you'd provided, however inadvertently. If the money came from you, I wanted nothing to do with it."

"My God!" Logan whispered, and sank backward onto the bumper. "*You* burned it? Do you know how sick and afraid for you I was, watching that house crumble beneath the flames? It was just an accident that I was in town when it happened. We all thought you were inside when it burned. They searched for your body."

"It was disappointing not to find it, wasn't it?"

Chance's accusation ripped at Logan's heart. He flushed and buried his face in his hands.

"Go home, Daddy," Victoria said. "Take a bath, doctor your face, and I'll be along later. We have to talk."

Sadness tinged her voice as she stared her father down. She breathed a sigh of relief as he nodded.

They watched him drive away.

"I'm sorry."

It was all she could say. Victoria was trembling, trying desperately not to break down and cry in the middle of the motel parking lot in broad daylight.

"You have nothing to be sorry for," Chance said. He wrapped her in a hug, patted her gently on the back, and nodded in agreement at Jenny's silent indication that she'd see him back in the room. "And, by God, neither have I!"

Victoria looked up and smiled. "It sounds good to hear you say that," she said. "Listen, enough of this."

She'd noticed Jenny's disappearance. "I'm going to leave now. I think you and Jenny need a little time alone. Ken will be home tomorrow. Please come out to the house and have dinner with us. He wants to meet you and Jenny. The boys will be ecstatic to learn they have an uncle."

"I don't know," Chance said. He had no desire to come into contact with Logan Henry again.

"Daddy won't be there," she assured him. "I'll see to that. In fact, I'd better go now. He and I have a long discussion ahead of us, and I intend to corner him before he can wangle his way out."

Chance nodded and then escorted Victoria to her car.

"Chance?"

"What?" he asked.

"I always wanted a brother."

He looked at that clear green gaze, once so familiar, and finally smiled. "You may have gotten more than you bargained for," he said.

"I don't think so." And then she was gone.

Chance didn't linger in the parking lot. Seeing Jenny again was suddenly the most important thing. The last thing he remembered was her beneath Cheyenne's hooves, only seconds away from death. Since then, much had come and gone between them, but not as far as Chance was concerned. He was still stuck in that time frame, sick with fear, hopelessly in love. He needed to hold her.

"Are you all right?" Jenny asked as Chance burst through the door, looking at her as if he'd seen a ghost.

He hung out the "Do Not Disturb" sign, slammed and locked the door, and scooped her off her feet.

"What?" Jenny was dumbfounded.

"I need to hold you," he said as he carried her to the bed. "I know a lot has happened between us, darlin'."
He stretched out on top of her, lifting himself above her with his elbows as he threaded his fingers through her hair. "But, mentally, I'm still caught in the fear of seeing you underneath that goddamned horse."

"Oh, Chance." She wrapped her arms around him.

Chance knew that he'd made love to Jenny numerous times. But in his heart, this would be the first. Remembering the last twelve years of their lives was going to make this time more special than anything that had gone before.

"Jenny . . ."

"What, Chance?"

"I want to make love to you . . . very badly."

She smiled. "It won't be the first time," she said.

"It will be for me, darlin'. It will for me."

The impact of his words brought tears to her eyes. Jenny knew just what to do. She nodded, let her arms fall to her sides, and waited, allowing him to do with her as he wished. The trust was implicit.

Chance saw what she offered. He had no words to express what he was feeling, but he could show her.

He tried to prolong the unveiling of Jenny by slowly removing one garment at a time, but the more that he saw, the more that he wanted. His hands were shaking, his breath coming in deep, aching gulps as she allowed him access to the buttons and zippers. The pink blouse slid away to the floor, followed by the matching pink slacks and shoes. An ivory teddy was all that remained of a barrier, and it too quickly disappeared.

He exhaled his breath in a soft grunt as he leaned back on the heels of his boots and saw blue heaven in her eyes. She was so tiny, yet so much woman. Her breasts enticed, her arms beckoned as she lifted them and began to help him unsnap his shirt.

And then he was lying, body to body, beside her. He closed his eyes and let his fingers trace what he could not see—peaked nipples, satin skin warm to his touch. Her heart was beating a rapid tattoo beneath his fingers as he lingered over her breasts.

And then Jenny's hands encircled him and brought him to life, instantly, achingly. His manhood pulsed under her caress, and then thrust forward uncontrollably as she teased him into a frenzy.

A sheen of perspiration broke out across his body as he slid his hand across her belly and beyond. She opened instantly, moving her legs enough to give him access to any part of her he chose. He chose it all.

He'd meant to wait. To bring her closer to fulfillment before he took her, but it was impossible. The sweet sound of her little moan in his ear, the sensation of her legs encircling him and drawing him inside were more than he could bear. He sank, deep and low, and shuddered, trying to maintain control of a maverick body that wanted to be turned loose inside the heat of Jenny.

Control was impossible. He could feel her pulling at him, warming, coaxing, and it was too much to resist. He moved once, twice, and then constantly, cherishing her with his body in a gentle but possessive way.

Jenny inhaled once, deeply, as he entered her. Joy

came and went with the touch of her man and what he was doing.

When she moved, he went with her. If she shifted on the bed, he went deeper, if she arched, he moved higher. They were on a fast ride to heaven.

Jenny could feel it beginning. The hum . . . the high-pitched signal of love that was starting to spiral through her. Words were impossible . . . and unnecessary. But she couldn't control her gasp of pleasure.

"Ohhh!"

Chance felt the whisper against his cheek as she moaned in passion. It felt good. It felt right. Jenny was his. She'd always belong to him. And then thoughts became jumbled as his blood coursed, building and building into an uncontrollable pressure that suddenly broke and spilled. From him, to her, with love.

Time meant nothing. Chance had no idea how long he'd been holding her, but he knew it would never be long enough.

Love for Jenny the girl and Jenny the woman were all mixed up inside him. She'd loved him her whole life— unequivocally, without restraint, without reservations. And she'd waited for him to admit his love, sometimes patiently and sometimes not, but she'd waited.

He buried his face in her hair and knew that he was the luckiest man in the world. Remembering the men that Marcus had dangled in front of her made him crazy. *I came too close to losing you, girl.*

"I love you, Jennifer Ann," he whispered.

She smiled and curled herself a little closer.

"I love you, too. And that's why I'm going to leave this afternoon."

Chance's stomach and arms tightened.

"No!" Shock and confusion warred inside him.

"Wait," she whispered, and feathered several small kisses across his chin. "Let me explain."

"Jenny . . . don't do—"

"Chance! After all the time I've spent trying to get you to admit you love me, do you actually think that I'm now ready to throw it away?"

He shrugged, refusing to look at her. He didn't want to hear whatever hair-brained scheme she had on her mind. He only knew he didn't want her to go.

Jenny sat up in bed and turned to face him. She cradled his hand in hers and traced his knuckles as she began to explain.

"The most wonderful thing has just happened to you, Chance. You've regained your memory. That means you're . . . you're you again. Do you know what I mean? But remembering everything about your life hasn't been easy . . . has it?"

Chance stared. He was beginning to see where she was headed, and as much as he hated to admit it, she was probably going to be right. He sighed.

"It was pure, holy hell . . . until I met you."

"There's a lot about you I don't know. And I don't want or need to know . . . until you can come to terms with it. That's why I think I should leave. If you're ever going to be completely and fully healed, you need to bury old ghosts. And you don't need me to do that. In fact, you *need* to do it alone."

Chance groaned. Letting Jenny go was not possible.

"Please do this for me." Jenny slid on top of him, fitting herself, curve to plane, ridge to valley . . . and waited, staring at him point-blank.

"I'd do anything for you, Jenny." The pain in his voice was thick. "But letting you go may kill me, even if it's only for a while."

"No, it won't," she said. "Just look forward to what's waiting for you when you get home." She grinned and kissed the tip of his chin. "Me!"

"You are a witch. A conniving . . ." a kiss feathered her eye, "scheming . . ." his hands cupped her backside, "lovable . . ." he lifted her up, "dangerous . . ." his body was taut and hard as she slipped down and over, "witch."

"Hocus pocus," Jenny whispered, and began to move.

Chance gritted his teeth, closed his eyes, and let the feelings swamp him. There was nothing in his world but the heat of her body, the honey melting around him, and the wave that came and washed him under.

"Is this the last bag?" Jenny asked, as Chance dropped it into the trunk of her car with a thud. She caught the disgruntled look on his face and knew that he'd finally accepted her decision to leave.

"Yes," he said shortly, and stuffed his hands in his pockets, already feeling the loneliness engulf him.

"I'll call when I get home, to let you know I've arrived," she said. "You hurry up and get through with what you need to do here, okay?"

"Okay," he muttered. His dark eyes raked her body as the breeze fluttered the fabric of her blouse and slacks, outlining her slender figure for all to see.

Just for a moment, Jenny hesitated. What was she doing . . . going off and leaving him here with people she didn't know or trust? And then she caught herself. Chance knew them, and once he'd trusted at least some of them. It was like he'd said . . . he was a big boy. He could take care of himself.

The next instant she was in his arms. He groaned as she wrapped her hands in his shirt, and clung to her as she returned his kiss in quiet desperation.

"My God, I'm going to miss you," he said, as he reluctantly let her go. Everything inside him was hurting. She was his world, and she was leaving him alone.

Tears burned bright in her eyes.

"I'm going to miss you too, you fool. And you better not linger. Don't forget. It's not long until Saturday night. From now on, I'm your only choice."

She drove away. Chance smiled as he remembered her last remark.

"You always were, Jennifer Ann," he said. "You just didn't always know it."

19

"Momma! He's here," the twins shouted, then each tumbled on top of the other in an effort to race to the front door. A red pickup had just pulled into their driveway.

Ken Oslow walked to the window overlooking the front yard. A twinge of nervousness pulled at his belly as he watched Chance McCall crawl out of his truck. It was a good thing he'd never seen Chance, or he'd never have had the nerve to try and fill his shoes.

The blue jeans, light blue western shirt, boots, and cowboy hat were normal attire for Chance. To Ken, a CPA who wore suits to the office and khakis at home, the man looked like he'd just stepped out of a picture of the Old West. The man's long legs and broad shoulders were intimidating.

"I'm damn near as tall," Ken muttered as he went to the door.

Chance was grinning from ear to ear at the look of awe on the two boys' faces.

"Gosh! He looks a lot like Grandpa," Kenny said. Mark nodded in agreement and mumbled, "Grandpa."

Chance was hard put to keep the smile on his face. That was the last thing he wanted to hear.

Ken saw the shock in Chance's eyes and quickly changed the subject by introducing himself and his sons.

"Chance. It's a real pleasure to finally meet you," he said. "I'm Ken. Victoria has told me a lot about you. And these two outlaws are Kenny and Mark."

Chance stared. Silent questions and silent answers passed between the two men, and then he smiled.

"It's a pleasure," he said quietly, and shook Ken's hand.

His grip was as strong as his unspoken promise. Ken breathed an audible sigh of relief. Victoria was right . . . as usual. He was probably going to like this guy, even if he did look too much like Logan.

The twins giggled and punched each other in embarrassment. Chance grinned again and knelt down to their level.

"So . . . which one's Kenny, and which one's Mark?" He burst into laughter when they each pointed at the other and then ran to the back of the house as their mother's voice called for them to go wash up.

Ken rolled his eyes, shrugged, and slapped Chance on the back as he ushered him toward the patio.

"Victoria's out back. She likes to barbecue in the summer. Says cooking too much in the kitchen heats up the house."

Chance smiled and nodded. "My mom always used to say the same . . ." The words froze in the back of his throat. He swallowed.

Ken saw the stricken look come and go. "Come on. I've got a cold beer with your name on it."

"It's about time you got here," Victoria said, as the men approached her. "Where are the boys? The food's ready."

"I'll get them," Ken said. The two of them probably needed a quiet moment together, he thought, and maybe Victoria would know how to put Chance at ease.

"Smells good," Chance said. He felt a little self-conscious at being here without Jenny at his side, as if he was off-balance without her.

"I wish Jenny could have stayed," Victoria said, almost reading his mind.

He nodded. "Sometimes she's too smart for her own good," he said with a sigh. "She's always known what was best for me . . . and the best way for me to do it. I have orders to . . . bury my ghosts." Then he teased, "Not that you're all that spooky."

Victoria was happy. Chance was going to be all right. Jenny Tyler would see to that. Victoria just didn't know what she was going to do about her father. Logan was adamantly upset about his part in the misunderstanding, but her anger was still justified. For his good as well as her own, she'd said her piece and left him to stew over it.

Like it or not, her father and his son were never going to love each other. She could learn to live with that. But they had to learn to get along. She couldn't bear it any other way.

"Come on, you guys," she said as Ken came out urging a boy with each hand. She smiled, her eyes filled with love for the tall, sandy-haired man, and leaned her face up for a quick kiss as he shoved the boys toward their seats. "Thanks," she said. "I don't know what I'd do without you."

"Don't worry," he said softly, for her ears alone. "You'll never have to find out."

Jenny stood in front of the window, staring down the long, dusty driveway.

"Are you okay, honey?" Marcus asked as he walked up behind her.

She nodded, and wrapped her arms around herself. "I'm just . . . I guess I'm lonesome."

"You love him a lot, don't you, Jenny?"

"Yes," she said.

Marcus heard the depth of her short response.

"I just miss him," she added. Then she turned and smiled. "But, you know what else?"

"What?"

"When I was in Odessa, I missed you, too."

Joy overwhelmed him. He hugged her tight. "Honey, I didn't think I'd ever hear you say that."

Jenny stepped back and grinned. "I didn't think you would either."

Marcus laughed, long and loud. There was one thing about Jenny that would never change. She didn't mince words. Her personality had been forged by her father. He couldn't disagree with her, it would be like arguing with himself.

"Was it bad for Chance . . . in Odessa, I mean?" Marcus hadn't asked her before. He'd read between the lines of Jenny's quick explanation as to why she'd come home alone.

"Oh, Marcus." Tears sprung. "It couldn't have been much worse."

"But he had you. You know that it had to help, knowing someone who cared was with him."

"I know." Her voice lowered to a whisper. "But before we knew him, before he ever left Odessa . . . I don't think he had anyone . . . except his sister . . ." Her eyes got a faraway look as she remembered the nursing home, "and a man named Charlie. I think he must have loved Chance . . . a lot."

"Then that's good. He didn't grow up unloved, Jenny. And if it's up to us, he won't grow old without love either."

She nodded and smiled and then pointed. "Here comes Henry." The little man was coming toward the house with a determined look on his face.

"He's probably coming to tell me some piddly-ass thing just for an excuse to see you."

Jenny grinned and went outside to meet the old wrangler.

"Hi, stranger," Henry said gruffly, letting his eyes feast on the welcome sight of his girl.

Jenny hugged him and planted a big kiss on his cheek. "Hi, yourself," she said. "Did you miss me while I was gone?"

He flushed and patted her on the back. "Didn't know you *was* gone," he teased. "Where you been?"

Jenny punched him playfully and then pulled him with

her toward the house. "Come on," she urged. "Juana made chocolate cake this morning. Let's go have a piece."

Henry grinned. "Don't mind if I do," he said. "Don't mind if I do."

"Say, Marcus," Henry said, as he walked into the house and saw his boss standing in the doorway with a smirk on his face. "We got another foal."

"Is that right?"

"Yep," Henry nodded. "We're gonna celebrate it by having ourselves some cake."

"Is that right?" he asked again. "Do you suppose I might have some, too?"

"Don't rightly see why not," Henry said. "After all, they're your horses."

Jenny and Marcus looked at each other and then burst out laughing. It took Henry a minute to realize that they'd been on to him all along as to why he'd come to the house.

"Well, don't be so damned smug about it," he muttered. "She's part mine, too. Even if it don't really count."

Jenny hugged him again. "Henry! You'll always count with me. Come on. Let's go get that cake."

Chance walked into his motel room and tossed the key onto the dresser. He stared at the clean, comfortable room and sighed. It was too damn empty.

He sat on the edge of the bed and thought about his sister and her family. There was still something he had to do. He picked up the phone book, searched the pages until he found the number, and then dialed.

"Hello?" Logan Henry's voice was low and subdued.

Chance heard the defeat and, for only an instant, a bit of sympathy surfaced. But it didn't last long.

"This is Chance," he said. "I want to meet with you tomorrow. There are things we need to say to each other, and I don't think either one of us wants an audience."

Panic surged through Logan, along with elation. Either his son was going to beat hell out of him, or . . . maybe there was a possibility of something else.

Logan was too quiet. Chance suspected it was fear. "I don't want to fight," he said. "Just talk."

"Will you come here?"

Chance inhaled sharply. Once he would have given a year of his life to have his father ask him that. Now . . . it was too late . . . simply too late for it to matter.

"Give me directions." He wrote quickly and then hung up without a good-bye.

Logan replaced the receiver, sat for a long moment in thought, and then buried his face in his hands and wept.

Chance knocked at the door to hell and the devil answered.

"Come in," Logan said, and stepped aside. The look on Chance's face mirrored the knot in his belly—hard.

Chance followed him into the den. A large wet bar ran the length of one wall. From the looks of the bottle sitting on the counter, Logan had been fortifying himself for this meeting.

He walked over to the bar, refilled his drink, and then offered one to Chance.

Chance shook his head.

Logan shrugged and tossed the fiery liquid down the back of his throat, relishing the quick kick of numbness that followed.

Chance frowned. He'd watched his mother drink herself to death. He drank an occasional beer, but he'd never been tempted to acquire a taste for the strong stuff.

"So, to what do I owe the pleasure of your company?" Logan asked.

Chance heard something in the tone of Logan's voice besides sarcasm. If he didn't know better, he'd have sworn it was regret. He yanked his hat off his head, tossed it on a nearby chair, and stared at the man who called himself his father.

Logan stared back. It was unnerving to look at a familiar face and know that the person behind it was a stranger.

"There's something I want to say to you," Chance said.

Logan held his breath. His fingers tightened around the glass until they turned white at the tips. He had no idea what was coming. But when Chance finally spoke, a band of pain that had been around his heart for the last twelve years finally broke and disappeared.

"Victoria and I . . . we never . . ." Chance hesitated and then continued. "We were never intimate."

Logan took a step back, reached blindly for the chair he knew was there behind him, and sank down onto it. He wiped his hand across his face.

"Thank God!" he said. "And . . . thank you for telling me."

"I didn't do it for you," Chance said. "I did it for Victoria. She deserves a clean slate. I don't give a damn what you think about me."

"Okay, I accept that," Logan said. "But I listened to you. Now you owe me the same privilege."

Chance frowned. As far as he was concerned, he didn't owe this man a thing, but still he sat there waiting.

"I did your mother a terrible injustice," Logan said. "I treated her badly . . . and I know it. It's something I'll regret for the rest of my life."

Chance's eyes narrowed. He didn't want to hear this, but Logan kept talking.

"What I did to her . . . and to you . . . is unforgivable." He held up his hand as Chance started to turn away. "Wait! Hear me out. No matter how wrong I was to become involved with Letty, I'm not going to say I wish it hadn't happened. There's one thing that Letty and I did that turned out right. We made you, boy, and I'll be forever grateful to her that she didn't have the abortion I wanted her to have."

Chance started to shake. All this was coming too late to matter.

"But there is one thing I wish hadn't happened." Logan stood up and walked as close to Chance as he dared. The look on his son's face kept him from touching him.

"I'm waiting."

"I didn't mean to hurt you, boy. That night . . . at the dance . . . and the fight . . . I just lost my temper."

Chance was quiet. Logan watched the emotion he was trying to deny coming and going in those dark, secretive eyes.

"Bad habit," Chance finally said.

Logan grinned. "That's what Letty always said."

An old pain dug into his belly and spun Chance around. "I'll be leaving now," he said.

Logan reached out, unable to stop himself. "If you wanted to, we could . . ."

"Don't say it!" Chance said. The bitterness he'd been trying to hide shot up with the threat. "Don't you dare be nice to me now, you bastard. I thought I needed acceptance from you, but that was before I knew who you were. I don't need you now . . . or anything from you."

He grabbed his hat, walked out of the room, out the door, and never looked back.

Logan sighed as he went back to the bar. The house echoed as the front door slammed shut. It was a lonely sound. He stared at himself in the plate-glass mirror over the bar.

"Yes you do, boy," he said softly. "You need it . . . and you need me. You just don't want it. But I do, Chance. By God, I do."

The sun had risen on a new day in Texas as Chance approached the retirement home. There were a couple of things he still needed to do before he could call this chapter of his life closed. One involved another visit to Charlie. And this time it would be special.

The first time he'd found him, he'd been a stranger and Chance had been looking for answers. Now, he remembered everything, and regret for what had happened to the old man was uppermost in his mind.

He stopped short at the door to Charlie's room. A short, middle-aged woman with curly brown hair was standing beside Charlie's bedside. Her slightly plump figure was encased in blue stretch pants and a loose fitting red and white top decorated with gold stars. She looked up at him and smiled. Chance had the strangest inclination to salute.

"Excuse me," he said. "I didn't know Charlie had company. I'll come back . . ."

"Come in," the woman said, and went to meet him. "I'm his daughter, Laura. I didn't know anyone ever came to see Dad. It makes me feel good knowing someone still cares. We live so far away . . ."

"You probably don't remember me," Chance said as he shook her hand. "My name is Chance McCall. I used to work for—"

"Yes, I do!" she said, and the smile on her face grew. "Dad talked about you for years."

Chance felt instantly at ease. She didn't look much like Charlie, but when she smiled, he got goosebumps. She was Charlie's daughter all right.

"Do you come often?" she asked.

Chance shook his head. "I live up in Tyler. In fact, this is the first time I've been back to Odessa since high school."

Laura nodded and walked back to her father's bedside.

Charlie seemed asleep but, then again, maybe he wasn't. His hands moved through the air and his mouth moved silently as he talked to whoever was presently occupying his mind. His eyelids fluttered as if he was trying to find his way back to reality.

"He's not doing so good this week," she said, patting her father's arm. "I just wish we lived closer. I feel so helpless."

"Why didn't you move Charlie close to you?" he asked, and then thought that the question might have been out of line. Thankfully, she did not seem to mind.

"My husband is in the service. We move around so much we don't have a place to call home. If I moved Dad every time we moved, he'd be lost and disconcerted . . . You understand, I'm sure. Right now we're in Virginia. But not for long. I don't know where I'll go when David . . . that's my husband . . . leaves again. He's going to the Persian Gulf. He'll be there at least a year, maybe more, and I'm not allowed. Not after the last mess."

"What are you going to do?" Chance asked.

"I don't know," she sighed. "We looked into buying here, but with the economy and our budget, it's not in the cards right now. We can either afford the lot, or the house." She laughed.

A lot was explained in that one answer. Charlie's daughter did love him, and she was doing more than most by making long trips back to visit him. What she said finally registered.

"You mean . . . if you had the land, you could manage to build a house on it?" he asked.

She nodded. "We think so. But . . . I've quit worrying about it. We've looked and it's no go. I suppose I'll rent . . . but it's so expensive and such a waste of money at our age."

Chance took a deep breath. This was going to come out all wrong, he just knew it. But he had to try.

"Laura . . . I don't want you to misunderstand, but if you're not real picky about neighborhoods . . . I have some land in town. I'll sell it cheap."

Laura smiled and patted his hand. "Thanks, Chance. But we couldn't manage a large mortgage right now."

"It's yours for a dollar, if you want it. And the neighborhood isn't dangerous, it's just not on the best side of town."

She stared. "A dollar! But, why? Why would you offer a total stranger such a thing?"

Chance looked down at the old man.

"I owe him," he said. "More than you'll ever know. Money could never repay what he's done for me. But now, the way he is . . . it's all I can do. If I do it for you . . . I do it for him . . . don't you see?"

Laura began to cry. The tears ran silently down her face. "Now I know why Dad thought so much of you," she whispered, digging in her purse for a tissue. "He always said you were special. He was right."

Right now, Chance didn't want to think about how special Charlie was to him, or he'd start to cry too.

"If you'll call this man," he quickly wrote down Ken Oslow's name and phone number, "he'll handle everything for you. I won't be in town much longer, but I'll try to come back as often as possible and visit."

"When you come," Laura said, "stay with me."

It was an offer he didn't refuse.

Ken was surprised to hear Chance's voice, and then what Chance asked of him made him grin with delight.

"I'll be more than happy to do that," he said, as Victoria walked into the room. "Boy, oh boy, it's a wonderful gesture, Chance. And you know what's even better? It's going to piss Logan off big time." He laughed. "Yes, that's right. He doesn't give anything away . . . ever."

Victoria smiled as she listened to her husband and brother's conversation. They were hitting it off, just as she'd predicted. But she wondered what they'd concocted that was supposed to aggravate her father. She found out as soon as Ken hung up the phone.

"Chance just gave away his land in Odessa to Charlie Rollins's daughter. He's selling it to her . . . for a dollar. That way she can be close to her father while her husband is overseas." He slapped his leg and laughed some more.

Victoria grinned. "You're right, I suppose," she said. "If Daddy knows that something he's paid taxes on for twelve years has just been sold for a dollar, he'll have a fit."

"It'll be good for him," Ken said. "And from the sound of Chance's voice, it was good for him, too. He really liked Old Man Rollins, didn't he?"

"He was the only father Chance ever had."

Ken nodded. The laughter disappeared from his voice as he hugged her. "Well, whether he likes it or not, now he has two. Logan seems hell bent on proving that he's not an asshole. Personally, I think it's a lost cause."

"Kenny!" Victoria said, and punched her husband playfully on his arm. "He's not that bad." And then she looked at the expression on Ken's face and sighed. "Well, maybe he is . . . but he tries."

They stared at each other and then broke into laughter.

There was one more thing left for Chance to do. And this time, it wouldn't be so easy to cure the pain that lingered inside. He couldn't get rid of it for a dollar. And it wasn't going to go away by getting mad. He had a score to settle and, strangely enough, it was with himself.

He cast a long shadow across the tombstones as he walked slowly along the pathways, his dark eyes somber as he searched the markers for the one bearing his mother's name. The sun was hot on his back. The wind was one long steady gust. He shoved his hat down tight on his head and narrowed his eyes against the searing heat.

He almost missed it. The small, flat stone was barely noticeable against the higher grass framing it. But there it was. *Leticia McCall. Rest in the peace you never knew.*

Chance's heart skipped a beat as the tears shot instantly to his eyes. He knelt.

"Well, Mom," Chance said softly, brushing away the dust on the marble, "I'm back. You always knew I would be, didn't you? But I came back for a reason. This time, I need something you can't give. I need your forgiveness."

His voice broke. He wiped tears with the heel of his hand and swallowed before he could speak again.

"I didn't mean to hurt you. I was so busy feeling sorry for myself, I didn't think of you." His voice softened, his touch lingering across the gray stone as he traced her name with his forefinger. "I love you, Momma, and I'm sorry I hurt you. I'm so, so sorry."

For long moments he knelt, absorbing the memories that flooded his mind as he remembered earlier days when he'd been younger, when she hadn't been so lost.

Then he stood and turned, brushed the dust off the knees of his jeans, and shifted his hat on his head. The

lowering sun caught him full in the face, highlighting
the strong planes and features that had been imprinted
by his parents' fleeting love. He started to walk away,
then stopped and looked back. For one long moment he
stared down at the tombstone. He could almost hear
her calling, "Chancey . . . is that you?"

"Yes, Momma. It's me." He touched the brim of his
hat, in a strange gesture of courtesy to someone long
gone, and said, "I'll be seeing you."

20

"*Juana, did you* get all the stuff to make enchiladas yesterday?" Jenny asked.

She nodded, and continued to shuck the fresh sweet corn piled high in the sink.

"Are we going to have corn tonight, too, or is that just for—"

"Jennifer, *niña,* would you please get out of my kitchen and let me do my work? If you say Chance comes home today, then he'll come. And if he comes, I will have food. If . . ." she stared pointedly, "you will leave and let me get busy."

Jennifer grinned. "I'm leaving," she said. "And of course Chance is coming home today."

Juana was puzzled. "What makes you so certain?" she asked. "Did he call?"

"No," Jenny answered. "But today's Saturday. He'll be home by tonight."

Juana rolled her eyes and went back to her work.

Jenny wandered through the house, anxious now that the time was near. Remembering the man who'd called himself Chance's father made her uneasy. Even though Marcus had all but ignored her at one time, he'd been a shadowy figure in the background of her life. It felt good knowing that their relationship had progressed.

"What are you doing?" Marcus asked, as his daughter paced the living room.

"Killing time." She fluffed the throw pillows on the sofa.

"Until what?" Marcus asked. If something was happening, he hadn't been told.

"Until Chance comes home." She carried an arrangement of flowers from the mantel to the table by the window.

"He's coming home today? When did he call?"

"He didn't. I just know that it's today." She stepped back and surveyed the room.

The assurance in her voice made Marcus worry. What if Chance didn't show up today? What made Jenny so all-fired certain it would be today?

"Okay," he said, trying not to let doubt seep into his voice. "But if he doesn't make it, I wouldn't worry. He'll be along . . . just like you said . . . when he's ready."

"Marcus! Quit trying to bolster my spirits. You don't understand. It's Saturday. He'll be home. You wait and see."

And then her face lit up as she remembered. "Wait here! I want to show you something."

She came hurrying back with a stack of magazines. He smiled as he saw the title of the magazine on top. *Bride.* It figured.

"I've found the perfect dress," she said. "Look, what do you think?"

Marcus took the picture she offered and tilted it toward the window for better light.

Jenny smiled, watching his intense concentration. She knew he didn't know satin from fur balls, but it was sweet that he was trying to get involved. And then she looked past him, out of the window.

"Oh, Marcus!" she whispered. "Look!"

He turned and lost his place in the magazine as it fell shut. A familiar red pickup truck had just topped the rise and was coming down the driveway toward home.

The rest of the magazines fell to the floor at her feet. Jenny began to move. She made it to the door without crying. But the minute she reached the porch, the tears began to flow. She hit the ground running.

It was late evening when Chance reached the last leg of his journey. Familiar faces and places had taken on new meaning. He could just imagine the look on Jenny's face. He wondered if he should have called, but he wanted to surprise her.

The pastures were in need of some rain, he'd noticed on the way to the ranch. It looked like their neighbor to the north had cut his prairie hay. When he came over a slow rise he saw a vehicle coming to meet him. He pulled over to let it pass, and smiled as he recognized two of the men from the Triple T.

"Hey, it's the boss!" They waved from their window. "Welcome home!"

Chance grinned. Damn, but it felt good to hear that!

The small pond in the north pasture was next in sight. The three cottonwood trees at the side of the spillway waved in the breeze. Even the landscape was welcoming him home. Chance's stomach twisted in nervous anticipation. The house was just over the next rise.

His fingers tightened on the steering wheel. He slowed down as he topped the hill, feasting his eyes on the Triple T and what it meant to be coming back.

And then he saw her, a small figure in white, coming out of the door and off the porch. She was running. Chance pressed down on the gas. Urgency overwhelmed him. He'd waited entirely too long to hold her again.

The closer he came, the faster she ran. He could see her face . . . and the laughter . . . and the tears. And then he was out of the truck and she was in his arms.

"Jenny, Jenny, Jenny!" It was all he could say. Holding her was the next best thing to heaven.

"I knew that you'd come today," she said. She wrapped her arms around his neck as her feet left the ground.

"How did you know that, darlin'?" he asked. "I wanted to surprise you." He was pressing urgent little kisses along the contours of her face and neck.

"Because it's Saturday night, you fool." She was smiling and crying, all at the same time, as Chance swung her around and around, stirring up a small dust cloud beneath his feet.

And then his laughter rang out, pure and long. Jenny Tyler loved him.

Epilogue

"*Did the caterers* get everything in place?"
Marcus asked, as Juana darted from the kitchen to the
buffet and back again.

"Yes." She sighed. "Go see to your guests. I'll see to
the food."

Marcus grinned and complied.

The wedding was all he'd expected and more. Jenny
made a beautiful bride. And walking down the aisle,
with her on his arm, had been the most uplifting experience of his life. He might have missed out on a lot of
things, but he'd finally been there when it had counted.

The front door to the house opened and closed with
constant regularity. Henry had stationed himself as offi-
cial butler for a day. He was dressed in a western suit
and brand-new boots that made his hobble more obvious than usual. But he'd sworn to be a part of Jenny's
special day, even if it killed him.

Marcus was anxious that everyone arrive for the reception before Jenny and Chance. They'd been detained at the church while the photographer insisted on more pictures, even though the guests had long since departed for the Triple T ranch.

The front door opened, and another small group of people entered. Marcus had seen them at the church, but had taken little notice until now. A young man and woman walked in, each firmly in charge of a blond little boy. Twins! Marcus smiled to himself. But it was the older man who walked in behind them that made him take a second look.

"Well I'll be damned," he said to himself. Even at this distance, through the crowd of people, he could see the resemblance. He didn't know whether to punch the man's face or shake his hand. From the little Jenny had told him, this man had given Chance nothing but grief.

"Marcus," Henry said, as he walked them over to where he was standing. "This here's Chance's sister and her husband," and then he grinned, "and their boys. Ain't they somethin'?" And then as an afterthought, he included the older man in his introduction, but Marcus could tell that Henry, too, was reserving judgment. "And this is Logan Henry." He muttered as he walked away. "Says he's Chance's father."

Logan would like to have complained about the lack of respect in the old man's voice, but in all conscience, he knew he deserved it. From what he'd learned in the last few weeks, Chance was a highly respected employee . . . and now son-in-law . . . of Marcus Tyler.

The look that passed between the two older men was reserved. Logan knew he was here on sufferance.

The phone call inviting him had been a surprise. When she'd identified herself as Chance's future bride, his attention had become instantly focused. She'd told him, in no uncertain terms, what she thought of his treatment of Chance. Then she'd invited him to the wedding.

Her reasoning still made his head spin. If he knew his women, and that was one thing on which Logan Henry was definitely an expert, his son had just married a tiger. He grinned. Those were always keepers.

He headed for the bar, grabbed himself a drink, and began to blend into the crowd of guests.

Jenny was fidgeting. She yanked on her sleeves and pulled at her veil. She smoothed the dark cloud of hair away from her face, and secured it back beneath the fluff of net and pearls that crowned her forehead. She pulled down the mirror over the visor and checked her makeup again, just to make certain that there was some left.

Chance had kissed her all the way from the church to the car, and then it had taken him five minutes just to put the key in the ignition and drive. He couldn't seem to keep his hands off of her. Jenny smiled. That was just the way she wanted it. Needy and begging like this, Chance was going to make tonight memorable, to say the least.

Chance grinned. He saw her smile. He knew what was on her mind, as well he should. He'd just spent the last twenty minutes putting it there. He watched her fidget with her wedding dress and was damned glad he didn't have to wear all that stuff.

"You okay, darlin'?" he asked, and slipped his hand beneath the yards and yards of skirt, trying to find his Jenny.

"Just drive," she said. "I can't wait to get home and get this off."

"Me neither."

She laughed, and then remembered. When they got to the reception, he was probably going to be mad.

The Triple T came into view. Jenny took a deep breath. Maybe she should prepare him. Maybe springing it on him unannounced wasn't such a good idea after all.

"Chance . . ."

"We're here, darlin'," he said. "Come on, let's get you and all that fluff out of the car. We've got cake to cut, champagne to drink, and a party to start. After that, they're on their own. I've been lonesome too long."

He was referring to the fact that she hadn't let him get too close to her, let alone make love to her, since he'd returned from Odessa. It had taken exactly two weeks to plan and execute this wedding, and she wanted their wedding night to be really special. As far as he was concerned, it had been two weeks too long.

She sighed. In a few minutes she'd know whether she would spend her wedding night alone or not.

They walked onto the porch.

"Chance," she said, "I should probably warn you . . ."

He saw worry clouding her eyes. What had she been up to now?

The door swung open, and Henry beamed, waving them inside as he called aloud to everyone assembled, "They're here!"

His family was the first group Jenny saw. She held her breath, turned a warning look toward Chance. and waited.

Chance felt the porch tilt. His grip tightened on Jenny's hand. He felt her return the gesture with a sharp tug of her own. He looked down.

"Jenny . . . what have you done?" His voice was stiff with disbelief.

Logan Henry was here!

"I know you don't like him," Jenny whispered. "I'm not asking you to. I don't care if you never resolve your differences. But you're going to have to learn to get along. I won't have the grandfather of our children be nothing but a faceless name for them . . . do you hear me?" Her vehemence was mixed with panic.

It was the word "children" that did it. He saw the small, dark-haired girl-child with scruffy boots, dirty jeans, and a torn shirt who'd wrapped herself around his heart and never let go.

"I hear you, Jennifer Ann," he said softly. "And you'd better hear me. You'll pay for this. Later tonight . . . you're going to pay dearly."

She turned and smiled. "I certainly hope so."

He caught his breath at the promise in her eyes and then swept her into his arms.

"Come on, darlin'." He laughed. "Let's cut that cake, greet the guests, and leave the rest of the partying to the family. I've got a lifetime of loving for you."

She leaned back in his arms, blessed him with a smile that nearly made him miss a step, and whispered in his ear, "I can hardly wait."